In memory of my parents... and with deepest appreciation
to William Alan Bales for
A Point in Time

My good friend, you are a citizen of Athens... are you not ashamed for caring so much for making of money and for fame and prestige, when you neither think nor care about wisdom and truth and the improvement of your soul?
Socrates, 399 B.C.

If you fail to work in public life as well as in private, for honesty, and uprightness and virtue—if you condone vice because the vicious man is smart, or if you in any other way cast your weight into the scales in favor of evil, you are just so far corrupting and making less valuable the birthright of your children.
Theodore Roosevelt, 1886

Are you kids willing to stick together and pull yourselves out of a hole? I've got an idea. Our folks think we're babes in arms, huh? Well, we'll show them whether we're babes in arms or not. I'm going to write a show for us and put it on right here in Seaport... We'll get every kid in town on our side, and we'll start right now. What do you say? Hey kids, let's put on a show!
Mickey Rooney in *Babes in Arms,* 1939

Prologue

"You'll never make the border...
You'll never even make the elevator."

Edward G. Robinson to wounded Fred MacMurray
in ***Double Indemnity*** *(1944)*

ELECTION DAY, 1981

Runner's high! There really is such a thing. I am Superman! Pick up the pace and an extra lap around the park. Or two extra laps. Maybe I'll run forever...

The sight of Brian Werth running through the streets of Sagamore, Long Island, was commonplace to the townspeople. He did it virtually every day. It was a real workout: four, five, six miles a stretch, about thirty miles a week. His blood pumped fast, muscles flexed and loosened, and sweat and warmth enveloped him. He felt utter contentment.

Over the hump and pounding out the last mile to home, Brian relaxed and daydreamed. Shore Road was the nicest part of his course. It ran the entire circumference of Sagamore Harbor: silver-blue water dotted with pleasure craft ranging in panache from transatlantic yachts to leaky dinghies with broken down outboards. Among the boats bobbed dozens of can-shaped lobster buoys, each one marking an underwater prison that might or might not contain crustaceans waiting patiently to be boiled alive, cracked open and savored with anything from Pouilly Fuisse to root beer.

Brian's running reverie instantly halted when a stabbing pain gripped him right where he imagined his heart to be. It was his body's way of telling him there was too much blood in his legs and not enough in his stomach where a chili dog devoured the night before still skirmished with his digestive juices. An experienced runner, Brian knew that a cramp meant his pace was too fast and he needed to reduce his speed to lessen the discomfort. Easing into a jog and feeling better already, Brian turned left away from the harbor and onto the street where he lived. Although he had passed it daily for nearly three years, he still smiled when he noticed the street sign denoting Skunks Misery Road. Streets allowed to keep their Native American names preserved the memory of those who were really here first. Brian surmised the Matinecock Indians had run across more than their share of skunks in the area. *Maybe they had camped right near here...*

A black and battered Chevy Camaro barreled off Shore Road and onto Skunks Misery. Brian laughed. It looked like one of those circus cars stuffed with clowns; heads and arms and legs protruded from every window. On the roof, a cardboard sign read "**BRIAN WERTH FOR MAYOR.**" The candidate glanced at it and felt a rush of excitement. It was finally Election Day after seven months of campaigning he would never forget. *Finally. Thank God.*

The Camaro coughed then stalled and coasted to a halt. He was barraged with shouts of encouragement.

"Good luck, Brian!"

"You're gonna win, for sure!"

"You're going all the way!"

Brian threw his fist into the air. "This is our last day, gang! Let's not let down!" he yelled back.

"We won't!" his supporters roared in unison.

The Camaro roared to life again and from the racket it was obvious the car had no muffler. Brian waved and put his hands over his ears as the car drove away. *At least no one in Sagamore will sleep through Election Day*, he thought.

Brian heard the other car just in time; the missing muffler on the Camaro had masked its approach. Without turning around and with less than a foot to spare, he dove off the road into the tall grass. A silver Cadillac limousine slammed on its brakes and whirled around one hundred and eighty degrees.

"You bastard!" Brian snarled, jumping up.

He backed up a few paces then started running away from the limousine in the direction of Shore Road. The limousine spun its wheels and began to accelerate. It was a race. Brian wanted to cross Shore Road and get onto the beach. The driver of the car wanted to run him down before he could get there.

Brian won. He sprinted across Shore Road, dove over the guardrail and tumbled about eight feet straight down onto a sand dune. A second later the Cadillac smashed through the guardrail and flew directly over him.

Brian had the wind knocked out of him but he managed to get to his feet. The limousine sat upright on the sand at the edge of the bay. Waves lapped at the front tires.

"You missed!" Brian yelled at the car, stumbling a couple of steps backward. He took some deep breaths. "You missed me you son of a bitch!"

The passenger door opened and a thickset man in his late fifties stepped out. A gash on his forehead streamed blood.

"It's you," Brian said.

The man reached into his pocket and pulled out a pistol.

Brian exercised his best option. He dove headfirst into Sagamore Bay.

"You'll die this time," the man said. He aimed and fired but his eyes were full of blood and he missed.

Brian swam frantically beneath the surface. Maybe it was his imagination but he thought he heard explosions up in the air and pinging all around in the water. He paddled down until his chest hit bottom. It was dark and cold and he forced himself to focus on his objectives, which were to hold his breath and swim out of range of the bullets. He got rhythmic strokes working for almost a minute until the pain in his lungs became unendurable. He knew he had to go up.

This has got to be fast.

His head broke the surface about fifty yards from shore. He gulped air until a splash in the water about a foot from his face sent him under again. Twenty yards farther out he had to surface again. He treaded water and squinted towards shore. This time there was no ping. Passing cars had pulled over to watch what was going on and the limousine was backing off the beach.

Brian tried to catch his breath and gagged on a mouthful of saltwater. Suddenly, he realized he might drown. He was more than seventy yards into Sagamore Bay—*in November!* The water felt deadly cold, his hands and feet would barely move and his head pounded as if it might split open. A definition of hypothermia raced through his brain. *Anesthesia produced by a gradually reducing body temperature. Damn. I've got to keep moving. My blood has got to flow.* He thrust himself towards shore and stroked and kicked as hard as he could even though his shoulder hurt like a son of a bitch.

He made it out of the water although he had to crawl about twenty feet before he could muster the strength to stand up. His knees would not bend and he could no longer lift his arms, but he found he could propel himself forward in a manner resembling... *that mummy that kept chasing Abbot and Costello in that movie... what was the name of it...*

"Come on, got to keep moving," Brian said out loud.

He stumbled across Shore Road and down Skunks Misery ignoring the gaping motorists who had stopped their cars. His body was numb but his mind asked questions. *Why? Why did I ever agree to run for mayor? God, this sucks. Come on, I've just got to stay alive until this election is over.*

Chapter I

"Politics? You couldn't get into politics. You couldn't get in anywhere. You couldn't get into the men's room at the Astor."

Jean Harlow to Wallace Beery in ***Dinner at Eight*** *(1933)*

APRIL 15, 1981, 7:15 P.M.

The campaign had begun over half a year ago after a much less eventful run around Sagamore Bay.

Thunder rumbled as Brian stopped in front of number seven Skunks Misery Road. That evening he arrived home just in time to beat the rain. In just a few moments April showers in southern Connecticut would roll across Long Island Sound and pelt the North Shore. He took a key from inside his sweat sock and unlocked the padlock on the wrought iron gate blocking the driveway. Locking and unlocking the gate was an irritating ritual because his modest house did not need the excessive security. But the mansion set back from the main road—known in Long Island's dusty social registers as "Wildwood"—did.

Wildwood was a Gatsbyesque mansion of seventy rooms located on three hundred acres overlooking Sagamore Harbor. Once bustling and home to more than thirty people, only an ancient Sicilian caretaker occupied it now. Brian viewed the structure as a monument to the excesses of a Jazz Age wannabe. The grandson of a robber baron, Harvey Whetherstone III had designed the house himself in 1936 as a present for his wife, Carmen. Great Depression be damned, his vision encompassed an Olympic sized swimming pool, a ballroom adorned with a ceiling of handcrafted gold leaf, and a master bedroom built in Tuscany, disassembled, then shipped across the Atlantic and reassembled. Three polo fields surrounded the Great House—three so the riders could compete any time of the day without sun in their eyes.

Luck was not with the project, as Carmen died six months before its completion. At the time, Long Island's gentry had made cruel jokes that she was lucky her death kept her from seeing her husband's monstrous creation. True enough, Harvey's amateur attempt at architecture ended in a dismal failure. He had zealously attempted to utilize every design concept he ever heard of—all within a single house. Anglo-Saxon, French, Italian, Dutch, Moorish and even Oriental motifs fused into mush. Gargoyles and a statue of Admiral Nelson perched uncomfortably side-by-side. Sheer size made the house uncomfortable to live in; the toilets were placed directly in the center of bathrooms so huge that the only way to reach the toilet paper was to hop off the bowl and somehow maneuver ten feet to the opposite wall.

When Harvey realized what he had done, he refused to spend even one night there and never returned to the property. A succession of freeloading offspring occupied the house until 1975 when rising property taxes forced Whetherstone to kick them out and put everything up for sale. There were no takers. Even the real estate boom in the late seventies bypassed Wildwood; it was simply too expensive to renovate and maintain. A desperate attempt to lease the property to the Nassau County Historical Society also failed. The Vanderbilts, Whitneys, Phipps and Morgans had built magnificent mansions upon Long Island; Whetherstone's Wildwood was just plain ugly. But to his credit, at a crotchety eighty-nine he was still refusing to sell the property to the drooling developers pining to tear the house down and subdivide the property.

Brian lived in the small carriage house on the edge of the grounds. He had found precisely the type of place he wanted by answering an ad in the *Sagamore Record*. The rent was manageable, the house was private and, most importantly, it gave him the opportunity for aimless wandering about three hundred acres of prime Long Island woodland. The ten-car garage notwithstanding, the five live-in rooms provided the perfect bachelor quarters. A woman moving in called for certain adjustments.

In the midst of sit-ups on the floor of his bedroom, Brian noticed Iva was late. The words boyfriend and girlfriend conjured images of teenagers going steady and necking at the drive-in, and they never used those terms to describe their relationship. Iva was the woman Brian loved, and the rain smacking against the window made him worry and wish she were home.

He lay prone and panting on the floor of his bedroom following sit-up number three hundred. Nearly eleven years after his last track meet at Princeton, Brian now kept in shape purely out of vanity, having vowed to fight the flab others at his ten-year college reunion had surrendered to. He glanced in the full-length mirror on the back of his closet door. *Thank God I've still got all my hair.* He grabbed at the flesh above his hips. It was tight. He had no love handles, something not many men of thirty-one could boast. The clock on the bureau chimed for seven-thirty and Brian frowned. Iva was still not home and at eight they had a dinner date.

That evening's meal was to be at the home of Alan Sansone, a man of indeterminate age over seventy-five who was the chairman of the history department at Wheatley College where Brian had been a faculty member for five years. As a teenager in 1918, young Alan had planted a victory garden in the backyard and kept it going ever since. In the fifties he erected a greenhouse so all year round dinner guests were certain to be treated to vegetarian delights snatched from their vines or ripped out of the earth just moments before their preparation. Brian, predisposed to meat and potatoes, dreaded his upcoming bout with Brussels sprouts and asparagus. He glanced at his watch and hoped he would have time to grab a quick snack before they had to leave.

In spite of the food, Brian knew they were going to have an entertaining evening. Alan Sansone always captivated his guests. For thirty-one years after the death of his wife in an automobile accident, he had buried his loneliness in history books. Erudite in everything from the Sphinx to the New Deal, Sansone would emerge from his solitary world selectively, usually only to teach his students or entertain his colleagues. Brian had impressed him immediately during his interview for the first teaching post in the history department at Wheatley to open up in thirteen years. It turned out both men shared a love affair with ancient Greece that involved impassioned reading on the subject and scrimping to pay for Hellenistic adventures poking about in the ruins themselves. Centaurs, Socrates, The Orestia and Zeus, and Brian had a job... a good job: associate professor of history—decent money, intellectually stimulating and not at all time consuming. There was time to write. And his recent appointment with tenure meant he could screw up or coast to his heart's delight. It was neat and secure.

Too damn secure, Brian mused as he soaped up in the shower.

"Brian?"

"Who's there?" he yelled, pressing his back against the wall and squinting through the lather.

"Who else?" It was Iva.

"Don't do that. How many times do I have to tell you don't sneak up on me in the shower?" Two nights ago they had watched *Psycho* on television and Brian was still jumpy.

"How much time do we have?" Iva asked.

"About twenty minutes, hurry up."

"You hurry up so I can get in there."

"Okay."

After he was dressed and while waiting for Iva, Brian wolfed down a bowl of Cheerios. He rationalized that he needed at least a small sustenance to avoid passing out from hunger during dinner; Sansone's Lima beans had to be avoided at all costs. Afterward, washing and drying the cereal bowl, he reflected on how Iva's moving in had changed his lifestyle. Dirty underwear on the floor had been impossible to defend in logical debate so he had promised to conform to at least a moderate degree of neatness. Changing to a Felix Unger after over thirty years as an Oscar Madison was no easy task, but lately he dutifully ironed, dusted and vacuumed. Even the immediate washing of the cereal bowl was new. He used to leave dishes in the sink long enough to cultivate an entire ecosystem.

"Are you ready to go?" Iva asked, entering the kitchen and standing with her hands on her hips. "Come on, we're supposed to be there in ten minutes." No matter that it was Brian who always waited for her, she had a way of making it seem the other way around.

Brian smiled; he loved that woman, gorgeous tonight as always. Clad in Calvin Klein jeans and burgundy silk shirt, top two buttons tactfully open, and suede riding boots, Iva really could pass as a fashion model. Champagne glass breasts meshed with a tall slender physique, and wavy dark shoulder length hair accentuated even darker eyes that framed the perfect—for Brian, Iva would have taken it a bit smaller—nose. Bespeaking her Jewish heritage, a Star of David descended sacrilegiously into her cleavage. Brian needed no such reminder; Iva's Jewishness consumed him. His isolated upper class upbringing had allowed him limited contact with Jews until he left home for college; there had been few Jews at his private Quaker high school and none at the Sagamore Country Club. His parents—blue-blood WASPs both of whom could trace their ancestry back to the 1630s—had been flagrantly anti-Semitic. As a teenager, Brian had found himself embarrassed by his parents' prejudice and actually intrigued by Jewish women. They were forbidden and different and... erotic.

"Let's have sex," he said, deadpan.

"Great, you go first," Iva answered.

Thcy laughed together and hugged.

"Brian, let's get going," Iva finally said. "We shouldn't keep Professor Sansone waiting. He's so funny no matter what he talks about."

Brian opened the door for Iva as they stepped into his midnight blue seventy-nine Volkswagen Rabbit. Once inside, she snuggled against his shoulder and he got a whiff of her *Opium*. It took an extra moment for him to find the ignition key.

Brian and Iva were not married. They were living together "without benefit of clergy" as Brian always said when he teased her. Driving down Skunks Misery Road, Iva's mind for some reason wandered to the subject. It had happened gradually. First they had slept together once a week, then twice, then suddenly seven. Then she had moved her belongings into Brian's house and was no longer a guest.

Only a few friends knew of the arrangement; at Iva's insistence appearances were maintained. She still paid half the rent to her old roommate so she could maintain a mailing address. To the best of her knowledge her father, a very religious man who would not understand, had not discovered the arrangement.

"Are you glad you met me?" Brian suddenly asked, purposely brushing her leg as he shifted into third gear. Like many men newly in love, he craved the security of frequent reassurance.

"Not really," Iva answered. She understood his need for encouragement, she needed it herself, but it had to be unsolicited to be real. "In fact, I'm going to leave you as soon as I find a guy with any kind of future."

"Thanks," Brian said. "I feel much better now."

"Good," Iva replied. After a moment she kissed him on the ear and said, "I am glad I met you."

They both were indeed glad they had met. It was a turning point in their lives although the initial encounter had occurred under somewhat less than enchanting circumstances: The Soundview Bar at two in the morning. Brian had been there with a friend and Iva had been there with a friend, and their friends had met and dragged them together...

"Come on, help me out with the tall one," Jeff Hollis had whispered to Brian. "Just talk to her, I think we have a shot."

Brian exhaled and shook his head. Jeff was an old grade school chum of his and they had been through the same routine too many times in too many bars. "Not tonight, I'm beat. Come on, let's get out of here."

"Are you crazy? They're both decent looking. Please!" Jeff's face contorted in a wild-eyed desperation that reminded Brian of alcoholics and compulsive gamblers. Jeff needed sex. It was a frame of mind he worked himself into whereby women merely became a means to an end. "Please," he said again, "Just this once do me a favor, please!"

"All right, relax. We'll have one more drink." Brian said.

He had to be sympathetic with Jeff; there had been times when their roles were reversed. Many times since college Brian had used one night stands to distract himself from his feelings, his rage. For a long time it worked but not lately. In the last couple of years sex had brought him nothing but guilt and loneliness and pain. His weekly visits to his psychotherapist—visits he told no one about—helped a lot. He was beginning to understand himself and like himself and even feel. One day he hoped sex could be an act of love, not anger.

"You've got ten minutes," he told Jeff.

Debbie Benson arrived back from the bathroom literally dragging Iva by the shirtsleeve. Their conversation had roughly paralleled Brian's and Jeff's:

"Let's just talk to them," Debbie had said to Iva.

"Why, why should we?" Iva asked.

"They might not be jerks. Come on."

Iva hated pickup scenes, so she strenuously suggested the evening would be best concluded over blueberry pancakes at the local diner. Debbie hated pickup scenes too, nothing good ever came of them, but one overriding consideration prevailed. She had not been with a man for over ten months.

Brian reacted to his introduction to Iva with a curt "Hi, how ya doin'?" and an automatic once-over that made her feel like a horse at auction.

"You want to see my teeth?" she snapped, catching him off guard.

"No, uh, sorry, I didn't mean to, uh..."

"Nice chatting with you, but I really must be going," she added.

"So long," Brian replied, recovering. "Let's not do it again sometime."

Angrily turning for their friends, they were greeted by the sight of Jeff and Debbie making out. Brian turned away to face the bar and with a sigh Iva plopped down on the stool next to him.

"You live around here?" he asked in a flat uninterested monotone.

"Yeah," Iva answered, "you?"

"Yeah."

Neither spoke for about a minute as Jeff and Debbie continued their public display two stools down the bar. Clearing his throat, Brian finally said, "I guess our friends like each other."

"Brilliant deduction," Iva answered. "Are you a detective?"

Brian smiled and for the first time really looked at whom he was talking to. Iva smiled back and also checked him out. Both were struck by each other's physical attractiveness and both assumed they were about to experience the old adage that—in bars especially—beauty and personality are mutually exclusive.

"Did you say you live around here?" Brian asked.

"I live with Debbie on Wolver Hollow Road," Iva replied.

They borrowed Jeff's car and headed to Geraghty's Diner, leaving Debbie and Jeff to continue their lonely revelry by themselves. Over blueberry pancakes Brian listened intently to a life story with, he felt, far more substance than his own. Without question, Iva Fidele at twenty-nine had been through a hell of a lot.

"What do people do on a kibbutz?" Brian asked. "I always picture them picking fruit and taking cover."

Iva grinned. It was difficult to explain her childhood to an American Episcopalian who had never been to Israel. *Probably,* she thought, *he's never even tasted gefilte fish.*

"We survive," she said.

It was a good answer. Childhood in the Jewish quarter of Jerusalem, adolescence in Tel Aviv, her twenties on Manhattan's upper east side, Iva Fidele survived the wars. Her mother and two brothers did not survive. Her father lived, his survival as yet unresolved. An agent of Israel's Mossad, Conrad Fidele had been unable to insulate his family from the ravages of his country's struggle to exist. Two elder brothers died within four hours of each other on Yom Kippur in 1973: Syrian artillery fire, cold, unromantic. Iva's ten-year-old reaction was to mourn for a time, continue growing older and promise never to forget.

Iva heard the gunshot that murdered her mother. Eleven years in anti-terrorist operations and good at his job, Conrad Fidele had many enemies. One afternoon a young Palestinian, barely sixteen, crowbarred his way through the back door of the Fidele house in suburban Tel Aviv. Father and daughter were pulling into their driveway as Lisa Fidele, pinned on the floor, died instantly by a bullet entering her skull at the temple. Iva recognized the sound as gunfire but she did not immediately compute danger and pain. Her father understood immediately. Gun drawn, he bounded through the front door in time to shoot the terrorist in the back. As he ran through the house screaming for his wife, he tripped over her body in the hall.

Conrad stood staring. His childhood sweetheart and lifelong companion suddenly gone, shock and disbelief gave way to unbearable pain. Vowing to mutilate every single follower of Mohammed, he reacted too late to block the only person left alive he loved from viewing the death scene.

The image of her mother lying dead in a mass of blood and torn tissue, eyes and mouth still frozen in terror, would endure in Iva for the rest of her life. Her teenage reaction was to mourn once again, continue growing older and promise never to forget.

"I'm talking too much," Iva said. "Would you like some more coffee?"

Brian did not answer. He was mesmerized.

"More coffee, Brian?"

"My God, I'm a plebe," he finally said. "What a story! I broke my arm in summer camp once but nothing like... when did you come to this country?"

Iva inventoried Brian's tall muscular frame and handsome face. *Chestnut hair, sky-blue eyes, high cheekbones, even a little dimple in his chin. God... he's gorgeous.*

"Right after my mother died my father retired and took a job as a security consultant for the El-Al Airlines office in Manhattan. I came here with him and enrolled at Barnard. I've been here ever since. Three years ago I found a teaching job at the Great Neck Academy elementary school and moved out to Long Island."

"How do you like the island?"

"Too much traffic everywhere. The north shore's nice."

Brian nodded. He knew he was about to be blunt but he was in a hurry to get to know this person. "You must feel guilty sometimes about leaving Israel," he said.

Iva put down her fork and turned away for a moment. Then she whipped her head around so fast her hair splayed over her face. All Brian could see were her eyes, the darkest brown eyes he had ever seen, angry eyes, eyes that had seen a hell of a lot. *Holy shit she's wild,* he thought. He felt himself getting aroused.

"I miss Israel very much," Iva said with such intensity Brian was taken aback.

"Hey, I believe you."

Her face softened. "Come on, you know all about me," she said in a hurry to change the subject. "What about you?"

"I'm dull."

"Come on."

"I'm boring."

"I doubt that."

"I'm too damn normal."

"I'll be the judge of that. Go ahead."

"But all I really love to do is watch old movies," Brian insisted.

Iva raised an eyebrow. *God, this is going too well.* "Me too," she replied.

"You know, grade B black and white flicks from the thirties and forties," he went on, leaning forward against the table. "When they really knew how to make movies. Movies where they had fun, the good guys against the bad guys, laughing in the face of danger... you know... "

"Believe me, I do know," Iva said. "My roommate at Barnard was a film major. We used to go to the Biograph all the time."

"William Powell,"

"Myrna Loy,"

"The Thin Man!" they both shouted simultaneously causing heads to turn. A couple of seconds went by and they both breathlessly whispered in unison, "Wow!"

Iva smiled and looked down at the tabletop. Brian cocked his head and tried to see through the hair falling forward to cover her face. Then he began to talk about growing up in a spacious house overlooking Long Island Sound, remembering a succession of private schools and tennis camps that insulated a young boy from the real world, and a high number in the Vietnam War draft lottery that had quite possibly kept him alive. Beaming, he revealed teaching to be his occupation also, meaning every word when he said there was nothing else he would rather do. For the first time to anyone, Brian talked about his long walks in the woods on the Wildwood estate. He described what he called Long Island's "treasure": forests, wetlands, beaches, some of the most precious landscape anywhere, and the mindless destruction propagated by green-eyed developers and politicians. Iva saw his indigo eyes blaze when he told her about the series of articles on the subject he had written for *Newsday*, the island's main newspaper.

"I pissed a lot of people off," Brian admitted with a satisfied grin.

"You sound like Ralph Nader," Iva said.

"No thank you, Nader's become a pompous egomaniac. I'd prefer Teddy Roosevelt. Just because he was a hunter he's totally misunderstood. He really cared about the land. He's a hero of mine."

"Theodore—I'm taking this canal and screw the Dagoes—Roosevelt?" Iva asked. "The big stick Anglophile to beat all Anglophiles? Do I have it right? Are we talking about the same guy?"

"Yup," Brian replied, "same guy. It's just that you have to understand him within the context of his own times. I'm pretty liberal and I'll say it again—he's my hero."

"I still don't get it," Iva said. "How come you're such a passionate environmentalist? I mean—a spoiled little rich boy from the North Shore?"

Brian did not like being called a spoiled little rich boy though in truth he knew the description was quite apt. Without thinking he said, "Listen, you don't have to have your family killed to really care about something." Iva blanched and

Brian realized he had been too blunt. "Sorry," he said quickly, "I didn't mean that."

"Yes you did," Iva replied. "It's okay. Just keep going."

"All right, why am I an environmentalist? No one reason. Maybe the first Earth Day when I was still at Princeton. It really struck me. We all marched around the campus in gas masks. We talked and watched movies about pollution. A TV movie with Hal Holbrook playing a candidate for the Senate who picks up a bird that can't fly anymore because of the smog. I'll never forget that. When I was a kid my parents sent me to camp upstate. I actually saw Lake Erie on fire. A lake burning! Look, I'm not bullshitting you. Even spoiled little rich boys can believe in something."

Iva nodded and said, "I deserved that, good answer." After a pause she asked, "What about your family?"

"Uh, it's just me and my parents. My mother never worked. My father was a writer and a good one—articles in *Life* and a couple of really good novels. But he stopped writing when I was in high school. My mother's father died and left us money so my father just sort of quit. We didn't need money so I guess he... well let's just say cocktail hour kept coming earlier and earlier. He still says he's going to get back to writing but I know he won't. I guess I was the last to know. Hey, I was twenty-five before I admitted to myself my father was an alcoholic.

"And now you write because your father won't," Iva said.

"Maybe," Brian admitted.

"It must be tough to love and hate someone at the same time," she added.

Brian said nothing. But the bile rising up in his throat betrayed the bull's-eye.

For almost a minute they poked at their food. Both were a bit embarrassed they had opened up so much so quickly. Brian finally cleared his throat and tried another tack. He started talking about ancient Greece. Iva deferred acceptance of his invitation for her to accompany him to Athens in the summer, but she did promise to read Edith Hamilton's *The Greek Way* as a start. Words flowed freely and as they did Iva realized she was in love. It just happened. Fast. No warning.

As Brian looked into the dark brown eyes scanning his face for approval, he knew. He knew he loved her and she loved him. And although he felt kind of nauseous he knew it would pass. *This is for real! I'm really in love! Fast. Insane. Just like the old movies.*

When Brian dropped Iva off at her apartment, he kissed her on the cheek. There would be sex later, but not now. Two people had just met, become friends and fallen in love. It was not a pickup; no one lied, no one mistrusted, no one hurt the other. Over the next few weeks Brian and Iva would see a lot of each other, even date to the surprise and delight of both. They never tired of finding out what the other was thinking, liked doing or dreamed about. The American staple of dinner and a movie became ecstasy, and blueberry pancakes at Geraghty's Diner provided an afterglow they could call their own.

When sex finally did happen a few weeks later, the moment was right for both of them. Their blood pumped fast, muscles flexed and loosened, and sweat and warmth enveloped them. They felt utter contentment. Cuddling afterward, Brian and Iva both said *I love you* for the first time.

Ten months later, driving to Professor Alan Sansone's house, Brian and Iva were still in love, more so if possible. Idiosyncrasies shared strengthened the bond. Iva enjoyed her initiation to Yankee Stadium as much as Brian enjoyed his first trip to the Museum of Modern Art. Jew and gentile, greens and meat, neat and not so neat—they could not understand their love or begin to define it, they just let it happen and allowed themselves to enjoy it.

"We're almost there," Brian said, turning onto Beaver Pond Road.

"Good," Iva replied, "Because I have to go to the bathroom real bad."

Brian chuckled. They had a running joke about Iva's always having to go to the bathroom while they were driving.

"You should have gone before we left," he said in a tone of parental authority. "Now you'll just have to hold it in. In a terrible German accent he added, "You vill learn zee bladder control and you vill like it."

At this Iva squirmed and Brian mocked her with sadistic laughter.

She played along. "How much farther?" she asked, her arms around her stomach.

"Poland then Belgium then France!" Brian thundered, and then turning into Sansone's driveway they both broke up.

There was no doorbell on the Professor's front door; he had removed it twenty years earlier in favor of an antique brass knocker in the shape of Mary Pickford's upper torso. The metal hammer designed to do the knocking did so directly on her breasts, still firm but tarnished.

"I'm not touching that thing," Iva said as they approached.

"Allow me with pleasure, Madame," Brian replied, bowing deeply and straightening his collar.

But it was not to be. Alan Sansone clairvoyantly opened the door thereby robbing Brian of his chance to engage in a bit of bad taste roaring twenties' style.

"Brian. Iva. Great to see you, come on in." He pumped their hands, beckoned them inside and, grinning ear-to-ear, announced, "I've made a gallon of hot buttered rum. Let's go into the den. I want to propose a toast."

Following them into the book-lined study, Iva noted fondly that the two men looked like they had been sent by central casting. The elder absent-minded professor costumed himself in baggy gray pants with cuffs, wingtips, and a brown cardigan over a white shirt and striped bow tie. Bushy white hair, flowing mustache and wire-rimmed spectacles added opening night perfection. Brian also looked right for his role as the rising still idealistic academic. Clad in an old Harris tweed over a lime green shirt, blue corduroys and brown loafers, he appeared how youthful scholars usually appeared in the movies: bright, willing to discuss the causes of the Peloponnesian War at the drop of a hat, but completely ignorant of the aesthetics of clothing combination.

"I sampled a bit of this rum before you got here," the Professor said with a wink as he poured mugs for his guests. "It's really quite acceptable."

"What are we toasting to, Professor?" asked Iva.

"Ah yes, the toast. It's important, serious, let's get right to it." He cleared his throat and looked at Brian. "Are you ready?"

"Sure," Brian answered, a bit surprised. He had expected something lighthearted. Professor Sansone brought his mug to his chest and held it there with a steady hand. He took a deep breath and said, "I propose a toast to Brian Werth, his past, his future, and the decision he must soon make." Raising the mug over his head, he nodded at Brian then Iva and took a long slow drink. Iva also drank; Brian did not, the toast was to him. Both wondered about the meaning.

"Mmmmmaaaah," Sansone uttered in a kind of half belch half sigh intended to verify that the rum concoction had delectably warmed his innards. He transferred remnants of froth from his mustache to his sleeve, looked at his guests and grinned: a wise old man with a special secret. "Wait right here, I have something to show you," he said, turning on his heels and literally running from the room.

"Say, what's going on here?" Iva asked, wondering as she spoke whether all those old movies they were watching were actually affecting her speech patterns.

"I don't know babe, just keep me covered," Brian answered, deliberately jumping into the same idiom. "Something's screwy, that's for sure." He laughed nervously then became serious. "Who knows what he means by toasting my future and some sort of decision I've got? I guess we'll just have to wait to find out."

"I've never seen him so excited," Iva said. "He ran out of here."

"It just proves he's in shape," Brian added, understating the youth of a man pushing eighty.

Point of fact, Alan Sansone radiated a vitality that belied his advancing years. Iva noticed it in his posture: head up, shoulders back, chest out—a passion for life fighting and winning against gravity and osteoarthritis.

"Just because there's snow on the roof doesn't mean the furnace has gone out," Sansone would boast to his friends. It was in his eyes: windows on a mind ablaze with activity.

"Maybe you are getting that promotion," Iva said, not looking at Brian as she spoke. She could not, it was a subject they had discussed earlier and agreed to dismiss. The frown she missed revealed resentment of the breach.

Brian said sharply, "Let's forget that."

He could not forget it though, not for a second. He had to admit there was a chance, albeit slim, that the evening would amount to more that just the spinning of yarns. Maybe, just maybe, Professor Sansone planned to recommend Brian Werth as the next chairman of Wheatley's history department.

Rumors of Alan Sansone's retirement had been floating around for ten years, but they were never riper. Lately, he had been dropping hints that he needed more time to finish his "master work," a voluminous treatise on the life of Socrates. Brian's own cause for hope derived from the infamous "younger man" remark at last Friday's wine and cheese reception for the history faculty and graduate students. In between crackers, Sansone informed his colleagues that the department "desperately needs youthful direction and fresh ideas." Brian had felt his eyes widen at the prospect of being promoted over eight older people with years more experience. His coworkers responded with icy stares, an indication they did not embrace the idea of a veritable adolescent rising past them to the exalted chairmanship.

"It's just that it's stupid to get worked up over something that will probably never happen," Brian said, sitting next to Iva on the couch.

"I know," she said.

"We shouldn't even think about it."

"You're right," she said.

"I have to admit it would be great. It would really make my night. I'd stay in a good mood even if dessert turns out to be Brussels sprouts."

"I hope it is Brussels sprouts," Iva said with a straight face that caused Brian to shiver and swallow hard.

"This is it!" Sansone announced, returning to the room with the same zest he left it. In two hands he held out a bulging black loose-leaf binder. "There's two years of hard work in here. It's good, really good."

"What is it, Professor?" Brian asked.

"Marcus Noble's master's thesis."

Brian nodded. He knew Marcus Noble and was impressed by him. Noble was African American and from the South Bronx, and he had somehow survived and done well enough in the New York public school system to earn a full scholarship to Wheatley. Vaguely, Brian had heard Noble was investigating corruption in the local political machine of Republican Frank Montesano.

"Right now, just read the section beginning on page forty-one," Sansone said. "Then take it home tonight and study the whole thing in detail."

"Okay," Brian said, curious, although such a big deal over just another master's thesis seemed a bit of an anti-climax.

"Iva my dear," the Professor said, walking over and extending his elbow, "I would be delighted if you would accompany me to my greenhouse. It's time to choose the corn."

"Charmed I'm sure," Iva answered, jumping up and taking his arm.

"You know the corn on the cob we'll be having will have been picked no longer than twenty minutes prior to our eating it. It's much better that way. When he lived at Sagamore Hill, Teddy Roosevelt used to insist on it."

"Boy, that Teddy Roosevelt must have been some kind of guy," Iva said, smiling and looking at Brian.

"He was," Brian and the Professor replied almost in unison, and they all smiled.

"Okay, I'm ready," Iva said, "let's go get that corn on the cob."

"You betcha. Pardon us Brian, we'll be right back."

Brian did not look up or acknowledge he heard: the section of Marcus Noble's master's thesis beginning on page forty-one immediately captivated him. Entitled *The Long Island Sound Crossing*, it began with a map diagramming secret plans for a humongous bridge. Outlined were the island's North Shore and the Long Island Sound across to the town of Rye, New York. The proposed route of the bridge and its access roads were marked in red and Brian saw blood streaming everywhere. Most of all he saw his hometown virtually destroyed. Sagamore stood to be the southern terminus for the bridge and as such would be the recipient of countless tons of steel and cement. The bridge destroyed homes, schools and churches indiscriminately. His woods were gone too; entrance ramps paved over them. Wildwood mansion ceased to exist; concrete abutments slammed right through it.

Noble's research was clear and thorough. Republican leaders, he charged, wanted to build the bridge for their own personal profit. With the GOP controlling the local governments on both sides of the Sound, the governorship, the state senate, and with plenty of money to bribe a few Democrats in the state assembly, they could very well pull it all off. Access roads included, the super bridge would cost the taxpayers approximately fifteen billion dollars, and Republican Frank Montesano possessed the power to gain control of the project. Although the governor theoretically could appoint anyone he wanted, Frank had to be the odds on favorite—come reelection time his Nassau County machine could make or break a governor. Covertly scheming for the bridge for nearly ten years, Boss Montesano stood well prepared to spread the spoils around, not forgetting himself, to the political allies who helped him keep his stranglehold on the municipal government of Long Island's most populated county.

Brian rubbed his eyes and suddenly realized he was hot and sweaty. If Marcus Noble's source was valid, and Brian desperately wondered who or what that source was, then his charges were within the realm of possibility. He took off his jacket. There was a lot more to read.

On the next few pages Noble went into detail as to how the Republican machine would profit from the project. Kickbacks from firms awarded construction contracts were one way. Real estate transactions were another. Vast amounts of land needed to be condemned to make way for the bridge and New York State's unassailable right of eminent domain would make it all quite legal. State public works officials, in a hurry to start construction and quite free with government money, could be counted on to offer considerably more for a property than it previously was worth. Noble detailed how Montesano, guided by his foreknowledge of the proposed bridge and its arteries, had been using proxies to buy as much Sagamore land as he could get his hands on.

"Come and get it!"

Iva's voice from the dining room snapped Brian out of his concentration. Placing the thesis on the coffee table and starting to walk from the room, he suddenly stopped in his tracks. Something told him not to leave the manuscript behind. Rationally he knew Noble must have made other copies but it still seemed too precious to just leave it there. He squeezed the thesis to his chest, walked into the dining room and forced himself to smile at the Professor. Sansone smiled back then both looked away, seemingly hurt by something.

Iva noticed this and Brian's cradling of the thesis. She became even more curious.

"We're having steak and potatoes and corn on the cob," Sansone announced. "Is that all right with you, Brian?"

"It sure is," he replied, amazed. *Real food.*

"I figured you'd feel that way," the Professor continued. "We're having your kind of meal because I want to ask you to do something."

"That's it, Professor," Iva chimed in, "get what you want out of him then spring the Brussels sprouts."

The Professor laughed, Brian did not. Brussels sprouts were never funny to him. Never.

"Careful Iva," the Professor said, "I need you on my side and Brian's going to need your help."

"For what?" Brian asked. "What do I need her help for? What do you want me to do?"

"Let's eat first," Sansone said, "then we'll get down to business."

The food really hit the spot. Among his many areas of expertise, Alan Sansone possessed considerable culinary acumen. The only minor drawback for Brian was that his steak was medium and not well done. But he had asked for it medium, having heard the Professor on more than one occasion state unequivocally that overcooked meat is an affront to the memory of a once noble steer.

Wondering what was up, Brian and Iva did not have their minds fully on the meal. Nevertheless, Sansone's dinner table discourse was, as always, great fun to listen to. From the cultivation of maize in pre-Columbian Mexico to Truman's firing of General MacArthur, the Professor seamlessly intertwined entertainment and education.

"Iva, let me tell you a little story about Theodore Roosevelt," Sansone said, dabbing his mouth with his napkin. "He's one of Brian's heroes."

"So I've heard," Iva said.

"Here we go," Brian said.

"Well," the Professor went on, "When Teddy left office in 1909, he headed straight for a big game hunt in Africa. His many enemies hoisted their drinks and toasted 'Health to the lions.' Conservatives joked that 'some lion ought to do his duty.' But after months of tramping through the wilderness, our man Theodore emerged bearing over three thousand trophies including nine lions, five elephants and thirteen rhinos. But Iva my dear, in reality Roosevelt was much too nearsighted to be a good marksman."

Brian chuckled. He knew what was coming.

"Every time he fired his rifle, four other rifles fired at exactly the same instant. You see, the safari leader and his men darn well knew Mr. Roosevelt had only an inkling of the general direction the animal was bearing down on him, and the life of a former president was far too important to take any chances."

The three of them laughed.

"Some say the cartoon character of Mr. Magoo was actually based on President Roosevelt," Brian added.

"As you can see, Iva," Sansone added, "there's no end to the useless and irrelevant information inside the head of a history professor."

They all laughed again. Dinner done, their host leaned back in his chair and uttered "Mmmmmaaaah," a Falstaffian figure with his innards warmed once again. Business, finally, was at hand.

"What do you think of the thesis?" he asked Brian without any preamble.

"Interesting," Brian replied calmly. Iva saw him clench his fist.

"They've really gone too far this time, haven't they?" the Professor added.

"They certainly have." Both fists clenched.

"They should be stopped."

Still low key, Brian said, "Yes, they should."

Iva stood up. "Would somebody please tell me what's going on here?"

Brian told her point blank, "The Republicans have secret plans to build a super bridge across Long Island Sound that will destroy countless acres of priceless landscape and displace thousands from their homes."

He took a deep breath after he finished and both he and the Professor stared at her. There was silence for a moment as no one spoke. As she sat down, the only response Iva could come up with was "Oh."

Brian continued: "We've got to get organized, Professor, start discussion groups, form committees, get petitions signed... "

Sansone smiled and shook his head. "You're not going to suggest a dance marathon to raise money are you?"

"Now that you mention it, why not?" Brian replied.

"Times have changed," the Professor said.

"What do you mean?"

"You want to relive your college days and I don't think it's appropriate. We're in the nineteen eighties now and new problems demand new solutions. Face it, Montesano won't lose any sleep over a bunch of college kids dancing till they drop."

Brian felt slapped, punched rather, in the face. Clearly, the Professor aimed to fight Montesano and his bridge, and he already had a battle plan mapped out—his way.

"What do you want me to do?" Brian asked numbly.

"Run for mayor," the Professor said.

The words stunned Brian. They made no sense. "Who should run?" he asked.

"You should dammit!" Iva burst in. "You'd be perfect! Take your message to the people. Campaign. Win. Use the system to break the machine. And then... then... then... long live Long Island!"

Alan Sansone nodded and smiled at Iva, gratitude in his eyes. *She'll be strength behind Brian*, he thought, *I knew it*. He felt his eyes starting to tear; Iva reminded him of his wife, Melanie, who had been gone nearly thirty years.

"You want me to run for mayor," Brian said, trying to digest the thought.

"That's right," Sansone said.

"Me?"

"Yes, you. You are a registered Democrat aren't you?"

"Sure, but why me? I have no political experience whatsoever."

"With your articles in *Newsday*, you've already established yourself as a thorn in the Republicans' side. You've got looks, good speaking ability, and you're young but not too young. I've already spoken to the Sagamore Democratic committee about you. They may support you for the nomination."

"Sounds like nobody else wants it," Brian said.

"None of the party regulars want it, that is truc," the Professor admitted. "You know Sagamore, for a Democrat it's a long shot."

Brian knew "long shot" understated the situation. The city of Sagamore had not had a Democratic mayor since 1896. It was a stronghold so staunchly Republican it served as the location for the GOP county headquarters.

For the past eighteen years Frank Montesano's long-time crony, Al Savino, had been mayor. Al ran routinely every two years and did not just defeat his opponents, he buried them. A freshman political science major could figure out why. First, there was more than a two to one Republican registration advantage, important because most Sagamore Republicans resembled marionettes in the voting booth. Second, the large Italian population blindly voted for anyone with a surname ending in "o."

"Why should I run if I have no chance of winning?" Brian asked the Professor.

"To play it safe and avoid offending the voters, Montesano will definitely hold off announcing his bridge plans until after the election. If we can get proof of what they're up to, concrete documentation that will stand up in court, you can hammer it home during the campaign. Then you will win. One thing history has taught us is the people love to vote the scoundrels out of office. The hard part is exposing the scoundrels."

Mayor Werth. Sounds nice. "There's no proof now?" Brian asked, hopefully.

Sansone shook his head. "Noble's source for his thesis has asked to remain anonymous. I don't even know who it is. It's going to take good old-fashioned detective work to nail Montesano and his crew. But make no mistake, we will nail them."

"I'm not sure, Professor," Brian said, "I'd have to leave teaching and give up my writing. You're talking a lot of time and effort, maybe for nothing. I just don't know."

Iva exhaled loudly enough to cause the Professor and Brian to turn and notice her displeasure. *I know what he's thinking*, she told herself, *he's thinking my life is comfortable now, why rock the boat*? This was the side of Brian she liked the least: too much dreaming and not enough practicable action... behavior her high school English teacher had called *Hamlet crap*. She wished there was a pitcher of ice water on the table so she could throw it in his face.

"I just don't know," Brian said again.

Alan Sansone leaned back in his chair and interlocked his fingers on his stomach. He uttered one word: "Areté."

Brian knew immediately what the Professor was driving at.

"What?" he said even though he had heard.

"Areté," the Professor repeated.

"What is areté?" Iva interrupted. "It sounds like an over priced cologne."

The Professor smiled.

Brian answered her seriously as if he was in front of a class: "Areté was the word the ancient Greeks used to define excellence. The Professor here is subtly reminding me that government service is not only a duty owed to the community, it is a duty we all owe to ourselves. In Golden Age Athens, the Greek with the greatest arête was the man most well rounded. The body and the mind grew together, neither favored. Arête demanded time be equally divided among the gymnasium, the battlefield, the theatre, and the Assembly. Completeness, including running for Mayor, that is arête."

Iva muttered "Hmmm" and appeared thoughtful. Then she asked, "What does it smell like?"

This time Brian grinned along with the Professor.

"Is it okay if he thinks it over?" Iva asked, sneaking a wink at Sansone, a wink he correctly interpreted as *If there's any problem, I'll handle it.*

"Sure," Sansone replied. "And Brian, you can keep that copy of the thesis. I've got another so does Noble."

"Right. Thanks. Thanks for an eventful evening."

"That's for sure," Iva added.

Walking to the front door, Brian turned to the Professor. "You know, when we first got here we thought you were going to tell us you're retiring."

"Me? Retire?" the Professor replied. "Not for another fifty years."

"That's the spirit," Iva said.

"But what about what you said last Friday about the department needing a younger man with fresh ideas?" Brian persisted.

"Oh that," the Professor said with a sheepish grin, "I was blasted."

A kiss on the cheek for Iva, a handshake for Brian and they were back in their car on the way home. Silence prevailed for a time, both lost in their thoughts. Brian, cursing the bridge and wondering whether to try running for mayor, gripped the wheel and stared straight ahead. Iva, trying to imagine what it must be like to be old and without a family, finally broke the quiet.

"We should have helped him with the dishes," she said.

"You know he never lets us," Brian replied.

"I know. He's such a nice man."

"He's one of the good people in this world."

"Yup."

As he unlocked the gate in front of their house, Brian used the light from the headlights to glance at his watch: twelve ten in the morning, April sixteenth, Iva's birthday. *She probably doesn't realize it's already her birthday*, he thought. *She's expecting me to give her a present tomorrow night. Maybe I'll give it to her now and surprise her.* He was excited about presenting the gift. He loved Iva more than anything in the world and her present was the absolute best he could do.

"I am bushed," Iva said as they entered the house. "It's late and it's a school night."

Brian cringed as he headed to the kitchen for some junk food. He hated that his chosen profession—teaching—still held him captive to the dreaded childhood admonition that it was a "school night."

"Want a cookie?" he asked Iva. "Chocolate chip."

"No thanks, I'm trying to quit," he joked. But then he took the biggest one in the box.

Brian swallowed the last of his cookie and went over and hugged Iva, hard. "Happy birthday," he whispered in her ear.

"Oh, that's right it is."

"Wait right here," he told her, taking her by the shoulders and sitting her down at the kitchen table. "I've got something for you so don't move."

"Okay," Iva said. *I'm getting a present,* she thought. *I can't wait.* Then her new age occurred to her. *Thirty-two. Damn. Not exactly menopausal but getting up there.*

Brian returned with his hands behind his back, a confident young man with a special secret. "This is for you," he said, revealing in one hand a small rectangular package wrapped in yellow paper topped by a green bow.

Iva accepted his gift and even before opening it threw her arms around his neck. "Brian, it's beautiful, thank you." She kissed him on both cheeks then hard on the lips. The contents of the package mattered little compared with the fact it was given by Brian. She loved that man.

"Open it," he said.

Ripping off the wrapping and peeking inside, Iva saw a necklace: a gold chain connected—not through a clasp or drilling but delicately by wire—to a stone the likes of which she could not immediately identify.

"That necklace is one of a kind," Brian said. "I had it specially made."

"It's quartz?" Iva guessed, noticing the dull white color.

"That's right it is quartz," he replied. "Look closely at it, it's cracked a little on the side but you can see the tip. It's an Indian arrowhead. I found it in the meadow behind Wildwood. It's probably from the Matinecock tribe of the Algonquian nation and could be old enough to date back to... who knows... before the Europeans came here."

"It's beautiful," Iva said, reaching for him. She wanted more hugging.

"Not so fast," Brian said, "there's more." In his other hand he held out a birthday card. "There's some of my writing on the inside. About the arrowhead... and, well, maybe my long walks in the woods will make more sense to you now."

Without a word, Iva sat down at the table to read. As she did, Brian took the necklace and from behind fastened it around her neck. Then he hugged her from the back and peered over her shoulder.

A POINT IN TIME
BY
BRIAN CHARLES WERTH

I have no idea on what errand it was sent. It lay on the ground, white and curiously lovely, a little mauled by time but crafted superbly and worthy of the astonishing person who made it.

It was an Indian arrowhead: unmistakable and splendid in the setting sun, its symmetry and terrible purpose making it different from all other stones around it. I picked it up and held it in my hand and knew that I was the first to do so, to test its still sharp edge, since he who had made it released the bowstring and watched it speed toward its target.

I was alone except for bird sounds and an autumn wind that moved across the meadow grass. What a pity the summer had given up so soon. The arrowhead was really quite easy to see. But now its creator was faced with a winter coming on, and there would be long hours spent making another. And it is unlikely that the finder, unless he be a kinsman, would return it.

I am a neighbor, at least, and a kind of kinsman, and I would be pleased to return this treasure to its owner. I waited for him that evening, hoping to hear him hail me from the line of trees beyond. But the sun moved low, the night grew impatient, and there was no call; I knew that he had given up the search and gone away. Perhaps for him, as for me, there was a dinner even now getting cold and a woman who would be displeased by such aimless wanderings. And so this marvelous instrument was lost to him.

But I'll come back, kinsman. Perhaps some evening we can sit together on that big stone at the western edge of the meadow, and I'll return your splendid arrowhead and we might talk for a moment.

How clever you were to make this arrowhead. I'm afraid the point has been broken, and the stem, too, has partially cracked off. But the work, the long hours you spent shaping this weapon, still shows in the gracefully tapered edges with their terrible sharpness.

Things have changed since you passed this way. The deer have gone. I see a rabbit occasionally. But some things are the same for both of us—morning mists and summer lightning, the first hint of red in the dogwood at harvest time and, in winter, bird tracks in the snow. Once, near here, just around that clump of trees, I saw a fox.

Ah, yes. Your arrowhead. What were you shooting at that day? An enemy fearfully painted and come from a distant land, and sworn by all his gods to kill you? Or was there a rabbit carelessly feeding on something green and tender, unaware of your slow and patient approach?

Or did you, by chance, fire your arrow at the sun. If so, you almost made it, you with your agile hands and impossible dreams. Of course, it was at the sun you fired this missile. There is something about this arrowhead, so marvelously contrived, so beautiful...

A squirrel, you say? And you missed? And you tried to mark with your eye the place where the arrow fell and you walked back and forth across this meadow but your precious arrow had vanished utterly, and it was almost night and everything you did was wrong. And there was no one there to tell you how wondrous you were, how almost like a god.

It grows late, kinsman, and you are anxious to be gone. I cannot see you in the dark. I gather you do not want your damaged treasure. Very well, I shall keep it and remember you by it and show it to you when next we meet.

And meet again we shall, my father, for it is our destiny that one day we shall journey far from our upland meadow, you and I, and, together, touch the stars.

Iva's eyes glistened with tears as she finished. Brian noticed this and was embarrassed. "Even little rich boys can believe in something," he said, shrugging his shoulders.

"It's beautiful," Iva said. She turned to face him. "And you know what? I want to touch the stars with you too. I want to be with you forever."

"You do?" Brian said.

Iva nodded, and a tear trickled down her cheek.

Brian stared at the tear, fascinated. She was crying because of him. In spite of himself, he found himself enjoying the proof he held such power over her. After a moment he moved in to stop it, another good feeling.

"Hey c'mon," he said, taking her face in his hands and brushing away the tear. "I want to be with you too. I want to marry you."

Brian stepped back from Iva and dropped his hands to his sides. He had not planned to propose marriage. Then suddenly he found himself feeling total exhilaration. *Iva and I should get married. That came out because it was meant to.*

He got down on one knee. "Iva Fidele, will you marry me?" he asked.

Iva stopped crying, in addition she stopped breathing; they both did. This was a crucial scene in their lives. Iva looked at Brian, vulnerable Brian, and fumbled for her line. *Relax and let it happen* she remembered her college acting teacher telling her as she struggled with Ophelia. Her hand brushed her cheeks and pushed back her hair. She relaxed. She let it happen.

"Yes, I will," she said.

The embrace that followed was long and hard. They separated when they both realized they needed to breathe.

"I'm very happy," Brian finally said.

"Me too," Iva admitted. "What a birthday!"

Brian went to the refrigerator and pulled out the handy leftover New Year's Eve bottle of champagne. "I want to propose a toast," he announced.

"To what?"

"To us?"

"Us?"

"Me and you."

"Don't you think you should open the bottle first?" Iva asked.

"Oh that's right. Wait. I have a better idea." He grabbed two glasses and handed everything to Iva. "Hold this, we'll drink it in bed." Before she knew it he scooped her up in his arms.

"What are you doing Brian?"

"Taking you to our love nest."

"Careful, don't rupture yourself."

"Don't worry."

"Am I heavy?"

"Can I say two words?"

"Sure."

"Diet tomorrow."

"You jerk," she said, playfully pounding on his chest, "you're just trying to play Superman."

"No I'm not." Then, pinching her rear, "I love you Lois."

They tumbled onto the bed, miraculously not breaking anything or anyone. Brian popped the cork, poured and made his toast again.

"To us."

"To us."

Iva played with his hair and kissed him on the top of his head. She hated to admit it but she found herself enjoying the obvious fact she held such power over him.

The doorbell rang, or more accurately, the gatebell. Brian and Iva reacted identically to the delay in the next item on their agenda.

"Sonofabitch."

"Damn."

"Someone's at the gate," Brian said.

"It's probably your parents," Iva said. "Mental telepathy. They don't want you marrying a Jew."

Brian laughed then realized Iva was right. There would be a problem—with his parents and her father. The gatebell rang again.

"I'll go see who it is," he said.

"Be careful, Brian, it could be robbers."

"Robbers do not ring bells."

"Polite ones do," Iva said. "I'm coming with you."

"Great," he replied, throwing her a sweatshirt, "now we can both become a statistic."

There was a hundred yard walk down the driveway to the gate, unlit and nearly pitch dark. They both felt... "Spooky," Brian said out loud. Down behind the bars they thought they could make out the silhouette of a single man.

As they got closer, Iva started whispering: "Lions and tigers and bears, oh my! Lions and tigers and bears, oh my! Lions and tigers and... "

"Knock it off," Brian said.

A flashlight snapped on in his face, completely blinding him.

"I'm Patrolman Bolster of the Sagamore police department," a voice said. "Are you Brian Werth?"

"Uh, yes," Brian replied, shielding his eyes.

The flashlight snapped off.

"Do you have a badge or something?" Iva asked.

"Check out the car and the uniform," Bolster snapped. "What do you think this is, Halloween?"

"What do you want?" Brian asked. Policemen always made him nervous, feelings left over from a pubescent fondness for firecrackers and, later, more than a little pot smoking in the Princeton dormitories.

"Professor Alan Sansone has been found dead," the patrolman said. As an afterthought and sounding totally insincere he added, "I'm real sorry."

Chapter II

"If you take the badge off, you muzzler, I'll make you eat it."

Spencer Tracy to cop Edgar Kennedy in ***Quick Millions*** *(1931)*

APRIL 16, 1:37 A.M.

Brian and Iva gripped each other's arms. The news did not make sense. *What the hell is going on?*

"Are you sure?" Brian heard himself ask.

"Positive. You and some woman were with him tonight, right?"

"Right," Brian answered. "This woman here, my fiancée." *Engagement and death... within minutes,* he thought.

"Good," Patrolman Bolster said. "They sent me to pick you up. The detectives at the scene want to ask you a few questions."

"How did it happen?" Brian asked.

"I don't know. Accidental, I heard."

"But we were just there," Iva broke in, composed but, as Brian noticed, just barely.

"Let's just get going," the officer said, "Okay?"

Only after they were seated in the back of the patrol car did they notice another policeman sitting zombie-like in the passenger seat. Patrolman Bolster did not introduce his silent partner. The stranger did not move or acknowledge their presence in any way, nor did he even bother to glance at Bolster who started the car and drove off. Brian and Iva both noted the conduct as odd but neither had time to wonder much. One of their dearest friends was dead and room had to be made to assimilate that. *When did it happen? How could it happen? Why?*

The muted Patrolman McGowan could not have cared less about the late great Professor Alan Sansone. All he knew was that the old man's death was keeping him and his partner on overtime. *Thank Christ for that.* He did not know when he could ever go home again, not after what had happened that afternoon...

It all started out so routine. Two teenage girls in a Chevy van pulled over for speeding found to have open beer cans in the front seat. Totally routine. It was his partner's turn to yell at them and write up the ticket. He did not even get out of the car. If he had, nothing would have gone wrong.

"I made a deal with them," Bolster had said, sticking his head back into the patrol car.

"What's the deal?" McGowan asked.

"They'll blow us both if we let them go."

McGowan rubbed his crotch. Yeah, he wanted it. "You first," he said, exhibiting the judgment that had kept him a patrolman after twenty-one years on the force.

"Okay," Bolster replied, "I'll be right back. You know it don't take me long."

McGowan laughed. *I'm glad the department teamed me up with this guy,* he thought. *It's gonna work out real good.*

True to his word, Bolster was not in the van very long: seven and a half minutes to be exact. "Not bad," was all he said when he returned.

"I'll probably be done quicker than you," McGowan sneered as he got out. "I don't need the romance."

The first girl he saw as he bounded into the back of the van made his mouth water. Sitting naked in the front seat, she looked young, seventeen at the most, with pigtails and a petite figure that reminded him of some of his favorite centerfolds. Motionless and unsmiling, she made a face like a child about to be forced to face up to some foul-tasting Caster Oil. The second girl remained in the back compartment snuggled under a blanket. Ripping it off her with a tender "C'mon baby," Patrolman McGowan had the single worst experience of his life. He recognized her.

"Daddy?" she said.

Words failed him. Any coherent thought failed him. Turning away immediately, he ran from the van as fast as he could.

"Wow, you are fast!" his partner said.

"Shut up and drive!" McGowan screamed, jumping into the car.

"What's the prob... "

McGowan grabbed Bolster's neck with both hands. "Drive or I'll kill you. My daughter's in there."

That was the last dialogue the men had exchanged over seven hours since the incident. Patrolman Bolster for his part could find no icebreaker. He knew what not to say. "Hey, she was good," would certainly not work. *Christ, a blow job from my partner's daughter. Way to go, asshole.*

McGowan felt numb. I've lost my daughter, he kept repeating to himself. How can I face her? If she tells her mother, I'll lose them both. *A wife and a daughter in one day. Way to go, asshole.*

Every light in Alan Sansone's house seemed to be on and four patrol cars sat in the driveway. An ambulance was backed up on the lawn facing the front door: *The meat wagon*, thought Brian. On the sidewalk, about a dozen neighbors stood huddled together talking softly.

"There's your Greek chorus," Iva pointed out.

"Yeah," Brian replied, but he knew he was not at a play. This night was real, more real by the minute.

"Let's go inside," Bolster said.

They got out of the car and left Patrolman McGowan, still unmoving, alone. As they walked up the front walk, someone called to them from down the street.

"Hey Brian!" The tall figure of a well-built black man in his mid-twenties sprinted at them. He cut across the yard and stood before them, panting and unable to speak.

"Iva, I'd like you to meet Marcus Noble," Brian said.

"Hello," Iva said.

Noble nodded and panted in her direction.

"Marcus, uh, how did you get here?" Brian asked.

Marcus took some more deep breaths and swallowed hard. "I guess you could say I hitchhiked. I just heard the news. I got here as soon as I could."

Brian and Iva both knew what he meant by "hitchhiked." A black man hitchhiking in Sagamore at two in the morning? Good luck. He had run the entire five miles from campus.

Two detectives met them in the front hall: no wrinkled trench coats, navy blue windbreakers instead, but detectives nonetheless. The detective who identified himself as Dolan, strikingly obese and living proof that the Sagamore police department paid scant attention to weight standards, ushered them into the living room. After perfunctory greetings and condolences he explained, "At approximately twelve-ten in the morning a neighbor, a Mrs. Pike, heard a scream apparently emanating from this house. She called 911. When the officers arrived about five minutes later, nobody answered the door. They entered anyway and upon a search of the premises located the body of Mr. Sansone in the upstairs bathtub. A plugged-in television set was in the water on top of him. We're treating this as an accidental death due to electrocution."

A television set in the bathtub? Absurd, too absurd to be believed, Brian thought. "How does a television set get in the tub?" he asked.

"It falls in accidentally," Detective Dolan replied. "A lot of people watch TV in the bathroom. It's not a good idea, but they do it. The Professor must have tripped and pulled the television in the tub with him."

"No," Brian said. "Professor Alan Sansone did not watch television in the bathtub."

"How do you know?" the other detective, Carroll, asked.

"He just wouldn't," Iva offered.

"I suppose you have first-hand knowledge of the Professor's bathroom habits," Dolan said to Iva.

"No but... "

"Hold on," Brian cut in, irritated at the detective's snide comment to Iva. "We are simply trying to let you know that the Professor hated television. He said so all the time. He could barely stand to even have one in his house. To suggest that he would set one up precariously on the edge of his bathtub is just crazy."

"You are suggesting that he was murdered," Detective Dolan said, staring at Brian.

"Yes, I guess I am," Brian replied, staring right back.

"Do any of you know anyone who might have had a reason for wanting the Professor dead?" Dolan asked.

Brian and Iva were stumped. Everyone liked Professor Alan Sansone; he had always avoided arguments, possessing an uncanny ability to make people think he liked them even when he did not.

Marcus spoke up, "The Professor was involved in an investigation of the Sagamore Republicans that could possibly ruin the careers of many of the politicians currently in power."

The detectives did not react to the statement; if anything, they looked bored. "Everybody investigates the Republicans, it's no big deal," Dolan said.

"This is different," Brian said.

"How?" Dolan asked.

Brian shot a glance at Noble. Their eyes met and they simultaneously agreed: *not yet*. Brian told the detectives "We're not yet ready to reveal that."

Dolan sighed and threw up his hands. "I'm sorry. There's got to be some reason, some motive. As far as I'm concerned, no murder investigation." He started to walk away.

Detective Carroll followed and added over his shoulder, "Listen, we will dust for fingerprints up there but I can't promise you anything."

"Wait!" Brian said in a loud voice. The two detectives turned around. "What channel was the television on when you found it?"

"What?" Dolan said, annoyed.

"What channel was the Professor watching in the tub?"

"Who cares?" the detective said.

It was a long shot but Noble caught on. "I'll find out," he said, running up the stairs to check the dial on the set.

"Aren't you gentlemen curious what show the Professor was watching at the time of his death?" Brian asked.

"No," Dolan said.

Detective Carroll grabbed his partner's arm to get him to leave but he shrugged him off. Brian and Dolan glared at each other.

"Channel eleven," Marcus said, returning.

"Channel eleven," Brian repeated, "and the scream was heard at twelve-ten. What's on channel five at that time?" He inhaled deeply. Not being a regular late night television viewer he had no idea whether he was about to inject reasonable doubt or look foolish.

"*The Dating Game*," someone said. Appropriately it was Patrolman Bolster who had just appeared in the doorway smoking a cigar and sipping a beer courtesy of the late Professor. "I watch that show sometimes." He smirked. "You know, when I don't want to wake up the wife."

"*The Dating Game*," Brian repeated. "*The Dating Game*." A point had been scored after all. Walking slowly toward Dolan he said, "You are telling us that Professor Alan Sansone, Ph.D. Columbia, chairman of the history department at Wheatley College, author of probably a dozen books, a man with an avowed aversion to television, died accidentally while watching *The Dating Game* in the bathtub." Their faces were inches apart.

"It would appear so," Dolan snarled through clenched teeth.

Brian's head pounded. *Professor Sansone murdered and two detectives deliberately treating it as an accident.* As he stared at Dolan, his pain fueled an anger that spread all consuming like a cancer. His vision blurred for a moment and he blinked his eyes. Strangely, Brian found himself remembering how helpless he felt the morning after his senior prom upon hearing of a classmate's death in a drunk driving accident. Tonight's anguish felt just the same. "You're a fucking pig," he said to Dolan.

The detective aimed a punch a Brian's face; sausage fingers curled into a rubber ball glanced outward with all the strength the blubber man could muster. Brian easily ducked it and offered a return blow that was sharp and swift and on target. Dolan's head snapped back and hit the wall, and he slid down into a sitting position. Marcus and Detective Carroll rushed at each other but both stopped short, having second thoughts about brawling. Like hockey players, they waited to see what was going to happen with the main bout.

Apparently, the main bout was over: Werth by a knockout. From his seat on the floor Dolan muttered to Patrolman Bolster, "Get them out of here."

Bolster, who had simply continued to sip his beer, said, "Okay folks, everybody outside."

For his part, Brian felt exhilaration. *I am Superman.* He wished Dolan would get up so he could beat him down again.

"Let's go champ," Marcus said, putting an arm around his friend.

"All right," Brian replied, turning away but glancing back to see if Dolan would have the balls to try to get back up.

Once outdoors the brisk April night invigorated them and they began to feel giddy.

"Brian," Iva said, "I can't believe you just belted a police officer!"

"Well I did," Brian replied, "and believe me it was the best thing I've ever done in my life!" He did a little dance step and mentally praised his daily running and calisthenics. "I could have killed him," he said matter-of-factly.

"A fucking cop!" Marcus said, incredulously. "I wonder why they didn't arrest you?"

"Hey, he tried to hit me first," Brian said. "Besides, they know the Professor was murdered and they know we know they are covering up. Arresting me makes things much more difficult... they still want to keep this quiet."

"So why was he murdered?" Iva asked.

"My thesis," Marcus answered, and Brian nodded. "Someone connected with the Republicans and the bridge project must have found out about it. It was my thesis."

Brian and Iva both felt they could see a look of guilt on Noble's face. His next words confirmed it.

"But why the Professor and not me?"

"I think I know," Brian said. "Sansone was well respected and nationally known. He could have broken the bridge story and people would have listened."

"Will they listen to us?" Marcus asked.

"I don't know," Brian replied. He turned and headed down the sidewalk. Iva and Marcus followed.

"Who killed him?" Iva wondered aloud.

No one spoke, no one knew. They reached Patrolman Bolster's squad car and stopped.

"Marcus, how are you getting home?" Iva asked.

He shrugged.

"We'll give you a lift," a voice cut in, incredibly belonging to the previously silent Patrolman McGowan. Taking Noble back to campus would take them twenty minutes out of their way—anything to postpone going home. "Come on get in," he added.

Brian, Iva and Marcus climbed into the back seat while Patrolman Bolster hopped behind the wheel, chuckling. "I gotta hand it to ya," he said to Brian, "punching Dolan took some serious *cohones*. I'm glad I got to see it. I hate that prick."

"Uh... thanks," Brian replied, too exhausted to be surprised. He looked down and noticed blood streaming from a gash across his knuckles. Iva pressed tissues on the wound as the car pulled away. Inside Professor Sansone's house Detective Dolan packed ice on a jaw he knew, if not broken, was at least badly bruised.

No one could think of much more to say. The next week or so would bring a wake and a funeral and a campus memorial service and plenty of time for speeches and quiet talks. Back on campus, Marcus shook hands good-bye and got out of the patrol car. He started away then turned back and rapped on the window. Brian rolled it down.

"I have to ask you this," Marcus said.

"Go ahead," Brian told him.

"Do you need a campaign manager?"

Brian realized Professor Sansone had taken Marcus into his confidence. He also realized that the Professor's death in no way relieved him of having to decide whether to try running for mayor. Iva's arm interlocked with his.

"You're damn right I do," he said.

"Yeah!" Marcus yelled, throwing his fist into the air and sprinting across the parking lot.

"I'm proud of you," Iva whispered.

Brian turned his head around and watched Marcus Noble's dormitory fade into the distance. *The Professor—dead. Me—running for mayor. Me.* He tried to swallow and realized his mouth felt like it was filled with cotton. Then he looked down and noticed his hands were shaking. He clasped them together hoping that would stop the trembling and Iva had not noticed. Then he squinted out the window and tried to think about anything else; facing what he had to do in the days ahead felt too overwhelming to deal with right now.

They passed another of the Wheatley dormitories, a drab gray building covered in ivy that reminded Brian of Princeton's Smithers Hall, his dorm freshman year. Now that was a Spartan lifestyle with community bathrooms and paper-thin walls that made privacy an abstraction that could wait until graduation. Brian would never forget good ol' Smithers Hall. He had lost his virginity there, and that was an encounter indelibly etched upon his brain for all eternity. Hopefully, he would never experience humiliation of such magnitude ever again.

The actual foreplay and intercourse had all gone so well, although quicker than he desired—under one minute. No matter. He was no longer a virgin. Sex with a woman: the American rite of passage achieved, true manhood forever his. He prayed that Jean Hanson, a sophomore Alpha Tau Sigma from Indiana, was sufficiently inexperienced not to take note of his brevity.

"Thanks a lot Speedy Gonzalez," she said, dashing his hopes.

It was then that he heard the applause from outside his door. First one person clapped, then two, then three, and then about twenty. Jean's high-pitched moaning—brief but vociferous—had permeated the dorm and attracted quite a rabble completely devoid of any sympathetic understanding of the situation.

"Good job, Brian!"

"Way to go you stallion!"

"Me next, please!" This from Brian's best friend Jeff Hollis, an eighteen-year-old with a raging sex drive who had never come remotely close to experiencing relief with another person. A libidinous vulture, he now circled the area looking for leftovers.

"Shut up, leave us alone," Brian yelled. And though Jean left an hour later, Brian stayed in his room, humiliated, for almost six hours. When he did leave it was just to go to the bathroom where, typically, he ran into Jeff Hollis.

"Wow!" Jeff exclaimed, deadly serious. "You must be great in the sack. We heard her moaning all the way across the quad."

"Thanks, I know what I'm doing," Brian replied, realizing things might be all right after all.

Patrolman Bolster turned sharply onto Skunks Misery Road. Centrifugal force threw Brian against Iva and snapped him out of his flashback.

"Sorry," he said.

"That's okay," Iva said. "You've been quiet. Are you all right?"

"Fine. How about you?"

"Fine. Were you thinking about the Professor?"

Brian was embarrassed. "Uh, no..."

"Were you thinking about your campaign for mayor?"

"Uh, not exactly. To tell you the truth I was thinking about a long time ago... my college days when I was young and stupid. I guess thinking about the future makes me a little scared."

"That's perfectly natural," Iva replied. She gripped his leg and with her free hand reached to touch her brand new arrowhead necklace.

Brian's watch read five after four when they finally rolled into bed for a couple of hours rest. The sleep did not come easily. Dead tired though they were, lying there waiting for unconsciousness made them hurt even more. Iva placed her head on Brian's chest and cried until slumber finally overtook her. Brian refused to cry. Crying he told himself would be too unmasculine—a symbol of weakness—so he willed himself not to cry while his stomach churned and bile rose up into his throat. He would not sleep this night at all. Lying there in the darkness, eyes wide open, feeling alternately sad then angry then completely helpless, clichés raced through his mind that precisely mirrored his feelings. *Why did it have to happen to him? He was such a nice man. Who could have done such a thing? I'll get them back.*

The alarm that woke Iva left her momentarily wondering whether the events of the previous night were real or a dream. Brian clarified the situation by grabbing the alarm clock and throwing it against the wall. Then he climbed out of bed and stomped towards the bathroom.

He stubbed his toe against the bureau. "Owww, shit, fuck, shit, fuck."

Sometimes he's so helpless, Iva thought.

"Cocksucker, motherfucker."

Iva knew the months ahead would not be easy for Brian. Watching him hop on one foot into the bathroom she promised herself she would help him all she could. The medicine cabinet slammed shut and she could hear him continuing to curse. Stepping out of her nightgown, Iva walked to the bathroom and went in without knocking.

Brian turned to face her and seemingly unaware of her nakedness said, "A television set. I can't fucking believe it... "

"Shhh," Iva said. She turned on the shower and started to pull down his pajama bottoms.

"Christ, *The* fucking *Dating Game.*"

"Quiet," she told him, stepping into the tub. "Get in here with me and relax for a minute." Without waiting for him to move, she grabbed his penis and pulled him towards her.

"Okay. Okay. Okay. Okay. Okay. Okay," he said.

Chapter III

Geoff: "A zombie has no will of his own. You see them sometimes, walking around blindly with dead eyes, following orders, not knowing what they do, not caring."
Larry: "You mean... like Democrats?"

Richard Carlson to Bob Hope in ***The Ghost Breakers*** *(1940)*

APRIL 22, 12:45 P.M.

Werth For Mayor
He's Young, He's Tough
And Nobody Owns Him

"I like it," Brian said, gazing at the sign over his newly rented storefront on Sagamore's Main Street. "Nice idea."

Up on a ladder Marcus Noble hammered one final nail through the sign. "It's definitely a good slogan," he agreed. "And I can think of one for Al Savino that says: Savino For Mayor. He's Old, He's Fat And Montesano's Machine Owns Him"

"That would be almost humorous if it weren't true," Brian commented.

A car horn honked and Jeffrey Hollis pulled up to the curb in his cherry red, '66 Mustang convertible. Everything about the car radiated *cool* with the possible exception of the pink panties dangling from the rear view mirror. Brian noticed them and muttered to himself, "Christ Jeff, how about reaching puberty?"

"Hi guys," Jeff called as he hopped out over his door.

"Hey Jeff," Marcus said from his perch on the top of the stepladder.

Although they had met several times before, Marcus still had to cover his mouth to stifle a laugh. *This Jeff Hollis is one weird dude,* he thought. *A good dude but weird.* True enough, Jeff's flaming red hair tied into a ponytail, wisp of a mustache, gold wire-rimmed sunglasses, worn boating sneakers, paint-splattered bell bottom blue jeans and tie-dyed tee shirt over the beginnings of a beer belly qualified him as a bit odd. Brian had lately been teasing him about his penchant for dressing like the Sergeant Pepper-era Beatles but Jeff had actually taken the jibes as a compliment. This afternoon he sported a maroon baseball cap emblazoned with the words: I AM THE WALRUS.

Hollis was currently employed at his father's masking tape factory in a job Jeff himself described as *Vice-President Of Doing Nothing And Waiting For The Old Man To Kick Off.* Actually, Jeffrey Hollis was intelligent and witty and fun to be around, except when he was drinking. Even mild intoxication brought out a mean streak and caused every other expression out of his mouth to be "Tape it easy." Brian had met him in gym class in seventh grade and they had been best friends ever since. They had even attended Princeton together although Jeff had needed an extra semester to graduate.

"Did you get *Newsday?*" Brian asked him.

"Yup. Your article's in there. Nothing like a little free publicity I always say."

Brian opened the paper to the Op-Ed page to take a look. His article appeared under an editor's imbecilic headline that read **H2OMyGoodness**. But the title of the piece was the only element tongue in cheek. Brian's text attacked a serious crisis facing all Long Islanders: pollution in the water supply. Not coincidentally, he named Frank Montesano and the Sagamore Republicans as the neglectful public officials exacerbating the situation. Traditionally, Long Island's vast mounds of garbage had been disposed of in local landfills. But in the last twenty years or so most of the landfills had become filled to overflowing. To solve the problem, Montesano's Republicans simply planned to designate more areas for dumping. Brian labeled the approach "shortsighted and disastrous." Already several overcrowded landfills were leaching toxic chemicals into the local aquifers. Long Islanders led the country in incidences of many types of cancer and women, in particular, knew that breast cancer struck their communities like the bubonic plague. Brian excoriated the Republicans for incompetence on all fronts, reminding his readers that several officials—one was a former United States senator—were being investigated by the Justice Department on suspicion of taking payoffs from firms awarded contracts at the landfills. His article ended with a call for positive new steps such as the construction of two new waste disposal plants and expansion of the current recycling programs.

"That's the last of your articles in *Newsday*," Marcus reminded him. "Now that you are officially a candidate they're not going to give you a free soap box."

"Maybe it's just as well," Brian said. "I'm sick of everybody reading my stuff, saying 'That's nice' and then never doing anything."

Iva walked out of the campaign headquarters wearing an apron and carrying a broom. "Well it doesn't look like a disaster area anymore," she announced. "Now it just looks like a slum."

"Hey, don't make me homesick," Marcus said with a smile. Around white people he trusted, Marcus often deliberately made self-deprecating jokes, little non-threatening reminders of who he was and where he was from.

"Sorry," Iva replied, smiling back. Then she read out loud, "Werth for Mayor, He's Young, He's Tough, and Nobody Owns Him. Hey, what is this? I thought I owned you."

"That's different," Brian said.

"I know. Listen, everyone's here. Let's get this meeting started."

"Great idea," the candidate replied.

Up until two weeks ago, Werth Headquarters had been Sagamore Discount Wines and Liquors. For more than forty years the local gentry had loyally patronized the place even though an actual discount had never been sighted on the premises. Three years ago a competing shop had opened five minutes away and the aristocratic scions proved a more frugal generation, deserting the place in droves for better prices. Long-time proprietor Martin Britton retired rather than stop gouging his customers in a manner that, he felt, wealthy people in the old days used to expect and even appreciate. Brian leased the place for a song until Election Day.

The interior of the storefront definitely needed some major sprucing. The small sixty by eighty foot room contained only one card table, several folding chairs and innumerable empty wine crates. Dust covered everything and sunlight streaming in the front window lit up particles in the air like snowflakes. On the wall where the cash register must have been a hand-lettered sign proclaimed: "We have an agreement with the bank, they don't sell booze, we don't cash checks."

"Everyone pull up a seat around the table," Iva said.

"The first meeting of the 'Werth for Mayor' Executive Committee is hereby officially called to order," Brian announced. He momentarily wished he had a gavel and something to bang it on.

There were seven people and six folding chairs so the candidate pulled up a wine crate. The rotted plywood slats splintered and he tumbled to the floor.

Everyone laughed, even Brian, and Jeff observed, "That's probably a bad omen."

"Never mind, I'll stand," Brian said, brushing himself off. "Now to begin I'd like to..."

"Excuse me, but we have doughnuts here," Iva interrupted. "Who wants what?"

"Chocolate," said Iva's friend, Debbie.

"Jelly," Marcus said.

"Do you mind if we start now?" Brian asked.

"Banana cream," Jeff said. Then after a look from Brian, "Sorry."

Brian continued: "I'd like to introduce everyone first. On my left is Marcus Noble, and he will be my campaign manager whose job it is to oversee all aspects of the campaign." Marcus smiled and gave a little two-fingered salute. "Next to him is Debbie Benson who will serve as our campaign's executive secretary." Debbie shook dirty blonde hair out of her eyes and said "Hi" while Jeff shifted uncomfortably in his seat.

Although Jeff had positioned himself so that he and Debbie could not look directly at each other, there still remained a certain awkwardness between them. Their nocturnal tryst had been nearly eleven months earlier, and upon chance encounters superficial greetings had been exchanged, but both still felt ill at ease in each other's presence. *A blowjob in the parking lot behind Burger King,* Jeff thought. *Christ, what was I thinking?* The situation was regrettable. In a different light, Debbie seemed not only pretty, but also a very nice person—too nice to have wasted on a one-night stand. Ms. Benson, Jeff found out from Iva later, was a graduate of Georgetown University who had majored in English Literature, and she had just in the past year written and illustrated and managed to get published a critically acclaimed children's book entitled, *The Monster Afraid Of The Boy Under His Bed.* Her current job teaching alongside Iva at Great Neck Academy left her feeling unfulfilled, bored, and hoping to complete another children's book or meet Mr. Right, preferably both. *A blowjob in the parking lot behind Burger King,* Debbie thought. *Christ, what was I thinking?*

"Next to Debbie is Iva Fidele, my... uh... personal assistant."

"No comment," Jeff said.

"The gentleman whose voice you just heard," Brian went on, "is Mister Jeffrey Hollis, our chairman in charge of fund raising, an area in which I might add..."

"Nowhere to go but up," Jeff interjected.

"Right. Now, I'd like you all to meet David England."

Brian gestured to a short slightly built man in a navy blue blazer, white shirt and tie who, upon hearing his name mentioned, began to clear his throat and fiddle with a pair of tortoise-shell glasses. The routine caused Brian to remember David's nickname in college: *Poindexter.* "Jeff and I both went to Princeton with David and for the past several years he has worked in campaign strategy on both the local and state levels in California and Michigan. In spite of a number of other commitments, he has graciously consented to function as our press liaison and work with Marcus on campaign coordination."

Everyone present politely applauded.

"Good to... ahem ahem ahem... be here," David said, adding, "Sorry, all this dust is murder on my sinuses."

Brian and Jeff both grinned. *Yup, that's Poindexter all right.*

"Poindexter" was actually a constitutional scholar who was unable to accept a university level teaching position due to a crippling fear of public speaking. David England nonetheless enjoyed a national reputation owing to his authorship of a series of articles for the liberal journal, *The New Republic*. After systematically demolishing conservative arguments against the Supreme Court's Roe versus Wade decision, William F. Buckley, Jr.—on national television—singled out David by name and called him "an arrogant, immoral, self-righteous fop completely incapable of ratiocination." Brian had looked up the word ratiocination and then been the first to call his friend to congratulate him.

To earn a living, David hired himself out as a campaign strategist to candidates in whom he truly believed no matter which party they belonged to. When Brian—one of his closest friends and an ideological compatriot—had called and asked for assistance he had not hesitated before answering in the affirmative. Two senatorial candidates and one candidate for the presidency of Costa Rica were bidding for David's services and offering impressive stipends... but friendship was friendship and principle was principle and that was that.

Next, Brian turned to acknowledge a man who appeared to be nodding off. Brian shook his head in disgust then raised his voice to wake him up, "Last but not least we have Mister Vincent Augustinelli who is here representing the Sagamore Democratic Committee."

Mr. Augustinelli opened his eyes, rose slowly and appeared to be in his late fifties. It was not yet noon but fresh tomato stains on his shirt indicated he had stopped for some pasta on his way to the meeting. He swerved and grabbed his chair for support, and it became obvious to everyone that wine had come with the meal.

"We can let you have fifteen hundred dollars," he said, punctuating his remark with a loud belch.

"We appreciate that, Mister Augustinelli," Brian replied, thinking that fifteen hundred dollars paled terribly next to the nearly two hundred thousand dollars that Al Savino would be spending.

"We'd give you more," Augustinelli persisted, at which point the alcohol removed any ability he might have had to be tactful, "but... hiccup... we don't think you have a chance."

"We understand this is not a high priority contest as far as your committee is concerned," Brian replied. Then he added, "It is high priority for us."

Augustinelli tried to stand up straight but he stumbled back a couple of paces. "The committee wishes you all the luck in the... hiccup... world. Remember... hic... the Democratic committee puts out a brochure in October that..." He stopped in mid-sentence and all the color drained from his face. "Oh God," he gasped, momentarily holding back vomit and running from the room.

"Thank you for your kind gesture of support Mister Augustinelli," Brian said.

"Now there's a guy who can't hold his liquor," Jeff said.

"What an asshole," Marcus said. "I bet the next time we see that guy is after we've won."

"And then he'll want jobs for him and his friends," Iva said.

"Please gang, let's show a little sympathy for the guy," Brian said. "After all, the last successful campaign he was involved in was way back when Roosevelt was President."

"Really?" Debbie exclaimed.

"He's kidding," Iva whispered.

"Oh... uh... I knew that," Debbie said.

Brian went on, "All I really want to say right now is that I appreciate your helping me in this campaign. There are a lot of issues, a lot of things we all want to say to the people of this city." He paused, took a breath and then continued, "First and foremost we have got to stop this bridge." Grim faces nodded and stared back. "I promise to work as hard as I can to get our message across. And even though we are desperately short on manpower and money, and whether or not any of you gets paid depends on how much we can raise, deep down I feel we can win and have a hell of a time doing it!"

"Here, here!" Jeff said.

"All right!" Marcus added, and there were general expressions of agreement from everyone.

"Well then," Brian declared, "let's dedicate the over four months between now and Election Day to the memory of Professor Alan Sansone... and get started."

No one moved. The mention of the late Professor cast a pall over the entire group. Marcus reacted first by slamming his fist on the table and stating, "Look, it's time to stop mourning and do something about it."

"Right," Jeff said, standing up. "I'll see you folks later. I'm gonna try to round up some furniture for this place."

"Debbie and I are going to the store to pick up some ammonia," Iva said. "We'll get this place cleaned up yet."

"I'll help you," David England offered. "Besides, I need some throat lozenges."

Marcus pulled Brian aside and said, "Brian, can I talk to you for a second?"

"Marcus, I know what you are going to say and the answer is still no. We can't release the information about their bridge plans until we somehow find a way to prove them. We would look like idiots."

"Come with me tonight," Marcus said. "I want you to meet someone."

"Who?"

"My source. She still wants to remain anonymous but if you'll agree to respect that, then maybe we can find out something that will help us to prove all this stuff without implicating her."

Marcus Noble's graduation present to himself was the purchase of a Harley Davidson motorcycle. Brian, with some trepidation, agreed to ride to their rendezvous on the back. Sure enough, Marcus drove recklessly and while they managed to steer clear of trucks, cars and pedestrians, one hesitating chipmunk became instant road pizza. For Brian it was the longest ride of his life that almost ended when a fellow biker heading in the opposite direction flashed Marcus the "power fist" salute. Marcus responded in kind and nearly ran off the road.

"Oh, that's just wonderful," Brian yelled in Marcus' ear. "Would you please slow down! I'd feel safer in fucking Iran!"

Ignoring him, Marcus sang out in a poor imitation of James Brown, "Livin' in America..."

Finally, they turned on to K Street. *What a boring name for a road,* Brian thought. They stopped in front of number 26, a colonial with yellow shingles. No lights were on.

"Looks like no one is home," Brian said.

"She said she'd be here."

"Who said?" Brian asked. "Would you please tell me now."

"Alright. It's Mrs. Ellen Fitzpatrick," Marcus said. "She's a widow. She was Montesano's personal secretary for over twenty years... just retired a few months ago."

"That's your source? How come she talked to you?"

"Pure luck. I came by to interview her at a time when she was very upset."

"Upset? Upset about what?"

"You'll find out," Marcus replied. "Let's go in." He rang the doorbell.

Mrs. Fitzpatrick opened the door almost before the bell stopped ringing. She was well into her sixties but a big bull of a woman who still looked strong and vibrant. With her silver hair tied up in a bun and dressed in a dark blue peasant dress, it almost appeared as if a time warp had just transported her from mid-nineteenth century Dublin.

"Come in quickly," she said with a hint of a brogue, and as they followed her into the parlor they realized the only light came from the kerosene lamp she carried in her hand. "The lamplight doesn't shine past the curtains," she explained. "I don't want anyone to think I'm home."

"Why not?" Marcus asked.

"About an hour after I talked to you this morning, the phone rang and a horrible deep voice with a strange accent said if I didn't keep my mouth shut about things that don't concern me, *bad things will happen.*"

"What bad things?" Brian asked.

"This is Brian Werth, the man I told you about who is running for mayor," Marcus added quickly.

Mrs. Fitzpatrick nodded and went on. "The voice just said *bad things* and hung up. I tried to call you today to cancel this meeting but you didn't answer. I have a son and three grandchildren. If anything happens I'll..." Her hand trembled and shook the lamp causing their shadows to flutter on the wall. "Look, maybe you gentlemen should come back some other time."

"We're on the same side Mrs. Fitzpatrick," Marcus said.

"I know," she admitted meekly, sitting down on the couch. "My goodness, how long have they been listening in on my phone?"

"Probably quite some time Mrs. Fitzpatrick," Brian said, glancing at Marcus.

"Yes, at least a couple of months," Marcus agreed. It was now obvious how the Republicans had learned about Marcus' research and Professor Sansone's involvement with it.

"Why did you leave Montesano's employ?" Brian asked.

"I know they want to build a bridge across the Sound," she answered. "I know because I typed the proposal. My Lord, all the things they've pulled... patronage, insurance kickbacks, and forcing Sagamore workers to give back one percent of their salary to the party... I didn't like any of that but I figured it was just part of politics. But this bridge... it's just for the money. I remember Long Island when it was really nice. I mean not crowded. Before they built the damn, excuse me, expressway and parkways. It used to be woods and fields and... you could ride a horse across the North Shore." Mrs. Fitzpatrick paused and took several rapid deep breaths.

Brian grew concerned she might hyperventilate. "We understand exactly what you are saying Mrs. Fitzpatrick," he said, trying to calm her down.

"How dare they!" she continued. "I saw the map. They're going to turn Sagamore into a collection of entrance ramps and tollbooths. And the pathetic thing is they took me totally for granted. They had me type up the details not even caring what I'd think. I mean if this bridge goes through... my church, my beach, my home... are all wrecked." Mrs. Fitzpatrick put her hands to her mouth, closed her eyes and tried, unsuccessfully, to hold back tears. "Oh Lord... I'm going to lose my home."

"You're not going to lose your home," Brian said firmly.

"I finally got up the nerve to question Mr. Montesano about the bridge proposal. I told him what I thought in no uncertain terms. He told me to mind my own business, like my home being destroyed is not my business. When I persisted he told me to shut up and get him some coffee. I quit on the spot, totally surprised him. And you know something, I'm glad."

"Good for you Mrs. Fitzpatrick," Brian said, putting his hand on her shoulder.

"Where is that bridge proposal you typed up?" Marcus asked.

"There are only two copies. The original Mr. Montesano has hidden where only he knows. The other is a xerox copy in the safe in his office. As a matter of fact, there are lots of records in that safe Mr. Montesano would not appreciate being made public."

"Do you know the combination?" prodded Marcus.

Mrs. Fitzpatrick did not hesitate. "Clear it to fifteen, two turns right to twenty-nine, three turns left to seven... for all the good it will do you."

"What do you mean?" asked Marcus, jotting down the numbers.

"There's a twenty-four hour guard in the lobby and he has the only key to the office."

"Hmmmm," Marcus murmured, "very interesting."

"You're not going to try to break in are you?"

"No, we are not," Brian said, getting to his feet. "Thank you very much for your time Mrs. Fitzpatrick, you've been very helpful."

"You're welcome," she said adding rapidly, "Please don't tell anyone you spoke to me, I fear for my safety and the safety of my loved ones. They are very determined men. Believe me, I know."

"We know it too, ma'am," Marcus said.

Mrs. Fitzpatrick looked away as if staring off at something in the distance, and her eyes brimmed with tears. "Twenty years ago when he was just a city attorney, Mr. Montesano was the sweetest man in the world. He used to buy me carnations every week for my desk. It's just that he's changed now." She paused and looked at Marcus then Brian and then folded her arms. "Now," she continued in grand understatement, "he's not very nice."

"I wonder if he's happy?" Brian wondered out loud.

"Give me a break," Marcus said.

"I'm sure he doesn't have time to even think about it," Mrs. Fitzpatrick said quietly.

Once outside Brian answered Marcus' question before he had a chance to ask it. "No way, we are not breaking into Montesano's office."

"Why not?" Marcus pleaded.

"Simple, because it's illegal."

They continued their argument on the motorcycle during the ride back to Brian's house. "Don't call me a stupid idealist and don't call me a wimp," Brian yelled into Marcus' ear. "We don't have to stoop to their level. There's no way I can sanction such... watch out... God that was close!"

Marcus, seemingly oblivious that had they hit that garbage truck their remains would be identifiable only by dental charts, yelled over his shoulder, "What's right and what's legal aren't always the same."

"Now you give me a break," Brian replied. "They'll slip up eventually. They've got to. And when they do we'll be there to catch them... legally... aaaahhhhh... a fucking wheelie?"

Brian invited Marcus in for a beer. Hopping off the motorcycle to unlock the gate he said, "It's how I feel right now. Please respect that."

"Okay. I just hope you realize it may be your only chance."

"It's how I feel."

"Okay man," Marcus said. Then he added, "Okay for now."

The sight of Jeff drinking the last beer in the house greeted them as they entered the kitchen. He had made himself completely at home, perusing the *Sagamore Record* with his feet on the table.

"Hey look at this," he said. "They announce your nomination on page one and print your picture, but underneath they spell your name wrong. WIRTH. Can you believe that?"

"Those are the breaks," Brian said.

"Henrietta Wilcox is an incompetent moron," Marcus said.

"Somebody should fire her," Jeff said.

"She owns the paper, Jeff," Marcus told him. "Who's going to fire her?"

"How about the ghost of Joseph Pulitzer and William Randolph Hearst?" Professor Werth offered.

Iva walked in carrying a gigantic coffee urn. "Look what Geraghty's Diner donated to our headquarters," she announced.

"That was nice of them," Brian said.

"Well, they got a new one and this one is broken."

"I'll tinker with it," Jeff volunteered.

Marcus looked at his watch: 10:05. "I've got to shove off," he said.

"Leaving so soon?" Iva asked.

"Got to. Gotta big date."

"Don't tell me you're going to pick up a date on that motorcycle," Brian said.

"No way. My dates pick me up."

"I'm impressed," Jeff said.

"See you tomorrow morning nine sharp at the King Kullen," Marcus called out to Brian as he pulled out.

"Right! I'm looking forward to it!" Brian yelled back. "Day number one of pounding the flesh." Then slapping Jeff on the back he said, "I think I feel like going for a run. Want to come along?"

"No thanks," Jeff replied.

"It's dark out," Iva said.

"Don't worry, I'll wear white."

"And..." Iva prompted.

"All right, I'll wear the stupid vest." Brian hated the mesh vest with the reflective orange strips even though he knew it made him more visible to passing cars. He usually wore it when he went running after dark but it still made him feel like a nerd.

"Sure you don't want to come Jeff?" he asked again.

"I would but I've got a nap scheduled," Jeff said.

Brian noted four empty beer bottles on the table and a fifth one rapidly draining, so he decided to make a point. "Let me ask you a serious question, Jeff. When was the last time you got some physical exercise of any kind?"

"That shows what you know," he answered. "Just two days ago I played a round of miniature golf."

"Really? How'd you do?"

"Passed out from heat stroke on the fourteenth hole."

"That's too bad," Iva said.

"Well you know me, I play hard," Jeff said, draining his beer and making his exit.

Brian turned to Iva with an exasperated look on his face. He could not think of anything to say so he just shrugged.

"He's so damn charming," Iva said, "and..."

"And he's legally DWI right now," Brian said. "Look, I promise I'll talk to him tomorrow."

"Tomorrow. It's always tomorrow."

"Story of my life," Brian said.

Brian's rapid indoctrination into the nitty-gritty of political campaigning began on the second of July. After about two hours of greeting people outside the King Kullen supermarket, the apprentice politician decided he hated politics and never wanted to see another potential constituent ever again. He had reason to be discouraged; his fellow citizens greeted him that morning with nothing less than indifference.

"It's not supposed to be easy," Marcus remarked as he stood ten feet in front of Brian and attempted to funnel people toward him.

"It's impossible," Brian replied.

The bulk of the shoppers were women and most of them simply took his flyer with a curt "Thanks" not even breaking their stride. Some ignored him completely. One said, "If you're running for Mayor, what are you going to do about these prices?" then left without stopping to hear his response. Another woman mistook him for a religious fanatic and yelled, "I hope you realize you're hurting your parents! Get a job!" Still another refused to shake his hand and threatened to call the police if he touched her. An emotional moment occurred when a young man in his early twenties struggling on crutches yelled, "Stop the war!" and then tottered away in tears. Brian and Marcus watched him in silence until they turned to each other and simultaneously said, "What war?" The most annoying encounter took place when a middle-aged woman actually wearing a mink stole glanced at the flyer and called to her companion, "Look Vivian, it's a Democrat!"

"Where?" her friend said.

"Right there," the woman replied, gesturing at Brian as if he were a leper.

"I didn't think there were any left around here," Vivian said. Then when she noticed Marcus she added, "Oh and look, he's with a Negro."

"Howdydodaday," Marcus replied in his best Steppin'fetchit.

The ladies' condescending tone infuriated Brian so he decided to bait them. "Tax the rich and give to the poor," he said with the sweetest smile he could muster.

"My goodness," they replied.

Marcus tiptoed up behind Vivian and whispered in her ear "Black Power! Burn baby burn! Stokely Carmichael lives!"

Both women gasped and ran to their Mercedes.

"Remember that's Werth for mayor in November!" Brian called out after them.

Brian and Marcus laughed but they both knew they had behaved badly. They reminded themselves that there would be plenty of times during the campaign when they would need to turn the other cheek to rude and obnoxious people. It would not be easy; public opinion polls annually placed politicians second only to auto mechanics on the list of the most mistrusted professions.

Eventually by bearing down and refusing to allow their confidence to be shaken they were able to generate some favorable responses. Two elderly women listened intently to Brian's conviction that Sagamore should subsidize low-cost housing for the aged and promised they would vote for him. A pinstriped banker glanced around to make sure no one was looking then whispered in Brian's ear, "I'm with you boy. I've been a Democrat all my life and I'm not about to change now. Give 'em hell as we used to tell good ol' Harry." One of Brian's students—a cherubic eighteen-year-old named Bill Nuss—was amazed and thrilled to learn his history teacher was actually doing something meaningful in the real world. A freshman, Nuss viewed Dr. Werth as his intellectual guru so he begged to be allowed to do some volunteer work for the campaign. Brian gladly accepted. But the last individual Brian and Marcus talked to raised them up then cast them down...

"Very impressive," a man in splattered painter's pants said after engaging Brian in a lengthy discourse on Rachel Carson's *The Silent Spring*. "You're exactly what this city needs as mayor."

"Thanks," Brian replied.

"I support you and believe me you've got quite a future up ahead."

"Thanks," Brian said again, beginning to feel a little surer of himself. "Can I count on your vote this November?"

"No," the man said.

"No? Why not?"

"I'm from Maine."

Iva did not know Brian had entered the house while she was talking to her father and overheard everything. The phone conversation between the two surviving members of the Fidele family proved to be precisely what they both knew it would—an argument between two people devoted to diametrically opposing positions. They spoke softly, jabbing gently, neither wanting to hurt the other.

"Papa, I love him and we are getting married. It's what I want to do."

"I understand sweetheart. It's your life, it's your decision to make."

"You're mad at me Papa."

"No Iva I'm not mad at you. A bit disappointed perhaps but not mad."

Father and daughter fell silent, both searching for a solution, a compromise, a rapprochement, anything to bridge the gap between them. Nothing came to mind. Brian appeared in the doorway.

"I won't change my mind about Brian," Iva said. "I can't."

"Don't forget our lunch date on Saturday," Conrad Fidele said, making a temporary tactical retreat.

"I won't. I'll see you at noon," Iva replied.

"Take care sweetheart. I love you."

"I love you too Papa. 'Bye."

Iva hung up the phone, turned around and saw Brian leaning against the doorjamb.

"Brian, how long have you been there?" she asked.

"About twenty seconds," he replied. "Long enough."

"How did it go at the supermarket?" she inquired nonchalantly, hoping that he had not heard anything.

"It went okay. Why doesn't your father like me?" A few seconds of overheard phone conversation had planted seeds of insecurity, and in Brian those seeds needed only micro moments to germinate, grow and flower in full bloom.

"You don't know that."

"I just heard what you said."

"You have no right to eavesdrop on a private conversation."

"I didn't eavesdrop, I just happened to walk in."

"It's none of your business what my father and I discuss."

"It is my business if it concerns me," Brian said, deathly curious whether his suspicions were true. If they were, and Mr. Fidele actually did not like him, he would count himself truly astonished. He had met Iva's father several times and up until now considered each encounter a rousing success. The swapping of jokes and stories and lengthy discussions of world affairs seemed to be evolving into a lasting friendship.

"He does like you," Iva said.

"Then why doesn't he want you to marry me?"

"You can't understand."

"Understand what?"

"It's nothing personal."

"Nothing personal? I'm not good enough for you... that's not personal?" Brian noticed that Iva was fighting back tears. He really hoped she would not cry because tears always disarmed him. If she cried he knew their argument would end abruptly with his apologizing for everything including sins not yet committed.

"It's just that..." Iva stopped, not sure whether she should finish a sentence that undoubtedly would infuriate Brian.

"It's just that... what?" he prompted, guessing what was coming.

Here goes, she thought, resigning herself to the inevitable explosion. "It's just that you're not Jewish."

"That's pathetic!" Brian yelled. "So you're not friggin' Episcopalian... big deal. Religious prejudice is so selfish, so old fashioned, so totally ignorant... your father has no right to foist his narrow-minded views on you to try and ruin our relationship."

"If you'd only try to understand," Iva said, refusing to raise her voice.

"Understand what... stupidity? I won't waste my time." Disgusted, Brian turned and started to leave the room.

"It is not stupid," Iva said in a tone stern enough to stop him in his tracks. "The thing my father loves most in this world is not me, not another person, it's Israel. He lost his parents at Dachau. Israel is his family now. All he cares about is making sure it's healthy and safe. To him all Jews should share in the struggle to keep their country alive. He knows fathers lose daughters, that's the way it's supposed to be, but he can't stand the thought of Israel losing me. He told me that if the family loses too many daughters it won't be strong anymore. I guess he's right. There's nothing personal towards you. I know he likes you very much. It's just that my mother and brothers are gone and he doesn't want me to go too." A single tear trickled out of her left eye. "My father is not stupid... he's... he's... he's my father."

The solitary tear did it. It flowed down her cheek and dissolved on her chin, and Brian gave in. "I'm sorry," he said, moving to her. "I don't know what to say."

"Don't say anything, just hold me."

He did.

David England's first real contribution to the *Werth for Mayor* campaign came in the form of a suggestion that Brian ride the Long Island Rail Road during rush hour to meet the commuters. Brian reacted favorably to the idea; several months back one of his articles in *Newsday* had addressed the line's deterioration.

Since its inception in 1834, the Long Island Railroad had grown to become the nation's largest commuter carrier. In 1980 more than 250,000 people a day were transported to their jobs in New York City—including many from Sagamore. Brian's article compared conditions on the trains to the hardships the pioneers endured in crossing the American west in Conestoga wagons. True, Indians rarely attacked but vandals did regularly throw rocks at the trains, perhaps deriving some perverse pleasure from the inherent possibility that a shard of glass might lodge in a passenger's eye. The interiors of the cars were filthy and heat and ventilation perpetually failed when desperately needed. Equipment breakdown and track maintenance problems made schedules hypothetical even on good days. Packed like cattle on their way to slaughter, Long Island's commuters found getting to and from work a slow and all consuming struggle for survival. As an added insult, the railroad's management lied about the delays and touted a ninety percent on time rate. The media, lazy and unquestioning, regularly printed and broadcast the rosy figures. The radio traffic reporter's "on or close to schedule" was pure fiction.

For decades, Brian believed, federal and state governments had been spending disproportionate amounts of their revenues pandering to the automobile at the expense of providing for decent mass transit. Building another bridge or tunnel never unclogged the traffic for very long. Governor Nelson Rockefeller had tried a unique approach in 1970, announcing an initiative that would make the Long Island Railroad the nation's finest commuter line in the nation—within six months. When the deadline came and went and very little had changed, Rockefeller simply announced that the LIRR—take his word for it—really was the best in the whole wide world.

"Great idea," Brian told David, concerning his idea that they campaign on the trains. "Let's start tomorrow. Let's tell the people it's time for new priorities. Don't drive your car so much, take a bus, ride a bike, try walking for a change. And let's fix the damn trains."

"I agree," David replied, ingesting enough of his Vicks inhaler to open every pore clear through to his brain, "but I can't go with you."

"Why not?"

"I'm prone to motion sickness. I'm sure I'd throw up all over the train."

"I doubt anyone would notice," Brian said.

To the surprise of no one, the 8:10 train the following morning pulled into Sagamore Station a full thirty minutes late. The apparent indifference of the riders to the delay amazed Brian until he realized most of them automatically expected to be detained. *Incompetence is so commonplace on this railroad it has become acceptable to these people.*

"Should we start in the front car and work back, Dr. Werth?"

"Makes sense," Brian replied.

His campaign assistant this morning was the studious-looking Bill Nuss, a freshman going-on-sophomore at Wheatley College. Brian liked Nuss, a severe dyslexic who had through sheer force of will had developed respectable reading and writing skills that now enabled him to make the honor roll. Nuss could easily pass as Brian's younger brother; they had similar haircuts and he always, like Brian, wore a corduroy jacket and tie when campaigning in public. He volunteered all the spare time he could find and his enthusiasm made him a pleasure to work with. Brian understood that Nuss looked to him as a mentor and he gladly accepted the role. For the sake of his campaign he wished there were a lot more where Bill Nuss came from.

"This should be fun," Nuss said, bounding onto the train ahead of Brian.

"All aboard," the conductor yelled. He looked up and down the platform then cleared his throat and spit on the pavement. That, plus the beard, earring and dangling toothpick would have made Norman Rockwell puke. His conductor's uniform—blue matching slacks and jacket and peaked cap—

looked as out of place as a nun's habit on a prostitute decked out in heavy make-up and painted fu-manchu fingernails.

"Come on, we don't have all day," he added, spitting again.

You seem to, Brian almost said.

"You go first with the pamphlets and I'll follow you," he told Nuss.

"Yes sir," Nuss replied.

Standing at one end of the car and looking down its length, Brian and Nuss saw that virtually all the seats were taken, most of them by faceless torsos hiding behind walls of newspaper. And though Brian's presence did not exactly electrify the commuters, they did seem more interested in talking to him than the shoppers had been. The main reason, Brian knew, was that they were trapped on their rickety benches for over an hour and had nothing better to occupy their time. Nevertheless, he soon determined that riding the trains should become a regular addition to his campaign schedule. Once they realized he did not want money, the commuters joked and tossed questions at him, and Brian thoroughly enjoyed himself. Several times he admitted he had no easy solutions for complicated problems. He had learned early on in his teaching career that it is better admit you don't know something rather than try to fake it. The riders, just like students, reacted favorably to his admitting ignorance. "Werth, eh?" one man said. "Good to see you out with the workers. I doubt Savino is even out of bed yet."

As they entered the last car of the eight on the train, Brian and Nuss were hit with a burst of hot air that smelled like a combination of sweat and urine.

"God, it must be eighty-five in here," Brian said.

"Try ninety," a balding fortyish man sitting to their right said.

It could have been a hundred. The first heat wave of the summer had hit two days ago and though only 9:30 in the morning the temperature outside already hovered in the mid-eighties.

"The heat is on," the man said.

"The heat!" Brian exclaimed. "What the hell for?"

"The fans weren't working and when they tried to turn them on they accidentally turned on the heat. Now they can't turn it off."

"Why not?" Brian asked.

"Most of this equipment is probably prewar."

"Which war?" Nuss asked, sarcastically.

"The Spanish-American," the man replied, stone-faced.

As if on cue, the train ground to a halt in between stations for no apparent reason. Groans of discontent echoed throughout the car.

"What now?" someone said.

"Here we go again," another said.

"Here we *don't* go again," the balding man corrected.

These people are angry after all, Brian realized, *that's good.*

"Hey I recognize you," Nuss suddenly said to the balding man. "You were in the paper. Aren't you the guy who last winter protested the lack of heat on the trains by organizing a one-day mass refusal by riders to show their tickets. You were on the news."

"That's me," he replied, his face softening. "Roger Dunlin, good to meet you." He shook hands first with Nuss then Brian.

"I heard the protest was very successful Mr. Dunlin," Brian said. "Thirty percent of the commuters refused to show their tickets."

"Thirty percent was the Long Island Railroad's figure," Dunlin said. "It was actually a hell of a lot more than that." He looked away and stared out the window. When he spoke again his voice was so low Brian and Nuss had to lean forward to hear. "Management met with us and promised improvements. That lasted about a month. Conditions are worse now, much worse. We're going to have to fight some more."

Roger Dunlin cut a pitiful figure sitting there, sweat dripping down his face, his shirt soaked through. Brian felt sorry for him, he felt sorry for anyone sentenced to ride these trains twice a day five days a week for most of their adult lives. A bead of sweat rolled into Brian's eye and he wiped it away; a mere five minutes in the sweatbox had started him perspiring profusely. Everyone was sweating, a single whiff of the air and a glance at the grimacing faces confirmed it. They were trapped and the other cars were packed, there was no place else to go.

The conductor entered and cleared his throat, preparing to make a statement. While composing his thoughts he took off his cap and rubbed a greasy hand through even greasier hair. In a burst of creative expression he told the captive assemblage, "We will be delayed until the train is moving again."

"Well, that certainly clears that up," Brian said.

Something snapped in Roger Dunlin. He leapt to his feet and yelled, "These conditions are intolerable! We won't stand for them!" The other passengers offered a smattering of applause.

The conductor's reaction, incredibly, was to laugh. "Why don't you just relax Dunlin," he said. "At least you finally got your heat." Laughing again, he strolled back into the adjoining car.

Dunlin sat down slowly and returned to staring out the window. He took off his glasses and used a tissue to wipe what might not have been sweat out of his eyes. Addressing no one in particular he said, "I swear some day I think I'm going to die on this train."

Chapter IV

"You've had no experience—you see things in black and white—and a man as an angel or a devil. That's the young idealist in you. And that isn't how the world runs, Jeff. Certainly not government and politics. It's a question of give and take—you have to play the rules—compromise—you have to leave your ideals outside the door with your rubbers."

Claude Rains to Jimmy Stewart in
***Mr. Smith Goes to Washington** (1939)*

AUGUST 2, 6:51 P.M.

Brian's early evening run left him with energy to spare so he danced around his living room throwing punches at the walls wherever he could find his shadow. He could feel his adrenaline flowing in anticipation of a big night. This evening, courtesy of The League of Women Voters, Challenger Werth would meet Champion Savino face to face in a no-holds-barred debate before a live audience in Saint Gertrude's parish—more accurately bingo—hall. When he took his boxing act to the kitchen, a right upper cut to the refrigerator caused Iva to inquire about his mental state.

"Having an acid flashback are we?"

"Come on, I'm just excited about tonight's debate, that's all. Whatever questions they throw at me, I'm ready. Fat Al doesn't stand a chance."

"I'm sure you'll win," Iva said, moving to give him a good luck kiss. As they touched she recoiled quickly. "Oh ick, you're all sweaty."

"And my stomach is rumbling," Brian said, hoping Iva might take the hint to make some dinner.

"Too bad, take a shower," Iva replied.

"I'm starved," Brian said, being less subtle.

"I'm about to have some gefilte fish."

"Gefilte fish, ugghh."

"Don't say ugghh, you've never tried it."

"I want something simple."

"Just taste it. One bite and I'll bet you get right on the phone and tell my father Israel should attack Syria."

Brian laughed. "My dear, for what I have to say you'd better sit down."

"Okay," she said, playing along.

"I want hot-dogs."

"I beg your pardon?"

"I want hot-dogs."

"You're kidding me. I offer to cook and you want hot-dogs?"

"Don't get me wrong, you're a wonderful cook. It's just that I love hot-dogs. I haven't had one since you moved in. A hot-dog on a bun with mustard... you can't beat it. Please don't be mad."

Iva shrugged her shoulders. "How have you managed to avoid anemia all these years?"

"Flintstone Vitamins," Brian replied.

Iva laughed. "Two Wilmas and a Betty every day, right?"

"You think I'm kidding?" Brian said with a straight face that made Iva wonder.

Thirty minutes later they sat down to dinner, Iva digging into an elaborate display of gefilte fish and tossed salad, Brian gulping two hot-dogs smothered in mustard. The contrast was striking, heightened when Iva turned off the overhead light and lit a candle. They did share a common beverage: blush wine from one of Long Island's increasingly competent wineries out on the North Fork.

"Ummmm, this is great," Brian said. "You grilled these just perfect."

"Thanks. It's something I learned from my mother who learned it from her mother who in turn..."

"I get the point," he said, raising his glass. "Now a toast. To you for putting up with me and me for putting up with you. I love you, you jerk."

"You're out of your mind," she said, clinking her glass against his and drinking. The look they exchanged confirmed what they both wanted it to; Iva saw that Brian meant what he said and Brian saw that she believed him.

The gatebell rang.

"I'll get it," Brian said, grabbing one more bite.

Delightfully scooping up more gefilte fish, Iva replied, "Good, because I have no intention of moving."

A silver Mercedes idled in front of the gate so Brian knew his parents were paying a surprise visit. *Damn, just when I need a clear head for the debate,* he thought. After opening the gate to let the car in and then locking it again, Brian hopped into the back seat for the ride down the driveway. He kissed his mother on the cheek and shook hands with his father.

"How's our boy doing?" his mother asked.

"Fine Mom," Brian replied.

"He's not our boy anymore," his father said. "He's the mayor."

"That's a long way down the road, Dad," Brian said.

"Just a matter of time son, just a matter of time."

Brian leaned back against his headrest. His father's breath smelled, as it always did, of scotch whiskey. He could not remember a time when his father did not smell like that though for most of his life he just thought of it as Dad's smell. But in high school he had begun to realize what caused the family fights and the cutting comments. His father was not a classic drunk, he did not stumble or slur his words, his alcoholism was much more devious. Just one or two drinks caused him to be mean, jealous, hateful, and childishly petty. Brian had come to understand through his weekly psychotherapy sessions that he had been an abused child—not physically—but he had been pummeled hard by words and thoughtlessness. Alcohol brought it all out in Harvey Werth, and the imbibing began in the morning. Brian had tried on a couple of occasions to talk to his father about his drinking but gotten nowhere. Harvey just smiled and nodded and kept on drinking. Brian's mother denied there was a problem, the classic behavior of *the enabler* his therapist had told him, and truly pathetic because she continually bore the brunt of his drunken spasms of cruelty. Brian stared at the back of his father's head and imagined how he could easily reach around and choke him to death. *You fucking son of a bitch. I always used to think it was all my fault...*

"I brought you this," Harvey said, turning around and handing his son a check.

"Ten thousand dollars," Brian read. There it was, the other side of the man, *the fucking doppelgänger.* Brian knew his father loved him in his own asshole way. Harvey Werth had always been capable of moments of great kindness. His eloquence and love of learning had molded Brian and taught a young child to love reading and writing and the history of the world. *I love him so much. God, I feel sick.*

"Thanks Dad, but you don't have to do this."

"I want to, you know I can afford it. Besides, usually we donate to the Republicans... but not this year." He chucked his son under the chin.

"I brought you a chicken casserole," his mother cut in, depositing the concoction on her son's lap. No way would she be outdone by a mere ten thousand dollars.

Brian held the check in one hand and balanced the casserole on the other. "Thanks, both of you. I'd say I'm in pretty good shape. Come on inside."

Iva leapt to her feet when she saw Brian's parents and immediately became a hostess. The silver-haired Mr. Werth entered first. Dressed in a white collared short-sleeve shirt and a blue country club tie, Bermuda shorts and knee socks, he could have stepped right out of the British Embassy in Jamaica. The matronly Mrs. Werth followed a few paces behind. Despite the weight gain on all fronts, she still showed traces of what once must have been striking beauty.

"Mr. and Mrs. Werth, how nice to see you again," Iva said. "Can I take your coats?"

"It's ninety degrees out dear," Mrs. Werth said. "We don't have coats."

"Oops," Iva said.

She desperately wanted them to like her. Although Brian had once taken his fiancée home to meet his parents and everyone performed properly, Iva had not been able to penetrate the formality to get a reading on how they really felt about her.

Harvey Werth stepped forward, took Iva's hand and bent low to kiss it. "Iva it is splendid to see you again."

"Same here," she responded.

"Yes, what a pleasant coincidence," Arlene said.

The remark caused an awkward silence. Arlene knew the couple was living together because Brian had made a point of telling his parents flat out. Calling Iva's presence a coincidence served as a not so veiled criticism of the arrangement. Father and son paid little heed, long ago used to mother's antics.

Iva was stung but she did not show it. "Can I get anyone something to drink?" she asked.

"No thank you dear," Arlene said, turning to peruse the kitchen.

"Nothing for me thanks," Harvey said.

Brian folded his arms and raised an eyebrow like Star Trek's Mr. Spock. It was... *illogical...* any time his father turned down alcohol.

Arlene strolled around the room like a drill sergeant, looking in the sink and running her fingers over the counters. Freshman cadet Fidele stood paralyzed, praying that nothing appeared unsatisfactory.

"I hope we didn't interrupt your dinner," Arlene said, noticing the accouterments of the unfinished meal on the table.

"We were just finished," Iva lied.

Mrs. Werth reached down and picked up half a hot-dog from Brian's plate and held it between her thumb and forefinger at arm's length. "I see Brian had hot-dogs, how nice," she said.

His mother's sarcasm caused Brian to leap to Iva's defense. "Mom, Iva cooked hot-dogs for me because I specially requested them. Let's just relax here."

Arlene's eyes widened and she took a quick breath that was almost a gasp. She was plainly taken aback; Brian almost never rebuked her. "You know I'm just concerned for you dear," she said. "It's just that you look so thin."

"I've never felt better in my life," Brian said, staring his mother down. He wanted her to understand: *I love you Mom, but I also love Iva and if you force me to choose one it won't be you.* To punctuate his point, Brian threw an arm around Iva and kissed her cheek.

"Excuse me, but we're running late," Harvey cut in diplomatically. "We're due at the Conran's in ten minutes."

"Oh, that's right," his wife said quickly. "We just came by to see how you're doing."

"We are doing just fine," Brian replied, accentuating the word *we.*

"Good-bye Iva, hope to see you again soon," Mrs. Werth said, avoiding eye contact.

"Good-bye," Iva said, "please come again soon."

"Oh... Brian," his mother continued, "don't forget to stop by next Tuesday for your Aunt Abby's birthday party."

"I'm kind of busy these days."

"Try dear."

"I will Mom."

With his wife on the way out, Harvey Werth waved good-bye, smiled and rolled his eyes skyward as if to say: *The woman may be eccentric but it's nothing serious.* Brian and Iva smiled back.

"Thanks Dad," Brian said.

"It's nothing," his father replied. "Good-bye and good luck... to both of you."

Brian whipped the check out of his pocket as soon as his father left the room. "Check this out," he told Iva. "And you said Episcopalian families never show affection."

Brian had to run down to the gate to unlock it for the departing automobile. From the outside all he saw were smiles and waves but inside sparks flew.

"Your conduct towards Iva was inexcusable," Harvey said, turning onto Skunks Misery Road.

"She's Jewish," his wife replied.

"I'm well aware of that dear."

"Well, what are you going to do about it?"

"Arlene, there is not a damn thing we can do about it. If we try we'll lose our son. You better just grit your teeth and accept Iva. There's really no other choice."

Arlene Werth took a moment to take a deep breath. In a soft, conciliatory voice she said, "You're right dear, she's a lovely girl."

Harvey nodded and stared straight ahead. A few moments later he pounded the steering wheel and muttered, "Damn."

The second of August heralded the first of four debates scheduled at various venues around Sagamore by the League of Women Voters, and a respectable number turned out to watch Brian and Mayor Savino match wits. Packed might have been an overstatement—an avaricious maitre d' could have found a few empty seats—but to the untrained eye Saint Gertrude's parish hall looked to be filled with about a hundred and fifty people.

The entire *Werth for Mayor* executive committee showed up in support of their candidate. Jeff Hollis arrived with Debbie Benson, having just that afternoon summoned the courage to ask her if she needed a lift.

"We might as well be friends," he had finally said.

"We might as well," she had replied.

Marcus Noble entered the hall arm in arm with a gorgeous woman he introduced as "Aida, an exchange student from Ghana."

Heads turned to view the hair braided with silver roping and the maroon wrap-around sari, but they would have turned regardless; Marcus and his date were the only black people present. David England attended the affair sans escort, with a dog-eared copy of the *New York Times* under his arm to indicate he had better things to do than socialize prior to the commencement of proceedings. Brian and Iva walked in together and greeted their friends warmly.

"We'll get him," Brian told the group.

"If things start going badly, don't forget I've got a car idling outside," Jeff joked.

"And the plane tickets to Paraguay?" Brian asked.

"In my pocket," Jeff said.

Marcus put his hand on Brian's shoulder. "Remember to relax and think before you speak. Don't try too hard. Let Savino make the mistakes."

"You relax too. Don't worry," Brian told him.

David England walked up and handed him a box of cherry cough drops. "Here, these might come in handy," he said. "And remember, project from the diaphragm. Try to keep your throat loose."

"Thanks Poindexter," Brian said.

"I beg your pardon?"

"Never mind, just thanks."

"You're welcome," David said.

"Oh, Mr. Werth... "

Brian turned to take the outstretched hand of the editor of the *Sagamore Record.*

"Hello, I'm Henrietta Wilcox," she said. "I've been appointed tonight's moderator."

"It's a pleasure to meet you," Brian replied, trying to remember whom the woman reminded him of.

"You and Mr. Savino will each be given five minutes to make an opening statement. The floor will then be open to questions from the audience. Both of you will have two minutes to respond to each question. I wish you the best of luck."

Alice. The maid on the Brady Bunch. She's the splittin' image of ... whatshername... Ann B. Davis. "Thank you, Mrs. Wilcox. I'm looking forward to it," Brian said, biting on the inside of his mouth to avoid laughing.

"I'll be very strict about the time limits."

"I understand," Brian said. He laughed out loud.

"Are you all right, Mr. Werth?" Henrietta asked, looking at him as if he was out of his mind.

"I'm fine, excuse me," Brian replied. He laughed again, failing utterly in his attempt to disguise it as a cough.

"I hope you'll adopt a more serious tone during the debate," an irritated Henrietta told him. She turned and walked away without waiting for a reply, completely at home in her role as the evening's school marm.

Brian watched her leave, shaking his head. *Get a grip. Come on, get serious.*

Across the room Bill Nuss entered followed by a retinue of six others of college age. Nuss had done an admirable job in recent weeks recruiting volunteers. He now marshaled a force of nearly twenty students who offered much needed help in the more mundane aspects of the campaign such as phoning voters, passing out literature and stuffing envelopes. Brian and Marcus made it a point to go over and greet the volunteers by their first names. They all wore red, white and blue buttons that read *Werth for Mayor*, and Nuss had an extra one he pinned on Brian. One volunteer, Betsy Brewster, had a surprise for him. Unsnapping and pulling back her windbreaker, she revealed a tee shirt with a caricature of Brian's face emblazoned on the front. Betsy's gigantic breasts bounced outward, giving his portrait a distorted bug-eyed look.

"I'm impressed," Brian said, realizing immediately what his comment sounded like.

Betsy put her hands over her mouth to stifle a giggle. A pretty girl, blonde and nearly six feet tall, she made no attempt to hide her infatuation with Brian. "Good luck tonight," she added, suddenly grabbing his neck and kissing him on the lips. Nuss looked jealous though he pretended not to be looking.

Brian politely but firmly pushed her back to arm's length. "Thanks," he said. "What I mean to say is, uh, thanks..." Marcus tugged at his elbow and pulled him a few paces away.

"Wow, did you see those... " Brian whispered.

"See them? I heard them coming," Marcus replied. "Listen, I just wanted to get you away from her. I don't want *Twin Cities* distracting you before the debate."

"Who?"

"*Twin Cities.* Look, she's originally from Minnesota, right?"

"So? Oh... very appropriate."

Unknown to the candidate, his fiancée had witnessed the tête-à-tête with Betsy and not been pleased.

"Oh great, the seduction of the professor scene from *People Will Talk*," Iva said to Debbie. "I swear all that Betsy Brewster wants to do is jump on Brian."

"Relax," Debbie told her. "What's she got that you haven't got?"

"Come on," Iva said.

"Besides that. Anyway, have you considered the fact that Brian might not like large-breasted women?"

"Come on," Iva repeated.

"Sorry, just a thought. Have you considered getting a training bra?"

"Debbie, I'm going to find what it is you love most in the world—and burn it," Iva deadpanned, straining to keep a straight face. Then they both laughed.

Jeff walked over and sat down next to the two women. "Boy, Betsy Brewster sure looks hot tonight," he said.

"Let's go kill her," Iva said.

"Save it," Debbie said, looking at the back of the hall. "Here comes the real enemy."

Mayor Al Savino, accompanied by Republican boss Frank Montesano himself, strode into the room. About three quarters of those present burst into wild applause. The two men stood arm in arm and waved as the ovation continued to build. It was anyone's guess as to which man carried more weight; neither of them weighed less than three hundred pounds.

"I've never seen so many chins in my life," Jeff whispered to Debbie.

The two men looked very much alike; their conservative gray suits, black greased back hair and darting beady eyes mirrored each other. Montesano's William Powell style pencil thin mustache set him apart a little bit as did his predominantly purple paisley tie. Their fixed smiles matched perfectly, though beneath them Montesano appeared cool and confident while Savino already glistened with sweat. Neither of them wanted to be there. Both Montesano and Savino dreaded having to debate someone they derided privately as "that young punk who might be too smart for his own good."

"You've got to show up," Montesano had told Savino. "You meet the voters rarely enough as it is. And we can't turn down The League of Women Voters. You'll be all right as long as you don't say anything too terribly stupid."

As prearranged, two of Savino's young daughters ran into his arms and allowed themselves to be carried down the aisle to the stage—a nice touch to a carefully orchestrated entrance.

"What a reaction!" Brian said, truly amazed.

"I was afraid this might happen," David said.

"What?"

"This hall is heavily papered."

"What do you mean?"

"I'll bet about three quarters of the people here are Sagamore city employees. They were probably told they better get down here tonight and whoop it up or lose their jobs."

"That means only about thirty or forty people here are actually interested," Brian said.

"I'm afraid so," David replied.

"What the hell, maybe we'll learn something," Brian said.

"You're damn right we will," Marcus cut in. "Get up there and good luck!"

"Thanks."

Marcus and David both shook Brian's hand.

Frank Montesano parked himself at a corner table reserved for him and directly beneath a **NO SMOKING** sign busied himself with the lighting of a monstrous cigar. Savino lumbered up onto the stage and into an enthusiastic bear hug from Henrietta Wilcox. Brian followed thinking *so much for objectivity from the moderator.* After Savino moved behind his designated podium, Brian walked over to extend a greeting. Offering his hand he said, "Good evening Mr. Savino, I'm Brian Werth."

Savino took the hand and replied, "So you're this Werth fella I've been hearing so much about. All I want to say is, may the best man win."

"I'll go for that," Brian said.

"Oh, one more thing Brian my boy," Savino continued, pressing his forefinger on Brian's tie. "This is very nice material."

"Thanks," Brian replied, instinctively looking down.

The downward glance was what Savino had counted on and he utilized the moment to raise his finger and twit Brian's nose. The sophomoric gesture drew guffaws from the Republican peanut gallery. Savino laughed loudly himself, apparently judging the move worthy of Charlie Chaplin. Montesano smiled and winked at his friend.

Brian stared at the man, more out of disbelief than anger. *What an asshole,* he thought to himself as he shook his head, turned and walked towards his own podium.

"What an asshole," Jeff said in a loud voice to everyone at the *Werth for Mayor* table. "Did you see what Savino just did?"

"I don't like it," David said, not looking at the stage but at the rear of the hall where a well-dressed group of about twenty-five had just filed in.

"What is it, David?" Marcus asked.

"Those people are part of the Right to Life movement. In fact, they're the most fanatical branch of it. They actually call themselves the Baby Protectors and they're opening new chapters all around the country. They're suspected of torching abortion clinics and even murdering a doctor in Chicago. When they don't sponsor their own candidate, they often put a lot of effort into defeating anyone who doesn't agree with them. I've seen them operate in California. They're bound to make a demonstration of some sort and get very ugly if things don't go their way."

"This is just bullshit," Marcus said. "The outcome of a local mayoral race has nothing to do with the abortion question. Not a fucking thing. It doesn't matter what Brian and Savino think about abortion, it has nothing to do with anything."

"This is America," David replied. "We're at the point where people in public life have to take a stand on abortion whether it's relevant or not."

"Fucking great," Marcus said. "You know Brian doesn't agree with them."

"I know, he's Pro-Choice," David replied. "And Savino does agree with them. In light of that, I suggest it would be in Brian's best interest to avoid the controversy."

"They're bound to press him. He won't lie."

"He doesn't have to. He can be vague. He should just keep repeating how he respects all life and leave it at that."

"I'll slip him a note suggesting that," Marcus said.

Brian took the note from Marcus just as Henrietta pounded her gavel to signify the start of proceedings. In a hasty chicken scratch it read: "Baby Protectors present—suggest you acknowledge importance of their point of view and say only you still have the issue under review." Brian scanned the room trying to pick out the group and immediately located them, shoulder to shoulder and looking very intense, against the back wall. He knew Marcus' suggestion was politically prudent but he did not like the idea of being forced to shun a subject he had strong feelings about—even if it had damn little to do with the office of mayor of Sagamore. He decided he would improvise.

Savino made his opening statement first, the order predetermined by a coin toss. It was a rambling and disjointed speech despite the fact that he read word for word from a prepared text. His poor delivery was due to a voice that never varied from a strident monotone coupled with a further inability to read more than a couple of sentences without stumbling. Once Brian noticed the word *the* threw him. Over and over Savino mentioned his lifetime of public service, references no doubt to Brian's inexperience in the field. He sounded calls for cuts in property taxes and decreases in spending, which Brian chalked up to pure election year hype since both taxes and spending had increased steadily during Savino's twelve years in office. "We held the line on taxes and spending this year," Savino declared proudly. "With your help we'll do it again!"

The captive Republican city workers frequently broke in with applause, right on cue. With thirty seconds to go in the five minutes allowed, Henrietta rang a cowbell that moved him to close with an expression of gratitude to "the great people of Sagamore for allowing me to serve them as their mayor.

My wife, three daughters and our new kitten named Buckwheat are eternally grateful."

Brian did not read his speech; he spoke extemporaneously with only sporadic references to a three by five note card containing a broad outline. His stage presence was impressive, honed through years of teaching. He smiled, made eye contact, and strolled out from behind the podium just as he always did in his classroom. Iva at one point thought he might assign homework. Brian wanted to save the frontal attacks for later and use his opening remarks just to introduce himself. Freely admitting his newness to the political game, he suggested a novice might provide a sorely needed fresh approach to the job.

"I don't owe any one person or organization anything," he said.

Nuss and his crew tried once to punctuate Brian's remarks with applause but were embarrassed when no one else joined in. Henrietta's cowbell clanged just as Brian finished asking those present to consider a local history lesson. The Republicans, Brian pointed out to the assemblage, consistently raised taxes and spending during the first three years of the mayor's term. It was only during the final year, preparing for a reelection campaign, that spending and taxes were restrained. "We won't get fooled again," he said, quoting from the rock classic of The Who. Then he wound up with a declaration of affection, heartfelt, for Sagamore and its people, and asked for an opportunity to improve the performance of their mayor. As an ad-libbed tag line he added, "I'm sorry I don't own a cat, but if you elect me I promise I'll get one."

The joke worked, with many of Savino's supporters laughing in spite of themselves. Brian's applause did not nearly measure up, but it was more than polite because the speech had allowed him to come across as a likable guy. That was all he had wanted from his opening remarks. His strategy: *Show them you're intelligent and sincere, then maybe they'll like and respect you. Once they like and respect you, then maybe they'll listen to what you have to say.*

A lectern was placed in the center aisle and the audience lined up, unscreened, to ask the candidates questions. A wide range of issues were raised, many of which would have been more appropriate for a congressional race. Sagamore mayoral candidates Werth and Savino were quizzed about the possibility of national health care, welfare reform and the feasibility of United States' participation in future United Nations' peacekeeping efforts in the third world. Brian understood why these irrelevant questions were being raised: the audience simply wanted to get to know him better and questions of national importance could be much more revealing than the vicissitudes of curbside garbage collection. Brian answered all the questions truthfully, the best he could. As he spoke he once again realized, as did everyone in the room, that he was a classic liberal. This infuriated the predominantly Republican crowd. Savino, meanwhile, pandered and recited nearly by rote the conservative policy pronouncements of right-wingers like the new President Ronald Reagan and televangelist Pat Robertson. But Brian did score points by attacking Savino's lack of commitment to the environment, which, according to his public record, amounted to complete indifference. Savino was on record, Brian reminded everyone, for a revision of local zoning codes—he wanted less acreage per new house. "Maybe he wants Sagamore to turn into Flushing, Queens," Brian said, hoping as he spoke that no one from Flushing was present. He also attacked Savino's support for the construction of a car wash on Main Street: "What the Mayor calls *free enterprise* is in reality "a noisy, dirty, ugly monstrosity which endangers the rural quality of our beautiful city." Brian even got a smattering of applause from the Republican minions when he called for a federal investigation into the high incidence of certain types of cancer on Long Island, particularly among those living close to power and recycling plants. "And don't forget," he reminded everyone, "Mr. Montesano and Mr. Savino were early supporters of the Shoreham nuclear plant. After what happened at Three Mile Island, shouldn't we learn our lesson? I say decommission it!" Even most of Savino's supporters applauded at that one.

As the debate progressed, exchanges remained sharp but tempers remained under control and voices were not raised in anger. But a deviation from protocol did occur when an elderly woman used her turn at the lectern to yell "Al Savino is the greatest! He's done a great job! I love him!" to a roar of approval from the Republican partisans and the obvious delight of Savino and Montesano.

"I love you, too!" Al bellowed.

Henrietta Wilcox prolonged the incident by jokingly asking Brian if he wanted to comment on the woman's statement. Brian said that he did and went on to thank Al Savino's mother for showing up in person.

Bill Nuss appeared next at the lectern with a question that immediately altered the mood in the room. He wanted to know why Savino had not gone on record for or against the controversial new quotas for commercial shell fishing in Long Island Sound. "Would the candidates comment, please, on the remarks yesterday by the Governor concerning the latest developments," Nuss asked.

The blank look and twitch on the upper lip of the fat man verified for Nuss that he had accomplished his goal of confusing Savino. All Al could do was wipe his brow and mumble something about needing more time to study the matter. Brian winked at his young friend then launched into a cogent analysis of the controversy. Savino was one of the only ones in the room who did not know what was going on; in recent months a lot of press coverage had focused on the plight of the local fishermen who stood to lose their livelihood because the oyster beds were polluted. Brian on the other hand had genuine compassion for the men who could no longer make their living on the sea. Then he went a step further. In a serious monotone he allowed how his sympathy for the baymen could not change the cold hard fact that contaminated seafood had to be banned to protect the public. He pointed out the real fault lay with the industrial polluters who should be tracked down and forced to pay for a clean-up and financial support for the fisherman until they could be allowed to return to their jobs. Most in the hall found themselves nodding in agreement: a point scored for Werth. It was an easy one, never would Brian be ignorant of a current news item. Unlike Savino, he made it a point to read the papers every day. As a final note, Brian suggested the reason his opponent was unfamiliar with the fishing controversy owed to his frequent absences from Sagamore. Al Savino, he pointed out to the assemblage, vacationed about four months of the year at his cabin in the middle of the St. Lawrence River—in Canadian territory!

Jeff asked a question he and Brian had set up as a test of Savino's ability to lie. "There are rumors going around," he said, in reality hoping he was starting them, "that after the election many Republican politicians intend to announce support for a bridge that would originate in Sagamore and span Long Island Sound. Would you please comment on that?"

All whispering and fidgeting in the room stopped. Everyone seemed to be trying to understand the ramifications of what Jeff had brought up. *A bridge across Long Island Sound? What the hell is this overgrown burned out hippie talking about? Why is he here? Is he on LSD?* Henrietta gaped at Jeff and struggled to comprehend the idea. Unsuccessful, she looked at Al Savino and waited for him to make some sense out of it.

Savino blinked and seemed uncertain what to say. He opened his mouth but said nothing and there was an awkward silence. Then suddenly came the sound of a loud chuckle. Savino glanced over and saw that Frank Montesano was laughing. Frank shook his head and giggled, then laughed louder, then burst into full scale guffawing. Savino got the idea and joined in. The city workers observed their leaders and mimicked them, even though they had no idea what they were laughing about. Laughter enveloped the hall. Almost everybody else found themselves laughing at the other people laughing. At the podium, after holding back as long as he could, Jeff finally broke down. Seeing Jeff, Iva got up, stormed over to him and demanded to know what the hell was so funny.

Jeff gripped his sides and tried to gain composure. Tears streamed down his face. "It's just that this is so pathetic," he replied, losing control again.

Brian and Iva and Marcus never laughed, not even close. They still remembered Professor Alan Sansone and how he died. For them the happy noise hurt.

After a signal from Montesano, Savino finally waved his arms to get everyone to quiet down. "The idea of a bridge across Long Island Sound is the most ridiculous thing I have ever heard," he said, patting himself with a handkerchief. "If there's anyone here who wants a bridge it's got to be my opponent, because he knows that after the election he's going to have to get off this island as fast as he can." Al laughed again prompting another burst from his supporters, but this time it sounded forced.

"Mr. Werth, would you like to comment on this?" Henrietta asked.

Brian picked out Montesano in the audience. "I am as completely opposed to a bridge across the Sound now as I will be after the election," he said, staring the Republican leader down.

Frank returned the look through two of the meanest slits Brian had ever seen. In a gesture calculated to show just how concerned he was with the whole Werth campaign, the boss leaned back in his chair, puffed on his cigar and proceeded to blow smoke rings.

Sitting in his seat, Marcus told himself how absolutely essential it was to convince Brian of the need for a break-in of Montesano's office. They needed proof of the secret bridge plans. It was the only issue that could swing enough voters to Brian to get him a win. Undoubtedly, his aggressive campaign was cutting into Savino's strength, but it would never be enough. It was only early August and the Republicans were still campaigning in first gear. Massive mailings and radio and print ads that Brian could not hope to compete with waited in the wings. Marcus' frustration grew when he remembered nice old Mrs. Fitzpatrick, their only legitimate source of information, bullied into silence.

When the turn came for the husky middle-aged woman in the beige tailored suit to speak, many people in the room knew what her question would pertain to. Brian knew; he had watched her move from her position against the back wall. Marcus and David crossed their fingers and hoped their man would not fall into a trap. Montesano and Savino were both on record as being Pro-Life and, though they preferred to avoid the controversial issue as much as possible, they were not at all threatened by the group's presence.

"Hello Eloise," Montesano said to the shorthaired former fifth grade teacher as she walked past him.

"Hello Frank," she replied.

"Go ahead with your question," Henrietta said.

"I'm Eloise Mosely," she announced in a stern nasal twang that made much of the crowd twinge. "I'm president of the Baby Protectors' Long Island chapter."

Fanatic, Brian thought, *how is this relevant to any of the problems we're dealing with here in Sagamore?*

"I guarantee that woman is a virgin," Jeff joked.

"What's wrong with that?" David said, a response that caused everyone at the table to turn and stare at him. "Don't get the wrong idea," he added quickly.

"Abortion is a plague," Eloise pronounced, "and our group is dedicated to its total eradication. The plain truth is that anyone who supports abortion is not fit to hold public office in this great land of ours."

Eloise's followers fanned out through the hall to pass out flyers. One bounded on stage to hand copies to the candidates and moderator. The picture on the top of the page struck Brian right away. It featured a sketch of a five-year-old boy dressed in a cowboy suit sitting on a tricycle. Behind the child a troll-like caricature of an abortion doctor crouched in the shadows clutching a dagger.

"Oh what an adorable little boy!" Henrietta exclaimed.

They attack with emotions rather than reality, Brian reminded himself. He scanned the sheet in front of him and saw that it contained a ranting diatribe claiming Pro-Choice activists controlled everything from the entertainment industry to the public schools. Meanwhile Eloise continued to speak, further escalating her propaganda blitzkrieg.

"Communist money supports many of the abortion clinics," she added, pounding a bony fist on the lectern. "They want to kill our children."

Brian could not contain himself. "Communism!" he exclaimed. "Are you out of your mind? You can't call everyone you disagree with a communist. What is this... another witch hunt?"

Eloise reared back, took a deep breath and prepared to excommunicate Brian from the human race. But before she could speak, Al Savino waved his hand and was recognized by Henrietta. "I welcome Eloise and her group here wholeheartedly," he said. "I have supported attempts to fight abortion in the past and will continue to do so in the future. Planned Parenthood thinks they are going to open a clinic here in Sagamore within the next year. I say..." Savino paused and held his right hand up as if swearing an oath... "Never, while I am your mayor! Never! Never! Never!"

With Eloise and her followers cheerleading, a rousing round of applause erupted from what looked to Brian to be almost every man in the room and about half of the women. Even Henrietta Wilcox clapped until she noticed Brian watching her.

Everyone at the *Werth for Mayor* table wondered what Brian would say. Brian wondered what he would say. He did not like the idea of abortion, far from it, but he disagreed with everything the Baby Protectors stood for. For Brian, abortion was between a woman and her doctor and possibly the father if she chose to include him. He supported the *Roe versus Wade* decision and fervently hoped it would never ever be overturned. He knew women who had multiple abortions and couples who cavalierly used abortion as birth control, and that revolted him, but as far as he was concerned it was not the business of government to tell a woman what she can and cannot do with her body. And the Catholic Church's prohibition against abortion, largely ineffective in the United States, helped make many areas in the third world ripe for a modern day grim reaper: a population explosion. But most of all it was the tactics of the Baby Protectors that appalled Brian: threats and violence that went far beyond any constitutional right to assemble and protest. In short, they were bullies and extremists and they were shameful.

"Mr. Werth?" Henrietta said.

Brian did not respond. It took the pounding of the gavel to snap him out of his rumination.

"Huh? What?"

"It is your turn to make a statement."

"Yes, thank you."

What should I say? Brian wondered. There were two voices in his head. One kept telling him to *Be a politician, don't make waves.* The other cut in frequently to say *Speak your mind. Go for it. What the hell, maybe you'll learn something.* Bill Nuss staring up at him caught his eye. The anticipation in his face showed just how much the hardworking young man believed in him. Brian chose to tell the truth because he knew in the long run it would be much easier to live with.

"Unlike my opponent, I am not a professional politician," Brian began. "Therefore, I've got to say that I respectfully disagree with the Pro-Life movement. I am Pro-Choice. No one on earth can tell others when life begins. That is a matter of individual conscience. And a woman has got to have sole jurisdiction over her own body and the right to make the choice for herself. *Roe versus Wade*, which the Supreme Court decided on the basis of privacy, is right and proper. I don't like abortion but the way to foster other alternatives is through education not intimidation. On the question of a family planning center in Sagamore, I support it. And I even favor the use of public funds, on the federal and state level anyway, to pay for a poor woman's abortion in the case of rape or incest or when the life of the mother is in danger. Ladies and gentlemen, sometimes liberty means freedom for others to choose for themselves."

A few women in the audience offered a smattering of applause. Eloise had held her breath and turned from pale to beet red as Brian spoke. When he finished she burst like a helium balloon and screeched at the top of her lungs, "Murderer!"

The hall had rafters and her shriek echoed in them. The outburst startled everyone including Brian, who responded by gripping the sides of his podium and staring right back at her. *I'm sorry this woman has such difficulty expressing her feelings,* he thought. Savino looked at Montesano for guidance and received a look back that said *stay cool.* Henrietta dropped her gavel.

"Murderer!" This time the call came from the back wall on the left.

"Murderer!" By the fire door on the right.

"Murderer!" Eloise again, escalating the insults into full scale heckling by all twenty-five of the Baby Protectors. The placards, previously held discreetly at their sides, bobbed up and down defiantly and a picket line formed in front of the stage. Brian noted some of the posters were actual photographs of physicians with the word **WANTED** printed above their face. ***WANTED. DEAD OR ALIVE*** *is what they're implying*, Brian thought. *The violence has already started. Doctors have been killed. It's these fanatics who are the real murderers.*

Overwhelmed, Henrietta yelled, "This meeting is now adjourned!" and ran off into the wings.

The audience, now all on their feet, stood around and wondered what was going on. Several arguments broke out between people with different views on the subject. Eloise's demonstration had taken only seconds to end the debate. No one had yet moved from the *Werth for Mayor* table.

"This is wild!" Jeff marveled.

"Oh my sinuses," David moaned, pinching the bridge of his nose. "I knew this would happen."

"I'm going to belt the next person who calls Brian a murderer," Iva declared.

"Murderer!" a man yelled and as she started after him, Debbie grabbed her arm and pulled her back.

"Let's go out this way," Debbie said, pointing to the back door.

"But Brian... "

"I'll get him," Marcus said, starting for the stage.

"Don't leave me!" pleaded Marcus' date from Ghana, obviously taken aback by all the commotion.

"Come with us," Debbie said. She took hold of Aida with her other arm and announced, "We'll all meet outside."

Marcus ran up onto the stage to where Brian was trying to extricate himself from a nose-to-nose argument with Eloise Mosely. He continued trying to reason with her in spite of her wide-eyed ranting.

"Look what you're killing!" Eloise persisted, thrusting the picture of a five-year-old on the tricycle into Brian's face.

"Mrs. Mosley," Brian replied in a level voice, "for your information, that is not a picture of a fetus in the first trimester. And I'd love to tell you where you can stick that tricycle."

Marcus took Brian's arm and said, "Let's go."

"I'm not through yet," he insisted, jerking himself free. "Mrs. Mosely, you and your group are without a doubt the most ignorant, the most selfish, the most... let me ask you a question. When you were a schoolteacher, how many children did you psychologically scar for life?"

Before Eloise could think of a reply, Al Savino tapped Brian on the shoulder. "Better luck next time kid," he said. He then turned to Eloise and said, "Goodnight Eloise."

"Goodnight Al," she replied, turning her back on Brian. "Here, let me walk you out." Arm in arm they strolled off leaving Brian standing there livid.

Tempers flared down on floor level. Nuss and several of his friends were engaged in a heated argument with the picketers. Brian heard Nuss tell one of them, "You had no right to disrupt this debate!"

"Get away from me wimp," the man said.

"You're wrong and you know it," Nuss said.

The man reacted by swinging the stick of the picket into Nuss' face. Nuss stumbled backwards, luckily into Betsy Brewster who, naturally, cushioned his fall. But the bridge of his nose bled profusely from a nasty gash.

Brian reacted with fury. Suddenly he knew what he felt like to have a little brother. He leaped off the stage on to the man's back. Several of the man's friends jumped on Brian. Marcus dove onto the pile. Punches flew and it was a western style free-for-all until a siren and red flashing lights outside prompted someone to yell, "Let's get out of here!" The Baby Protectors scampered out the back door. The Werth Gang headed for the side fire door.

Brian regrouped his forces in the parking lot and announced a general campaign meeting at the headquarters for nine the next morning. No one appeared hurt except Nuss who sported a wicked cut on his nose. To avoid further trouble, everyone agreed it would be best to get to their cars as quickly as possible and leave the area.

"I wanted to join the fight," Jeff explained, "but I couldn't since I have glasses."

"I've never seen you wear glasses," Debbie said.

"Sure, I just don't have them with me tonight."

"I've got mine," David pointed out.

Brian and Iva offered Nuss a lift to the emergency room in case his cut needed stitches, so they hurriedly said goodnight to everyone.

"Marcus, I'm sorry," Brian said.

"For what?"

"I guess I have a temper."

"I got in a few shots too, you know."

"Think I should have been more diplomatic back there?"

"Nope, I've changed my mind. Be honest. That's what we're here for."

"Thanks," Brian said.

"Thank you," Marcus replied.

"Nice to meet you Aida," he said to Marcus' date. "Sorry things worked out the way they did."

"I think your country is very strange," she said.

"Sometimes it is," Brian admitted.

In the car on the way to the hospital Nuss showed no signs of being troubled by his injury. He seemed elated about the whole evening. Iva could hardly get him to sit still long enough for her to press a bandanna against the still bleeding wound.

"What a great time!" Nuss exclaimed. "I haven't had this much excitement ever in my life. And I think I learned a lot."

"What did you learn?" Brian asked.

"I learned to duck the next time a raving maniac swings a stick at me."

"How do you think I did against Savino?"

"I think you slaughtered him," Nuss affirmed.

"All right!" Brian yelled. He turned around and slapped five with Nuss.

"Would you please watch the road," Iva said.

The cut on Nuss' nose required three stitches but the doctor promised there would be no permanent scar. The white strip covering them looked like Indian war paint, and Nuss whooped in delight when Brian told him he had been promoted to membership in the *Werth for Mayor* executive committee. The parting words of the newly christened Coordinator of Volunteers were borrowed from America's first naval hero... John Paul Jones. "I have not yet begun to fight," Nuss declared.

Exhausted, Brian and Iva went straight to their bed as soon as they arrived home. They threw their clothes on the floor and climbed in, perfectly natural for Brian but a remarkable testimony to Iva's tired condition. She rested her head on his chest and put her arm across him.

"You haven't told me what you think about all this," Brian said.

"I'm not sure," Iva replied, squeezing him.

He stared at the ceiling. "I wonder what the Professor is thinking right now. I guess he's pretty disappointed."

"I don't think he's disappointed," she said. "I'll bet he's watching us and is damn proud we're doing our best to win this thing."

"Do you really think so?"

"I do."

"Good, then so do I."

Chapter V

"Rocks is a magnificent specimen of pure viciousness."

Edward G. Robinson describing Humphrey Bogart in ***The Amazing Dr. Clitterhouse*** *(1938)*

AUGUST 9, 11:21 P.M.

"Ach mein Gott! Was ist das?" Wilhelm Weltsmirtz jumped back from the spider and hit his head on a ceiling beam, hard. *"Ow Verdammt!"* He grabbed at the spider, caught it and held the wriggling thing in his fingers by one leg. It was a daddy longlegs. With his free hand Weltsmirtz felt the back of his head and the rapidly expanding goose egg. "*Verdammt!* This fucking darkroom is the size of a closet." He threw the spider on the floor and crushed it under his heel.

While waiting for his film to develop, Weltsmirtz closed his eyes and tried to take his thoughts off his splitting headache. But what streamed into his consciousness made his head hurt all the more as his mind drifted back to the mid-sixties when he had been in charge of a darkroom half the size of a city block at CIA headquarters in Langley, Virginia. Those were salad days... a long time ago and gone forever. Now he was a small timer, a year or two from retirement and completely unappreciated. But it had not always been that way. In late 1967 the intelligence agency had "loaned" his services to the suddenly resuscitated presidential campaign of Richard Milhous Nixon. Christened with the ubiquitous title of Logistical

Coordinator, he soon impressed his new employers through a series of sophisticated "ops" run during the Republican primaries of the following year. The procurement of potentially embarrassing photographs was his specialty, and a number of prominent politicians had been successfully prevailed upon to shift their support to the former Vice-President. But in the summer of '68 at the GOP convention in Miami something had gone horribly wrong. Governor Nelson Rockefeller of New York—*a fucking liberal*—stood a halfway decent chance of beating out Nixon for the nomination. Hidden cameras were set up in Rockefeller's hotel suite and a transvestite—beautiful, undetectable—hired to seduce the Governor. The objective had been to catch Rockefeller with penis in hand so to speak. But the transvestite, probably retarded from too many hormone injections, had gone to the wrong room. The wrong fucking room! Room two-fifty-six instead of room three-fifty-six. She-he-it-whatever failed to follow the simplest instructions. And as luck would have it the wrong room was really the wrong room, occupied as it was by Nixon's campaign manager John Mitchell who had not been part of the loop. The stupid cunt-cock-whatever, probably too high on drugs to realize the mistake, had gone right on ahead and seduced an all too drunk and willing Mitchell. The future Attorney General did not discover the true gender of the person he was cavorting with until his hand grasped a hot-dog where there should have been a doughnut. Then the shit really hit the fan.

Weltsmirtz had been fired and stripped of his government pension. Cooler hotheads prevailed and Rockefeller was destroyed by more conventional means: employees of the Gallup organization were bribed and a key poll showing the Governor in the lead among independent voters was altered to show Nixon in front. Rockefeller's growing momentum ground to a halt and *Tricky Dick* held on to enough delegates to win. The Plumbers had gone on without Weltsmirtz. Political espionage. Sabotage. Dirty tricks. *And Watergate... a bigger fuck up then anything I ever did wrong. Ha! At least that's something,* Weltsmirtz thought.

Amid the euphoria after the squeaker victory over Vice President Hubert Humphrey, a sheepish John Mitchell had been clear-headed enough to worry that a disgruntled Weltsmirtz might someday talk about the "campaign irregularities" he had been a part of. To keep him employed—and quiet—his pension was restored and he had been shuttled around the country to local Republican organizations under orders to hire him as a "security consultant." It was all small time stuff after what he had been used to, but at least he was guaranteed a job. For the last four years he had worked for the Sagamore Republicans as nothing more than a part-time chauffeur and night watchman at their headquarters. He had to pinch himself when the Boss actually asked him to do something substantial. "Destroy Brian Werth," had been Montesano's exact words. Weltsmirtz clapped his hands... *One last chance to kick some liberal ass.*

He rubbed his temples. Damn this headache. Both of his ex-wives had continually called him a "fathead." Since they had conjured up the insult independently of each other, Weltsmirtz reluctantly admitted to himself that he did indeed have a fat head... and a round one... with virtually no neck. Classmates in high school had not been kind when they dubbed him "Cro-Mag" and listed him in the yearbook as "Most Likely To Evolve Into A Lower Form Of Life." At fifty-eight, he regularly reminded himself that *I'm still solid enough to kick the shit out of all of those assholes.* Luckily for his classmates, Weltsmirtz had not bothered to attend any of his class reunions.

Images began to appear on the photographic paper in the fluid in the tray in front of him. Weltsmirtz took a swig from his ever-present brandy flask and waited. What crystallized as the blurring cleared caused him to break into a wide toothy smile. One of the squares on the contact sheet was a work of genius. Full figure front stood Father Jamison, the priest who had organized those Alcoholics Anonymous meetings he had given up on. Right next to him in a perfect exposure was that Werth guy.

"Boy will the bitch love this one," he said out loud.

Henrietta sure did. She ordered her staff to stay up all night to rush out the next issue of the *Sagamore Record* the following morning. "Extra! Extra! Read all about it!" she sang out loud over the din of the printing press.

Jeff Hollis burst in brandishing a copy during Brian's campaign meeting with his volunteers. Prominently featured on the front page of the *Sagamore Record* was a shot of Brian gripping a man by the clerical collar and aiming a punch at his jaw. A bold-faced headline plastered above trumpeted: **CANDIDATE WERTH BRAWLS WITH PRIEST.**

"My God," Brian gasped.

He declared a recess and everyone crowded around trying to take a look. Fourteen volunteers were there; word of the action the night before had fueled their interest.

"A priest!" Jeff cried incredulously. "He punched a priest!"

"I can't believe it," David moaned. "This is a public relations disaster."

"Wow Brian, you actually hit a Catholic priest!" Debbie exclaimed.

"The guy wasn't dressed like a priest," Marcus said, "so I can't really criticize you. Besides, I tackled a nun."

"At least it wasn't a rabbi," Iva said, trying to lighten the mood.

Brian refused to offer any apologies. "Take a look at Nuss' nose if you want to see what turn the other cheek means to this guy," he said.

Fortunately for the campaign, Jamison refused to press charges. Montesano sent Weltsmirtz as an emissary to ask him to, but the Father politely demurred. The dozen or so witnesses who had seen him strike a defenseless young college student would make it a sticky business. The Lord would handle any punishment, the Padre explained.

Passions began to cool after a few days. Marcus sent out a press release regretting the emotional outburst on both sides. An initial deluge of letters, which David noted was running 97.4 percent unfavorable, slowed to a trickle. Probably due to a preoccupation with the crash of a Continental Airlines DC-10 fifteen miles off the coast off Montauk on the same night as the debate, *Newsday* never picked up on the fight nor did any of the local television newscasts.

"We're damn lucky that crash happened when it did," Brian said, only half kidding.

"That's sick but definitely true," David replied.

"We can shake this off," Marcus declared. "We've only been hit, not knocked out."

The League of Women Voters refused to take any more chances. They flat out canceled the remaining three debates. Savino was euphoric. Brian was extremely disappointed; he needed the exposure much more than the incumbent did and three golden opportunities to portray Savino as the idiot he was had been lost.

"I won't punch another priest," Brian promised his supporters at another general campaign meeting a week later, "unless of course I feel like it."

The bravado brought applause from the group, now swollen to twenty-one.

"He wouldn't really do it again, would he?" David whispered to Jeff.

"Stranger things have happened," Jeff replied.

"He'd better not," David said.

"Who knows, maybe next time I'll get in some shots of my own," Jeff joked.

Debbie overheard and could not resist teasing him. "Face it Jeff, the only way you'd ever join a fight is if everybody else is already unconscious."

"Are you insinuating that I'm a coward?" he asked, pretending to be deeply hurt.

"I don't know if *coward* is the right word."

"How about *wimp*?"

"That's it."

"Let's change the subject," David said.

By the middle of August, the Werth campaign rolled along in full swing. Furnished with metal card tables, folding chairs and a perpetually jammed Xerox copier, the Sagamore headquarters became the focal point for a myriad of activities and its decor looked right for the controlled chaos. The walls featured **Werth for Mayor** bumper stickers and giant blow-ups of his face, and colored demographic maps that looked good but no one except David really understood covered leftover space. They also had an AM transistor radio and a portable color television set with rabbit ears though Brian as yet remained undiscovered by the broadcast media.

Perhaps the most important feature of the headquarters was the two phones. One was kept as an open line but a rotation of volunteers continuously made calls on the other phone from twelve noon to nine at night. Strategy called for all independent voters and registered Republicans to be contacted and pitched for Brian. There was neither the time nor the manpower to call everyone. It was hoped the Democrats would generally support Brian regardless and capturing the majority of independents plus a fair number of defecting Republicans could make an upset victory possible. David England gave each volunteer an index card containing guidelines on how to conduct the calls:

> ***Hello (their name). I'm (your name) and I'm not selling anything or asking for money. I'm calling to remind you that November fourth is Election Day. I'm a volunteer for Brian Werth who is running for mayor. Do you have any questions on where Brian Werth stands on the issues?" (If the person says "yes," engage him or her in discussion. Be totally honest about Brian's positions even though the person may disagree. Above all, be courteous and friendly. Sign off by saying: "It's been great talking to you, please remember Brian Werth for mayor on Election Day!" If at any time the person on the line becomes irritated or abusive, diplomatically say "Thank you for your time." and hang up. Remember, you may curse out your fellow citizens only after you have hung up the phone.)***

David made the first few calls to demonstrate phone technique to the volunteers. The first three calls went very well but on the fourth call a woman kept him on the line asking him question after question. David obliged convinced he was converting a diehard Republican to the zen-like peace and tranquility of *Werthism*. But when David asked the woman if she had any more questions, her response left him stunned.

"Do you mind if I touch myself?" she asked.

David was speechless. The volunteers watching him wondered about his gaping mouth and glassy eyes.

"Please... just talk to me... I'm about to come."

David cleared his throat and tried to politely extricate himself. "Nice to talk to you. Remember that's Werth for..."

"No don't go. I'm almost there."

David got angry and whipped off his glasses in preparation for telling the woman off. Jeff, who was watching, was reminded of Clark Kent heading into a phone booth.

"Listen madam, I sincerely hope you vote for Brian Werth in November. But it is rude and inappropriate for you to... "

"Oh yes! Yes!"

"... expect me to stay on the line if you are doing..."

"Aaaahhhh! Oh!"

"... what I think you are doing. Good day madam."

"Wait! Please! I want to thank you, that was great. I'm definitely going to vote for Brian Werth," the woman replied, giggling and hanging up.

David slammed down the phone. "Unbelievable," he said, "that woman wanted sex over the phone!"

Everyone laughed and applauded. The general consensus was David had handled the situation quite well. But he was not amused.

"There are lots of sickos out there," he said.

"What are you complaining about," Jeff said. "It's the latest thing. Usually phone sex is twenty-five bucks for fifteen minutes, and you have to have a major credit card."

"Really?" David replied, allowing himself to smile. "Hey, I guess that's one vote we don't have to worry about."

Bill Nuss organized literature drops. Every few days the Executive Committee issued a position paper depicting Brian's stance on a relevant issue. Volunteers would then fan out to parking lots all over the city to place them on the windshields of cars. Getting the position papers together proved to be great fun. Brian had the final say but he was open to suggestion, and committee members would stay up to all hours of the morning in heated debate. Frequently their enthusiasm led them on tangents far from the municipal politics of Sagamore. One morning it was past three when Iva finally stood up and declared, "That's it. Debbie and I are out of here."

"Yeah, I give up. They don't allow women into combat anyway," Debbie added, rubbing her eyes.

"A good thing," Jeff said, opening another beer.

She just looked at him, too tired to argue.

"Tape it easy," he said.

"All I'm saying is the Soviet Union is going down," David went on. "And China is ready to rock. Our armed forces need to stay ready for whatever happens."

"Okay," Brian said sarcastically, "if you really think that's going to happen, why don't we just come out in favor of Armageddon?"

"What's Armageddon?" Nuss asked.

"It's a final and conclusive battle between the forces of good and evil," Professor Werth replied.

"Savino's already taken that position," Marcus said.

They all chuckled despite how tired they were.

"Let's go to bed," Brian said.

Financial donations did not exactly roll into the Werth camp. Finance Chairman Jeffrey Hollis agonized over his inability to get local businesses to give money. He wrote letters and made follow-up phone calls but ran into an Ebenezer Scrooge at every establishment.

"Doesn't anyone even need a tax write off?" he moaned.

No one blamed him for their financial woes; he was obviously doing the best he could. The local business people knew a Democrat running against one of Montesano's boys stood virtually no chance of winning. They figured why donate money to a sure loser who would never be in a position to return the favor.

Jeff's persistence eventually did pay off modestly. The Landolfi Bus Company donated one thousand dollars. "Montesano screwed me out of a city contract," the president of the company explained to Jeff over the phone. "He gave it to his cousin. I'll send a check right over."

A Washington-based abortion rights organization called Choice for the Future donated two thousand dollars. Jeff had written them a letter containing a blow-by-blow description of the disruption of the debate. They called once to verify the story and a check arrived ten days later. Roger Dunlin remembered Brian's pledge to work to improve the Long Island Railroad: *Commuters for Decent Mass Transit* gave three hundred dollars. Marcus added up their assets:

$1,000	Nassau County Democratic Committee
$10,000	Harvey Werth
$1,000	Landolfi Bus Company
$2,000	Choice for the Future
$300	Commuters for Decent Mass Transit
$5,000	Hollis Adhesives, Inc.
$19,300	

"If Savino spends as much as he supposedly did on his last campaign, he'll outspend us by about one hundred and eighty thousand dollars," Marcus pointed out.

"A nine point three to one spending ratio," David immediately observed.

"We'll make that up by working harder," Brian said. Everyone nodded in agreement, at the same time thinking that another one hundred and eighty thousand dollars sure would make life a hell of a lot easier.

"We may be reduced to begging," Jeff said.

"In some cultures begging is perfectly honorable," Marcus informed him.

"In some cultures it's polite to fart at the dinner table," Brian cut in. "This is America and we aren't going to beg. We'll make do on what we have."

Brian spent his own money on the campaign without telling his friends. His savings drained week by week; by

Election Day all seventeen thousand of it would be gone. His attitude was... *What the hell, you only live once.*

Iva, the only one who knew, told him, "You won't be able to live off me. I'm broke too."

"We'll starve together," he replied.

One big expenditure was the fifty-fifteen by eight foot-plywood signs that were ordered. Red, white and blue and emblazoned with the **WERTH FOR MAYOR: HE'S YOUNG HE'S TOUGH AND NOBODY OWNS HIM** slogan, they were slated to go up all over the city on September fifteenth. And though expensive, a citywide mailing of a *Werth for Mayor* pamphlet was planned for about a week after that. Financial realities prevented any television or radio advertising, and print ads in the Sagamore Record were going to be restricted to one-quarter page in each of the four editions the month before the election.

Brian worked sixteen-hour days, determined to meet as many voters as he could. Accompanied by a volunteer or two or sometimes by himself, he faithfully rode the trains in the mornings and reserved the afternoons for visits to shopping centers, beaches, church picnics, the bowling alley—anywhere people congregated. Hundreds of people shook his hand every week. Sometimes they touched him. One woman described the hardships of caring for a son with some sort of an immune disorder the doctors couldn't figure out. The episode nearly moved him to tears and placed the whole campaign in perspective. *I'm helpless*, he realized. *A mayor is just a mayor, this woman's son is down to ninety-seven pounds.* He was seeing a lot of real life, and learning much more than he ever had on a college campus.

Most moving was the loyalty shown Brian by his friends. Iva, Marcus, Jeff, David, Debbie, Nuss and many of the volunteers sacrificed selflessly for the campaign. No one accepted any salary. Everyone managed to scrape by although Marcus, unable to meet his September first rent payment, was forced to sleep on the couch in Brian's living room. When school started up again the first week of September, Iva's first instinct told her to continue working full time for the campaign.

Brian, himself on sabbatical for a year from Wheatley, insisted she return to her job.

"I won't let you sacrifice your career for me," he explained. "It's not really right and in the long run it won't make you happy."

So Iva went back to teaching, pushing herself hard to put in several hours at the headquarters each night. Bill Nuss also pushed himself. Though he started his sophomore year at Wheatley College, no one noticed him contributing any less time. Brian finally had to order him to make at least a token appearance in his classes.

September tenth marked the day the Republicans revved up; previously, the Savino campaign had been on automatic pilot. All Al had done was show up at ceremonial events and interviews—functions he couldn't miss.

"Let Werth dick around all summer," Montesano dictated, "he's doing minimal damage. Come September we'll blow him away."

Marcus and David had researched past Republican tactics so they knew Savino would lay low until after Labor Day. Then the inevitable barrage would be unleashed... a campaign cacophony that would build to a crescendo the day before the election.

"When it happens, we just keep going," Brian said. "Slow and steady wins the race. We're the tortoise, Savino's the hare, the big fat hare."

"Too bad fables aren't real," Marcus commented.

The Republicans' first move was to mail a picture and personal history of Savino to every registered voter in Sagamore. Remarkably, they planned one mailing a week for the remaining seven weeks. The first Savino pamphlet infuriated the Werth campaign because it contrasted Savino's "meritorious service in the Army" with Brian's lifelong civilian status as "a member of the Woodstock generation." It was revisionist history of which "Tail Gunner" Joseph McCarthy would have been proud; in reality, Al Savino had spent the entire Korean War stationed at Fort Dix, New Jersey working in the Army's division of camera repair.

Republican radio commercials started playing on three of the area's highest rated stations. Listeners heard paid professional actors masquerading as average men and women sing the praises of Al Savino three times each morning during "drive-time." Phone canvassing began with a bank of ten phones and the manpower to call every registered voter in the city three times. Montesano personally placed a full-page ad in the Sagamore Record—featuring a smiling Savino arm in arm with President Reagan—to be repeated in every edition until the election. Massive foot canvassing commenced. City workers just happened to volunteer their time to go door to door for Savino; every house and apartment would be hit by the first Tuesday in November. Two hundred orange and blue **SAVINO FOR MAYOR, FOR A STRONGER AMERICA** signs sprang up everywhere.

"I'm sure Montesano has city workers doing campaign work during business hours," Brian said at an executive committee meeting. "That's a violation of the Hatch Act of 1939."

"That was a federal law," David pointed out.

"Whatever..." Brian replied. "If only we could prove it."

"We can't seem to prove much of anything," Marcus added.

The Werth forces found it increasingly difficult to shrug off the Savino onslaught as September rolled on. He was buying the election. One radio ad could reach more voters than Brian could in a month of pounding the pavement. The mood of excitement and fun waned as the weather turned cooler and reality intruded on the dream. Work continued apace at the headquarters, but there was less smiling and fewer wide eyes. Just about everyone realized that Brian would probably lose.

On the evening of September thirtieth Brian went to bed early to catch up on some sleep. Alone in the darkness he admitted to himself that the way things were going he would certainly be defeated. The thought made him angry. *How do you fight a machine?* He was not in a conciliatory mood when the phone rang. Iva walked in a minute later just in time to see Brian slam down the receiver.

"Are you okay?" she asked.

"Yeah, I'm okay."

But she could see him, tense and aggravated.

"Who was that?"

"Well, it's kind of strange."

"What's strange?"

"That he would call me. I mean Sagamore is really just a small town."

"Who called?"

"A U.S. senator."

"Really?" Iva said. It was hard to believe but then she remembered the debate debacle. "Who was it?" she asked.

"The honorable Jesse Helms of North Carolina. At least that's who he said he was. It sounded like him. He had that stupid accent."

"What did he want?"

"He wanted to know my position on abortion rights."

"What did you say?"

"I told him the truth—Pro-Choice all the way."

"Then what?"

"Well, I believe I called him a *dick.*"

"I beg your pardon?" Iva said.

Brian laughed, crossed his legs and clasped his hands behind his head. "Yes, I do believe I called the senator a *dick.*"

Iva shook her head and smiled. "What did you do that for?" she asked.

"Because he is a *dick*," Brian answered. "That senile North Carolinian asshole. This is a local election on Long Island. He should stay the hell out of it."

"What did he say?"

"He said he would make sure I lost the election. He guaranteed that all five hundred Baby Protectors in Sagamore would vote against me."

"No way Sagamore has five hundred Baby Protectors," Iva said. "That's ridiculous."

"Who cares," Brian replied. "The man's a *dick*. Come on to bed."

Simultaneously, they spread their arms and came together in a hug. Then they looked at each other for a moment and broke into exhausted smiles.

On the first day of October, Iva's yellow Honda Civic sedan happened to be in the shop so Brian swung by Great Neck Academy to pick her up after school. He was happy to do it; their schedules allowed them little time alone. When they were together they were usually at the headquarters, in a group and always working. At home they ate and slept and got dressed to leave again.

"Howdy stranger," Brian said, walking into her classroom.

"Hi," Iva replied, getting up from her desk.

He went to kiss her but she stopped him by pointing to a child sitting all alone in the corner.

"This is Gary Leach," she said.

"Hi Gary," Brian said.

"Yeah," the kid said.

"I had to keep him after school," Iva whispered. "He's a real discipline problem. He's only nine but he acts twenty-seven. Everyday it's something. Today he was especially bad."

"What did he do?"

"Go ahead and ask him."

"All right, I think I will." Brian walked back to Gary's corner. "Gary, why were you made to stay after school today?"

Defiantly, Gary replied, "I told Miss Fidele to go fuck herself."

"I see," Brian replied. He walked back to Iva. "What's the big deal? I tell you that all the time."

Iva refused to smile in order to appear stern before the boy. "Brian, this is serious. Gary's father died before he was four. He's an only child and his mother spoils him. He needs someone to look up to. He needs a father figure."

"I'll handle this," Brian said. He walked back to Gary. "Gary, my name is Mister Werth and Miss Fidele and I are engaged to be married. I don't approve of people using foul language toward her. If I ever hear of you doing it again I promise you I will personally come and find you and punch you in the face... hard!" He slammed his fist on the desk in front of the boy causing him to jump in his seat. "Do you understand me?" He slowly moved his face about two inches from Gary's.

The young man had never been spoken to that way. "Yes sir," he replied, using the phrase for the first time in his life.

"You're not going to do it again, are you?"

"No sir."

"All right, you can leave now."

"Thanks, 'bye," Gary said, scampering out at warp factor seven.

Brian turned to Iva. "I think we related," he said.

Iva frowned and squeezed the bridge of her nose. "Brian, that was too much."

"Come on, that was exactly what that kid needed."

"I said he needs a father figure, not a Hitler figure. I think you really shook him up."

"Wait and see if there are results."

"All right. Maybe your way is worth a shot. God knows nothing else has worked."

"Can we go now?" Brian asked.

"No, first I want you to come with me to the auditorium."

"Why?"

"The sixth graders are putting on *H.M.S. Pinafore.* I designed the set and I want you to see it."

"Great, I love westerns," Brian said.

"How were your grades in school," Iva asked.

"Low, very low."

"I'm not surprised."

They walked through deserted corridors to the auditorium, even though it was only 3:15.

"Where is everyone?" Brian asked.

"Are you kidding? When school ends at 2:45, most teachers beat the kids out."

"That attitude stinks," he said.

Iva threw open a double door and led Brian into a musty old auditorium that had not been renovated since the early fifties. Still, there was a certain charm to the place. Arched cathedral-like windows ringed the room and the four hundred seats were leather upholstered, a luxury no school district in the lean early eighties could even contemplate. Graffiti laden seat backs contained random adolescent scribbling and resembled small obscene billboards: names and dates carved by decades of children seeking to alleviate the boredom of annual assembly programs on such topics as *Pedestrian Safety, The Four Basic Food Groups,* and *Mister Tooth Decay.* One carving read *Herb 55,* an enduring testimony to the youth of a man now in his forties.

The floor sloped down to an orchestra pit, empty save for a once majestic grand piano. From backstage Iva pulled and pulled and pulled open the curtain. Slowly, the deck of Her Majesty's Ship of the Line *Pinafore* materialized on the stage. There were masts and barrels and, off to the side, the captain's cabin with the poop deck on the roof. It looked the same as every *Pinafore* set has and will for as long as there are footlights.

"It's terrific," Brian said. "Did you design this yourself?"

"All myself," Iva said.

"It's great, just great."

"Thanks," she replied. "You know, our production is going to be really special. The girl playing Buttercup is positively gifted."

Brian jumped up onto the stage and looked out over the empty seats. He cleared his throat and thrust his back and shoulders into ramrod position:

"I am the very model of a modern Major general,
I've information vegetable, animal, and mineral,
I know the Kings of England and I quote the fights historical,
From Marathon to Waterloo in order categorical."

Iva giggled and threw the blackout switch.

"Hey," Brian said.

"Sorry, that was Gilbert and Sullivan all right, but the wrong show."

"So I took a shot," he said. "By the way, I can't see a thing."

Iva snapped on a single spotlight. "Watch me," she said. She walked into the circular glow:

"O Romeo, Romeo! Wherefore art thou Romeo?
Deny thy father and refuse thy name;
Or, if thou wilt not, be but sworn my love
And I'll no longer be a Capulet.
'Tis but thy name that is my enemy;

Thou art thyself, thou not a Montague.
What's a Montague? it is not hand, nor foot,
Nor arm, nor face, nor any other part
Belonging to a man. O, be some other name!
What's in a name? that which we call a rose
By any other name would smell as sweet."

"Hey honey, you know I fuckin' love you," Romeo Werth said in his best Brooklyn accent. He grabbed his crotch for emphasis. "You're hot stuff baby."

Iva laughed. Brian walked into the spotlight and took her hand. The white ball blinded him.

"You know, I wasn't always into history," he said, squinting. "My freshman year I was a theater major."

"Why did you switch?" she asked.

"I stunk as an actor. Besides, I couldn't recite Shakespeare without drooling down my chin." He led her out of the spotlight.

Iva went to the light board and turned off all the lights. Pitch darkness enveloped the auditorium; the red glow of an exit sign was the only thing visible. "We're supposed to turn off all the lights when we leave," she explained. She walked back on stage and took his hand. "Here, follow me up the aisle."

Brian pulled Iva into his arms and kissed her.

"Ummmm, what was that for?" she asked.

"For being so beautiful."

"You can't even see me now."

"You feel beautiful."

"You feel beautiful, too," she said. They kissed again.

"You know something," Brian whispered, wondering whether to finish the thought.

"What?" Iva finally asked.

"Well, I've always sort of had this fantasy.

"What fantasy?

"Uh, a fantasy about fucking on a stage."

"Why on stage?" she asked.

"I don't know. It's supposed to be a public place. We might get caught. It just turns me on." He slipped his hand between her legs.

"Brian, someone might see us." She did not push him away.

"You said the place was empty."

"I'm not positive."

"We'll be quiet."

"Suppose we get caught?"

"Don't worry."

"I could lose my job."

Brian let go. "I guess you're right," he said.

"Well, don't stop now," she said.

They assumed a horizontal position on the cold wooden floor—amidships on the *H.M.S. Pinafore*—and proceeded to enact Brian's fantasy. There was no time for formalities; all they took off was one leg of their pants. They also dispensed with foreplay because it immediately became clear they did not need it... Brian was hard and Iva was wet. As their bodies intertwined and convulsed in the darkness, both admitted to themselves they were having the best of times. Iva told herself the experience was worth it even if the principal walked in, fired her and barred her from teaching ever again. Brian kept repeating to himself over and over... *What a great idea!*

The heightened eroticism of the moment caused him to climax in less than two minutes. Such rapidity was atypical for Brian; normally he held back, thinking about Brussels sprouts if necessary, in order to give Iva equal opportunity to reach orgasm. His speed on this occasion embarrassed him. What he did not realize was that Iva climaxed twice before he did.

Wow, she thought, *that's the fastest I've ever come!*

"Sorry, that was a little fast," Brian said.

"No problem, right on the money," Iva replied.

"Ah my little Buttercup."

"Shut up and get off me."

A shaft of light shot across the room. Someone was opening the side door, away from the stage so the light hit the far wall. Brian and Iva held their breath and, still coupled, kept as still as they could. The door creaked open wider. Iva bit her lip and kept silent even though the muscles of her vagina continued to contract. The darkness on the stage went from pitch to murky and now they could make out each other's eyes, terrified. Brian found himself remembering the time the police caught him throwing eggs on an adolescent Halloween night. Iva just focused on her heart, which she supposed pounded loud enough to be heard a mile away.

No one walked into the auditorium. After what seemed like an hour but was really only a few seconds, the door slammed shut. Again, there was blackness. Footsteps echoed in the hall and died.

"Let's get out of here," Brian said. He pushed himself up and away.

"Fast," Iva added.

Brian fell backwards as he scrambled into his pants. "Where's my goddamned shoe," he grumbled.

Iva handed him his shoe. "Here it is. I'm sure I've got a heel print on my ass."

"Let's hurry," he said.

They ran up the center aisle to the main door. Just before they went out Brian whispered, "Act natural. Nobody can tell anything."

They strode briskly through the halls.

"Why is it I feel like Hester Prynne with her scarlet letter?" Iva wondered aloud.

"Relax, there's no *A* on your dress," Brian told her.

"I know. But I feel like there's a capital ***F*** tattooed on my forehead."

"There isn't, it's all in your mind."

Nothing impeded their escape. The school still seemed empty. Upon reaching the parking lot, they involuntarily sprinted to their car. Brian ignored two speed bumps and zipped them away as fast as he could. Both relaxed a little bit as the car sped off school property.

"Do you think anyone saw us?" Iva asked.

"I hope not."

"But what do you think?"

"I think we got away with it."

Iva suddenly realized they had just had sex without taking any precautions, and at definitely the wrong time of the month for that sort of thing. "Uh oh," she said.

Brian was thinking the same thing. "Uh oh is right," he said.

They drove along in a worried silence for a while. Finally, Brian smacked his head and said, "I can't believe I forgot all about birth control back there. It never entered my mind."

"I forgot too," Iva said.

Nobody spoke for about a minute. Then Brian said, "You know I think I have a different perspective now on all the those people in the ghetto who have unwanted pregnancies all the time. I used to think most of them were just idiots."

"It can happen to anyone," Iva said.

"Yup." Brian agreed, squinting ahead and tightening his fingers on the steering wheel.

After another minute or so of silence Iva said, "Relax, I'm fine."

Chapter VI

"Well, all the jokes can't be good!
You got to expect that once in a while."

Groucho Marx speaking directly to the audience in
***Animal Crackers** (1930)*

OCTOBER 5, 8:15 P.M.

"This is right out of a movie," Jeff said with a smirk.

"Or *The Honeymooners*," Brian replied.

"I really can't believe this," Jeff went on. "These guys are actually wearing antlers!"

"Shhh, don't let them see you laughing at them," Brian told him.

The Sagamore Moose organization boasted a membership of one hundred thirty-nine, made up mostly of blue-collar workers who shared the common bond of having served in the armed forces. No women were members, not because they were not allowed but because no one was interested; the regularly scheduled stag parties were a total turn off. Headquartered in a refurbished warehouse, the clubhouse boasted a spacious wood-paneled bar, dining area and billiard room. Pennants and emblems representing military units adorned the walls. The main thrust of the fraternity aimed at providing its members an opportunity to get away from it all and enjoy a drink or meal together with comrades. Brian found nothing wrong in the idea especially since the Sagamore

Moose performed a useful function in the community by quietly donating to local charities. But those crimson cowboy hats with antlers they all wore sure did look silly.

"Where's Teddy Roosevelt?" Jeff wisecracked.

"Shhh, keep it down," Brian said.

This monthly meeting had been underway since 5:30 and it was now nearly 8:15. Every year the Moose invited local candidates to speak and afterwards by voice vote they made an endorsement. Tonight the turnout amounted to ninety percent of the membership, the main lure being the free drinks and post meeting buffet. Brian and Savino were slated last on the agenda, but just as their turn came a fuse blew plunging the lodge into darkness. Candles appeared and the meeting delayed pending repairs. Liquor, already flowing fast, flowed faster. And with the electric soda dispenser out of commission, the spirits came undiluted.

Empty stomachs combined with unlimited alcohol soon took their toll. A festive atmosphere evolved and the men split into groups to swap war stories. There were two World War II groups—one for the Pacific theater and one for the European theater—and one group each for Korea and Vietnam. Burton Francis Holmes—ninety-nine years old and a veteran of World War I—sat in his wheelchair alone, gripping an empty mug and forgotten.

"Where's the Woodstock group?" Jeff joked.

"It's just me and you," Brian said.

One bunch that included Al Savino started singing:

"Praise the Lord and pass the ammunition,
Praise the Lord and pass the ammunition,
Praise the Lord and pass the ammunition,
And we'll all stay free!"

"Makes war seem kind of romantic, doesn't it," Brian commented.

"Where have all the flowers gone..." Jeff sang just loud enough for Brian to hear.

"Oh you hippie you," Brian whispered.

Frank Montesano walked in wearing antlers and carrying a candle. He joined the group of singers and slapped Savino on the back. The two men appeared to exchange pleasantries, but Brian and Jeff saw him firmly remove the drink from Al's hand and place it out of reach. Then Montesano took Savino by the arm and guided him into the lavatory.

"Looks like Fat Al has had a little too much to drink," Jeff observed.

"Oh, I hope so," Brian replied.

In the bathroom Montesano railed at Savino. "You're drunk," he yelled, throwing some water into Al's face.

"Hey, what's the big deal?" Savino mumbled.

"What's the big deal? You've got a speech to make."

"Speech, smeech, they support me every time I run."

"Don't be stupid. You can't take it for granted. You've got to go up there and thank them for supporting you in the past and respectfully ask them to support you again this year."

"Stupid? Why do you think I'm stupid? Why are you always telling me what to say? I'm going up there to say what I want to say."

"What is it you want to say, Al?" Montesano asked calmly.

"I don't know but I'm definitely going to say it." Savino pushed his way through the bathroom door.

"Moron," Montesano muttered under his breath.

The electricity surged on again. Sagamore Moose President Bob 'Buck' Krasinski, as drunk as anyone in the room, called the meeting back to order by shouting into the microphone, "All right everyone, shut the fuck up!" The singing stopped and the Moose got quiet.

"I personally took care of the electrical problem," Buck announced.

"Half an hour to change a fuse and the man is proud," Jeff whispered.

"Benefit of the doubt," Brian whispered back, "maybe he couldn't find a fuse."

"Or maybe he's drunk and out of control like everyone else in this room," Jeff said.

"That's probably more accurate," Brian admitted.

Buck continued: "Would the two guys running for uh... uh... whatever they're running for please come up to the microphone."

Brian and Savino walked to the front. There was polite applause but most of the men started chatting. Savino elbowed Buck and Brian out of the way and grabbed the microphone. "I'm goin' first," he announced. He cleared his throat. "All right, how do you get four fags on a bar stool?" Al inquired of the assemblage.

"You should know you fat homo!" someone yelled, followed by a collective guffaw from the membership.

Savino ignored the heckle and delivered the punchline, "You turn it over!" he bellowed. He got a small response, everyone had heard the line a million times.

"Try again!" an anonymous Moose yelled out.

"More!" another called out.

Nary a Moose wanted a political speech. They wanted jokes and more drinks.

"How did Helen Keller burn her fingers?" Savino continued.

"How?" a good portion of the crowd countered.

"She tried to read the waffle iron." There were no laughs, just derisive booing and hissing. Frank Montesano buried his head in his hands. Insults flew at Savino from all parts of the room.

"Get off!"

"Next!"

"Get the hook!"

"Gong!"

Buck took the microphone out of Savino's hands and handed it to Brian. "You're on kid."

"Thanks," Brian replied. He looked out over the herd of antlers. His worst fears had come to pass—the Moose were all drunk and seemingly crazed out of their minds. *Okay, get a grip. It doesn't matter whether they support me or not as long as they don't attack. Well, at least I won't bomb any worse than Savino.* "Hello, my name is Brian Werth and I'm happy to be here," he began. "I'm running for mayor."

"Tell a joke!"

"Make us laugh!" Whistling and stomping commenced.

Always give the audience what they want. Who was it that said that? Jolson? Durante? Mussolini? Brian could not remember. "Okay, I'll tell a joke," he said, desperately searching his brain for something funny to say. One joke came to mind, his all time favorite he first heard over twenty years ago at summer camp. *What the hell, it always works at parties...*

"Okay here goes," he said, removing several frogs from his throat. "Two little kids are sitting at the kitchen table. Their mother turns to the first kid and asks, 'What would you like for breakfast?' The kid says, 'How about some fuckin' French toast?' The mother is upset. She slaps the kid across the face three times. Slam. Slam. Slam. 'Don't let me ever hear you talk like that,' she says. 'How dare you be so rude.' As the kid starts to run upstairs the mother says, 'Come back here.' Wham. She slaps him again and kicks him in the crotch for good measure. Crying, in terrible pain, the kid runs into his room. Next, the mother turns to the second kid and says, 'Now what do you want for breakfast?' 'I don't know,' he says, 'but I sure don't want the fuckin' French toast.'"

The Moose roared. The laughter cracked off clean and solid, and they applauded wildly. Savino grabbed the microphone back.

"What did the Polish mother say after her daughter told her she was pregnant?" Al yelled at the top of his lungs as if louder also meant funnier. "Are you ready? She said, Are you sure it's yours?"

Nearly half the Moose membership was Polish and the men grew silent. *Wrong choice of material Al baby,* Brian thought to himself. Montesano stormed out of the room. Buck Krasinski stepped forward and shouted, "I'll have you know I'm Polish!"

"Then I'll talk slower you dumb Polack," Al bellowed.

The room became so eerily still that Brian could actually hear crickets outside in the bushes. Buck's face turned beet red and his hands at his sides balled into fists. Savino finally realized he had offended everyone but he was drunk and his attempt to extricate himself only made matters worse.

"Hey—the Polacks, the Irish, the Jews, it's all the same. Come on. I'm a WOP. First I'm an American but I'm also a WOP. It don't bother me."

Someone threw a glass that shattered against the podium. Next to the Polish, Italian Moose numbered the most. Buck grabbed the microphone and shoved Savino back against the wall. "How many of you vote not to support this asshole?" he yelled.

A unanimous roar went up.

"Now get the fuck out of here you fat tub of shit," Buck told Savino.

Wilhelm Weltsmirtz suddenly appeared next to the befuddled Savino, grabbed him by the shoulders and dragged him towards the nearest exit. Buck turned to Brian and said, "We all support you, kid. Good luck."

"Thanks, 'bye," Brian replied, offering a little three-fingered Boy Scout salute and heading out.

Buck adjourned the Moose meeting with a cry of "Let's eat!"

Brian could not leave as fast as he wanted because Moose after Moose kept grabbing his arm and pulling him back. Great joke, they told him.

"Now you need an agent and a booking on *Carson*," Jeff told him.

"What I need is to get the hell out of here," Brian replied. "No, I don't know any more jokes," he told another Moose.

Finally out in the parking lot they had to walk past a limousine where slumped against the hood a rapidly sobering Al Savino was receiving a stern lecture from Frank Montesano. Weltsmirtz sat silently behind the wheel, listening. Brian could not resist throwing a comment over his shoulder.

"Better luck next time, Al," he said.

Weltsmirtz opened the car door and started to go after Brian but Montesano put a restraining hand on his shoulder.

"Not now," Frank said. "Not now."

An hour later Brian, Jeff, Marcus and David left their headquarters and walked the half block to Geraghty's Diner. They slid into a booth and ordered three coffees and for David a small club soda with no ice.

"I'm sure they're all going to vote for me," Brian told his friends.

"I'm sure they will," Marcus replied.

"It was a riot," Jeff said. "Savino was drunk out of his mind."

"I believe you," Marcus said, clearly in a bad mood.

"What's wrong?" Brian asked.

Marcus exhaled and looked away. David straightened and unstraightened and straightened his tie and cleared his throat. "Uh... it's... uh... it's my poll." he admitted.

"What poll?" Brian demanded.

"Well, we called over three hundred people to find out who they plan to vote for."

"And?"

"A lot of them still haven't heard of you. And a lot of them are going to vote for Al Savino."

"Give it to me straight," Brian said.

"Uh... well... uh... there's a margin of error... "

"Brian," Marcus cut in, "with a month to go you are trailing by more than a two to one ratio."

"We'll cut that down," Brian said.

"How? We're broke and Savino's campaign is stepped way up."

"He beat the last guy three to one," Brian pointed out.

"Right, and we all agree the progress you've made is nothing short of incredible. I'm sure the Republicans have polls of their own and are worried shitless about the support Savino's lost. But that still doesn't alter the fact you are going to lose big."

Brian felt a knot in his stomach. He knew Marcus was telling the truth. He could not think of a thing to say.

"Brian," Marcus continued, "how many **Werth for Mayor** signs did you guys see on your way back from the Moose meeting?"

"Come to think of it, none," Brian answered.

"Hey, we didn't see any," Jeff said.

"That's right, you didn't see a single one. We put up fifty signs last week and now they're all down. Not only down, they're gone, vanished.

"They're gone all over the city," David said.

"Who... " Brian started to say.

"Come on, who do you think?" Marcus said.

"Duh," Jeff said, tapping Brian's head. "Anybody home?"

Brian swiped Jeff's hand away and stared at Marcus, unsmiling. "Go ahead and say what you're going to say," he said, sensing where his friend was heading.

"All right," Marcus continued, looking Brian right in the eyes, "I propose, once again, that we break into Montesano's office to get evidence of their bridge plans and whatever else we can find. It would be relatively simple after that to release the evidence to the press and reap the benefits of the inevitable public outcry."

"I... uh... agree with that," David said.

"It makes sense," Jeff said.

"In other words," Brian said, "you'd all like to stoop to the same stinking level the Republicans are on." He sat back and folded his arms. "I know, let's all pretend we're the Watergate Plumbers. I'll be G. Gordon Liddy. Who wants to be John Dean?"

No one smiled or said a word.

"I still don't know," Brian finally said.

An explosion ripped through the air outside the diner. Their window rattled as did the cups on the table. Everyone ran outside. Half a block away, two bodies lay prone on the sidewalk. Horrified, Brian recognized one of them as Iva. He rushed to her, knelt down and took her head in his hands. She was alert and at least outwardly unhurt.

"Are you all right?" he asked.

"I think so," she said.

Debbie lay on the ground next to Iva and Jeff cradled her. "We were loading some stuff in my car and we got knocked over," she said.

"A bomb went off in our headquarters!" Marcus announced. It was an obvious deduction; the windows were blasted out and debris littered the sidewalk."

"Oh God!" Iva cried. "Nuss!"

"Nuss!" Debbie gasped.

"Nuss is in there!" Iva yelled.

"Jesus!" Brian shouted, leading the charge into the building.

Chapter VII

Rick: "That was some going over your men gave my place this afternoon. We just got it cleaned up in time to open."

Renault: "I told Strasser we wouldn't find the letter here. But I told my men to be especially destructive. You know how that impresses the Germans."

*Humphrey Bogart to Claude Rains in **Casablanca** (1942)*

OCTOBER 6, 10:45 P.M.

"We go tomorrow night at midnight," Brian said.

Marcus, Jeff and David nodded.

"You're all clear on what each of you is supposed to do?"

They nodded again.

"Anything further to discuss?"

All eyes automatically focused on David.

"I have a question," David said.

Marcus and Jeff made no attempt to hide their displeasure. The four men had been planning their break-in of Frank Montesano's office for the better part of the day, and gone over detail after detail, but David kept coming up with things that could go wrong.

"Don't tell me," Jeff said. "You want to know what to do in case of a tornado."

David ignored him. "Tell me again what we do if the alarm goes off while we are still in the office," he persisted.

"I think you want things to go wrong," Marcus said.

"It's a good question," Brian cut in. "Let's review the alternative escape routes one more time." He stood up from his wine crate and walked to the front window. There was a jagged hole in the glass and the breeze blowing in held few traces of the hot summer gone past. The chill made him shiver. He wondered if he would find some time to do some skiing in the upcoming months. *Alternative escape routes. Swish and around the mogul in a sea of white.*

Brian turned to face his comrades, true friends willing to risk arrest with him. "I want you to realize you're not obligated to help me with this break-in," he said. "It will be bad if we get caught. I'll understand if you want to back out."

Three grim faces stared back with a solemnity heightened by the disorder in the room. The bomb had devastated the interior of the headquarters. File cabinets, tables and chairs were knocked over, phone jacks torn off the wall and the copy machine damaged beyond repair. Mountains of campaign literature and envelopes that had piled high on the tables lay scattered everywhere. No one knew whether the crucial mid-October mailing could be salvaged.

"Shut up," Jeff said.

"Don't worry," Marcus said.

"We were talking about alternative escape routes," David said.

"Thank you," Brian replied, truly touched.

Iva and Debbie walked in. Everyone waited for them to say something.

"Well," Brian pressed, "any change?"

"No," Iva replied. "Nuss is still sedated. They won't let him have visitors until tomorrow."

"He's not any worse is he?" Brian asked.

"No, they still think he's going to have a full recovery. No permanent injuries."

Everyone heaved a sigh of relief.

"We'll see you guys tomorrow," Debbie said.

"Don't stay up too late," Iva added, waving goodnight.

The Sagamore police force assigned Brian's favorite detective, Dolan, to investigate the incident. The next day Dolan announced that there was no evidence of a bomb, only a fire that had almost certainly been accidental. "Maybe these young kids got a little careless smoking pot," he had joked within earshot of half a dozen reporters. Reality, of course, was something else. Brian and his friends had easily observed that an explosion ranging in force from one or even two sticks of dynamite had detonated from inside a waste paper basket. Bill Nuss had been in the room when it went off, luckily about twenty feet away and facing the other direction. As he bent over a drawer of a file cabinet, the blast threw him forward and knocked him unconscious. He fractured his collarbone and hit his head hard enough to receive a severe concussion. A three-inch strip of metal from the waste paper basket lodged in his rectum.

Ten minutes was all it took for an ambulance to arrive and whisk him to Sagamore Community Hospital two miles away. Brian rode in the back with Nuss, who kept drifting in and out of consciousness and calling for his mother who had been dead for nearly two years. It was with the siren wailing, lights flashing and Nuss lying there bleeding that Brian swore he would do whatever necessary to beat *that fucking Montesano and Savino and the machine and the bridge and Dolan and Henrietta Wilcox and Baby Protectors and Jesse Helms and all the assholes like him and...*

I am not afraid.

The media finally discovered Brian Werth. The injury to Nuss plus the fire or bombing or whatever it was made for a great story, so hordes of paparazzi descended upon Sagamore. Ironically, Al Savino received as much coverage from the incident as Brian did. After hearing from the doctors that Nuss was resting comfortably, Brian returned to his headquarters to find Al Savino standing on the front steps making a statement to the press.

"The Sagamore police will investigate this entire incident," Savino was assuring a bevy of reporters. "Although preliminary indications are that this is only an accidental fire, if vandalism is involved we will get to the bottom of it. Ladies and gentlemen, we must never let ourselves forget that the two-party system and free-spirited competition are what makes this country great. Towards that end, I hereby announce that the Sagamore Republican Committee is pledging the sum of five hundred dollars to help with the reopening of my opponent's headquarters."

Brian leaped onto the steps next to Savino. A torrent of questions flew at him from all sides.

"I'd like to make a statement," he said, holding up his hand for quiet. "This act of terrorism will not intimidate me or any members of my campaign team. We will now work harder to achieve our goal on Election Day. And we do not believe for a minute that this bombing—mark my words, bombing—was accidental or a random act of vandalism."

"Do you have any idea who might do such a thing?" a pretty blonde television reporter up front asked, thrusting a microphone into Brian's face.

"It could be any number of groups opposed to the positions I've taken," Brian replied. He paused to ponder his next few words. *No more politics. No more bullshit.* "Or it could even be my opponent in this election."

It took a moment for the reporters to absorb the impact of Brian's statement. Here was a real story: an incumbent Republican mayor accused by his Democratic challenger of bombing his headquarters. Marcus, Jeff and David standing on the sidelines heard Brian's words and agreed with them completely... *to hell with prudent political rhetoric.*

"Would you comment on your opponent's accusation?" another reporter asked Savino.

"You're damn right I'll comment," Savino replied, his face red with rage. "I feel sorry for Mr. Werth. His campaign is floundering and he's a desperate man. It's entirely possible he staged this whole thing just to get attention."

The inference that Nuss had been deliberately injured infuriated Brian. With the reporters taking it all in, he said, "Listen to me Savino. I think the Republicans are responsible for this explosion and you know it. Face it, you'd kill your own grandmother if Montesano told you to." He accentuated this last statement by bouncing his fingers off Savino's chest. When an irritated Savino looked down, Brian had the pleasure of twitting his nose. "A nose for a nose," he said.

Savino tried to grab Brian's neck but was restrained by Wilhelm Weltsmirtz who had come up behind him. Before Brian could take a step towards Savino, someone grabbed him in a hammerlock from the back. Brian twisted around to see who it was and found himself embraced by Detective Dolan.

"Go ahead, struggle," Dolan whispered in Brian's ear. "Please, I want you to struggle."

Brian made it obvious to everyone he was not offering any resistance so Dolan had to let him go.

"Thanks," Brian said. "By the way, how much are they paying you?"

Dolan smiled and used every ounce of his self-control to stop himself from drawing his gun and firing into Brian's midriff. Marcus and Jeff pulled Brian off to the right while Weltsmirtz escorted Savino in the other direction, their latest encounter done.

"That was great," David said, running alongside Brian to his car. "I wish I could do something like that... just once."

Savino evaded reporters when Weltsmirtz shoved him, rather roughly, into the back seat of a black limousine where a shrouded Frank Montesano sat waiting. As soon as the door slammed, Al started to say, "Hey, did we plant a b..."

"Shut up you idiot," Montesano snapped.

The reporters with their notebooks, tape recorders and videotape recorded the entire confrontation, but because of the late hour most people did not learn of the incident until the news reports of the following day. It was front-page material for *Newsday* and all the New York City newspapers except the *Times*, which did feature it prominently in its section of Long Island news. One tabloid, the *New York Post*, remained true to its tradition of yellow journalism by printing a large picture of Savino lunging at Brian along with a banner headline reading: **DEM SAYS GOP BOMBS HQ.** Another crisis in the Middle East led off the local radio and television news broadcasts but Brian and Savino came next and were extensively covered. Dan Rather even cited their encounter on his national radio broadcast calling it "a perfect example of how American politicians love to head for the gutter."

The media treated the story almost uniformly. First, they detailed the "fire and alleged bombing" and reported on Nuss' condition. Then they covered the candidates' confrontation of the steps of the headquarters. Brian's refusal to rule out Republican complicity in what he called a bombing was continually quoted as was Savino's description of Brian as a man desperate enough to say and do anything. Detective Dolan, speaking on behalf of the Sagamore Police Department, explained they had no leads whatsoever but promised the investigation would continue. Savino and Brian obliged legitimate news reporters with interviews but both turned down offers to appear on *Geraldo* and *Sally Jesse Raphael.* Savino wanted to fulfill a lifelong dream of going on those shows but Montesano had told him, "Forget it Al, the more you talk the more you fuck up." Brian rejected the offers flat out on the grounds that he found the shows vapid garbage from which participants rarely emerged in a positive light.

"Who's coming off better?" Brian wondered as he turned the dials on the headquarters' radio that, miraculously, still worked.

"What you mean is... who's coming off worse?" David said. "Both of you look real bad."

"All right, who's coming off worse?"

"Impossible to say."

"At least more people have heard of you now," Marcus interjected.

"I still can't understand why Montesano would do something like this," Brian said.

"I'm sure he's not happy with how it came out," Marcus said.

"But what's the point?" Brian continued. "Polls show Savino creaming me. Why not just leave it alone and let it happen?"

"What was the point of Watergate?" David said. "Ted Kennedy never even got the nomination and Nixon creamed McGovern."

"There's the point, don't you see?" Marcus said. "Liars lie, cheaters cheat."

"Killers kill," David added.

"That's right," Marcus said, nodding at David. "People do what they do. It doesn't matter whether they really need to or not."

"People are what they are," Brian said slowly, instinctively trying to sum up a lesson learned.

Silence in the room signaled agreement.

"I think there's something else," Jeff finally said.

"What?" Brian asked him.

"I think you've made Montesano mad,"

Brian stood up and started pacing wildly. "He has Professor Sansone murdered, puts Nuss in the hospital, and I've made him mad? You must be kidding me."

"I agree with Jeff," Marcus said. "Two to one is not enough of a victory margin for him. Remember, Montesano is part of a dying breed. He's a throwback, a real political boss in the tradition of New York's Boss Tweed and Wilbur Doughty in the old days here on Long Island. Just winning isn't enough for him. He wants... no... he needs to destroy your campaign, your career and you."

"And build his bridge and get rich," Brian added.

"Right," Marcus agreed. "I can't think of a powerful political machine that acts with restraint. I don't think it's possible."

"Let me get this straight," Jeff cut in. "Montesano is mad so he'll keep attacking until..."

"Until we all run off to South America," Marcus interrupted, "or..."

"Or I'm dead," Brian finished.

They all thought about that for a moment, four young men who suddenly felt very grown up.

"We can't go to the police because Montesano controls them," Marcus pointed out.

"And we can't go to the media because without any evidence we'll look like bigger clowns than we already do," David added.

"That's right," Marcus affirmed.

"We're fucked," Jeff said.

Brian faced his three friends. "Obviously, the logical thing to do is give up. Maybe we should all hit Club Med for a few weeks. But to tell you the truth, I don't feel logical right now. I feel anger, more anger than I've ever felt in my life. So I'm going to continue."

"I'm with you," Marcus said.

"I thought we all agreed on that before," Jeff added.

"Can we go over alternative escape routes?" David said.

Brian smacked a fist into his palm. "I want a gun," he said.

No one thought they heard him right.

"A what?" Jeff asked.

"A gun," Brian repeated.

Jeff laughed nervously. "What are you going to do with a gun? Have you ever fired one?"

"Well, just a BB gun," Brian admitted.

"Oh my God," Jeff said, throwing his hands up and turning away.

"Listen, I've got to be able to protect myself."

"Brian, you're on record as being strongly in favor of restricting access to small firearms," David reminded him.

"I know, I know, I know, we all agree the NRA sucks. But somebody's trying to kill me."

"I'll get you a gun," Marcus said.

"And where are you going to get a gun?" Jeff asked him.

"I'll give him mine."

The revelation that Marcus owned a gun surprised everyone.

"You own a gun?" Brian said, in a kind of awe.

"Yup."

"What kind?"

"It's black with a barrel and a trigger."

"Very funny. Come on."

"It's a twenty-two.

"Why do you own a gun?" Brian asked his friend.

"You have to remember I grew up in the South Bronx," Marcus replied. "All my friends had guns and so did I. I still have mine because it has sentimental value. It was a gift from my parents on the occasion of my first Communion."

"You're kidding," David said. "Please tell me you're kidding."

"Okay, I bought it on the street," Marcus owned up.

Jeff scratched his scruffy red whiskers. "Hmmmm. I guess when we white guys on Long Island were trading baseball cards..."

"We black guys in the South Bronx were taking target practice in an abandoned lot."

"Does the gun still work?" Brian asked.

"I guess so. I haven't fired it for years though."

"I need it," Brian said earnestly.

"Okay," Marcus agreed.

"Great, just great," Jeff said, disgusted. "Now answer me this. Are you going to tell Iva there are likely to be further incidents like the bombing?"

"She knows," Brian replied without hesitation. "I know she knows. She probably figured it out before we did. But I won't tell her about the gun." He drew a mock pistol and knelt on the floor. "Werth, FBI!" he yelled, though his impression more resembled an altar boy than a G-man.

"Always fire from a crouch and with two hands," Marcus said.

"Oh God," David moaned, visibly upset. With trembling hands he took out a bottle of nasal spray and shot twice into each nostril. "I can't tell whether you guys are serious or not."

"I don't think we know for sure," Brian said, walking over and throwing an arm around his friend. "Don't worry though, buddy. I promise we're not going to do anything stupid."

David cleared his throat and straightened his glasses. "Could we..." He stopped; his voice had come out falsetto. He cleared his throat again. "Could we get back to work? We were discussing alternative escape routes."

"Right," Brian said. "Alternative escape routes. Any suggestions?"

Montesano's Republican organization rented a three-story office building in downtown Sagamore. Originally built in nineteen hundred and six as a Masonic Temple, with the Republicans occupying it the venerable old structure still remained a place for secrets and whispers. Located directly across the street from City Hall, the location was fortuitous since city workers could unofficially stop by during the day to help out with whatever happened to be the current project.

With an election upcoming, Republican—they were virtually all Republican—city officials unabashedly ordered their underlings to get over there and assist the campaign. Frank Montesano, with no official government job himself, liked being close to the action. He held tight the reins of city, town and county government. No important officeholder made a major decision without his approval. The County Executive, County Commissioners and Town Supervisors were all his vassals and, guided by decades of tradition and precedent, regularly paid him homage. Sagamore was the seat of Frank Montesano's kingdom, the fiefdom he kept for himself.

Montesano's office on the third floor was spacious, a suite with a private bathroom, kitchenette, bar, and ample space left over for an antique mahogany desk, matching coffee table and three sofas. One door of the office opened into a reception area where a secretary—a newly hired young redhead whose shapely legs and pointed breasts had rendered her resume irrelevant—screened all calls and visitors. Another door opened into a conference room containing a large table around which twenty people could comfortably sit. The conference room also had a door connecting it directly to the reception area.

The skylight in the ceiling of the conference room provided the means the Werth burglars planned to use to enter the building. Their scheme called for Jeff to park his car in an adjoining alleyway. While he waited in the getaway car, Brian, Marcus and David were going to stand on the hood and lift themselves up onto the fire escape. Roof hopping would get them to the skylight and a diamond glass-cutter would cut a hole. Brian and Marcus planned to climb down a rope ladder into the conference room while David remained on the roof to offer advice, keep lookout and throw down any tools they might need. The lock on the door leading into Montesano's office posed no barrier.

"I'll handle it in about thirty seconds," Marcus had promised.

"Let me guess, you're from the South Bronx," Brian had commented.

Mrs. Fitzpatrick had revealed the combination to the safe so no problem was anticipated there. It would then be a piece of cake to clean out the safe and climb back up the rope ladder to the roof and hustle back down to the car. In case anyone happened to notice the car pulling out, five blocks away Iva and Debbie would be waiting in the cab of a Jiffy Tape Company truck procured by Jeff from his father's factory. A ramp leading up into the back of a truck would be in place so Jeff's car could make a quick disappearance from the street.

Of course, things could go wrong. The guard downstairs might hear them. A hidden burglar alarm might be tripped. The combination to the safe might have been changed. They would not give up in the event of the latter. First, Marcus would try to pick the lock by using a doctor's stethoscope and listening for clicks. Failing that, David would send down an acetylene torch and they would try to cut their way into the safe. They all prayed the torch would not be necessary since none of them—including Marcus—had any experience with one and had only seen them used in the movies.

Brian brushed the hair off his forehead and threw his pen on the wine crate in front of him. "It appears the only way to get out in time if a burglar alarm goes off is for me and Marcus to lower a rope out of one of the office windows and climb down to the ground."

"Extremely dangerous but the only way," Marcus agreed.

"David, you just go back across the roof the way we came as fast as you can. Jeff will wait for all of us," Brian added.

Jeff nodded that he understood. David also nodded but thought to himself, *If I don't settle down I'm going to hyperventilate and pass out.*

"Okay, then we leave from my house tomorrow night at midnight," Brian said.

"Right," Jeff said.

"Right," Marcus echoed.

All eyes focused on David.

"No further questions," he said.

Chapter VIII

"I hate the blasted army, but friendship, well, that's something else."

Douglas Fairbanks, Jr. explaining his reenlistment to fiancée Joan Fontaine in Gunga Din (1939)

October 7, 12:09 A.M.

Brian felt like the blood vessels in his brain were about to burst. He had a wicked headache and a throbbing right at the nape of his neck. *Great, a cerebral hemorrhage,* he thought. As he slipped behind the wheel of his car he caught a glimpse of himself in the rear view mirror. *Is that really me?* He grabbed the mirror and aimed it at his face. An exhausted man he barely recognized peered back with pale skin and bloodshot eyes with, not bags exactly, but a subtle hollowness underneath. *Are those crowsfeet? God, I've been tired before but I've never seen myself look tired. Thirty-one going on thirty-two. Am I old?*

"Man, I'm beat," Marcus said from the passenger seat.

Marcus looked the same as he always did; he was twenty-six. Brian placed his hands on his temples to check his hairline. *Still holding firm thank the Lord.* He turned the key in the ignition and was about to pull away when a police cruiser pulled up in front of them preventing them from moving.

"What now?" Marcus moaned.

"They can't pull me over before I've even started driving," Brian said. "That's absurd, even around here."

The policeman made no move to get out of his car.

"I guess I go to him," Brian said, hopping out. He walked around to the window of the patrol car and immediately recognized the driver as the officer who had come to his house bearing the news of Professor Sansone's death.

"Hello Werth," Patrolman Bolster said.

"Uh... hi," Brian said.

"Look, I was just driving by so I thought I'd let you in on the preliminary findings of the investigation into the... uh... fire at your headquarters. The preliminary findings are that there are none. No clues, no leads, no nuthin'."

Brian forced a sarcastic laugh. "I expected as much."

"Don't hold your breath waitin' for progress."

"I won't," Brian said.

Bolster picked at his nose and flicked a snot ball out the window. Brian had to dodge it.

"Werth," he said, "I don't know what you've been doing to piss off all the top brass, but if I were you I'd watch my ass."

Brian nodded, not fully paying attention. His mind was on the night Bolster had driven them to the Professor's house with total indifference to the fact that a man had died. *His partner never even turned around...*

Bolster seemed to read his mind. "Hey Werth," he said, "remember my partner?"

"The conversationalist?" Brian replied.

"Yeah, well, I can explain that. He had a nervous breakdown. He was havin' it that night. He's in the loony bin now, totally cracked up. His wife and daughter left him and he couldn't take it."

"I'm sorry to hear that."

"All part of being a cop," Bolster said solemnly.

"What does all this have to do with me?" Brian asked. "What are you trying to tell me?"

"What this means is... if you fuck around they're going to get you. They're trying to get me, run me out a few months before I get my pension... the cheap bastards. So I'm on your side Werth. I hate these prick bastards as much as you do. I'm just tellin' you to watch your ass and don't fuck around."

"Thanks," Brian said, amazed that this misfit cop was apparently an ally. "We're going to keep trying."

Bolster flicked another snot ball, and this time out of respect for Brian he aimed it into the back seat. "For Christ's sake watch your ass," he added one more time.

Brian nodded and walked back to his car thinking about the old adage that politics makes for strange bedfellows.

"What's up?" Marcus asked.

"To explain his wartime alliance with Josef Stalin," Brian answered, "Winston Churchill said he would get into bed with the devil if the devil was fighting Adolf Hitler."

"What are you talking about?"

"That cop... " Brian began.

"... is on our side?" Marcus finished.

"I guess so. Something about how they want to fuck him out of his pension."

"But why?"

"Who knows? Let's just get out of here. Everything's getting insane."

Iva was already asleep when Brian slipped under the covers next to her. He gently rolled her on her side and placed her head on his chest. She murmured something incomprehensible and kept on sleeping. Brian kissed the top of her head and tried to sleep himself, but he could not. It was one of those times when he was too exhausted to sleep. *Man am I wound up, come on... I've got to sleep...*

With the side of her head on Brian's chest and her ear over his heart, Iva could hear and feel the vibrations of his pulse. The rapid pounding woke her up. *My God, the man's a veritable powder keg. His heart's racing.* "Honey, are you okay?" she whispered.

He kissed the top of her head again. "I'm fine, thanks."

"Are you sure?"

"Just a little tired, that's all."

Iva sat up and said, "Roll over onto your stomach."

He obeyed. She straddled him at the waist and started rubbing her fingers over his neck and shoulders.

"Oh, that feels great."

"Just relax."

"Okay."

Iva pressed harder. She moved her hands all around his back, twisting and turning, soothing the tense muscles. Then starting at the base of his spine, she walked her fingers up towards his head massaging one vertebra at a time. Brian lay there motionless, aware of the pent up anxiety flowing out of him.

"Thank you," he murmured.

"You're welcome."

She continued top brush her finger tips over his skin, lightly touching, tickling. Brian took a deep breath and relaxed. He knew he was going to be able to sleep after all.

"You're so good to me," he whispered.

"I know." She kept her hands drifting from back to shoulders to neck and back again.

"Iva, I love you so much, oh this feels great."

She leaned forward to kiss the back of his head. Then still straddling him, she jerked bolt upright. *My mother, my brothers, please not Brian. God, I'm afraid.* At about the same time Brian fell asleep lying on his stomach, Iva laid down on her back next to him and could not sleep for a long time.

Man do I hate hospitals. The next afternoon as he walked through the corridors of Sagamore Community Hospital, Brian knew his blood was rushing to his head and his face probably projected a pale shade of crimson. *Come on, I've got to look like I'm in control,* he told himself. He took a right at the water fountain then a hard left down the hall past radiology to room thirty-two where the sticker on the door read **WILLIAM NUSS**. Brian took a deep breath, brushed his hair off his forehead and walked in. Nuss was sitting up in his bed sporting a white wraparound bandage for his head and slings for both arms to restrict potentially painful movements. His buttocks rested on a pink silk pillow. *Twin Cities...* Betsy Brewster sat at his bedside, spoon-feeding him ice cream.

"Hey baby, what's shakin'?" Nuss sang out upon seeing Brian.

"Hi Dr. Werth," Betsy said. "It's the pain killer, it makes him kind of goofy."

"I guess so," Brian said. He could feel himself relaxing.

Nuss giggled and said, "I asked the doctor if I would be able to play the piano and he said, 'Sure' so I said 'That's funny, I never could before.'"

Brian smiled.

"What's the matter, don't you get it?" Nuss asked.

"I get it," Brian said.

"Here, have some more ice cream," Betsy said, shoveling a wad of chocolate chip mint into Nuss' mouth. It was her way of shutting him up. Brian pulled up a chair.

"I brought you a present," he said, producing a brown paper bag. "No big surprise... it's a book."

"Thans a wof," Nuss responded because the ice cream had numbed his tongue.

"It's Gore Vidal's *1876,*" Brian continued. "Vidal's an arrogant son of a bitch, but he sure as hell can write."

"I'll read it," Nuss said.

Brian had no doubt he would. "So, how are you feeling?" he asked.

"He's feeling much better," Betsy answered for him.

"My butt hurts," Nuss said. "Or at least it used to until Betsy gave me this pillow." He lifted himself up to offer a better view.

Brian observed that Betsy had embroidered on the pink satin pillow *TO BN LOVE BB.* They looked longingly at each other and clasped hands, and Brian happily realized Betsy's affections had found a more suitable direction.

"Well," Brian said, getting to his feet. "I just came by to say hello and see how you're doing. Looks like you're doing just fine."

"I'm getting better," Nuss said.

Brian walked to the door and turned around. "Take care you two."

"Dr. Werth..." Nuss said. He did not finish his sentence.

"Yes?" Brian finally asked.

"Why..." There was another pause.

"Why what?"

Nuss shook his head and rubbed his eyes trying to clear the sedatives out of his brain. "Why... uh... why am I here?"

Brian walked back to the bedside and leaned over his young friend. "You're here because sometimes our system screws up. You're here because sometimes men get too powerful and arrogant. You're a victim of that."

"It's not fair," Nuss said softly.

"We're fighting back," Brian told him. "We're not going to take it. We're going to do whatever we have to do to fight back."

Fogged though he was, Nuss knew what Brian was alluding to. As a member of the Executive Committee he had been privy to discussions concerning a possible break-in of Montesano's office. "What changed your mind?" Nuss asked.

"I'm looking at him," Brian replied.

"But... "

"We're fighting back."

Tears welled up in Nuss' eyes. "Good luck. Just please let me know..."

"Thanks, I will. You just get better." Brian gave a little wave and left the room.

Nuss opened his mouth to say good-bye but was silenced when Betsy shoved in another spoonful of chocolate chip mint.

Brian strode through the oppressive white halls wanting nothing more than to get out as soon as he could. *Man do I hate hospitals.* The conglomeration of medicine smells jogged memories of freshman biology class. Dissecting that fetal pig may have been the most disgusting thing he had ever done in his life. And when the ever-amusing Jeff Hollis cut off the pig's ear and squished it in Brian's English anthology, their friendship had been strained for nearly ten minutes.

"It's not fair," Brian repeated Nuss' words out loud. "It's not fair." *Damn. How can you explain to a college kid who wants to go to law school and someday become President that politics frequently relegates basic right and wrong to a peripheral consideration. What kind of pure and unadulterated crap am I spewing in my classes? The constitution... checks and balances... separation of powers... judicial review... it's all bullshit.*

"Professor Sansone, this running for mayor isn't what I thought it would be," Brian said out loud.

Seemingly on cue a cloudburst exploded just as he stepped outside. There was nothing to do but get wet. He jogged to his car, his mood turning foul. *Areté, what a pain in the ass.*

"Where would you like this cabinet," Miss Fidele?" Mr. Majid asked, poking his head into Iva's classroom.

"Oh, thank you. Right in that corner will be fine," Iva told the man who had been at Great Neck Academy longer than anyone: twenty-six years as its head custodian. Arshad Majid and his parents had escaped the Shah of Iran and his secret police in the late fifties although once in America he always told everyone he hailed from "Persia." He wore a green janitor's outfit with a purple turban and there was never any doubt that this Jewish private school was cleaned every day by a Muslim. Thousands of miles from the Holy Land nobody gave it a second thought, least of all Majid; it was a peaceful job and he made more money than most of the teachers. Both the faculty and students liked him and the flying carpet jokes behind his back lacked any venom.

"Here you go baby," Mr. Majid said, wheeling a hand truck bearing a metal file cabinet into the room.

Iva was stunned. *Baby?* she thought to herself, continuing to grade papers. *He's never called me baby before.*

Mr. Majid deposited the cabinet and turned to go. When he got to the door, out of the corner of her eye Iva distinctly saw him wink and flash a toothy grin. "See you later my little chickadee," he added and was gone.

Iva leaned forward and put her head in her hands. Normally she would find amusing the incongruity of a man with a thick Farsi accent producing a serviceable W.C. Fields impression. But this time she had other concerns. *Oh God, I hope he didn't see anything... shit...* Then Iva smiled. *So it was good old Mr. Majid. Maybe he got a thrill. Praise Allah... it sure could have been a lot worse.*

"Well everyone's here," Marcus said, "except... "

"Except David," Jeff cut in.

"Is he chickening out?" Debbie wondered.

"You're all too tense," Brian said as he paced and cracked his knuckles. "It's only a few minutes after twelve. He'll be here."

The gatebell rang.

"There you see."

"I'll get it," Iva said, running outside.

David's appearance in the doorway drew looks of astonishment from everyone. The man was dressed to the hilt for a clandestine adventure clad in black high-top basketball sneakers, black pants, black turtleneck, black ski cap and black gloves. He had even smeared his face with charcoal. Doubled over under the weight of a large duffel bag, and consequently every few seconds having to push his glasses back up his nose, he looked absolutely ludicrous.

"I'm ready," he announced, gasping for breath.

"David, what do you think this is... a James Bond flick?" Jeff said.

"Maybe he's from the French Underground," Debbie added.

"It wasn't necessary to dress like that," Marcus said.

"Look, he can dress any way he wants as long as we can just get going," Brian said.

David's knees buckled. Brian grabbed the duffel bag just in time to keep him from falling forward onto his face.

"Wow, this thing weighs a ton?" Brian said. "What's in here?"

"I call it my contingency bag," David replied. "I'm prepared for anything that might go wrong. There's extra rope, lots of tools, rain gear, all sorts of stuff. I've even got a sledge hammer."

"Your contingency bag is going to be a pain to carry," Marcus said. "Are you sure it's necessary?"

"It is definitely necessary," David replied.

"I hope you didn't forget the emergency flares," Jeff kidded.

"Nope, I've got four of them."

He actually has flares everyone realized.

"And I've got sandwiches and doughnuts," he added.

"Doughnuts," Jeff repeated.

"Yup. Banana crème."

"I'm sorry I made fun of the way you're dressed," Jeff said.

"I'm sorry too," Debbie said. "I myself frequently overpack on short overnight trips."

"I'll put those sandwiches in a cooler if you like," Iva offered.

"What is this, a fucking coffee klatch?" Brian interrupted in a loud voice. "Let me remind you we are all about to go commit a major felony."

"I think we're all ready to go now," Marcus said calmly.

"Let's synchronize our watches," Brian said. "I have 12:14."

"Oh no!" David cried, gaping at his naked wrist. "My watch. I forgot my watch!" He was clearly agitated.

"You can take mine," Iva said.

"Thanks," he replied, starting to calm down.

Brian moved to the front door and threw it open. "All right, if there's nothing else, let's roll!"

Everyone started to follow him.

"Wait!" It was Iva. "I know you're going to think this is stupid, but I seriously think if anyone has to go to the bathroom, it is best they go now."

They all exchanged glances but no one admitted anything.

Brian finally spoke up. "Now that you mention it, I do have to go."

Now that she mentioned it, they all had to go.

Chapter IX

Sorrowful Jones: "You never heard my courage questioned."

Gladys O'Neill: "I never heard your courage mentioned."

Bob Hope and Lucille Ball in Sorrowful Jones (1949)

OCTOBER 8TH, 12:56 A.M.

Wilhelm Weltsmirtz put his feet up on his desk and leaned back in his chair. This was the lowest he had ever sunk: night watchman at a smalltime Republican headquarters from midnight to eight in the morning. "Take the ten bucks an hour or you're fired," Montesano had said. *The Boss had said a lot of other things as well,* Weltsmirtz mused, *none of them true. The bombing of the Werth headquarters had been a master stroke of improvisation and individual initiative. So what if the bomb goes off prematurely and injures some kid. It's not my fault the press makes that Werth punk out to be some kind of a martyr. Controlling the press isn't my department.* Inept, incompetent, retarded, Montesano had railed at him. G. Gordon Liddy and John Erlichman had reamed him out the same way about thirteen years ago. *Fuck 'em all, they were all assholes.*

Weltsmirtz' stomach rumbled. He rubbed it and yawned then ran his hand through hair thin and gray not thick and blond like it used to be. He glanced at his watch: after one in the morning. He was supposed to check the locks on all exterior doors every half hour and stroll up to the second and third floors to look in on the offices there. *ZurHolle damit. At ten dollars an hour they're lucky if I do it at all.* He yawned again, took a sip of brandy from his trusty flask and tipped his hat over his eyes. *Assholes. If they want to pay me ten dollars an hour for sleeping, fuck 'em I'll take it.* About a minute later he was snoring, dreaming of decades ago... and imagining himself in charge of a coup in Guatemala that had gone off without a hitch. Weltsmirtz did not hear the Mustang convertible pull into the alley next to the building.

By standing on the hood of Jeff's Mustang convertible, Brian was able to jump and pull himself up onto the fire escape. Marcus followed and together they pulled up David and his contingency bag. Luckily, a garbage dumpster effectively hid the car from anyone peering down the alley from Main Street.

"Wait for us here unless you hear differently," Brian reminded Jeff.

"Right," Jeff replied in a whisper.

The night was overcast, moonless and very dark. The three men climbed the ladder past the second and third floors and hoisted themselves up onto the roof. They tiptoed toward the skylight as quietly as they could but David, despite a desperate effort, could not keep the contents of his contingency bag from clanging together.

"Go ahead... make some more noise with that thing," Brian said. "They can't hear you in Tibet."

"Sorry," David said.

"Quiet," Marcus snapped.

Finally they reached the skylight and peered inside. Blackness. David handed Marcus the glass cutter, a wrench-like instrument with a diamond point. Brian attached two suction cups with handles to the window so the severed panel could be pulled outward. Marcus set to work cutting the glass as close to the frame as possible to avoid jagged edges. The cutter made a sound resembling the high-pitched purring of a kitten; it was barely audible but as nervous as they all were it may as well have been a saber-toothed tiger. David kept glancing around like a Neanderthal Man after dark.

"So far so good," Brian said, glad there was someone else there to be more nervous than he was. Marcus kept telling himself there was too much work to be done and no time to be nervous.

The glass came out cleanly. They tied one end of a rope around the leg of a ventilation unit that seemed sturdy and threw the other end into the hole. Brian put on a pair of gloves, slipped his flashlight into his back pocket and lowered himself into the darkness. He hit the floor next to the conference room table about five feet from the locked door of Montesano's office. Marcus joined him and the two cat burglars surveyed their surroundings holding their fingers over the lenses of their flashlights to mute the light.

"Looks just like we expected," Brian whispered.

"Yeah," Marcus whispered back.

They peered into the reception area and noticed the door to the hallway had clear glass for its upper half. They decided to close the conference room door so someone walking by would not notice the flickering of their flashlights.

"Hurry up!" David pleaded from above.

Using a thin metal instrument resembling a dentist's probe, Marcus, true to his word, picked the lock on Montesano's office door in about fifteen seconds.

"There," he whispered as he heard the bolt slide back, "quite a talent, huh?"

"Yes," Brian replied, "as long as you realize the talent is not genetic but rather a response to continuous economic deprivation."

"You white liberals make me sick," Marcus said.

They both grinned.

"Hurry up!" David pleaded again from above.

Brian pushed the door open. It squeaked and they all held their breath. By the light of their flashlights they quickly located Montesano's safe in the far corner behind his desk. Marcus walked right to it and tried the combination Mrs. Fitzpatrick had given them.

"Clear it to fifteen, two turns to the right to twenty-nine, three turns left to seven... for all the good it will do you." Well, Mrs. Fitzpatrick, let's hope it does us a lot of good, Brian thought, praying desperately the combination would still work.

Marcus completed the numbered sequence and snapped the lever. It did not open.

"Try it again," Brian said.

Marcus did. It still did not open. He tried a third time. Nothing.

"They've changed the combination," Marcus said, producing a stethoscope. "Let me see if I can pick this thing." He spun the dial back and forth a few times. "It's no use," he said. He pulled the plugs out of his ears. "This lock is sophisticated. I can't hear a thing."

"Let's tell David to throw down the torch," Brian said.

"Okay"

The two men walked out into the conference room. The overhead light snapped on blinding them.

"Get your hands up," Wilhelm Weltsmirtz said, aiming his pistol with two hands. "Hey... it's Brian Werth. This must be my lucky day!"

Brian and Marcus put their hands up. It was a weird feeling being caught and held at gun point for the first time in their lives. That guy really could kill them by just squeezing his finger. Marcus immediately saw lunging at the gun would not work; the guard was too far away and could easily fire a clean shot. Brian momentarily considered trying to explain they were not really burglars, just students doing research for a class project.

"Lucky thing I was making my rounds and I happened to check this office," Weltsmirtz said. That was a lie; the only reason Weltsmirtz had stumbled across them was because he had begun to search the upstairs offices for a comfortable couch to snooze on. Still aiming the gun, he side-stepped to a small red alarm box on the wall and pulled the switch. A loud bell started ringing throughout the building and a tiny red light began to blink at police headquarters about a mile away.

"The cops will be here in a few minutes," Weltsmirtz said. He took one hand off his gun and reached for his flask. His hands quivered so most of the liquid spilled down his front. He wiped his mouth on his sleeve, put the flask back in his pocket and resumed holding his gun with two hands. *Brian Werth,* Weltsmirtz thought. *You're the reason I'm being punished. You're the reason people think I'm a fuck-up. My bomb should have convinced you to quit. This is all your fault. People who fuck with me pay for it. That stupid transvestite found that out. Her next hormone shot was spiked with strychnine. Ha. That worked perfectly. Now it's your turn, Werth.* "I want you to turn around and place your palms on the wall and spread your legs," Weltsmirtz told them.

Brian started to obey but Marcus yelled, "Don't! He'll shoot us in the back and claim we were trying to escape!"

"I said turn around," Weltsmirtz repeated.

"No," Brian said.

"We're not moving," Marcus said.

Weltsmirtz shrugged. *Shot in the back while escaping or shot in the front while escaping. I guess there's no real difference. "Gute nact und aufwiedersehen,"* he said, smiling at his sense of the dramatic.

He pulled the trigger.

David England's contingency bag slammed into the side of Weltsmirtz' head just as the gun discharged. The bullet, previously aimed at Brian's chest, was diverted slightly into a harmless path between him and Marcus. Weltsmirtz fell down face first and lost his grip on the pistol which rattled a few feet away. He was groggy but not unconscious and instinctively he raised himself to his hands and knees to begin feeling for his gun. Brian took a step forward and kicked him squarely on the cheekbone with the instep of his right foot, a move he had executed countless times in high school soccer games. But Weltsmirtz' head did not fly through the air into an opponent's goal. It snapped back and then forward and then down as he fell onto his face and lay motionless.

The alarm bell kept ringing.

"Get back up here and let's scram!" David yelled through the skylight.

"Scram?" Brian and Marcus both repeated the word simultaneously.

"You know what I mean," David persisted. "Let's get out of here."

"But the safe... " Brian said.

"There's no time... "Marcus said.

"Come on," David begged.

"Wait," Brian said. "David, go back down to Jeff and tell him to back the car under the window of Montesano's office."

"But..."

"Just do it!"

"Okay," David said. He scampered away.

When Brian pulled out another length of rope, Marcus knew what he wanted to do... tie it around the safe and lower the entire thing out the window.

"I hope we can lift it," Marcus said.

"So do I."

It took only a few moments to throw two loops of rope around each side of the safe. Brian tied the knot and said, "This will have to do. Let's go." They each took an end of the safe—half the size of a refrigerator and one hundred fifty pounds if was an ounce—and grunting and groaning lifted it onto the window sill. They threw open the window and saw Jeff and David backing the car underneath, three stories down. There was no sign of the police in either direction.

"We're lowering the safe, watch out!" Brian yelled down.

"What did he say?" David, now sitting in the back seat, asked.

"He said, *We're lowering the safe, watch out!,*" Jeff told him.

They looked up and saw the safe on the window sill starting to tilt outward. They jumped out of the car faster than they had ever moved in their lives. Standing safely off to the side they looked up and saw the safe descend slowly for about the first ten feet then appear to fall freely. It slammed into Jeff's car right where David had been sitting, ripping the upholstery and embedding itself.

"I'm going to be sick," David said.

"Campaign funds are paying for that," Jeff said.

Three stories above, Brian and Marcus both grimaced in pain. The nylon rope had been too slippery for them to maintain their grip and it slid through their hands burning the palms off their gloves along with some skin underneath. Marcus threw David's contingency bag out the window and started the painful climb down the rope to the ground. Brian followed.

The alarm bell kept ringing. Two police cars arrived just in time to get a glimpse of four men jumping into a car and speeding off. One cruiser stayed to investigate the office building and the other took off in pursuit. Jeff's Mustang had about a one hundred yard lead.

"Move it!" Brian told Jeff. "If we can just get this thing in the back of the truck and close the door, we'll lose 'em!"

Jeff grunted "Yeah," and kept his eyes moving back and forth from the speedometer to the road ahead, about five hundred yards of deserted straight-away. *Seventy... seventy-five... eighty... eighty-five... ninety... ninety-five... one hundred.* Brian and Marcus turned around and noticed they were gaining on the police car. David sat rigid, one hand pressed against the dashboard, the other pressed against his chest to monitor his pulse.

Nine blocks away, Iva and Debbie sat in the cab of a Jiffy Tape Company truck parked halfway down the block of a side street. The engine was idling and a ramp leading into the back was in place. If everything went right, the plan called for the Mustang to drive up and into the cargo area and the back door to be shut immediately. Iva would then drive a mile or so to a secluded section of road then pull over and let Jeff drive the rest of the way home. She was not at all comfortable driving the truck. Although that afternoon Jeff had given her two hours patient instruction, she still dreaded having to shift the heavy gears and steer a vehicle of such monstrous size. For someone who had never driven anything larger than a station wagon, the truck handled like a Brontosaurus with an attitude.

Debbie checked her watch. "2:15. Getting late. They should be here by now," she said.

"They'll be here," Iva said.

"I'm worried."

"Me too."

The Mustang's tires screeched as they swerved onto the street where the truck was parked. Jeff drove up the ramp with such speed he crashed into the panel behind the cab. He knocked out his headlights, the only source of light in the compartment. The impact jarred everyone, including Iva and Debbie up front.

"Oh my God!" Debbie yelled.

"Well, I guess they're here," Iva said.

"Let's go!" Debbie said.

Iva jammed the gear stick into first and took off even before the men in the back had time to pull up the ramp. It clattered harmlessly to the ground. Brian and Jeff each grabbed a side of the rear door and started to pull it down, but they were not in time. The police car turned the corner and the two officers inside got a good look at the door closing and the truck starting off.

"They're in the back of that truck!" Patrolman Bud Armstrong screamed, thrilled that he was finally going to see some action and maybe even face danger. This was his first chance to prove himself: five months out of the police academy, at last his first high speed chase.

Hunched over behind the wheel, Patrolman Randolph Bolster winced. The volume of his rookie partner's running commentary was severely exacerbating his hangover-induced headache. *First a transfer to the overnight shift and then this asshole—who probably lives with his parents and jerks off to reruns of Dragnet under the covers—as a partner.* No doubt about it, the department aimed to make the last five months he needed for his pension as unpleasant as they could make them. *The bastards, they want me to wash out. Fuck 'em, I'm going to get my money.*

"Keep your fuckin' voice down," Bolster growled at the cherub sitting next to him.

Iva heard the siren and saw the red flashing lights in her side mirror. "Oh shit, now what do I do?"

"Lose them," Debbie said.

"How? How can I lose them?"

"We've got to try! Just keep going!"

"Okay," Iva said. She pushed the accelerator further down towards the floor and managed to achieve the whopping speed of forty-one miles per hour.

Spirits were pretty low inside the back of the truck and the pitch darkness only made things seem more hopeless. They could not find their flashlights.

"Those cops saw us," Brian said.

"Yeah, I think they did," Marcus said. "We're cooked."

"What can we do?" Jeff asked.

Neither Brian nor Marcus had any ideas. They heard the sound of David sniffing his Vicks inhaler. "I have four smoke bombs," he said, "in my unnecessary contingency bag."

Iva took a sharp turn causing the four men to tumble against the side of the truck. The shelf above them broke and hundreds of loose rolls of masking tape poured on top of them.

"This is absurd," Brian said. "We need some light."

"I've got flares," David said.

"We can't light a flare in here, we'd suffocate" Marcus said. "Shit, I can't see a thing. Anyone got any matches?"

"I forgot matches," David said.

"There's a cigarette lighter in the car," Jeff said, refusing even in crisis to miss the opportunity for a joke.

"Jeff..." Brian started to say.

"I know... shut up," Jeff finished for him.

Iva turned sharply again causing them to roll over against the opposite wall.

"What the hell is she doing?" Jeff said.

"She's not stopping," Brian said. "She's trying to lose them. Atta girl!"

Patrolman Bolster slammed his fist against the dashboard. "Shit, they're not stopping. Why do people always have to make my life so much more difficult?"

"I'll make them stop," Patrolman Armstrong announced, drawing his gun and aiming it out the window. He fired three shots in rapid succession that ricocheted off the back of the truck.

Bolster slapped the side of his partner's face with the back of his right hand. "Cut that wild west shit out," he snapped. "You want to hurt somebody? Get on the radio and tell them where we are. And for Christ's sake, relax." Armstrong obeyed, duly chastised and looking like his dog just died.

The bullets bouncing off the back of the truck reverberated like Fourth of July fireworks on the inside.

"The cops are shooting at us," Brian said, thinking as he spoke *I can't believe I just said that.*

"Iva should stop," Marcus said. "There's nothing she can do. She'll get hurt."

"I agree," Brian said.

Inside the cab, Iva and Debbie were nothing short of petrified.

"Bullets!" Debbie exclaimed. "They're shooting bullets!"

"They can't hit us from back there," Iva said.

"What are you going to do? We can't seem to lose them."

"I guess we should pull over," Iva said. But in fact she did not pull over. She pushed the pedal that last fraction of an inch to the floor.

"Just a little farther," she said. "Maybe they'll blow a tire or something."

A burst of static over the police car's radio signaled the start of a message from the officers on the scene at the Republican headquarters: "Suspects are to be considered armed and dangerous. One is black about six feet tall, medium build. Another, Caucasian, about the same height and build, has been tentatively identified as Brian Werth." Bolster was astounded. *Werth! Brian Werth! Werth broke into the Republican headquarters! Werth and his crew are in that truck! The cast iron balls on that guy.* A tight smile came to Bolster's lips as he pondered his next move. *I told him to watch his ass.* With his partner Bud Armstrong squinting straight ahead like a hunter with a high-powered rifle closing in on Bambi's mother, Bolster lifted his foot off the accelerator and used his knee to knock the ignition key into the off position. The engine stopped and the car began to slow down.

"What the heck is going on?" Armstrong exclaimed.

"I don't know," Bolster told him. "The engine just conked out. Get out and check under the hood while I radio our position."

"Oh for gosh sakes," Armstrong said, hopping out.

"Fuck 'em Werth, fuck 'em hard," Bolster said under his breath as he watched the truck turn out of sight. In reporting over the radio they had engine trouble, Bolster correctly named the street Iva had turned onto but made a deliberate one hundred eighty degree error in reporting her direction.

Debbie stuck her head out the cab window and forced herself to look behind them for a full ten seconds despite the fact she risked getting shot. "I'm telling you there are no cops following us," she said.

"Well, where are they then?" Iva asked.

"I have no idea."

"Maybe there is a God."

"Maybe, maybe not. I'll let you know later."

"I think I'll just head home," Iva said.

"Yeah, as fast as we can," Debbie added. She brushed her hair back with both hands and pressed on the sides of her head as if she could literally hold herself together.

In the back of the truck the men remained trapped in their dark compartment.

"I don't hear any sirens," Marcus said. "Maybe Iva lost the cops."

"How could someone driving a big slow truck like this for the first time in her life out race a police cruiser?" Brian said.

"The same way certain species of seals migrate thousands of miles each year," David said.

Everyone let the remark slide; no one had any idea what the analogy was, least of all David. When nervous he often spoke without fully formulating his thoughts.

"I'm going to lift up the door and take a look," Jeff said.

"And if the police are back there..." Marcus said.

" ... you could be shot," Brian said.

"To hell with it," Jeff said. "David, do you think you could feel around for those doughnuts?"

Iva drove to Shore Road without being sighted by police; Bolster's misdirections had neatly thrown off the six squad cars called in on the chase. Frustrated in their search, the officers were ordered to stake out Brian's house in case the fugitives showed up there. The truck and a police car met from opposite directions just as both were preparing to turn onto Skunks Misery Road. The officers flipped on their siren and flashing lights and swung sideways to block Iva's access.

"Damn," Iva said. "There is no God."

"Go straight," Debbie said.

Iva did. She drove around the police car and swerved around the bend on Shore Road temporarily out of sight of the cops.

"I'm going to hide us," she said.

"Where?"

Iva did not answer because she was not exactly sure. Then she remembered the few times she had done some sunbathing during the past summer... and how she had walked to the beach. Immediately, she extinguished the headlights and turned onto a tiny dirt path that led to about a hundred feet of sand on the edge of Sagamore Bay. The police car drove past them up on Shore Road, its own siren masking the noisy truck engine. She started driving along the water's edge.

"They might see us here," Debbie said.

"I know. There must be some place we can hide."

They kept bouncing along until they were blocked by the large poles supporting the Sagamore fishing pier, a narrow wooden ramp that extended from Shore Road to some eighty feet into Sagamore Bay.

"Think we can fit under that?" Debbie asked.

"Let's find out," Iva replied. She drove under the pier and stopped. Both the front and rear ends stuck out.

"They can still see us here," Debbie said.

"Look at how dark it is down by the water," Iva said. Without waiting for Debbie to respond, she slammed the gear stick in and out of forward then reverse and somehow managed to turn the vehicle around ninety degrees. Then she forced the stick one more time into reverse and backed the truck up directly under the pier to the water's edge. Tiny two-inch waves lapped at the rear tires. She turned off the engine. Up on Shore Road, police cars sped by oblivious that down on the shoreline their quarry sat hidden by moonless darkness, fog and Sagamore pier.

"We're hidden," she whispered to Debbie.

Debbie nodded but did not reply. Neither of them moved.

"The engine's turned off," Brian said. "We've stopped. Let's get out of here." He threw open the cargo door and leaped off the truck, landing knee deep in sea water and toppling over backwards.

"What the hell..."

Iva jumped out of the cab and ran towards him. "Shhh... quiet," she said, wading in after him and helping him up. Thanks to the half moon they could just make out their silhouettes.

"Where are we?" he gasped, wiping saltwater out of his eyes. The darkness, sand and water seemed incomprehensible to the men emerging from their sensory deprivation.

"We're right by the water under Sagamore pier," Iva explained. "A cop car blocked the entrance to our street so I had to hide us real fast."

They all walked around to the front of the truck.

"You did great," Brian said, arching his body forward to kiss Iva on the cheek without dripping on her. He shivered as his lips touched her skin. It was not a terribly cold morning for early October, mid fifties, but soaked Brian felt a definite chill.

"Here's a towel," David said, never ceasing to amaze everyone with the amount of stuff he had packed.

Huddled around each other, they took a few minutes to fill each other in on what had happened. Clearly, they were fortunate not to be in police custody and no one could believe they had even gotten this far.

"We'll figure that out later," Marcus said. "Right now we've got to plan our next move. There still appears to be a lot of police activity in the area."

"We've got to figure out a way to get the truck to a safe place where we can open the safe," Brian said. "Then maybe we can deal."

"Right," Marcus agreed.

"What..." Iva and Debbie both started to say at the same time.

"We brought the whole safe back with us," Marcus explained.

"Why?" Iva asked.

"It's a long story."

"We have time."

"No we don't," Brian interrupted.

Up on top of the pier a police cruiser was driving towards them.

Chapter X

"I'm giving you till sundown to get out of town."

Brian Donlevy to Joel McCrea in ***The Virginian*** *(1946)*

October 8, 2:49 A.M.

"Nobody move," Brian ordered. "And total silence."

David hiccupped.

"Don't even remotely consider doing that again," Brian snapped.

David nodded and put his hands over his mouth. The police car stopped directly over them. The engine shut off, doors opened and two officers got out.

"This is the area where they disappeared," one said. "Check the shoreline with the binoculars."

"Right," the other said.

The radio squawked and one of the cops got back into the car. For nearly two minutes the fugitives barely breathed. Then the officer in the car rolled down his window, "See anything?"

"Nope, it's so dark I can't see a fuckin' thing."

"The hell with it. You might as well get back in here and get comfortable. We've been ordered to stay put and keep a lookout."

"Okay." Footsteps echoed on the planks then a door opened and closed.

"We're going to have to wait them out," Brian whispered in Marcus' ear.

"It's five till three," Marcus whispered back. "About three hours of darkness left."

Brian nodded. Hopefully the police would not stay till dawn. Everyone sat down in the sand. Brian and Iva held hands and they noticed Jeff and Debbie did too. There was nothing to do but wait.

No one dared speak because the police car above had its windows rolled down. Clearly audible to those below, the talkative lawmen passed the time discussing baseball in a manner—particularly galling to Brian—of unsurpassable asininity.

"I know for a fact Reggie Jackson is a fag," one of the officers said.

"Really?" the other said.

"Yeah, him and a bunch of the other Yankees are total homos."

"How do you know?"

"There's no doubt. My old man has a friend with season tickets who knows a guy who's a vendor at Yankee Stadium."

"Jeez!"

Brian grabbed a handful of sand and squeezed it. *These idiot cops are assholes. When is our society going to get beyond persecuting people because of their sexual orientation? It doesn't make a bit of difference.* He threw the sand down causing Iva to pat him on the leg and give him a look saying *Just relax*. Brian glanced back *All right.* Then he closed his eyes and thought back to when his father had taken him to games at Yankee Stadium. The two of them had actually been in the upper deck for Mickey Mantle Day in 1968.

After a few more minutes, David tapped him on the shoulder. Brian put a finger on his lips to signify they had to keep quiet.

"But it's important," David whispered as softly as he could.

Brian nodded *Go ahead.*

"The tide is coming in."

It took a moment for Brian to comprehend what David was trying to say. When he did he quickly turned to take a look towards the back of the truck. The water level measured halfway up the rear tires with the waves breaking under the truck at almost its midpoint. The tide, indeed, was coming in.

"Look at the barnacles on the pier," David whispered.

Clumps of the tiny white shellfish clung tenaciously to the poles, some of them rising to a height a foot taller than the top of the truck. Brian smacked his palm against the side of his head. *Why didn't I notice this earlier*, he thought. No verbal communication was necessary to make everyone aware of the situation; the rapidly encroaching water spoke for itself. It was obvious they had taken their position just as the tide had turned inward from dead low and the truck would be swallowed up completely if they did not move it. But the police above would hear if they started the engine... a dilemma, no doubt about it, a real crisis. Jeff, keenly aware of his Mustang parked in the back of the truck, looked upset.

What are we going to do? he mimed frantically.

It will be all right, Brian gestured back. He took Marcus aside and whispered, "What do you think?"

"At the rate the water's advancing, we probably have about another half an hour where we can still move the truck out of here."

"We wait until the last minute to see if the cops move," Brian whispered. "But if they don't, you and I have no choice but to run for it in the truck before the tide gets it. When the cops chase us hopefully the others can sneak away in the opposite direction."

Marcus nodded.

Word of the plan passed from ear to ear. Iva walked over to Brian and said, "No."

"What do you mean *no*?" Brian whispered.

"We all stick together no matter what," Iva whispered back.

"But Marcus and I are the only ones they can positively identify."

"Doesn't matter."

Brian glanced behind Iva and saw Debbie, Jeff and David all nodding agreement. *Man, these are friends.* "Okay," he said.

With the police car still above them all they could do is stand around and stare at the advancing waves. The time ticked by excruciatingly slowly. After twenty minutes, the water lapped at the front wheels of the three-axle truck. Jeff finally put his hands on his hips and stared at the scene with a big grin on his face.

"Are you okay?" Debbie whispered.

"I refuse to believe any of this is real," he whispered back.

Flashing lights sped by up on Shore Road,

"It's real all right," Debbie breathed in his ear, punctuating the moment with a kiss on his lobe that turned into a bite.

Jeff looked at her and even in the near complete darkness and cold, not to mention the desperate situation they were in, they both realized it would not take much to make each other horny. "Baby, we got a problem," he whispered.

"You and me both," Debbie whispered back.

Twenty-six minutes passed. The rear tires were almost entirely under water.

We can't wait any longer, Brian signaled. He turned to Iva and so did everyone else. She had done such a good job hiding them under the pier that they all wanted her to be the one to drive them out. Iva realized this, nodded and climbed behind the wheel. Brian sat next to her while the others moved a few feet up the beach to be ready to get into the back of the truck as soon as it cleared the water.

Iva gripped the ignition key. "You know those cops up there are going to hear us," she said.

"Yup," Brian said.

"I'll drive up to Shore Road and try to lose them." After a pause, "I guess our chances aren't too good."

Brian's jaw tightened and he stared straight ahead. "Well... let's do it."

Iva reached for the ignition key.

Directly above, the police car roared to life. Iva jerked her hand back a fraction of a second before the truck's engine would have turned over. The cruiser's headlights came on and it rolled down the pier and turned onto Shore Road in the direction of Brian's house. It disappeared around the bend.

"Beautiful!" Brian shouted. "Now let's get out of here."

Iva started the engine but before she could shift into gear the sand on which the rear wheels were sitting collapsed. They were both thrown forward against the dashboard as the truck lurched backward and the back end sank about three feet deeper. The sudden creation of a forty-five degree slope in the rear compartment jarred Jeff's car causing the transmission to slip out of first gear into neutral. The Mustang—with Montesano's safe still in the back seat—rolled slowly off the back of the truck and into the water and sank like a rock out of sight. Iva applied full power to first gear and the truck, suddenly front heavy, roared out of the water. Iva stopped safely out of reach of the advancing tide and with Brian ran down to the water's edge. Jeff stood there staring at the spot where the water had swallowed up his cherry red classic.

"I'm sorry," Brian said.

Jeff kept staring silently.

"This is all my fault," Iva said. "I never should have parked down here."

"I owe you a car," Brian added.

Jeff turned to face the group. He was actually smiling. "Hey, forget it. So I lost a car, it's no big deal." He shrugged. "As a matter of fact, I feel pretty good. Selfless sacrifice... I hate to admit it but it's a new feeling for me. I think I like it."

"This is a new Jeffrey Hollis," Debbie said, throwing an arm around his waist.

"She's right," Jeff agreed. Then he glanced again at his car's watery grave. "And I feel like I'm going to puke."

"If you puke, I'll puke," David said.

"Listen, at the next low tide you can get the car towed out of here," Marcus said.

"Sure," Jeff replied. "Unless of course I'm in jail."

"You won't be in jail," Marcus said, starting to strip off his shirt.

"What are you doing?" Brian asked.

"I'm going in after that safe."

"It must be twenty feet out by now."

"I don't care. I've got to get it."

"We've all got to get it. But it's out of reach right now."

"Why? It's just under some water."

"This whole strip of beach is closed to swimmers," Brian told him. "There are wicked rip tides and currents. People drown around here."

"Jimmy Whalen," Jeff remembered out loud, recalling a ninth grade classmate of theirs who never resurfaced after a dive off the pier.

The danger was real. Beaver Pond flowed into Sagamore Bay about a hundred yards to the south. About the same distance to the north, a series of underground streams converged to add more fresh water to the salt. This infusion created a series of random and indefinable currents that made the northwest quadrant of Sagamore Bay, however great for fishing, deathly hazardous to swim in. Even water skiers were warned off.

"I'm not being a coward when I say it's too dangerous to go in after the safe right now," Brian said.

"For God's sake, it's dark and foggy and freezing," Iva said.

"All right," Marcus said. He buttoned his shirt back up, but he kept staring at the spot where he imagined the safe to be.

"Those safes are designed to be waterproof," David said. "We can easily get it tomorrow."

"Uh, I hate to bring this up," Debbie said. "But aren't we about to be arrested the minute we show ourselves? After all, they know who we are."

"They only got a look at me and Marcus," Brian said.

"But they probably got the license plates off my car and the truck," Jeff said.

"Hold it," David said. "They might not arrest us."

Brian, Iva and Marcus immediately grasped the line along which he was thinking.

"Yes... " Marcus nodded.

"For all they know we've had time to break into the safe and remove a load of incriminating evidence," David went on.

"He's right. They might think we have a stalemate," Brian said, explaining David's theory. "They won't arrest us as long as we don't release the evidence."

"No police cars have driven by for a while," David said. "They may have taken that position."

"And maybe not," Marcus said. "So, in case they do arrest us, we've got to refuse to talk about anything that happened tonight. When they ask about the safe, don't admit anything. Maybe we can bluff them into a stalemate."

"I don't think they'd dare arrest us," Brian said. "Montesano has much too much to lose having his bridge plans revealed to the public."

"I hope you're right," Marcus said.

"We'll get the safe tomorrow," Brian said, slapping Marcus on the shoulder. "Let's go."

Brian and Iva hopped into the cab, everyone else climbed into the back. There was no reason to hide anymore so they left the rear door up. Iva drove the truck out from under the pier, off the beach and up onto Shore Road. There was no sign of the police.

"I certainly hope they don't arrest us," Iva said.

"Your hiding us under the pier was brilliant improvisation," Brian said. "It bought us time. As far as they know we've had plenty of time to stash lots of incriminating evidence."

"That's if there was any in the safe to begin with."

"Don't be a party pooper. Let's see how this plays out."

Iva turned onto Skunks Misery Road and headed for their driveway. It was still night and dark and everything looked normal. They both took deep breaths as they approached the final curve before their house.

A bizarre sight greeted them outside the gate. Two single file lines of parked police cars sat pointed at the driveway, four cars on each side. No headlights were on but each car had two occupants, just sitting. A limousine sat at the back of one line.

"What in the world is this?" Iva said.

"Just keep going," Brian said.

They stopped in front of the gate and Brian hurriedly jumped out to unlock it. None of the police made a move to stop him, they just kept on sitting. Iva drove through the gate, stopped and waited for Brian to lock it again and get back in the cab. Still, the police just sat and watched. Walking back to the truck, Brian forced himself to move slowly. *I've got to show them I'm not afraid.* As soon as he sat back next to her, Iva drove up the driveway and stopped by their front door.

"Bizarre," Marcus commented, jumping off the truck.

"Fucking weird," Brian replied.

"What the hell is going on?" Jeff said as he hopped off.

"Quickly, let's go inside," Brian said.

The first instinct everyone had upon entering the house was to run around barricading all the windows and doors. Brian sensed the mood and said, "It's not like they're Apaches out there. If the police want to come get us, they will. There's nothing we can do."

"That reception line proves they think there's a stalemate," David said.

"Yeah, but for how long?" Marcus said.

The phone rang. Everyone started and glared at the instrument like it was an enemy intruding upon their fortress. "I guess we find out how long," Brian said. He let it ring four times then picked it up. "Hello?"

"Werth?"

"Speaking," Brian said. He recognized the voice.

"This is Frank Montesano."

"I know who you are. What do you want?"

"Werth, I want you listen to me and listen to me good. You've got twenty-four hours to return the contents of that safe to Republican headquarters. Repeat, twenty-four hours. If you don't, or prior to that any of the contents are made public, you and your friends will be hurt and hurt bad."

Brian swallowed but did not speak.

"Arrested for burglary and assault and hurt bad."

Brian tried to compose himself and organize his thoughts. "Now you listen to me," he said. "We have the evidence and if anything happens to any of us it will be released immediately."

"Twenty-four hours," Montesano repeated. Then there was a click and the line went dead. Brian slowly replaced the receiver.

"How long?" Marcus asked.

"Twenty-four hours."

"Then what?"

"Then I guess we meet the big Republican in the sky."

The joke was not funny; it was too real to be funny. The room became silent and everyone paled except Marcus who would have if he could. David was white enough to spare some.

Iva broke the tension. "Anyone want some coffee? I'll make it."

"I'll help you," Debbie said, following her into the kitchen.

Jeff trailed after them. "A beer!" he shouted. "My kingdom for a beer!"

"Excuse me while I use the facilities," David said, hurrying out.

Brian and Marcus were left alone in the living room. "We've got to get the safe out of there this afternoon at low tide," Brian said.

"And then..."

"And then we take the evidence to a federal agency that can't possibly have any connection to Frank Montesano... like the FBI for God's sake... and we demand protection."

"Makes sense," Marcus agreed. "Man, we've got to get that safe."

"We sure do," Brian said, suddenly realizing he was exhausted. He glanced out the window and noticed a glint of light glimmering in the eastern sky and birds up and chirping away.

Iva, Debbie and David made omelets. There were plenty of doughnuts, an angel food cake and because they were out of orange juice everyone joined with Jeff in gulping down bottles of Budweiser. When the meal was served they all chomped away at their food without conversing, too tired too think about anything but chewing and swallowing.

A gunshot sounded outside. Everyone stopped in mid-gulp. A few seconds went by then another burst fired, then another and another and another. Then a volley exploded.

Iva threw her hands over her ears and squeezed her eyes shut. The sound of gunfire always made her remember that one special shot she heard as a young girl. Brian recognized immediately what she was feeling and threw his arms around her. The gunfire continued. They all instinctively moved away from the windows, up against the wall and then down into a sitting position on the floor. Jeff backed into the hot stove.

"Oww! Definitely not my night."

"It's coming from the direction of the road," Brian yelled over the noise.

"They're not hitting anything," David said.

"They're not trying to," Marcus said. "They're firing into the air."

The volley ceased. There were a few more individual shots followed by silence, total silence, no bird dared make a sound. Then doors slammed, engines started and cars drove away.

Brian got up, sat down at the kitchen table and forced himself to resume eating his omelet. "I guess they just wanted us to know their position is firm," he said as nonchalantly as he could.

"Great, I appreciate subtlety," Jeff said.

"That was frightening," Debbie said, sitting back down. Her hands trembled. So did Jeff's but when he gripped Debbie's they both managed to keep still.

"That was the idea," Marcus said.

"We'll get at that safe in a few hours," Brian said. "Then we'll take it from there."

"I think everyone should stay here tonight," Iva said. "There's only time for a few hours sleep anyway, and it's much safer than splitting up right now."

Everyone agreed. Brian produced all the pillows and blankets he could find and they all bedded down for some much needed rest. He and Iva slept in the upstairs bedroom like they always did; Jeff and Debbie put two couches together in the den. Marcus pulled out his cot in the living room and was amazed when David took only a blanket and proceeded to lie down on the floor.

"What are you... a monk?" Marcus asked him.

"Sleeping this way is great for your posture," David explained.

"You're nuts, do you realize that? Do you always sleep that way? I imagine some women would object to it."

"I have a bed at home," David said, "just in case."

Marcus exhaled, lay down and closed his eyes.

"A waterbed," David added. Marcus opened his eyes but did not comment.

"Psst Marcus." It was Brian, standing on the stairs in is underwear. "Quick, while Iva's in the bathroom, give me your gun."

"Are you sure you want it?"

"Positive."

Marcus pulled his forty-four-caliber revolver out of his suitcase and dropped it into Brian's hands. "It's loaded and the safety's on. Be careful with it."

"Wow, it's heavy," Brian said, hefting the instrument in cupped hands as if it was big rock. "This is much heavier than a squirt gun."

"Brian, how about we forget this..." Marcus started to say.

"I'm kidding, okay?"

"All right, just be careful."

"I will. I don't know if it's going to do any good, but I'm going to keep it with me from now on. It'll make me feel like I'm at least making an attempt to protect myself."

"I understand."

"Thanks. Goodnight."

"Goodnight."

Brian ran upstairs and managed to slip the gun into his jacket pocket seconds before Iva emerged from the bathroom. Marcus lay back down on his cot, his mind on Brian in bed with Iva and Jeff on the porch with Debbie. *Maybe I'll give whatshername from Ghana... Aida... a call*, he thought. The sound of David England snoring wafted up from the floor below. *Wouldn't you know it, that little guy snores like a lumberjack.* Marcus got up and took another look at the tide table in the newspaper that sat on the coffee table. *October 8: low tide at 3:58 p.m.* He slipped back under the covers. *We've got to get that safe.* David snorted and rolled over. *And somehow I've got to get some sleep.*

Upstairs, Brian hopped out of bed to triple check the tide table on his bureau.

"It still says the same thing, right?" Iva said.

"Yup. Low tide in less than ten hours. We've got to get that safe."

"We will. Try to get some sleep."

"Okay."

Remarkably in light of such an eventful night, sleep came quickly for both of them.

Chapter XI

"Don't cry. She mustn't see you've been crying."

Vivien Leigh to Leslie Howard in ***Gone With the Wind*** *(1939)*

October 8, 3:05 P.M.

The guard who had surprised them could plainly identify Brian and Marcus so they determined Jeff and Debbie would be the ones to return to the beach to retrieve the car and safe. With the help of Richardson's Towing Service, the plan called for the Mustang to be recovered as soon as the tide receded. A tarp would then be thrown over the car at once in case any suspicious police happened by and the vehicle towed to Brian's house without delay. There the safe would be broken into immediately.

"Are you sure there's a car out there?" Junior Richardson asked. He was sixty-seven but his moniker would never change; even his children and grandchildren called him Junior.

"Positive," Jeff replied. Then he thought, *Suppose it's not out there. Impossible. Absurd. No, it's out there.* He and Debbie were sitting next to Junior in his tow truck.

"I'm warnin' you. If you're tryin' to pull some prank I'm still gonna charge you for my time." Black spittle ran down Junior's chin. Several months back doctors had removed a cancerous lesion from his lower lip causing him to shift his chewing habit from tobacco to something much more benign but just as disgusting... black licorice.

"I promise you there's a car out there," Debbie said.

"You know back in '68 I pulled a Dodge out of the front window of the Valley Drug Store," Junior said. "This'll top that." He spit a black mass out his window but his aim was off and he covered his driver's side mirror.

Jeff surveyed the area. They were parked under the pier waiting for the retreating tide to reveal his car; it was five after three so it would be any moment now. Fortunately, the beach was deserted. The few fishermen on the pier who noticed the tow truck beneath them paid it no mind. Nothing bothered them as long as the striped bass were not disturbed.

Junior snickered. "What were you kids doing out here last night anyway?"

"Uh... we got lost," Jeff said.

"You kids don't expect me to believe that, do you?"

"I don't care what you believe," Jeff said.

First the water began to look a little darker in one spot, and then inch-by-inch the Mustang began to poke itself out of the waves. For the first few minutes the only thing exposed was the radio antenna, reminding all of them of a submarine's periscope.

"Well I'll be damned!" Junior exclaimed. "There is a car out there. In a little while we'll be able to get at it."

"Good." Jeff was enormously relieved. The car looked exactly the same as it did the day before, just wet. The safe still sat wedged in the back seat.

"Well, I hope you kids learned your lesson. Next time you're lookin' for a place to park and... do it... be more careful."

"I beg your pardon?" Debbie said.

"Doin' it. That's all you kids care about."

"No comment," Jeff said. Debbie rolled her eyes but kept her mouth shut.

They hooked the winch to the front of the Mustang's chassis and hoisted the front wheels off the ground. Jeff threw a tarp over the car.

"What's the safe back there for?" Junior asked as he drove the tow truck off the beach and onto Shore Road.

Debbie, deciding to be deliberately rude to this lout, spoke up before Jeff could think of something to say. "I keep my extra hymens in there. I never know when I'm going to want to get laid so I keep extra hymens with me at all times. They're in the safe so I don't lose them."

Jeff laughed. Junior seemed to take her comments seriously.

"What else is in there?" he asked.

"Oh... some condoms of course... and some chains and a whip."

Jeff looked at her as if to say *All right, how far are you going to take this?* Debbie looked back *Sorry but the old fart pissed me off.*

"What's a hymen?" Junior finally asked.

They did not encounter police cars or anything out of the ordinary during the drive back. Brian, Marcus and David had the gate open and were waiting when they arrived. Junior maneuvered the tow truck so the car ended up inside the garage. They paid him in cash and after he left they locked the front gate.

"This is it," Brian said, pulling the garage door down.

Brian and Jeff lifted the safe out of the car and onto a workbench. Marcus put on a clear plastic face guard, grabbed an electric drill and attacked the safe.

"I'm going to cut through the bar that keeps the door closed," he explained. "It may take a while."

Everyone stood around nervously while Marcus sliced away from within a cascade of white-hot sparks. Jeff busied himself by trying to wipe some of the dried salt off his car.

"I'll get this thing running again," he said. He slipped behind the wheel, ignoring the seaweed and sand on the vinyl seats. "The battery's shot, there's salt in the carburetor and probably a whole bunch of parts will have to be replaced, but I'll get this baby running again."

"I'll pay for it," Brian said.

"Don't worry, it's insured," Jeff replied, sliding over to the passenger seat and continuing to wipe off the dashboard. Without warning the glove compartment fell open and something snakelike and slimy flopped into his lap.

"Aaahhh!" he screamed, brushing the thing off and jumping out over the door. "What the hell is that?"

Debbie looked at what had fallen to the floor of the car. "Well my fearless friend, it looks to me like it's a dead eel."

"Thank God," Jeff replied. "I thought I was having an acid flashback."

"Or the DTs," Debbie said, giving him a look.

"There's a dragon on your shoulder," Brian added.

"Funny, real funny," Jeff replied.

Marcus stopped drilling and lifted the visor on his face guard. "I think I'm through it."

Everyone crowded around. Brian inserted a crowbar into the opening and pushed causing the safe door to droop almost all the way off. Water poured out onto the floor.

"But these safes are supposed to be waterproof," David said.

"Yeah, well this one leaked," Brian replied.

The safe contained two large ledgers and a loose-leaf notebook. Brian reached in and grabbed the sopping wet blue binder. The first page was blank. The second page was gray because it was covered in black ink that had completely smeared. He tried to turn to other pages but they ripped in his hands. After about a minute's frantic perusal it became evident that the salt water had caused the ink to run and nothing was readable, not a word. *This notebook contained the secret bridge plans,* Brian realized, *and now it's worthless.*

"Damn, these ledgers are completely wrecked," Marcus said. "And I'll bet they contained the Republicans' confidential financial records."

"The Republicans enter their data with a fountain pen," Jeff said incredulously. "The old bastards. A ballpoint would never smear."

"These safes are not supposed to leak," David repeated.

"This one fucking did!" Brian yelled. Then he caught himself and put a hand on David's shoulder. "I'm sorry David, I'm sorry."

Brian walked a few feet from the group and stood still with his back to them. The situation was clear. The safe had leaked and salt water had destroyed its contents. Nothing had been gained from the break in. It was a total failure. No one knew what to say or do so they just stared at the floor not wanting to look at each other.

After a few seconds Brian turned to face them. "Even though it looks like we've lost," he said, "I want to thank you all for helping and taking the risks you did. No one needs to take the blame for this. We all did the best we could. No apologies are necessary when you've tried your best." No one was looking directly at him except Iva. "I think it is best we try to keep the Republicans thinking we have the evidence in our possession. We'll just ignore the deadline and try to keep the stalemate in place. That way hopefully they'll leave us alone." He saw Marcus nod at the floor. "Now if my memory serves me correctly, we have a general campaign meeting scheduled for tomorrow morning at nine. I hope I'll see you all there. And again, thank you. Please believe me, thank you."

He walked out of the garage and into the house. Iva followed a few seconds later. Brian headed towards his bedroom having just experienced the greatest disappointment of his life. *What a disaster. I needed those bridge plans so bad*, he thought. At the top of the stairs a tear trickled down his cheek. He quickly brushed it off. *Come on get a grip.* He entered his bedroom and closed the door behind him. Out came another tear. *Everything's lost. I don't have a chance now.* Another tear came out. He threw himself on his bed and buried his face in the pillow. He couldn't help himself; the dam broke after holding for years and he sobbed uncontrollably.

Iva halted before she entered the bedroom. She could hear him crying on the other side of the door. *That's good for him now,* she thought, *and it's probably best I leave him alone.* She walked back downstairs.

Out in the garage the remaining members of the Executive Committee stood around wondering how to deal with their disappointment.

"I'd love a beer right now," Jeff said, "but the way I feel I'm sure I'd keep drinking until I'm unconscious."

"How about some frozen yogurt?" Debbie suggested. "Would you like to go out for some frozen yogurt?"

"Yogurt. Yeah, let's go out for some yogurt."

"You guys want to come along?" Debbie asked Marcus and David.

"No thanks," Marcus said. "I think I'll give a girl a call."

"Who?" Jeff asked.

"I don't know. Some girl, any girl, it really doesn't matter."

"How about you, David? Want some yogurt?" Debbie asked.

"No but thanks for the offer," David replied, misty eyed. "Believe it or not I think I'm going to go to the library. I'm behind in my reading. I'm going to try to relax and read a book." He looked at Marcus. "Some book, any book, it really doesn't matter."

Brian cried solidly for a long time. He couldn't stop himself and gave up trying. Soon he realized he was crying about much more than the safe. He had a lot of pain he had just stuffed inside and never dealt with. *Alan Sansone... my father... my sister I never knew... Christ, even John Lennon and Harry Chapin.* Brian also cried about a called third strike with the bases loaded in a Little League game twenty-six years ago. *Why didn't I swing?* After about half an hour he began to calm down and was amazed at how much better he felt. *That was great*, he realized. *I've got to do that more often.*

There was a knock on the door. Brian ran into the bathroom and threw water on his face. Iva walked in carrying a tray.

"I made you a chocolate milkshake and brought you some doughnuts. I thought it might cheer you up."

Brian poked his head out of the bathroom. His eyes still looked red despite the water. *She knows I've been crying*, he thought.

He knows I know, she thought.

"Thanks," Brian said, taking the food and leaning forward to give his fiancée a kiss on the cheek.

She kissed him back and they sat down next to each other on the bed. Brian took a large gulp of his milkshake.

"Man, that really hits the spot," he said.

"Brian, I don't know what to say."

"There is nothing to say. We tried our best. We lost."

"Are you giving up?" she asked, already knowing the answer.

"Tonight I am. Tonight I'm pretty fed up. Tomorrow's another day."

He walked into the bathroom and turned on the shower. Speaking over the sound of the water he said, "Come on in here with me, you're the one who showed me how a good long shower can help you forget your problems."

She followed him into the bathroom and they stripped each other. Steam, hot water, soapsuds and strawberry smelling shampoo soothed and relaxed them. The outside world began to feel farther and farther away as they caressed and played with each other. First they performed the acrobatic feat of intercourse standing up under the shower stream. Then they let the tub fill and made love under water. Next they moved out of the shower and onto the bed. Then it was back into the tub. They went crazy and really let themselves go. Iva lost track of her orgasms early on. Brian kept count—he had four and was immensely proud. *Four! Four you old son of a bitch!*

Afterwards, Iva lay on top of Brian in their bed. They were both exhausted and could feel sleep closing in, sleep they would both welcome with open arms.

"Boy, that was great," Brian mumbled.

"It was okay I guess."

He looked at her and she smiled and then he smiled.

"I love you."

"I love you too."

As they drifted off to sleep, Brian and Iva were happy together, and that was more important than Republicans and Democrats and campaigns and bridges and safes and... peaceful dreams comforted them through the night and into the morning.

At ten minutes to four Brian woke up and stared at the ceiling. *Was it a dream?* Whatever it was, he had an idea... an idea to beat the bridge. Legally. *It's a long-shot but it might work and I can handle it myself. The hell with all this break-in stuff.* He got out of bed, grabbed a piece of paper and pen off his bureau, walked into the bathroom and sat down on the toilet. He knew he rarely remembered dreams so he scribbled the rudimentary contours of his inspiration down on the paper. *I'll keep this to myself. If it doesn't work at least the others won't have to deal with another disappointment.* The last thing Brian did before dozing off again was set the alarm: six in the morning so he could get an early start.

Tomorrow's another day.

Chapter XII

"We'll never give in... We won't be beaten. We won't. We just won't!"

Joan Fontaine to Tyrone Power in ***This Above All*** *(1942)*

OCTOBER 9, 9:35 A.M.

Brian got a booster shot when he showed up at his headquarters the following morning. Twenty-seven volunteers were there and the place was jammed. What four days earlier had looked like a scattered mass of garbage now looked good as new. Piles of envelopes sat stuffed and stamped: the city-wide mailing ready to go. The Nuss Brigade, angered by the bombing and injury to their leader, had worked around the clock to undo the damage to the campaign.

Brian made no attempt to hide his appreciation, and he strolled around the room shaking hands and clapping backs. Although everyone knew one mailing was no match for the Republican machine, at least the Werth campaign would get its message out. Standing alone, that was important.

Most of the volunteers were college students Brian knew; some he had taught, some were friends of Nuss, and some were political science majors looking for hands-on experience. But about five of them looked much too old for college—late thirties and forties. Brian did not know these individuals so he introduced himself. Without exception they turned out to be veterans of the sixties—ex-hippies, yippies, SDS members,

Vietnam War protesters—who had read newspaper accounts of Brian's confrontation with Savino, sensed what was going on and been unable to resist coming by to help out. *Peace. Love. Woodstock. Again.*

"Don't let my pinstripes fool you," Roger Dunlin, the president of Commuters for Decent Mass Transit, told Brian. "Even though I'm an insurance salesman, I've been to more political rallies than I can count. I volunteered for Eugene McCarthy and was involved in the effort we had for George McGovern around here."

"What made you come here this morning?" Brian asked him.

"You impressed me on the train. Listen... there are lots of things I believe in despite the direction the country seems to be moving these days. You're still a liberal despite the shifting winds and I like that."

It was a compliment intended and a compliment received.

"Thank you," Brian replied. He discreetly tapped a two-fingered peace sign on Dunlin's chest and they both nodded solemnly.

Bill Nuss' condition was the first order of business once Marcus called the meeting to order. "He's doing fine," Betsy Brewster told the group. "He's been up and walking and they're letting him go home fairly soon."

A loud burst of applause greeted the good news. "And he thanks you for all for the get well cards," she added.

Brian rose to address the group. Smiling broadly he said, "Our campaign is moving again. I think you all ought to give yourselves a hand for saving our city-wide mailing."

The volunteers applauded themselves wildly; they were not being pretentious, they had worked hard and were deservedly proud. Their enthusiasm wafted over the room making it easier for Brian, Iva, Marcus, David, Jeff and Debbie to continue to deal with the disappointment of the previous day.

"Kids today, where they get the energy I just don't know," Jeff joked.

Standing next to him, Debbie smiled and whispered, "Pipe down and take your Geritol."

Brian reached into his pocket and unfolded a piece of

paper. "I'm afraid I'm about to ask you to do some more work," he said. "I wrote this this morning and I think copies should be made so they can be included in the mailing. I think it's really important."

No one knew what was on the paper except Brian. Iva had heard him up and pounding the typewriter at six in the morning but they had not discussed it. He cleared his throat and started reading:

> "Dear Neighbor,
>
> I've learned that the Sagamore Republicans, headed by Frank Montesano and assisted by my opponent Al Savino, are secretly planning to sponsor the building of a bridge from Sagamore across the Sound to the town of Rye, New York. The impact of such a bridge would be disastrous for all New Yorkers, not just those in the areas forever devastated by the construction. A tax burden would be created that will hang over our grandchildren.
>
> Please ask yourself the following questions: Do we really need to bulldoze countless acres of precious North Shore landscape? Do we really need to throw thousands of people out of homes they have lived in all their lives? Do we really need more concrete and cars in our community? Should the public trust be abused in such a manner?
>
> I hope you'll agree with me and answer with a resounding NO!!!
>
> You may well ask—why do the Republicans want to build such a bridge? The answer is for profit. They have plans to embezzle a substantial portion of the over one billion dollars that would ultimately be earmarked for the project.
>
> Absolute power corrupts absolutely. The Sagamore Republican machine has been allowed absolute power. They are corrupt. That is why they tear down my campaign posters and signs. That is why they make personal threats against my staff and me. That is why they bomb my campaign

headquarters and nearly kill a volunteer. THAT IS WHY THEY MURDERED PROFESSOR ALAN SANSONE, the man who originally uncovered the bridge conspiracy.

Please vote for me on Election Day. I promise to fight the Republicans. I promise to beat the bridge. I promise to return honest government to Sagamore. Above all, I promise to do my best for what I believe is right. For the sake of true democracy here on Long Island, the two-party system must be allowed to exist. We must have a choice. We need a change.

Respectfully yours,
Brian Werth
Democrat for Mayor

No one seemed to be moving or breathing when Brian finished; there was total silence in the room. Then someone started to applaud. Someone else joined in and the clapping multiplied. One person stood up and everyone followed. It became a standing ovation.

Brian was taken aback, embarrassed and thrilled all at once. "Thanks," he said as the tumult died down. "I guess I'll take that as a vote of confidence."

"That was great," Roger Dunlin called out. "Give it to me and I'll start making the copies right now."

"Thanks," Brian replied. He noticed as he handed Dunlin the paper that there was some semblance of color back in the man's face; he did not exactly radiate health but at least now he looked like he could survive the week.

David leaned forward and whispered in Marcus' ear, "Without proof those statements could be considered libelous. We'll be sued."

"Good," Marcus answered over his shoulder.

"Yeah, fuck 'em." David added.

Marcus turned, looked at David and smiled. David shrugged and smiled back, surprised and pleased at himself.

Brian next recognized David England to speak. David had requested time to put forth a plan for beefing up Brian's campaign effort in the final days. He stood up and stared at the faces. *Public speaking, not my favorite activity*, he thought. Addressing large groups of people was something he had loathed ever since he had vomited all over the crèche in the middle of his Sunday School Nativity play. Frankincense and myrrh were even more putrefying then cigar smoke. Even though his glasses were straight, he straightened them. And even though his throat was clear, he cleared it.

"As you all know," David finally said, "Republican workers tear down our signs and posters as soon as we put them up. In the campaigns I worked on in California, we had a tactic to combat this. We called it commando raids."

What David had in mind was highly illegal. He proposed that small groups of volunteers—"commando squads"—converge on certain neighborhoods night after night at four in the morning. Armed to the hilt with staple guns and **WERTH FOR MAYOR** posters and flyers, these squads would plaster them all over—trees, fences, telephone poles, store windows, anywhere conspicuous—so the awakening citizenry could not help but notice.

"Of course the posters will get ripped down by noon, but by then we will have made our point. We will have made more people aware of our candidate and what he stands for."

Everyone looked at Brian for some sign of how he viewed the idea. "I like it," he said without hesitation. "We're fighting back, hitting them hard." After burglarizing a building and fleeing from the police, putting up illegal posters gave him no pause at all.

Marcus adjourned the meeting and volunteers wanting to sign up for the nocturnal mischief immediately surrounded David. The adventures offered a rare opportunity: the thrill of doing something unlawful while at the same time being convinced of the rightness of the act.

"You know something?" Brian whispered to Iva. "David may look like a Poindexter on the outside but on the inside he's got a lot of strength."

"He was great during the break-in," Iva agreed.

"He's got balls," Brian said.

"*Chutzpah*," Iva added.

In another corner of the room Debbie mapped strategy for the increased distribution of campaign literature in parking lots. A few feet away Jeff spoke to a group of phone canvassers; new phones were being installed that afternoon and the calls would continue apace. Marcus approached Brian with a folder containing the layouts for the election week newspaper ads.

"You've got to go over these and approve them," he told him.

"Okay," Brian replied, putting his arm around Marcus. "Look at this place... it's a beehive. We're not dead yet."

"What you mean is we're going down swinging."

Brian bit his lip and did not speak.

"The deadline for us to surrender the safe's contents has passed," Marcus continued. "Nothing's happened yet but this letter we're sending out is going to really freak out Montesano. Especially the part about Professor Sansone. They'll probably file a libel suit. And don't forget he can still arrest you and me for breaking and entering."

"I don't give a shit about a libel suit," Brian replied. "And if Montesano wants to arrest us, here we are," Brian said. "I don't think he will. Putting me in jail means much more publicity of the kind he doesn't want. And I'd be entitled to a hearing where they would have to produce the evidence they have. And we could produce ours."

"But we don't have any," Marcus said.

"They don't know that. Let them arrest me, my campaign will continue with me behind bars. I'd still be on the ballot."

"Montesano won't have you arrested," David, who had walked by and overheard, said. "What might come out of that is too unpredictable for him. He'll probably tell the press you are emotionally unstable and a liar and sue you for libel, a case that won't be heard for months or even years. Right now he's going to totally focus on making sure Savino wins. Once you lose the election you're just a gnat he can swat away any way he wants."

"Well then," Brian replied, "we better not lose."

"Any ideas how to keep us from going down?" Marcus asked him.

"Somehow locate another set of bridge plans, but I have no idea how," Brian said.

"Neither do I," David said.

"It would be nice if we could come up with something," Marcus said.

"Yes, it would," Brian agreed.

"Brian..." David began.

"Yes?"

"You'd better be very careful between now and the election."

"I was thinking the same thing," Marcus said.

Before Brian could reply, a group of volunteers approached them and they found themselves absorbed in commando raids and phone canvassing and literature drops and... Marcus' gun was tucked into Brian's belt under his jacket.

Chapter XIII

"We McDonalds—we're high tempered.
We fight amongst ourselves, but let trouble come
from outside and we stick together."

Agnes Moorehead to Lew Ayres in ***Johnny Belinda*** *(1948)*

OCTOBER 14, 9:15 P.M.

The citywide mailing created quite a stir and the local media clamored for proof of the charges. When Brian responded that his statements were entirely true but there was no proof to corroborate them, it was widely editorialized that unsubstantiated charges during an election campaign constituted nothing more than dirty politics. Savino told anyone holding a microphone that Brian Werth was most likely "mentally deranged." He also called the charges "an insult to all decent Americans" and filed suit to collect damages and stop Brian from making any further accusations. Overall, it was difficult if not impossible to assess the political consequences of the last minute addition to the mailing.

"Well, its gotten people thinking," David observed.

"Yeah, but thinking what?" Marcus wondered.

"One of two things. Either Brian is a caped crusader fighting for truth, justice and the American way or..."

"Or what?"

"Or a total idiot."

"Which one is it?"

"We'll find out on Election Day," David replied. "It should be very interesting."

Even though the Savino campaign added a sound truck that cruised the city blaring **"AL SAVINO FOR A STRONGER AMERICA"**, all the adversity actually energized Brian's supporters and morale at the Werth headquarters improved day by day. The number of volunteers stopping by to help out grew steadily and the old optimism of the summertime returned. Phone canvassing and literature drops increased and Brian maintained his hectic pace of public appearances. The word *upset* was bandied about with ever increasing frequency.

Commando raids went off as scheduled. Every morning a different section of the city awoke to find itself plastered with *Werth for Mayor* paraphernalia. The Republicans quickly realized what was happening and organized a task force to tear down the odious propaganda, but they were never in time to void the effect. Marcus and David led several volunteers on the four in the morning forays that, as it turned out, everyone enjoyed immensely. Once when Roger Dunlin scraped himself jumping into a rosebush to avoid detection by a passing police car, David reached into his contingency bag and produced a first aid kit.

Montesano had not been heard from again. There were no further physical attacks against Brian or any of his friends. They all knocked on wood as each day passed without violence—everyone still remembered all too well his threat that they would be *hurt and hurt bad.*

"Frank probably figures the reason we won't release any proof of our charges is we're afraid he'll have us arrested if we do," Brian told his Executive Committee.

"Let him think that," Jeff said. "I like being alive."

"Agreed," David said.

"Montesano knows Savino is still clearly ahead and he doesn't want to risk any drastic action unless it's absolutely necessary," Marcus added.

Debbie Benson raised her hand to speak, reminding Brian of one of his students. "Just go ahead Deb," he said, "you don't have to raise your hand."

"Sorry, old habit," she replied. "Let me see, how should I put this? Okay. We are all working very hard. Us and the volunteers. Are we going to lose? Should we prepare ourselves emotionally to lose?"

"Yes," Brian told her without hesitation. "There's a chance we'll win. I believe there's a real chance. But the odds are we'll lose."

"Thanks for being honest about it," Debbie said.

"We won't lose if we can break into Montesano's home," Marcus cut in.

There was a collective groan from around the table.

"Oh God," Debbie said.

"*Oy Gevalt,*" Iva said.

David took out his saline nose spray.

"Marcus," Brian said, "certainly no one can question your commitment to all this."

"You're not using my car," Jeff said.

Marcus' formal motion for another break-in lost by a vote of five to one. There was nothing to indicate Montesano kept any records at his home, and even if he did they did not know where to begin a search. His wife, suffering from severe rheumatoid arthritis, lived as a semi-invalid and rarely left the house. A security system almost certainly protected every conceivable entrance. It was a mission beyond their competence.

"We're desperate," Marcus pleaded after the disheartening referendum, "we've got to try something."

"I agree," Brian said. "But we can't jump half-cocked into things that will do more harm than good."

"I hate to lose," Marcus said, dejectedly.

"So do I," Brian replied. "So do all of us. That's why we've got to come up with a constructive idea that makes some sense. Any other suggestions?"

There were none so the meeting was adjourned.

"Oww... Dammit." Iva swore as she used her fingers to grab a hot-dog out of boiling water. There was never time to really cook anymore. As soon as she got home from work it was a quick change, something simple to eat and straight down to the headquarters. Brian left the house at seven in the morning and never returned before ten at night; lately he found time to run only one out of every three or four days. Details like housework and laundry went unattended to. That morning she had noticed him putting on his pants without underwear...

"Oh Brian dear, you forgot your underpants. Let's not be a lowlife now," Iva had said in her sweetest voice.

"My underpants are all dirty. Real dirty. I've been out for a week."

"Oh my God. All right, I'll do a wash for you today."

"Iva, you don't have to do my laundry. We don't have that kind of a relationship."

"I know. But I want to do it this time. Human beings in civilized societies have got to wear undergarments... "

"I understand. Thanks."

"Careful zipping up your fly today."

"You've made your point."

Iva took a bite of her hot-dog and promptly started to gag. Only with great effort did she manage to chew and swallow. *I'm eating vulcanized rubber*, she thought. *Oh well, the damn election is in less than three weeks. We're in this thing to the finish.* She held her nose and took another bite.

The gatebell rang. Iva walked outside, grateful for any excuse to postpone her forced feeding. She stopped in her tracks. A big black limousine sat outside the gate. *Frank Montesano. Al Savino. They've come here to get us.* Her mind reeled with visions of Alan Sansone dead in the bathtub and a bloody Bill Nuss being loaded into an ambulance. She thought about running but her legs started moving her mechanically towards the gate. As she got closer she had a premonition of a masked man jumping out of the car and shooting her at point blank range. Her breathing quickened and blood rushed to her head. When she reached the gate she grabbed the bars and stared through them like a death row inmate. The sun reflected off the windshield so she could not see inside and the car's headlights gazed impassively back at her. The rear door started to open. Iva felt faint, her legs buckled...

"Iva! Sweetheart! Are you all right?"

"Papa? Oh God! Papa!" She recovered herself, unlocked the gate and ran into her father's arms. "Oh Papa!"

Conrad Fidele cradled his daughter's face in his hands. "Iva, what's wrong? You're white as a ghost. Are you sick?"

"I'm all right. I'm just surprised to see you, that's all."

Iva relaxed and returned to normal as they sat down to some iced tea in the living room. Conrad immediately put his daughter at ease.

"Nothing's wrong at all, honey," he said. "I'm sorry I didn't call you before coming out but I couldn't get a hold of you. I kept calling but I got no answer. Don't you have one of those answering machines?"

"It doesn't matter, Papa. I'm just glad you're here."

Conrad stood up and strolled around the room, still a commanding presence at fifty-eight. Shrapnel had destroyed his right eye in 1967 so he wore an eye patch like Moshe Dayan, but rue the poor soul who jokingly made the comparison. His thick head of jet-black hair and a close cropped beard flecked with gray topped off a muscular six-foot frame that—carried with the posture of a career military man—appeared taller. In contrast, his face looked aged beyond its years. Constant exposure to desert wind and sun had taken its toll so he was permanently ruddy and handsome in a rugged sort of way. He flexed his elbow and grimaced.

"Oww. Racquetball, damnable sport these Americans play. But I must admit I'm getting quite good at it."

"You look good Papa. You look like you're in shape."

Conrad beamed, clicked his heels together and took a little bow. "One sixty-six, thank you." Then *sotto voce* he added, "I won't tell you how much my health club membership cost."

Iva smiled. Conrad sat down and took her hand.

"Iva be truthful. How are you doing?"

"Fine. I'm doing fine."

"How about financially? Do you need some money?"

"Thanks, but we're both doing just fine."

"Speaking of that, where is Brian?"

"Out on the campaign trail somewhere. He won't be back till late."

"How is he?"

"Tired, working too hard, but fine."

Conrad scratched his beard and looked away. "Iva, this really isn't a social call." He turned back. "Though God knows I wish it were. We don't see nearly enough of each other."

"What is it, Papa?"

"Something's come to my attention... just what the hell have you and Brian gotten yourselves into out here?"

Iva did not reply right away. Then she said simply, "Bad politics."

"Dangerous politics I would imagine." Conrad squeezed his daughter's hand tight. "Now I want you to tell me exactly what the situation is. Tell me everything."

"But why?"

"It's important I know. Come on now, from the beginning."

Iva told him the whole story. She left nothing out: the bridge, Alan Sansone's murder, the bombing, the break-in, all were included. Conrad frowned and continually folded and unfolded his arms as he listened. When his daughter finished, he exhaled loudly and pulled at his his beard.

"Is that it?"

"Yes Papa."

"Why haven't you asked for my help?"

"You're supposed to be retired, Papa. Besides, we can take care of ourselves."

"I'm not so sure about that. The folder," he said.

A clean-cut sport-coated young man in his mid-twenties materialized to deposit a manila folder in Conrad's lap. Iva started, she had not realized there was anyone else in the house. "Hi," she said but got nothing but a nod and a hint of a smile in response.

The youthful stranger wordlessly backed a few paces behind his superior and stood at attention with his arms at his sides. Iva looked at him and then back at her father and knew instantly her suspicions had been correct. Conrad took an eight by ten photograph out of the folder and handed it to her. She did not immediately look down. "Oh Papa," she sighed, in two words giving voice to her mixed feelings of fear and love.

"Oh Papa nothing," he replied, embarrassed and a little bit ashamed because he could sense what his daughter was thinking. "Iva, just look at the picture."

She did.

"Ever seen that man?"

The picture was of Wilhelm Weltsmirtz, in sharp focus though obviously taken without his knowledge through a telephoto lens. Iva had never seen him so she shook her head. "But wait! I do recognize the front of that building. It's the Republican headquarters in Sagamore... the building we broke into."

"Correct," her father said. "That's why I'm here. This sort of investigation is usually not my concern but..."

"But I figured I'd butt into your life because I have nothing better to do," Iva finished for him. She was smiling.

"Sweetheart..." Conrad opened his hands palms up like a marketplace vendor who can't lower his price another shekel. He was also smiling.

"Boy, security consultant for El Al Airlines sure is a far reaching job," Iva went on.

"It sure is," Conrad affirmed.

"There's no chance this El Al job is just a cover for continued employment in the Mossad is there?" She had stopped smiling.

"Oh, no chance of that."

"It wouldn't be that you read about our predicament in the papers and—unofficially, completely on your own time—used your connections to do some snooping around."

"Perish the thought."

"You haven't done this because you love me and you couldn't resist."

"Absolutely not."

"Oh Papa." They understood each other and they hugged. The young Mossad agent cleared his throat, shifted his feet and looked down at the floor.

"All right, who is this guy?" Iva asked, tapping the photograph.

"The man in the picture is Wilhelm Weltsmirtz."

"What a creepy name."

"He's a creepy guy. German-American, he's an old CIA man who worked in security for Nixon's campaign in 1968. Apparently he's always been a bit of a screw up. They keep him working in Sagamore just to make sure he's out of the way and quiet. He freelances occasionally as a photographer for the local newspaper and works nights as a security guard at the Republican headquarters. And we found out the Republicans also use him as a part-time strong man. When city workers are slow with their monthly donations, this guy Weltsmirtz collects."

"Why doesn't somebody just arrest him?" Iva asked.

"The authorities here in the States don't have any proof against the guy. He's suspected of killing at least three people over the years: one in Florida, one in New Hampshire and maybe another here on Long Island."

Iva looked down at Weltsmirtz who suddenly looked very sinister. She shuddered and gave the picture back to her father. "What do you have in mind to do Papa?"

Conrad stood up and walked over to the young agent. "Wait for me at the car please, Jacob."

"Yes sir." Jacob moved swiftly out.

Conrad turned to his daughter. "Sweetheart, as I guess you've always suspected, I'm in charge of the Mossad's operations here in the United States. If we keep this low key, and by low key I mean completely secret, I can unofficially bring some of my resources to bear to help you and Brian."

"Protect us, you mean," Iva said.

"I mean help you. But you're still my daughter and if I have to protect you, I will."

"But how?"

"Well, I think we should bug Frank Montesano's office. Let's find out what we're up against. If you're in any real danger—and I think you are—we'll deal with it. Who knows, Montesano, Weltsmirtz or Savino might incriminate themselves on a tape you and Brian might just happen to find in your possession."

"Papa, I just don't know. Can you just..."

"Iva, your old man is a bit of a big shot. I really have quite a free hand over here." Conrad smiled and sat back with his hands behind his head. "Of course if we get caught it will be a huge diplomatic incident and I'll be court-martialed. But at my age I couldn't care less about that. Besides, you're my daughter for God's sake."

"How do you do something like this?"

"Technically, it's easy. We have a flower arrangement with a camera and wireless transmitter hidden in the stems. It's completely undetectable. Someone can even pick it up and smell the flowers and still not notice anything. We'll have someone pose as the maid to plant the thing. As a matter of fact, I have an agent flying in a few days who's perfect for the job."

Iva stood up. "We're desperate. A few days could be too late. We need to get the evidence as soon as possible so Brian can use it in his campaign."

"Don't worry," her father said, "we'll get someone else then."

"I want to be the maid," Iva declared. "None of the Republicans know who I am. I want to do it."

"Absolutely not," Conrad said.

"I want to do it," Iva repeated, stamping her foot like a spoiled ten-year old. "I want to do it for Brian. I want to do it for Alan Sansone."

"You're my daughter. It might be dangerous."

Iva pursed her lips, widened her eyes and pleaded with him the way she always did. "Please Papa! Please!"

Conrad looked away. He knew what would happen next, he knew he would give in. Iva had always gotten her way, particularly after the murder of her mother. He loved her so much he could not bear to deny her anything it was in his power to give.

"You're not employed by us. It's highly irregular," he insisted, pleading his lost cause.

"You can arrange it, you said you're a big shot. I want to do it... I want to do it... for you and Brian."

Conrad looked sharply at his daughter. "If you really want to do something for me, you'll move back to Israel with me when my appointment here is finished."

Iva looked hurt. She dropped her eyes and sat back.

"I'm sorry," Conrad said quickly, realizing he had hit back too hard. "Okay, you can be the maid. You can plant the bug."

"Thank you," Iva said.

Conrad stood up and walked to the window. He could see his young aide de camp waiting for him behind the wheel of his limousine. *I'll die if anything happens to her,* he thought.

He turned back to Iva. "You really love Brian, don't you?"

"I do, I really do."

"I really loved your mother."

Iva moved to her father and they hugged.

"I still love her," Conrad said. His voice cracked and his eye watered.

"We both do Papa."

He gripped her by the shoulders and stared into her eyes. "For God's sake, be careful when you're doing this. I'll be waiting right outside. If you're a second late coming out, I'll..."

"I'll be careful," Iva said.

Chapter XIV

"Tell you what. I got a proposition for you. Now you sing us your song, and you can have a drink."

Edward G. Robinson to Claire Trevor in ***Key Largo*** *(1948)*

OCTOBER 17, 8:03 A.M.

Iva walked out of the Republican headquarters and turned left. About ten yards down the sidewalk she climbed into a van marked *Continental Maid Service.* The man behind the wheel nodded to her and pulled away from the curb. A small metal strip slid back on the partition behind her seat.

"You're three minutes late," her father said. All she could see were his eyes, actually one eye and an eye patch.

"Sorry Papa. It went fine. I walked right in, cleaned the office and planted the flowers. Nobody was around."

"Is the camera aimed properly?"

"Right at Montesano's desk."

For Conrad Fidele and the Mossad the bugging was routine. In just over twenty-four hours they had procured sophisticated surveillance equipment along with the personnel to monitor it. They also arranged for Iva to substitute indefinitely for Montesano's regular maid.

"The fewer people that know about a clandestine operation the better," Conrad had said over and over, so Iva promised not to inform Brian nor anyone else of what they were doing. She was relieved not to tell Brian because he would almost certainly construe her father's assistance as meddling. Since their engagement the two men, though courteous on the surface, always seemed to be competing against each other. *Brian pushes himself hard enough without giving himself something else to be stressed about,* Iva decided. *If we're successful then I'll tell him.*

The van drove about a mile and pulled to a stop in a side street. Iva got out and walked around to the back door. It opened and as her father climbed out she caught a glimpse of two men in headphones hunched over an elaborate tape console.

"Let's go," Conrad said. "They'll get in touch with me immediately if they pick up anything interesting."

The two agents were to continuously monitor the audio and video received from the bug in the flower vase. The apparatus was activated by a motion sensor so all they had to do was wait. Iva needed to retrieve the vase during the evening cleanup so the batteries could be replaced. Fortunately, Montesano demanded fresh flowers daily. Like Mrs. Fitzpatrick had said, he preferred chrysanthemums, and he began his office routine by smelling them. That morning, after taking a deep whiff, he thought they smelled particularly pungent.

"Ward five was a piece of cake last night," David said. He blew into his cup of hot chocolate. "We plastered the whole downtown area in less than twenty minutes."

"Uh huh," Marcus replied, staring off into space. The two men were alone; a group of phone canvassers was expected about ten.

"No one hassled us," David continued. "Mission accomplished... smooth as silk all the way."

"Yeah." Marcus crumpled his paper cup and threw it over his shoulder just like he had once seen his father toss an eviction notice.

"Is there something wrong?" David asked.

"No. Well..." Marcus swung around so fast David took a step back. "All right, there is something bugging me," Marcus said. "Don't get me wrong, I'm not complaining, I knew what I was getting into when I signed on, but this damn campaign has taken up so much of my time I've had no social life to speak of for months. I swear there are moments when I need sex so bad I feel I'm going to die."

David blinked, taken aback by Marcus' frankness. He commenced his ritual throat clearing and glasses straightening.

"How do you deal with it?" Marcus asked.

"Deal with what?" David replied, turning and starting to put on his jacket. This conversation made him uncomfortable and he would put an end to it, even if he had to walk out.

Marcus stood in front of the door to block his exit. "How do you deal with it when you want a woman?" he persisted.

David retreated, took a seat, leaned on his forearms and stared at the floor. "All right, I'll tell you," he said. "I think about my grandfather naked."

"You what?"

"Uh... whenever I get... uh... aroused when I don't want to be, I think about my grandfather naked. He had dementia for about five years before he died at ninety-one. All hours of the day or night he used to wander around the house totally naked except for black socks. Wrinkles, drooling, it was a disgusting sight."

Marcus stared incredulously at David not sure whether or not he was joking. David stared back inscrutably like the Sphinx.

Brian and Iva walked in.

"Of course, you never met my grandfather," David said.

"What did you say?" Brian asked.

"Never mind, you don't want to know," Marcus said.

Brian clapped his hands together. "I feel good," he said. "I'm getting good responses from the people I'm meeting out there. It's been weeks since anyone's called me a baby killer or a crazed Communist traitor."

"Except me," Iva cut in. "He gets aroused when I call him that."

"Drives me crazy," Brian agreed. He and Iva laughed at their joke; Marcus rolled his eyes.

David changed the subject. "Things are going pretty well," he said. "We're in good shape as we head down to the wire."

Jeff and Debbie burst through the door. Both brandished copies of the *New York Times.*

"Look at this!" Jeff said, thrusting the editorial page at Brian. "The *Times* has endorsed you! The *New York* fucking *Times*! Listen, they say "the charges and counter charges will be settled in a court of law over time but in the meantime..."

"...Brian Werth has youth, energy, and a fresh approach," Debbie read from her copy. "He sounds alarms that need to be heard."

"Yes!" Marcus yelled, throwing a fist into the air.

"Tremendous news," David said. "Absolutely tremendous."

Brian kissed the paper. "This is beautiful. I'm going to have it framed."

"I'll go out and buy five hundred copies," Iva said.

"Don't bother, we'll make copies," Finance Chairman Jeffrey Hollis said.

"Good thinking," Iva said.

"That's what I don't pay him for," Brian said cheerfully.

"Well, we broke even," Marcus said soberly, bringing everyone back down to earth. He was referring to the reality that during the past week the conservative leaning *New York Post* had come out in favor of Savino calling him "a proven talent with an excellent track record. Brian Werth," the *Post* continued, "seems rash and impetuous and has the potential to become a dangerous demagogue." With *Newsday* and the *New York Daily News* thus far remaining neutral, they had traded major print endorsements even up. Of lesser impact but still important, the *Sagamore Record* had exhibited a marked Republican bias: its latest headline trumpeted **AL'S THE ONE!**

"Remember, some multimillionaire corporate prick from Australia recently purchased the *New York Post*," Brian said. "He's turned it into a right wing waste of time. Hardly anyone reads the *Post* on Long Island, anyway."

"Great sports section though," Marcus said. After a look from Brian he shrugged and added, "I'm just sayin'..."

"So what is *Newsday's* fucking problem?" Jeff said for the umpteenth time. "I really thought we had a chance to get their endorsement. Come on, what is this neutral bullshit?"

"I'll tell you what their problem is," David said. "They're torn. They know a bridge across the Sound is something to be concerned about. They might even know that it's wrong. But a bridge would mean more jobs and businesses and ultimately more population on Long Island. That means more money and more profits for *Newsday*. That's why they're remaining neutral and have been negligent in investigating Montesano. They're stuck between doing what's right for Long Island and doing what's right for their business."

"We really need another major newspaper here on Long Island," Brian said.

"Competition," David agreed.

Brian looked down and read his plaudit in the *Times* one more time. "This is still great news," he said.

"We'll add copies to this afternoon's literature drop," David said.

"Great," Brian replied.

"Maybe there's a chance for an upset after all," Marcus said in an attempt to cheer himself up.

"Damn right there's a chance," Brian said.

"We've definitely got hope," David said. "Without hope we've got... "

"...we've got jack shit," Jeff cut in.

"Very nice, very poetic," Debbie told him. "The noble Bard himself couldn't have put it any better."

"Shakespeare?" Jeff said.

"No, Tony Bard, a friend of mine," Debbie said.

Jeff laughed. "You've been spending too much time with me," he said.

"...youth, energy and a fresh approach," Brian read out loud again.

Iva giggled. "That's funny, I haven't noticed any fresh approaches lately."

Brian looked at her and frowned. "What do you mean by that?"

"Oh nothing."

"Tell me."

"Nothing, I was kidding."

"Seriously."

"Don't be so sensitive. I was just teasing."

Brian was not appeased. "Did I do something wrong?"

Iva gestured at the other people in the room. "Can we discuss this later?"

"I have to know what you meant."

"Brian, relax and shut up," Iva said.

"Maybe I should show them a picture of my grandfather," David whispered.

Even Marcus had to laugh.

Iva reclined in her favorite easy chair in the living room and rubbed her temples; she had a major league headache. After five days the surveillance of Montesano's office had revealed none of the hoped for incriminating evidence against any of the Republicans. Montesano, it turned out, preferred to conduct business from a corner table at Mama Liapetto's Italian Restaurant down the block. When he did use his office it was more for the purpose of socializing. One afternoon, in the manner one might ask for chicken salad on rye, he called an escort service and ordered a prostitute to go. "A tall blonde not too fat with big tits." And hold the mayo.

The chrysanthemums worked perfectly. The Mossad now possessed crystal clear audio and video of Frank Montesano copulating—and sweating and grunting—with a short, brunette and decidedly chubby prostitute. She did possess huge breasts that, in the opinion of Conrad's Mossad operatives, must have been somehow surgically enhanced. It was a bizarre scene to watch, even for intelligence agents well indoctrinated in the field of sexual blackmail. Montesano had produced a nun's habit and the hooker had—for an extra fifty dollars up front—donned it and performed a striptease. She concluded the dance completely naked by straddling her manic client and demanding that he "Confess." Iva refused to attend a screening of the session, insisting to her father that under no circumstances was that the sort of evidence she was after. Sooner or later something incriminating of a political nature would occur in that office. It just had to. Besides the episode with the prostitute, all they had recorded were benign situations such as Montesano arguing over the phone with his wife over the virtues of whole versus skim milk.

The phone rang and Iva answered it. Her father was on the other end.

"Looks like we've got it, honey. Just what we want."

"What happened Papa?"

"My people just called to tell me Montesano finally opened his fat mouth. So did Savino. So did Weltsmirtz. And it really is Weltsmirtz."

"I can't believe it."

"I'm coming right over to pick you up so you can go and retrieve the bug. Then I'll show you what's on the tape."

Iva walked in the front door of the Republican headquarters and took the elevator up to the third floor. She did not attract any undue attention. The glances she garnered from most of the males she passed in the hall were normal; her black cleaning service uniform was short and tight she looked good. Once again she entered Montesano's office without being questioned and—as had been the case for her twice-daily visits for the past five days—there was no sign of the Boss. There was no need to go through the charade of cleaning the office any more, everything they needed had been recorded by the camera hidden in the chrysanthemums. She walked directly to the flower vase, bent over and scooped it up in her arms.

"I told them I wanted a redhead this time," Montesano said, checking out Iva from the back.

She whirled around.

"Hey, not bad. I'll take it," Frank said. He closed the office door.

"I'm the maid," Iva said quickly.

"Oh, of course," he replied, disappointed.

"I'll just be going now," Iva said, starting for the door.

Montesano stepped in front of her. "Where are you going with my flowers?" he asked.

Iva looked down at the flowers and began to improvise. "Oh these. Uh, they need water. I was just going to water them." She walked into the bathroom, turned on the tap and started filling the vase. Her father had told her the apparatus was insulated against watering.

"Just go about your work," Montesano called out, taking a seat behind his desk. He peeled off his jacket and tie, kicked off his shoes and plopped his feet up in front of him. Foot odor rivaling the most pungent areas of industrial New Jersey wafted through the room and nearly felled Iva when she emerged from the bathroom. She pretended to smell the flowers as she rushed to open the window. Thank God they even smelled real.

Montesano leaned back in his chair and interlocked his hands behind his head. "Ah, the work of a public servant is never done," he said, grabbing the phone and dialing the Foxy Lady Escort Service.

"Yes sir," Iva said, dusting the room and waiting for her chance to steal away with the flowers.

The line was busy and Montesano slammed down the phone. He did not like being kept waiting under any circumstances, especially when he felt like relieving himself. Sex to Frank was like going to the bathroom, when he had to go, he had to go, and it ached to hold it in. He put his elbows on the desk and leaned his head in his hands. His eyes zoomed in on Iva's ass: tight and perfect and undulating a bit as she walked. He panned down her shapely legs: *awesome. Is she wearing a bra?* He could not get a clear view from the front.

Iva turned and noticed him staring at her. She smiled and went back to work.

No bra... and a beautiful face. Frank stood up, walked over to the dimmer switch by the door and turned the lights down.

"Hey, what's going on," Iva said, actually realizing but having no idea what to do about it.

"We've both been working too hard," Frank said. "Let's take a break."

Before Iva could respond, he pushed a button that caused the couch she was standing in front of to spring out and become a bed. She leaped out of the way just in time. Frank laughed and pushed another button. A compartment in the wall slid back to reveal a fully stocked bar.

"Pretty impressive, isn't it?" he said. "Would you like a drink?"

"Uh... nothing for me, thanks," Iva replied, trying desperately to figure a way to get out of there with the flowers and without making a scene. No good to run for it—Montesano blocked the door.

"I think you should loosen up," Frank said. "Believe me, I'll make it worth your while."

He took a step forward. Iva backed up a step. The door behind Montesano opened a crack and Al Savino poked his head in.

"Hey Frank, I just wanted to know if you've heard anything from Welt..." Suddenly he noticed the mood lighting and his leader's infuriated face. "Look, if you're busy I'll come back later, he said, checking out Iva. He liked what he saw. "Hey, you better believe I'll be back later... for seconds."

"Get out!" Montesano yelled.

The door slammed.

Down the block in the Continental Maid Service van two agents of Israel's Mossad restrained Conrad Fidele from charging into the Republican headquarters with his gun drawn.

"I give the orders around here," Conrad yelled. "Let me go!"

"We're just asking you to think for a second," the agent named Jacob said.

"My daughter's in there! That bastard is trying to rape her."

"It's because she's your daughter you're not thinking straight," the other agent said. "Charging in there and shooting the place up will ruin everything. Your daughter's a big girl. Give her a chance to get out of this herself."

Conrad shook himself free from the two men and punched the side of the truck. He turned back and shook a bloody fist in their faces. "If she doesn't get herself out of there in the next sixty seconds, I'll take care of it myself. And that fat fucking Guinea WOP prick's going to be sorry he was ever born."

"Would you like some decaf?" Jacob asked.

Montesano riveted his eyes on Iva's breasts. "They're nice," he said.

Iva put her hands on her hips and stood as tall as she could. "Don't you dare touch me you disgusting piece of shit," she said.

"They're real nice," Frank repeated, still staring and so mesmerized he was oblivious to the insult. Then he actually licked his chops.

"I'm warning you, I won't let you touch me," Iva said.

Montesano wiped his mouth on his sleeve and put his hands out like he was about to adjust shower spigots. "Please, I've got to touch them. I've got to. Please."

"Fuck you," Iva said.

Montesano only heard what he wanted to hear. He took a step forward. "Thanks," he muttered.

Iva backed up a step. "Get away from me you fat son of a bitch Republican pig."

"I want you," Montesano said. He lurched forward and backed Iva up against the wall. His sweaty palms reached for their targets. "Just want to touch them. Just..."

Montesano's fingertips brushed Iva's breasts at the precise instant the toe of her shoe impacted with his groin. A spasm of pain flared down his legs and up through his chest to his head. He yelped and doubled over. Iva stepped around him and ran to the door. It was locked.

"You whore," Montesano snarled.

He straightened up and lunged at her, and this time his hands aimed at her throat. Iva sidestepped the uncoordinated glob and moved behind the desk. Out of the corner of her eye she noticed rectangular discoloration on the rug where the safe must have been.

Iva grabbed a pair of scissors and aimed the point outward. Montesano's eyes widened but before he could do anything the pain between his legs became so intense he began to feel dizzy. His vision blurred and he moaned and doubled over. A key turned in the door. It burst open and the doorknob slammed solidly into the side of his head. He fell forward onto his stomach, one hand holding his head the other his groin.

"You okay, Frank?" Savino asked, understanding nothing of what was going on. "What are you doing on the floor?"

Montesano did not answer nor lift his head. He started to cry softly. "Bitch," he moaned.

Iva put the scissors down and walked out from behind the desk. She picked up the flower vase from the coffee table, stepped over the weeping hulk on the floor and moved past Savino out the door.

Over her shoulder she said, "Good day gentlemen, and I use the term loosely."

"Uh, good day," Savino said. He turned to his friend who was still sobbing on the floor. "Hey, come on Frank. So you didn't get her. There's no reason to be that upset."

Frank Montesano swore that as soon as his strength returned he would remind the Mayor what a good swift kick in the balls feels like.

Iva literally ran into her father in the lobby on her way out. He looked panicked having just realized he had charged into the building without first ascertaining the location of Montesano's office. The relief showed when he recognized his daughter.

"Iva, are you all right?"

"I'm fine, let's get out of here."

"Where is he?" Years of training be damned, with his daughter involved he wanted to kick the crap out of the guy.

"He's upstairs, forget about it. I've got the camera, let's just go."

Conrad gripped his daughter's shoulders. "Are you sure you're all right," he asked.

"I'm sure."

The day security guard walked over to them. He was a freckle-faced nineteen-year-old working his way through community college. "Is there something I can help you with?" he asked.

Conrad wheeled around and snapped, "Young man, I suggest you mind your own business."

"Yes sir," the guard replied. He retreated to his seat. The last thing he wanted to do was aggravate someone important.

Iva nudged her father towards the door. He still seemed undecided whether to leave or go punch out Montesano. She finally grabbed him by the arm and pulled him outside.

"Papa, we have the evidence. You've got to calm down."

"All right, I'll calm down."

"Thanks Papa, let's go."

The van was waiting for them out front and they climbed into the back. An agent immediately took the flower vase from Iva. Conrad rapped on the wall behind the driver and they sped away.

"Give me the tapes," Conrad told his men.

"Yes sir," one said, handing him two videocassettes.

"I'm sure we got everything," the other agent said, thinking what a pain in the ass it was to work directly with the head of American operations.

"For your sake I hope so," Conrad said, realizing as he spoke that he should go easy on his men who were there on their own time doing him a personal favor. "Strike that, Jacob," he added quickly.

"How did Montesano incriminate himself?" Iva asked.

"The whole thing is incredible," Jacob answered.

"What is it? What did he say?"

"We'll see everything when we play the tapes at your house," Conrad said.

Chapter XV

"Put it on his ears, his nose, his mouth,
put it every place on him, every place."

*Wallace Beery orders Joseph Schildkraut covered with honey and staked out for the ants to eat in **Viva Villa** (1934)*

OCTOBER 23, 6:02 P.M.

"I really do not want to ride that roller coaster," Brian said. "Maybe they'll let me just cut the ribbon, pose for a picture and then leave."

"You have to ride it," Jeff replied. "That's what you're here for."

"But I've always hated roller coasters. What's the point? Scare yourself to death, scream your lungs out and then vomit, what fun is that? You know I puked at Disney World once."

"Space Mountain?" Jeff said.

"No, one of the restaurants."

Jeff laughed. "Good one," he said.

"Thank you," Brian replied. "But I'm serious, I really don't want to ride this thing."

"Sorry, but you're a candidate for public office."

"So?"

"So... that's what campaigning is all about... you force yourself to do things you hate and smile your way through it all."

Brian and Jeff threaded their way through the crowd to the platform in front of the Deep Space Rocket Ride. It was finally time for what had been billed as "The Most Outrageous Experience East of the Mississippi" to open to the public after more than eighteen months of construction, six more than planned. It was an extravagant addition to Island Funland, an amusement park that already included a state of the art video arcade, twelve batting cages, a golf driving range, two miniature golf courses and two dozen kiddie rides.

Brian was present to participate in the dedication ceremonies. Dominick Belsky, owner and president of Belsky Amusements, Incorporated, had initially invited the Mayor but Savino had declined upon hearing he would be required to accompany Belsky on a ceremonial inauguration of the Deep Space Rocket Ride. Al cited scheduling conflicts as the reason for his regrets but in reality he was concerned his bulk would make it impossible for him to fit into one of the ride's seats. Brian agreed to fill in at the last minute though now he regretted it.

"How do you do, Mr. Belsky?" Brian said as he mounted the platform. "I'm Brian Werth, Democratic candidate for mayor."

"Glad you could make it, Werth," Belsky replied. He turned to his wife. "Sugar, this guy's running for mayor. He's respectable."

"Don't count on that," Jeff cut in.

"Ignore my assistant," Brian said. "He's an imbecile."

Brian and Jeff looked at each other and cracked up. They both realized the endless campaigning was finally beginning to make them goofy and they were behaving like Abbott and Costello.

"Hiya," Roberta Belsky said, smiling and popping her gum at the same time.

"Hiya," Brian and Jeff responded at the same time, causing them to laugh again.

"Do you have any more gum?" Jeff asked.

"Stop," Brian told him.

The Belskys were made for each other; both were pudgy and greasy looking. Dominick's suit was unpressed and at least two sizes too small. Brian and Jeff noted to themselves that he was a "hair looper"—someone who parted his hair just above the ear and combed it over to cover a completely bald crown. The tactic fooled no one and outside with the wind blowing Belsky resembled Bozo the Clown. His wife Roberta had on a striped tent dress that called attention to rather than hid her weight problem, and with every breeze it billowed up like a parachute.

"We'll be getting underway any minute now," Dominick said, "just as soon as the photographer from *Newsday* gets here."

"Nice turnout," Brian said, scanning the nearly one thousand people crowded around. He noticed with regret that virtually all of them were under the voting age of eighteen and pounding the flesh would be a waste of time. *Oh well, at least a picture in the paper should come out of this,* he thought.

"Everyone rides free tonight," Dominick said. "Starting tomorrow, it's five bucks a shot."

Jeff blew into his hands. "It's a little nippy," he said.

The remark infuriated Belsky and he wheeled on Jeff. "Tell me about it," he said. "Do you think I want to open a roller coaster in late October? I have no choice. We were supposed to open last May but the damn thing was just finished last week. The fucking unions ruined everything. And the fucking permits—from the state, county and even little fuckin' Sagamore. What a crock of shit. I'd love to wail till next spring to open but my creditors sure as hell won't wait. I've got to start taking money in right away."

"Sorry I brought it up," Jeff said.

"I'm going to keep this thing going until the first snowfall," Belsky added.

Jeff thought for a moment then smirked. "After the first snowfall, why don't you change the name from the Deep Space Rocket Ride to the White Mountain Toboggan Ride? That way you can keep the thing going year round."

Dominick Belsky's eyes widened as if he had just heard a viable suggestion. "What's your name?" he asked.

"Jeffrey Hollis."

"I like you, Hollis."

Dominick's wife elbowed him in the ribs and said, "The photographer's here, let's get going."

They all hustled over to where the first roller coaster car stood waiting for its maiden voyage. It looked like any roller coaster car except it was painted in silver sparkles and had the words **BLAST OFF!** stenciled on the side. A blue ribbon ran from the front safety bar to the back bumper. Brian and Dominick picked it up and held it between them. Dominick's wife handed her husband a battery powered megaphone.

"Ladies and gentlemen and children of all ages..." he intoned. In an aside to Brian he whispered, "P.T. Barnum is my hero." Back into the megaphone: "Welcome to super-fantastic and stupendous Island Funland and the official opening of the largest and most outrageous roller coaster in the East." Everyone in the crowd cheered and whistled. In another aside much louder this time Belsky said, "Fuck Great Adventure." Brian and Jeff both responded with solemn nods, not wanting to mess with a man on a roll. "And now with the official dedication," Belsky continued, "I introduce to you Mayor Brian Werth."

Jeff started to correct the misstatement but Brian stopped him. "Let it slide," he told him, "I like how it sounds." He took the megaphone. "Hello everyone. My name is Brian Werth and I'm running for Mayor."

"I'm freezing," someone in the crowd yelled out. "Get on with it!" The adolescents on line for their free ride, fearing a speech by a politician, began to hiss and boo.

Brian decided to shorten his remarks. "So let's get going," he concluded, handing the megaphone back to Belsky who then put his arm around Brian, handed him a pair of scissors and told him to pose as if he was about to cut the ribbon. Mrs. Belsky and their four young children crowded around on both sides. The photographers were about to click away when Dominick yelled, "Hold it! Hollis, come on and get in the picture."

"Me?" Jeff said.

"Yeah you, come on!"

"Don't mind if I do." He sauntered over.

Dominick elbowed his wife over a space. Jeff stood between them and picked up their three-year-old daughter in his arms. On cue they all said "**Cheese Louise!**" Strobes flashed capturing all smiles save for the much put upon Mrs. Belsky. Brian cut the ribbon and the crowd applauded.

"Okay, it's you and me on a ceremonial first ride," Dominick told Brian.

"Are you sure it's safe?" Brian asked, looking out over the seemingly endless twisting and turning track. *Holy shit, there are three loops that will turn us completely upside down!*

"Of course its safe. Inspectors have been up my ass for months. I got all the permits I need. There's nothing to worry about."

Dominick squeezed into the car first. Reluctantly, Brian followed. Mrs. Belsky snapped the safety bar into place, extra hard because she was angry. Brian noticed a sign that read...

LIFT HEIGHT: 173 FEET
TRACK LENGTH: 4160 FEET
SPEED: 66 + M.P.H.
RIDE TIME: 2 ½ MINUTES
STATE OF THE ART TECHNOLOGY UTILIZES A DUAL COMPUTER CONTROL SYSTEM WITH ON SCREEN DIAGNOSTICS SIMILAR TO THAT ON APOLLO MOON MISSIONS.
HALF A MILLION WATTS OF LIGHTING ILLUMINATE THE EXCITING TWISTS, TURNS AND DIVES.
GUESTS EXPERIENCE ALMOST 3.5 "G's" AS THEY RACE DOWN THE 55-DEGREE ANGLE ON THE FIRST DROP.

... and wished he were someplace else. *Calcutta... the dentist... anywhere far away from this stupid ride.*

PLEASE REMOVE EYEGLASSES AND ALL LOOSE OBJECTS FROM YOUR PERSON. KEEP HANDS AND FEET INSIDE CAR. BELSKY AMUSEMENTS, INC. IS NOT RESPONSIBLE FOR LOST ARTICLES OR INJURIES INCURRED DUE TO A FAILURE TO COMPLY WITH REGULATIONS. PERSONS WITH ILL HEALTH SHOULD CONSULT PHYSICIAN

BEFORE RIDING. NO ONE UNDER THE AGE OF EIGHT ALLOWED. NO ONE UNDER 4 ft 6 in (137 cm) ALLOWED. NO PREGNANT WOMEN ALLOWED.

No pregnant women allowed, Brian mused. *What kind of a pregnant woman rides a roller coaster? Maybe someone way past their due date desperate to induce labor.*

"Take it away, Carlos," Dominick said to a tall lean Puerto Rican teenager wearing a leather jacket and sunglasses.

"*Adíos Señor Belsky*," Carlos shouted. He opened what looked like a fuse box and pushed a red button. An electric motor under the platform whirred to life and Brian was actually relieved there was no sort of an explosion.

"Carlos has roller coasters in his blood," Dominick said. "His father and grandfather worked the Cyclone at Coney Island."

"Very interesting," Brian replied. He wondered how a break for his car would look. Carlos gripped a five-foot lever and shifted it from the ten o'clock position to two o'clock. The brake holding Brian and Dominick let go and they began to creep forward, their car pulled by a chain driven by the electric motor. A second car rolled into place to wait for passengers. The photographers went to work again. Dominick smiled and waved. So did Brian in spite of the bile rising up in his throat.

"Nice knowing you," Jeff called after them.

There was about twenty feet of straightaway before the car had to climb a ninety-foot incline... when released from the tow chain at the apex, downward force would provide momentum for the remainder of the trip: a two and a half minute journey through curves and rolls designed to frighten the hardiest of souls.

Kids lined the fence along the straightaway and shouted encouragement. Brian waved and gave the thumbs up sign, but he was wishing he had not eaten that day.

"God bless the little peckers," Dominick said through a toothy plastered on smile. "Starting tomorrow they're all money in my pocket."

Brian received the shock of his life as the car neared the foot of the incline. Lined up along with the kids was... *that guard who surprised us at the break-in. The guy I kicked in the face. The guy who threatened Mrs. Fitzpatrick. Montesano's bodyguard. What the hell is he doing here?*

Brian gaped at the guard whom he noticed was wearing a neck brace. The guard sneered back and raised his hand to his forehead in a salute. The car started its slow climb. Brian and Dominick were thrown back against their seats.

Weltsmirtz admitted to himself the trap he had set was not original; it was definitely in a mode similar to what the French Underground had utilized with great success during World War Two: piano wire strung across dark roads to sever the heads of German motorcyclists. *Décapiter!* At that moment a thin virtually invisible strand, taught and anchored firmly between two support beams, stretched at neck level across the tracks at the beginning of the third and final loop. When Brian and Belsky hit the razor-sharp wire at over sixty miles an hour, decapitation would occur in a fraction of a second.

The roller coaster chugged up the hill. Brian immediately concluded Weltsmirtz was there to kill him. *But how? Is he going to shoot me? No, there are lots of people around. This roller coaster! He's going to kill me while I'm on this roller coaster. He's planted a bomb! Sabotaged the tracks! Set up snipers! Snipers? Christ, get a grip on yourself.*

"We've got to stop this thing," Brian shouted.

"Relax Werth," Dominick said. "Enjoy it."

"No, it's not safe! We have to get out!"

"Too late now. Just close your eyes, it'll all be over soon."

The roller coaster closed in on the top of the hill. Brian threw the safety bar forward and tried to climb out. "Someone's trying to kill me!" he yelled.

"Hey, what are you trying to do?" Belsky said. He grabbed Brian, sat him down and pulled the safety bar back into position. "Werth, don't be an asshole."

The towline disengaged about two feet from the top of the hill, leaving the car with just enough momentum to get it to the point where gravity could take over. It seemed for a moment the car would not make it and would stop and roll backwards, but it inched up to the crest. Off in the distance they could see rooftops and tiny headlights moving on the roads. Brian reached under his jacket and felt Marcus' gun tucked into his waistband. He did not pull it out. *What the hell is there to shoot at?*

The car tilted downwards and picked up speed. Brian's vision blurred and air ripped at his face. He grabbed the safety bar and stared straight ahead. He felt more terror than he ever had before, and the most helpless.

We're going to die on this thing!

Chapter XVI

"The 39 Steps is the name of an organization of foreign spies collecting information for..."

Wylie Watson is shot before he can reveal ***The 39 Steps*** *(1935)*

OCTOBER 23, 6:35 P.M.

As soon as they got to the house Iva, her father and the two Mossad agents went directly into the living room. Brian was not home so the results of their spying would be revealed only to those present at the screening.

"There's the video player," Iva said, pointing to it.

"Be careful with that tape," Conrad said. "We haven't had time to make a copy."

"Yes we have, sir," the agent inserting the cassette said over his shoulder.

"Papa..." Iva began.

"... sit down and relax," Conrad finished for her. He let out a big sigh and complied.

Iva thought she caught fleeting smiles on the lips of two agents. "Would anyone like a beer and... popcorn," she offered. "We've got popcorn already popped."

The two men looked mournfully at her and Iva could tell they were starved. Neither spoke up, worried Conrad might consider the consumption of beer and popcorn unduly cavalier during the screening of a surveillance tape. But Conrad noticed his men were ravenous so he answered for them.

"Popcorn and beer would be great honey, thanks."

Iva walked to the kitchen grateful to have something to do; the wait was making her a nervous wreck. She pinned all their hope for victory on the contents of the tape and she wanted Brian to win more than anything else imaginable, infinitely more than anything she wanted for herself. *I guess this is love,* she thought as she carried a six-pack of beer and a gallon tub of popcorn back to the living room.

"Thanks," Conrad said. "Have a seat, we're all set to go."

Iva sat next to her father on the couch.

"Lights," Iva said.

"Camera," the agent working the tape player said as he pushed the ON button.

"Action!" Iva said. Her father looked sternly at her. She giggled and said, "Have a beer, Papa." He took one and smiled, and then put his arm around her.

After a twenty-second blank leader, the tape spit fuzz and came into focus. Frank Montesano could be clearly seen sitting behind his desk clipping his toenails.

"Men make me sick," Iva declared, deliberately reversing the gender in Humphrey Bogart's line from *The Big Sleep*.

"That's Montesano all right," Conrad said, scowling at the picture.

<u>Montesano</u>

(He speaks into the intercom.)

Send Savino in here right away.

<u>Savino</u>

(He enters almost immediately.)

What's up, Frank?

(Montesano does not answer. He picks up a folder and throws it to Savino who opens it and reads.)

This is not good, Frank. This poll says my margin has slipped to only two to one point six five.

That's too close.

Montesano

Way too close. There's a chance Werth could win. We cannot allow that.

Savino

What are we going to do?

Montesano

Kill Werth

(He clips one last toenail and it arcs through the air like an Arab scimitar. It hits Savino in the shoulder who brushes it off. Montesano starts to put his socks and shoes back on.)

Savino

But Frank... are you sure? Do we have to? I mean I'll go along with it but you said no one would have to be killed except for that professor guy.

Montesano

Do you want to lose?

Savino

No but...

Montesano

Do you want a Democratic mayor fighting my bridge?

Savino

Our bridge.

Montesano

All right, our bridge.

Savino

But how will you do it.

Montesano

I'm going to give the old man another chance. Of course if he blows it again, he's through.

(He speaks into the intercom.)

Send Weltsmirtz in here.

Secretary

(Her voice is heard over the intercom.)

Yes Mr. Montesano

(Weltsmirtz enters.)

Montesano

Mr. Weltsmirtz, come on in, take a seat.

Savino

Hello Wilhelm.

Weltsmirtz

(He sits.)

Good day gentlemen. How can I be of service?

Montesano

Well, we have a job for you.

Savino

A job you screwed up the first time you tried it.

Montesano

Shut up, Al.

Weltsmirtz

I presume that is an indiscreet reference to the bomb at the Werth headquarters.

Savino

It is.

Montesano

I said shut up, Al. Listen, uh, Wilhelm, it is imperative that Werth be disposed of. And it absolutely must look like an accident.

(Weltsmirtz reaches into his pocket and pulls out his flask but finds it empty. Montesano pushes the button that reveals his bar.)

Feel free to fill that.

Weltsmirtz

(He walks over to the bar, fills his flask with Jack Daniel's and takes a large belt.)

I'm forever in your debt.

(He walks to the door.)

Savino

Hey, what about Werth?

Weltsmirtz

Consider it done, gentlemen. After he kicked me in the face I swore I'd kill him. And I will soon.

Montesano

Weltsmirtz, what the hell have you done?

Weltsmirtz

You'll see. I'll give you one hint, it's a work of genius.

Montesano

A word of warning. It will be very unpleasant for you if you fail again.

Weltsmirtz

I will not fail. Aufwiedersein, mein heirs.

(He walks out and closes the door behind him.)

Savino

Fucking Kraught asshole.

Montesano

Shut up, Al.

Iva took another handful of popcorn, passed three more beers to her father and his men and then took one for herself. None of them took their eyes off the television screen.

"This is in-fucking-credible!" Iva said out loud. *Ooops,* she thought, *that's the first time I've ever cursed in front of my father.*

Conrad did not notice nor divert his glance. "We've got the fucking sons of bitches," he said.

The videotape rolled on.

Savino

Why the hell are we using Weltsmirtz for this job? Why aren't we using someone more reliable?

Montesano

We will if he fails again. But I have a feeling he'll do it right this time.

Savino

I've never understood why you hired him in the first place.

Montesano

His resumé impressed me.

Savino

What?

Montesano

His resumé listed murder and torture experience in Nazi Germany.

Savino

His resumé said that?

Montesano

I swear you're brain dead, Al. What actually happened was President Richard Nixon himself called me to request I give Weltsmirtz a job as a personal favor. Actually, I had no choice.

Savino

Why?

Montesano

Why? Because I really believed Nixon would have me killed if I refused.

Savino

(He visibly shudders.)

Geez.

(The intercom buzzes. The voice of Montesano's secretary is heard.)

<u>Secretary</u>

Excuse me, but there are like twenty Boy Scouts in the conference room waiting to meet you and the Mayor.

<u>Montesano</u>

We'll be right there. Hey Al, did you see where I put those fucking merit certificates.

Agent Macy turned off the tape player. "That's all of it," he said.

Iva jumped up. "Papa, they're going to kill Brian. What do we do?"

"Don't worry," Conrad replied. "I've had a man tailing Weltsmirtz all day for just this eventuality. We won't let him anywhere near Brian."

"But he said it was *already done*. What does that mean?"

Conrad forced a smile and stroked Iva's cheek with the back of his hand to hide his concern. "Listen to me," he said to her. "It's time we went to Brian and explained the situation. This tape's going to make him a mayor."

The phone rang. Iva answered it and handed it to her father. The news on the other end made his face red with rage.

"Find him!" he yelled, slamming down the phone.

"What is it?" Iva asked.

"Our men lost Weltsmirtz," Conrad said, keeping his voice calm. He glared at his men. "The Mossad lost a fifty-eight-year-old drunk." His fists clenched and his knuckles were white. The young spies stared silently back at their superior, thankful not to be in the shoes of the agent in question. "Where is Brian?" Conrad asked Iva.

"Oh my god, I'm not sure."

"Find out, honey."

Iva hurriedly dialed the number of the headquarters. David answered.

"David, this is Iva. Is Brian there... Something's come up, I have to know where to find him... Yeah, I know the place, on Hicksville Road... No, everything's all right... Thanks, 'bye." She hung up the phone and turned to her father. "He's at Island Funland. I know where it is."

"Let's get going," Conrad said.

They all ran out to the van.

The roller coaster tilted and dipped and swerved. Brian felt that at any moment he would be shot or—even more grotesque—the car they were riding in would fly off a section of sabotaged track and send them plunging to their deaths.

Loop number one. *Christ, I'm upside down!*

"Oh baby, this is fucking great!" Belsky screamed.

Loop number two. *I don't want to die.*

"Great, just great! I'm going to be rich!"

Loop number three. *Please God, don't let me die.*

Brian felt a wave of nausea so he closed his eyes, turned his face sideways and put his head down by his knees.

"Wow, what a gr..." A razor-thin wire whipped over the roller coaster and decapitated Dominick Belsky. It missed Brian by about two seconds and a few feet. Belsky's head—severed at the top of the third loop—dropped down and lodged in the second seat of the coaster at the bottom of the loop. His headless torso, hands still gripping the safety bar, remained upright in the front seat. His head sat in the seat directly behind, face front, eyes and mouth open, and definitely missing something.

Brian remained in his fetal position, safe and unaware but vaguely conscious of a wetness on his back. After one last death defying curve the roller coaster leveled off and slowed to a crawl. Thirty feet remained for the riders to compose themselves before the car would turn into the discharge area. Brian sat straight up and looked around for any potential danger in the last few seconds of the ride. All looked normal.

"Well, we're through it," he said. "Sorry I freaked out back there."

There was no answer. Brian turned to face Belsky and saw the headless corpse. His first instinct told him not to believe his eyes. *This is a joke, a Halloween joke,* he told himself, *Jeff had something to do with it.* The roller coaster chugged along. Blood gushed out of Dominick's torso like a fountain. Brian felt his back and realized he was covered in blood, and then he saw that at least half an inch of it covered the floor. *It's real! Oh god this is real!* He looked at the body and then up at the neck. The bloody mass of torn tissue was incredible... bones and muscles and arteries stuck out between Belsky's shoulders and he looked like the *Six Million Dollar Man* waiting his turn in the repair shop. Brian was not revolted yet, he was overwhelmed, so he just stared.

The crowd waiting at the discharge area cheered when the roller coaster rolled into sight. The sound built to a crescendo then quickly died off. Everyone with a view fell silent as the car slowed to a stop. Jeff was the first person to speak.

"Holy Christ, there's blood! Brian, are you all right?"

Brian did not answer or move. He continued to stare at the body.

"Hey Brian!" Jeff slapped him on the shoulder and Brian jerked around. The sight of his friend jolted him out of his shock but when he opened his mouth no sound came out.

Jeff leaned over and gripped Brian under the armpits. He pulled him out of the roller coaster with great difficulty because Belsky's hands still held the safety bar in place. Once free, Brian found his legs were too weak to support him so he sat down on the platform. Jeff kneeled next to him.

"Are you okay?"

"Yeah... yeah, I'm okay." He pointed at Belsky's body. "Look at that!"

Jeff looked and grasped that a decapitation had taken place. There were shrieks of terror as other people came to the same realization. Mrs. Belsky fainted first with a groan and a thump as she hit the metal platform. Others, both male and female, followed and within a few seconds there were about a dozen people unconscious. Most of the crowd up front turned in panic to run away. Those in the back sensed something exciting up front and tried to push their way forward. The result was total chaos—people tripped and trampled each other.

Carlos stepped forward and said, "His head's chopped

clean off. Must be a wire across the tracks. No more rides tonight *gringos*."

"A wire!" Brian exclaimed. "A wire across the tracks that was meant for me." He grabbed Jeff by the arm. "Listen, I saw that Republican guard before."

"Where, here?"

"Yeah, against the fence."

Before anyone could stop her, Belsky's three-year-old daughter toddled over to the roller coaster car. To their horror, she addressed herself to the head that sat upright in the seat behind her father's body. "Daddy?" she said.

"Christ, get her away from there!" Brian yelled.

Jeff swooped her up and carried her off. Brian got to his feet and told the other three Belsky children to follow the man with the red hair even though he knew it was too late to prevent a lifetime of nightmares and psychotherapy. Then he grabbed the megaphone and addressed the panicked crowd: "Everyone stop pushing. Stand in place. Stop pushing. Everything will be all right. Stop pushing. Just stand still."

The crowd, thankful to have some authoritative direction, started to calm down.

"Please give those who have fainted room," he continued. He saw a patrol car pull into the parking lot. "And make room for the police to get through."

Brian ran to where Jeff was shepherding the Belsky children off the platform. "Stay with the kids and Mrs. Belsky," he told his friend. "I'm going to see if I can find that guy."

"Okay," Jeff said.

Weltsmirtz was not where he had been earlier. Brian raced to the parking lot and searched among the terrified crowd rushing to get away. None of the faces belonged to that Republican guard. He climbed up on to the hood of a car to get an overview. Still there was no sign of Weltsmirtz. A teenage boy walked by, gaped at him and exploded in vomit. Brian looked down at himself and realized his appearance had caused the discharge; his clothes were drenched in Dominick Belsky's blood and his back felt soaked through and sopping wet. He jumped off the car and looked at his hands. They were covered in blood and it had even seeped beneath his fingernails. He tried to wipe his hands but his clothes were saturated wherever he touched. Brian took two steps and vomited himself. *I've got to get this blood off me,* he thought. *A shower! Please, I've got to take a shower.* His head pounded and his vision blurred. He stumbled to his car and headed home.

It was a tortuous drive. Uncontrollable heaves seized him every couple of minutes. The first time he pulled over. The second time he hung his head out the window and nearly drove off the road. After that he threw up on his passenger seat and console, getting home as soon as possible being his only consideration.

"Come on, stop shaking," he said out loud to his hands.

When Brian reached his house, he left his car running and jumped out of his car to unlock the gate. Just as he stuck the key in the lock a gunshot ricocheted off one of the bars about a foot to his right. He did not turn around; he turned the key, squeezed through and ran. Another shot went off. It missed but Brian felt a pulse in the air near his ear. He dove off the driveway and slashed through the thorns and bristles the rest of the way to his house.

Wilhelm Weltsmirtz pounded the hood of his car and cursed. Then he slugged from his flask and took two bullets out of his breast pocket. Gun reloaded and drawn, he stalked his prey down the driveway.

Brian tried his front door but found it locked. *Fuck, my keys are back in the gate.* No one answered his knocking so he ran around to the back. It was locked too, and inside looked dark. Searching his pockets frantically on the chance he might have a spare key, his hand brushed the gun tucked into his waistband. *My gun! I totally forgot I've got my own gun! I don't have to run, I can protect myself.* He pulled the gun out.

Leaves rustled around the corner. Brian leaped off the stoop and crouched behind a rhododendron. The silhouette of the Republican guard moved into view. Brian took careful aim at his chest. *Always use two hands.* He put another hand on the gun. Weltsmirtz walked closer and he was now about twenty feet away. Brian fired: click. There was no gunshot. He fired a second time: click, again. The gun did not work. A startled Weltsmirtz turned and aimed his own weapon, but then he had to duck when Brian threw his defective gun at him. Weltsmirtz straightened and fired but his shot went wide and Brian managed to scamper around the side of the house, up a small incline and into a clump of trees.

The thick woods were a mélange of oaks, maples and firs, and in the dim light of dusk Brian collected lots of cuts and scrapes as he dashed through them. He knew his appearance probably resembled something out of *Night of the Living Dead* but only one thing really mattered: escape from the man trying to kill him. He hoped if he could cut across the Wildwood property and get down to Shore Road, someone in a passing car would stop and help him.

Brian paused under an oak tree and tried to keep his panting down so he could hear any pursuit. No one seemed to be following. He took a few more seconds to catch his breath and squinted ahead, but it was impossible to see much of anything. His mind drifted for a brief moment to how the forest looked in the daylight: beautiful, especially with the autumn color at its zenith. *About another hundred yards to the meadow then on the other side about a quarter mile of woods to the road. I've got to make it.*

Brian faced a choice when the woods thinned out; he could either run across the meadow or remain in the forest and circumnavigate. He listened for his pursuer but there was nothing but the stillness of the gathering night all around him. To his front stretched nearly two hundred yards of knee-length grass, wild and unkempt now but once the site of one of the estate's three manicured polo fields, each angled differently so the players never had to ride with the sun in their eyes. The long way around would take a lot of extra time and might allow the killer to catch up. But sprinting through the turf would be a risky short cut. He listened again and there were still no predatory sounds in the rear. Brian took off–straight ahead.

Runner's high! There really is such a thing. I am Superman! Maybe I'll run forever...

I know I'm tired but I don't feel tired, Brian thought as he raced across the meadow. Iva's image materialized in his head and he swore to her he would not let himself get killed.

He ran faster, not afraid really, just completely consumed with survival.

A shot rang out when he was about halfway across the meadow. The sound startled him and he tripped and sprawled head over heels. Not hit, he immediately sprang up and kept going. Another shot exploded and... *wait, it came from the front... I think... wait.* Another shot. *From the side... but I'm not sure... I don't think I'm hit yet.* A bullet flew overhead and he dove to the ground. *This is fucking stupid... I'm a sitting duck.* Brian knew he had to get to safety fast—but which way? He twisted around in a circle. Woods surrounded him on all sides except for up front where the Wildwood mansion stood, dark and indifferent. It was the closest cover and no shots had come from there. He got up and ran in that direction.

More shots rang out. One bullet pierced the back of his right shoulder a few feet before he would have reached the stairs leading up to the patio. The force of impact spun him around and he ended up laying on his back on the first few steps. He realized he had been shot and his pain was caused by a bullet inside him. *It missed my heart,* Brian told himself, *I'm still alive.* He pulled himself up and stumbled up the steps, tripping twice and bouncing from banister to banister like a pinball.

Brian tilted backwards on the top step and nearly fell back down, but somehow he regained his balance and pushed forward. *I am not Superman, I'm hurt,* he realized. He crossed the patio and began to pound on the sliding glass door leading into the house. "Let me in! Please! I'm hurt. I have to use the phone."

It occurred to him that Wildwood might not even have a working phone but he kept on pounding anyway. "Come on, open up!" Upstairs in his third floor bedroom, Vito the caretaker snorted and rolled over, sound asleep in a burgundy induced coma that could not have been disturbed had he been grabbed by the shoulders and shaken.

"*Stirb Amerikaner! Stirb!* " Wilhelm Weltsmirtz called out in his native German. Brian turned and saw in the moonlight the man trying to kill him. That Republican guard was about thirty feet away, aiming a gun and curling his lips into a crooked smile. "They think I'm too old," Weltsmirtz said, "but I'm not."

Brian had a brief flash of an ancient Greek amphitheater and a *deus ex mahina* descending from the sky to save the day just when everything seemed the most hopeless. *Different time... different place*, he thought as he jumped, back first, through the plate glass patio door. Weltsmirtz fired and missed. The glass shattered and splintered into a million pieces, and Brian landed inside the house on his injured shoulder. He cried out in agony and willed himself not to pass out. Shards of glass cut into his back and neck and peppered his hair, but with his good arm he managed to drag himself away from the outside. Pitch dark surrounded him. When he bumped into a wall, he inched along the baseboard until he came to a doorway. He crawled a few feet through and stopped and tried to be quiet. Keeping silent was no easy task in his condition. So many places hurt he thought he might go out of his mind... or die. He shoved a wad of his shirt in his mouth and bit down to keep from crying out.

Abruptly the lights came on throughout the mansion. Brian blinked and wondered whether he had been unconscious. Lying on his back, the first thing he saw was the ceiling, a sight that really disoriented him: blue sky and hand-painted white clouds. *Am I dead?* he wondered. He looked around him... sheets covered all the furniture. He tried to sit up. *Pain.* His shoulder still had a bullet in it and now his back was soaked in Belsky's blood and his own. Reality came roaring back. He remembered that all he had done was crawl into the first room he had come to. Somehow the lights had come on and he could expect to be found at any moment. *I've got to hide,* he realized. He crawled to the closest place he saw: behind a screen in place to conceal a dumbwaiter right next to the door.

Brian looked back at where he had lain. Red splotches covered the floor and a crimson smear trailed him to his hiding place. *When that guy comes in here I'll have to do something fast,* he told himself. He noticed a suit of armor a few feet away and thanked Divine Providence that it still held a sword.

Who the hell lived here... the Addams Family? He stood up and limped over to it, using all his strength not to cry out.

The hollow knight surrendered his grip on the sword easily. It was surprisingly heavy and Brian had only one arm he could maneuver. He carried his medieval weapon back behind the screen and leaned against the wall. He swung the sword to where his injured arm lay limply at his side and poked his finger at the tip. It was sharp and he pricked himself hard enough to draw blood. He actually chuckled silently to himself over the insignificance of the injury given the fact he was already leaking like a sieve. Then he noticed the side of the blade looked sharp enough to slice off a man's head. *Now that,* Brian thought, *would be justice.*

Footsteps sounded outside in the ballroom. They made a crunching sound on the broken glass and then echoed louder as they headed straight for him. Brian gripped the handle of his sword, choking up a bit because he knew he would get only one swing. A gun protruded through the doorway first followed slowly by an arm. Underhand, Brian brought the sword forward a short distance, then down and up and around in a full circle. At the last moment he turned the blade sideways so the flat edge made the contact with Weltsmirtz' skull causing him to collapse in a heap to the floor. Brian hovered over the body and checked if it was still breathing. It was.

"I let you live," he said. "I don't know why."

Brian stepped over Weltsmirtz and tried to walk out into the ballroom. Dizziness forced him to stop and grab hold of the doorjamb. Now his only concern was his physical condition. Two injuries took immediate precedence: the bullet in his shoulder and a huge gash on the back of his neck. Pain was not his biggest problem; Brian realized he had lost a hell of a lot of blood. *How much can a human being afford to lose?* He could not remember. *Is it one or two quarts... or is it pints?* He looked down at the blood that covered him and shivered. *I've got to find a phone fast,* he told himself, *or trip a fire alarm... something to help me get out of here.* He pushed himself out into the ballroom. Light from a crystal chandelier glistened and forced him to shade his eyes. Always the historian, he noted that the chandelier had originally been built for candles and only later converted to electricity; tiny black wires ran from the ceiling to alongside the candlesticks. He glanced around and noticed the hole his precipitous entry had made in the glass door. It was jagged and surprisingly small, and just beyond it he could see the darkness of night. The room he was in was nearly empty, filled with just a few pieces of sheet-covered furniture, so he decided to try another. He spied a door to his right and started to stumble towards it.

Brian had taken only a couple of steps when a loud clang shook him and stopped him in his tracks. He threw the one hand he could still move over his ear and bent over. The clang sounded again, so loud it actually felt like a strong wind pushing against him. He lifted his head and tried to figure out where the hell that damn noise was coming from. Not thirty feet away those two detectives who had been at the scene of Professor Sansone's murder stood facing him. Detective Dolan aimed a rifle at him. Detective Carroll was next to him holding a large mallet and preparing to strike for a third time the large Chinese gong that decades ago had served to call the aristocratic multitudes to their repast. Dolan took one hand off his rifle and grabbed Carroll by the arm.

"That's enough," he said. "Do you want to make us deaf?" He addressed Brian. "Sorry, but we had to get your attention."

Brian coughed and spit up blood. His legs buckled and he fell to his knees. The room began to spin and the walls undulated like waves. Dolan and Carroll appeared to be reflections in a fun house mirror.

"I... You... Don't... " Brian rasped. His mouth trickled blood.

"Shut up and die like a man," Dolan said. He shoved the rifle into the crook of his shoulder and sighted it.

Brian closed his eyes and thought of Iva. A shot fired and he cried out, but after a moment he realized he had not been hit. He opened his eyes and looked at Dolan. He was still standing there holding his rifle but he had a startled look on his face and a red dot in the center of his forehead. He dropped the rifle and fell to the floor. Carroll reached for his pistol but another shot rang out and a similar red dot materialized in his forehead. He dropped down on top of Dolan.

Brian remained on his knees, coughing and spitting. Conrad Fidele ran up behind him, tucking an Uzi into a holster.

"Brian, it's me, Conrad Fidele. We were back at your house and heard the shots. We're going to get you to a hospital."

"I don't feel so good," Brian said softly.

"You're going to be fine," Conrad said, not positive that would be the case. The kid looked in pretty bad shape. He noted Brian's shoulder and neck wounds and as gently as he could laid him out flat. "Just lie here and keep still," he told him.

Brian did. "I hurt," he mumbled, barely audible.

Conrad reached into Brian's back pocket and pulled out his wallet that fortunately contained a blood donor card. "Call an ambulance," he snapped to Agent Macy, "and tell them the patient will need a massive on-site transfusion of blood before he is moved. Blood type is A positive."

"Right," Macy replied, pulling a walkie talkie out of his coat pocket.

"Levinson," Conrad said. "Clean up the two dead men and get Weltsmirtz. Completely, before the ambulance gets here. You know what I mean."

"Yes sir." Levinson ran off.

Iva stuck her head through the hole Brian had made in the glass. "I'm not waiting in the car any longer," she said.

"Maybe you shouldn't... " Conrad began.

She saw Brian. "Oh my god!" She stepped in and ran to him. "Brian! What happened? Are you okay?"

"Hi," Brian said softly.

"Oh Brian, you're alive."

"I know," he said.

Iva threw off her coat and pulled her shirt over her head. Tearing with her teeth, she ripped her blouse in two; half she pressed onto Brian's neck, the other half she applied to the bullet wound in his shoulder.

"An ambulance is on the way," Conrad said. "He's lost a lot of blood."

Iva nodded but did not look up. *Don't die,* she pleaded silently. *Please don't die. I can't lose you, too.*

Brian twisted his head and tried to speak, but his mouth was full of blood so he just gurgled.

"Don't talk, just lie there," Iva told him. "Help is on the way, you're going to be all right." *God, I hope so.*

"I love you," Brian managed to whisper.

"I love you, too," Iva replied. "I love you more than anything in the world. Now shut up and lie there." She pressed harder on Brian's wounds trying to stem the bleeding but his blood continued to ooze through her fingers.

She loves him more than anything in the world, Conrad repeated to himself as he stood over them. *She really does. If he lives I'll leave them alone. I should have before.* Suddenly he noticed his daughter was topless from the waist up, no bra, nothing. He took off his coat, knelt down and wrapped it around her.

"Let me give you a hand," Conrad said, grabbing one of the white sheets off the furniture.

Chapter XVII

Nick Charles: "I'm a hero. I was shot twice in the Tribune."

Nora Charles: "I read you were shot five times in the tabloids."

Nick: "It's not true. He didn't come anywhere near my tabloids."

William Powell and Myrna Loy in ***The Thin Man*** *(1934)*

OCTOBER 23, 11:36 P.M.

Brian did not die. His injuries all proved survivable once his blood loss problem was dealt with: one bullet removed from his shoulder, fifteen stitches in the nape of his neck, bandages on all the cuts and bruises, complete recovery expected. He woke up as an orderly was wheeling him out of the operating room. Iva walked alongside.

"Where am I?" Brian asked. He really did not know.

"You're in the hospital," Iva answered. "You're going to be fine."

"I feel numb."

"Oh Brian, not here, not in the hospital."

He blinked at her through anesthetized eyes. It took him a few moments to get the joke. "Very funny. That's not what I meant," he said. He managed a weak smile.

"I know. Listen, you're sedated. They want you to rest."

"I was shot," Brian said. It was as much a question as a statement. *Is any of this real?*

Iva opened her hand in front of his face and said, "Here's what's left of the bullet." The doctors had given her a souvenir: a metallic object about the size of a thimble, twisted and bent.

This is all real, Brian told himself. He shuddered and looked away. "Am I really okay?" he asked.

"Yes you are. Nothing permanent. They said you'll heal right up."

"Will I be able to play the piano?"

"What?" Iva asked.

"Never mind," Brian said, giggling stupidly.

He was wheeled into an elevator. The orderly pushed button number three and the doors closed. Brian took Iva's hand.

"Can you stay a while?" he asked.

"As long as they'll let me."

"I love you," Brian said.

"I love you too," Iva replied, casting an embarrassed glance at the orderly, a huge black man with the physique of a linebacker.

"Don't worry," the orderly said in a surprisingly high voice. "I see mushy stuff all the time."

Once Brian and Iva were alone in his room, a nurse stuck her head in to say visiting hours were long since over but she would make an exception under the circumstances. Iva could stay for ten minutes then Brian had to sleep.

"How do you feel?" Iva asked him.

"Drugged," Brian replied. "It's like I know I'm hurting but I just can't feel it. I'm afraid when this stuff wears off I'll be in a lot of pain and have a mental breakdown from the whole experience."

"Really?" Iva asked, smoothing is hair.

"No, I won't have a mental breakdown."

"That's good."

Brian rolled onto his stomach but that felt even more uncomfortable so he rolled back onto his side; his side was going to be his only option for a couple of days. Iva noticed his rear end stuck out of a hospital gown that was not fastened tight enough. *I'd offer to fix it,* she thought, *but it's just too adorable.*

"I've got to get out of here before the election," Brian said.

"You will. The doctor said you'll only have to be here a few days."

Brian closed his eyes but fought off the sleep. "Iva... "

"Yes Brian?"

"Iva, I have to get straight in my mind what went on today. I have to get it clear."

"You will."

"It's almost like a dream to me now."

"We'll talk about it tomorrow morning,"

Brian looked at Iva but he was so tired he could barely even focus. "What was your father doing at Wildwood?" he asked.

"Looking for you."

"But why?"

"We'll talk about it tomorrow. Now listen to me. My father told me to tell you not to say a word to the police. They may try to question you because hospitals are required to report gunshot wounds. Seriously Brian, not a word."

"Two cops tried to kill me today," Brian said. "No way I'll ever talk to any of them." Then he realized what he had just said and became immediately afraid.

Iva sensed his fear and even felt it herself. It was obvious Brian was suddenly worried about being murdered in his hospital bed. "Mr. Macy," she called out. "Brian, my father has posted a man outside your door. You have nothing to worry about."

Agent Macy stuck his head in. "There's nothing to worry about Dr. Werth," he said.

"Thanks," Brian said. He took Iva's hand and Macy ducked back out the door. "I still can't understand why your father would be out there in a position to rescue me. It doesn't make any sense. None of this makes any sense."

"You'll see tomorrow, we'll both be here at nine o'clock sharp. You rest now, get some sleep." Iva leaned forward and kissed him on the lips and at the same time pinched his exposed rear end.

"I didn't even feel that," Brian said.

"Want me to try again?"

"No, just bring me some pajamas tomorrow."

"Okay, anything else?"

"Yes. Please call an Executive Committee meeting for right here in this room tomorrow afternoon. I'm still in an election don't forget."

"You're in it more than you know," Iva said. She smiled and left the room. Brian wondered what she meant by that but he was too tired to dwell on it. He closed his eyes and within thirty seconds fell fast asleep.

A blonde nurse with Annie on her name-tag woke Brian at six-forty-five the following morning. She gave him some codeine pills, which he gratefully swallowed because his shoulder still throbbed. Then she announced she was going to give him a sponge bath before breakfast.

"I'm going to help you remove your gown," she told him.

Brian noted that even though Annie was probably in her forties she was one of those older women who kept in shape and still looked quite attractive. The idea of a sponge bath embarrassed him so he gave no indication he had heard hoping she would forget the idea. Annie ignored his reticence and walked behind him. She began to fiddle with the knot at the back of his gown.

"Uh, don't you think you should at least take me to dinner first," Brian said.

"I'm a registered nurse," Annie replied, unsmiling. "This is my job."

Duly chastised, Brian allowed his ablutions to commence. His face was shaved and then his body washed all over. He did not become the least bit sexually aroused when she sponged his groin; Annie, a nurse for eighteen years, kept the water uncomfortably cool. After he was dried and dressed in a fresh hospital gown she asked him if he had ever used a bedpan before. Brian lied that he had.

"Good. You're to use the one that's here, you're not to try walking around just yet."

"I understand," Brian said. Annie turned to go. "Uh, thanks for a job well done," he added.

She turned and scowled. "Mr. Werth..."

"I know," Brian said, "you're a registered nurse. Well, thanks anyway."

"You're welcome," she replied, and then she smiled and left.

Brian immediately got up and walked to the bathroom. Never would he use a bedpan until at least the age of ninety. His shoulder throbbed during the short walk and he felt a bit lightheaded but he would never... never urinate like some kind of an invalid. Bladder empty and slipping back under the covers, he said out loud, "Mission accomplished." He mused that he should slip some apple juice into his bedpan so no one would be the wiser. *God, it's great to beat the system, he thought.*

He ate a breakfast of powdered eggs that were so bad they made him fret about whether or not there was such a thing as powdered chicken. He figured he would find out at lunch. After Annie took the tray away, a doctor inspected his wounds. There were no complications and almost immediately he fell asleep.

Iva and her father arrived promptly when visiting hours commenced at nine. Finding Brian taking a nap, they decided to let him sleep. They waited for an hour in the coffee shop downstairs and then checked on him again. This time Brian was sitting up in his bed wide awake. "Hi, would someone please tell me what the hell is going on," he said as soon as they walked in.

"Nice to see you too," Iva replied.

After a sincere inquiry into how he was feeling, Conrad launched into a thorough explanation of the bugging of Montesano's office. Brian listened impassively; what he was hearing was so outrageous he chose silence as the safest response for the time being. His first flare of emotion came when he heard Iva had been the one to retrieve the hidden camera.

"What were you thinking of? How could you risk letting her do that?" he demanded of Conrad.

"I insisted," Iva interjected. "It was up to me."

"She insisted," Conrad said. "She's difficult to argue with. I'm sure you've noticed that by now."

Brian had to admit he had noticed that. "Did you have any problems?" he asked Iva.

"None," Iva lied. Montesano's sexual assault was something she would tell him about later, way later.

Conrad described the contents of the tape they had obtained.

"Incredible," Brian commented. "Those bastards are truly as evil as we thought they were."

"Worse," Iva said.

Brian nodded but then took a deep breath and frowned. "Something else is really bothering me," he said.

"Here it comes," Conrad said, figuring Brian would get to this sooner or later.

"What?" Iva said. "What is it?" She looked at her father then back to Brian.

Brian locked eyes with Conrad. "I'm forever grateful you saved my life, but it's still wrong," he said.

"Go on," Conrad said.

"It's wrong for Israel to spy on the United States, her staunchest ally and supporter. The clandestine operations you obviously maintain are illegal and a violation of America's sovereign rights as a nation."

"What is this, a lecture?" Conrad said.

"I'm just speaking my mind," Brian said.

"Here we go," Iva said, throwing her hands up and turning away from the bedside.

"Oh, you mean Israel does to the United States what the United States has done to the rest of the world for the better part of this century," Conrad said.

"It's not the same thing," Brian said.

"Yes it is." Conrad nearly shouted.

"Papa, please keep your voice down," Iva said.

"I'm sick and tired of your American double standards," Conrad continued. "Vietnam, Indonesia, Chile, all of Central America... Christ, the United States has been everywhere. Israel needs to survive and that is more important then silly platitudes about sovereignty."

"What a good friend Israel is," Brian said, facetiously.

"Your alliance with Israel is greatly to America's advantage," Conrad said.

"The Rosenbergs, Jonathan Pollard, the *USS Liberty*, what are friends for?" Brian went on. "You ever wait on a gas line?"

"Brian, you would be dead now if it wasn't for the Mossad," Iva cut in. "Would you please realize that? You know, you could be grateful,"

"This is the real world..." Conrad persisted.

"... not a classroom," Brian finished for him. "I understand that." He closed his eyes and as gently as he could lowered his head back onto his pillow. He knew he was losing the argument and, worse, sounded like an ingrate. "Thank you with all my heart for saving my life," he said. "I didn't mean to... "

"The issues we're discussing are complicated," Conrad cut in diplomatically.

"Yes they are," Brian agreed. *I'm not sure what's right anymore,* he thought to himself, *but I do know that "saying things are complicated" is not a sufficient justification for bullshit behavior.* His head started to hurt. He decided to let the matter drop for the time being. "Thank you, again, for saving my life," he said.

"No thanks are necessary," Conrad said. "Now would you please tell us what happened to you before we got there."

Brian recounted the roller coaster incident as best he could remember it. Iva interjected she had heard on the news that Dominick Belsky's death was accidental.

"They're covering up," Brian said.

"Of course," Conrad said. "And notice the Sagamore police are not even bothering to question you about how you got shot. They know how." He adjusted the strap on his eye patch. "Go on now, what happened after you drove home?"

Brian told of his flight from Weltsmirtz across the Wildwood property. He found it difficult to find the right words to describe the peculiar exhilaration he felt after the bullet entered him and he realized he was still alive. "You feel lucky and you get a sense of being at the mercy of something like fate... or... God... or something."

"Go ahead please," Conrad said with a hint of impatience at Brian's philosophizing.

Iva interrupted immediately to diffuse the potentially awkward moment. "We drove home after we couldn't find you at the roller coaster." she said. "We heard the shots in the distance. That's when we drove up to the mansion."

Brian nodded and went on with his side of the story. Iva gasped out loud when she heard Weltsmirtz had held him at point blank range on the patio. When Brian told them he had deliberately jumped through the plate glass door, Conrad nodded openly in admiration. *This kid's got one hell of a survival instinct,* he thought to himself.

"And I finally knocked out Weltsmirtz," Brian continued. "I didn't kill him, did I?"

"No, you didn't," Conrad answered him. "You should have, he got away. We searched the house and grounds as best we could before the police got there, but there was no sign of him."

"You mean he's still out there?" Brian said.

"He's still out there," Conrad affirmed. "But he won't be for long. My men are looking for him. Weltsmirtz is a wounded animal on the run. We'll get him."

"He'll come after me again," Brian said. He had no doubt.

"Papa's supplying you with a bodyguard," Iva cut in. "And you're not going anywhere alone."

"A bodyguard is at your service twenty-four hours a day," Conrad explained, "provided you accept the protection."

"He accepts," Iva said.

"I accept," Brian agreed. "I'd be stupid not to." *I'm not going to die for some stupid principle.* He exhaled and looked at the ceiling. "I should have killed him," he said.

"We'll kill him," Conrad said flatly.

"Good luck to you," Brian replied.

"Thanks," Conrad said. "Now you listen to me carefully. It's important we handle this whole thing a certain way."

"I'm listening."

Conrad's main concern was that the Mossad's involvements in the affair remain a secret. "Our operations in this country are clandestine and must at all costs remain that way," he explained. Towards that end he asked Brian and Iva never to reveal the source of the surveillance tape. "And as far as the deaths of the two detectives are concerned, you know nothing about that. They've already been found in a car alongside the service road of the Expressway burned beyond recognition."

Iva looked at the floor. This was a side of her father she had never seen. She supposed she had always known it was there but seeing it in person for the first time repulsed her. The barbaric realities of his profession had turned him into a brutal man. She felt sorry for him and at the same time thankful for his strength and support.

"You've got my word," Brian told him, thinking as he spoke how his own morality had changed in the past few months. *Here I am acquiescing to an illegal cover-up simply because it's for the cause of good,* he thought. Apparitions of H.R. Halderman and John Ehrlichman flickered across his mind. *God, it is possible to think like that.*

"I promise too Papa," Iva said. She still could not look at him.

"Oh, on the subject of Weltsmirtz..." Conrad began.

Brian nodded. "Weltsmirtz is a dead man, isn't he?"

"Yes he is," Conrad said. He clapped his hands together as if at a party. "I guess I'll be on my way. Now as far as the surveillance tape is concerned I suggest..."

"We've got a big problem with that," Brian interjected. "It's illegally obtained evidence—*the fruit of the poisonous tree* we call it in this country. It's not admissible in court. There's no way around it."

"Yes there is," Conrad said.

"How?" Brian said.

"Welcome to the real world, Brian," Conrad said.

"How?" Brian repeated, raising his voice.

"Calm down, both of you," Iva said.

"Just tell me," Brian said.

"We—the Mossad if you will—have connections with certain officials in Washington. The fact that Weltsmirtz is suspected of crimes in other states theoretically makes it possible for the Justice Department to become involved. The United

States District Attorney in Brooklyn will take the tape, a judge will post date a warrant, and he'll claim his office legally conducted the surveillance."

"I can't believe it," Brian said incredulously.

"Believe it," Conrad said.

"The Mossad..." Brian paused to gather his thoughts.

"The Mossad is deeply connected inside the United States' government," Conrad finished for him. "You wouldn't believe how deeply. Just as the Central Intelligence Agency is deeply involved in the Middle East." He shrugged. "It's... it's..."

"Symbiotic," Iva said.

"It's illegal," Brian said.

"Precisely," Conrad said. "You're both right." He smiled and patted his daughter gently on the top of the head. Iva felt like a twelve-year-old again and did not like the feeling.

"It's absolutely unbelievable," Brian said.

"Yes it is," Conrad said. "And little risk for the U.S. Attorney because no one would ever believe such an outrageous scenario much less be able to prove it."

"Well..." Brian said.

"Thank you," Iva said.

"Yes, thanks for everything," Brian said. He felt absolutely helpless.

"You're welcome," Conrad said. "See you around." He shook hands with his future son-in-law, kissed his daughter on the cheek and was gone.

Brian and Iva looked at each other then she walked to him and they embraced. He responded with the one arm he could move. They closed their eyes and did not bother to speak for about a minute.

"Iva," Brian finally whispered, "I feel..."

"I know," she whispered back, "I feel the same way."

"Dirty."

"Yeah, dirty."

"But right now I can't think of any other way to..."

"I can't think of one, either."

Brian pulled back and looked in Iva's eyes. "We do what we've gotta do to survive," he said.

"Yes," Iva said.

They embraced and fell silent again.

"Uh, I have an even bigger problem," Brian said after about a minute.

"What is it?"

"I have to call my parents to let them know I'm in the hospital."

"You haven't told them yet?"

"No, I've been putting it off. My mother will overreact... to put it mildly."

Iva picked up the phone and placed it next to him on the bed. "Go ahead, you've got to do it."

Brian reached his father first at home and it was still morning so he took the news with unruffled dignity. Harvey Werth was shocked and concerned for his son but relieved the emergency had passed and everything was on the mend. When Brian interrupted his mother in the middle of hostessing a Sagamore Garden Club brunch, as predicted, she did not take the news well. She cried, "Oh my boy, I'll be right there!" and dropped the phone before he could even begin to calm her down. Static crackled in his ear and the line went dead so Brian carefully hung up the receiver and rolled his eyes at Iva.

"I expect my mother will be here presently," he said.

Iva laughed. "She loves you. I'm sure she'll settle down once she realizes you're going to be all right."

"I need you here for moral support," Brian said.

"Okay, you've got it," Iva replied.

Arlene Werth burst in seventeen minutes later. She was clad in a transparent rain hat and a full-length mink coat. She gasped and put her hands to her mouth when she saw Brian's bandages.

"Try to relax Mom," Brian said quickly. "I'm going to be fine."

"They... they... told me you've been shot," his mother cried.

"That's true," Brian replied, "But everything's going to be okay."

Arlene started to swoon. Iva helped her into a chair and got her a glass of water. She sipped at it and then walked tentatively to the bedside. She kissed her son on the forehead and stroked his cheeks.

"Are you sure you're all right dear?"

"Positive. I'm getting out in a couple of days in plenty of time for the election."

"You look pale. I'll bring you a casserole."

"That would be nice. Any food not powdered would be greatly appreciated."

"My poor boy," Arlene said, still stroking his cheek.

Iva reached into her pocket and held out her hand. "Here's the bullet they took out of him," she said.

Arlene swooned again.

"I'm really sorry," Iva said. "I didn't mean to..." She helped Mrs. Werth back into the chair and got her another glass of water.

"I'm so sorry," Arlene said, fanning herself. "It's just that the thought of a bullet inside my Brian makes me..." She shuddered.

Iva slipped the bullet back into her pocket and Arlene Werth once again approached the bedside.

"It's all over now, Mom," he assured her.

"Listen Brian," his mother began, "This political thing you're involved in is much too dangerous. I wish you'd give it up."

Brian looked away. He knew what was coming, he had heard it too many times.

"You know I can still talk to Ralph Hayes at Morgan Brothers. He said he'll take you on any time."

"Mom, I've told you before I'll die before I become an investment banker." *Whoops, I almost did,* he realized.

Iva smiled, trying to picture Brian in a pinstriped suit. He deftly changed the subject and the three of them chatted for about fifteen minutes before Arlene finally left, promising to return in the evening with some food and his father.

As soon as his mother left Brian remarked to Iva, "Nice move with the bullet."

"Sorry," Iva said.

"Don't worry. Overall, it went well. My mother did not insult you once. I think she's beginning to accept you."

"Sure, like most pregnant women accept morning sickness."

"What?"

"Nothing."

Iva insisted that Brian take a nap before the Executive Committee meeting at one. He readily complied and slept for about an hour while Iva sat reading a magazine and occasionally straightening his blanket. A nurse woke him for lunch at 12:15 and at least the baked chicken breast and cottage cheese were edible and real. After lunch Brian had to admit he felt a bit better; his shoulder still hurt but maybe a little less. He rubbed his eyes and tried to brush his hair into some semblance of order but the bed-head cowlicks prevailed.

"Please get your father's men to bring over the videotape," he asked Iva. "I can't wait to see this thing."

"Sure," Iva replied.

The Executive Committee arrived en masse at one o'clock sharp. Debbie bought two dozen red and white carnations. Marcus gave him the latest edition of *Playboy.* "Can you believe they're triplets?" he said, pointing to the front cover. Jeff produced a six-pack of beer from beneath his jacket and placed it under the bed. "Just so you know it's there," he explained. David proffered the latest edition of the *Wall Street Journal's Guide to Managing Your Money.*

"But I don't have any money," Brian said, smiling.

"You can dream can't you?" David said.

"Thank you all," Brian said.

Marcus walked to the foot of the bed. "I hereby call this meeting to order," he said. "And I think I speak for all of us when I ask you Brian, what the hell is going on?"

"Okay, here goes..." Brian began.

The door opened a crack. "Wait for me!" a voice pleaded. An orderly pushed a wheelchair containing Bill Nuss into the room.

"I stopped by his room and invited him," Iva whispered.

"Hey... way to go!" Brian exclaimed.

The entire Executive Committee cheerfully surrounded their late arriving member. They patted him on the back, but gently; a bandage still covered the top third of his head and his left arm remained in a sling. Iva and Debbie kissed him on his cheeks at the same time.

"Aw... shucks," Nuss said, hamming it up. The orderly deposited him next to Brian and left. "As one victim of the system to another," Nuss said to Brian, "welcome to Sagamore Community Hospital."

Brian nodded solemnly. "Thanks."

"What happened to you?" Nuss asked.

"That's what we'd all like to know," Marcus said.

Brian recounted his roller coaster to Wildwood ordeal, noting with a certain satisfaction his friends' looks of amazement. He did not mention Iva's father or the Mossad and Detectives Dolan and Carroll were left completely out of the story; Brian lied that after knocking out Weltsmirtz he had found a phone and called for an ambulance himself. The stares and open mouths persisted as Iva revealed the bugging of Montesano's office and the results. She concluded by explaining only that it had been "arranged."

"There are certain things we can't tell you," Brian cut in. "Please understand. I've even got to ask you to keep your speculations to yourselves."

There were general nods of assent. It was obvious Brian and Iva had received external assistance and everyone had a pretty good idea where it had come from. They all knew Iva well enough to be aware her father used to work for Israeli intelligence... probably he still did. Iva guessed her friends were adding two plus two...

"Please don't ask who helped us," she said, "even if you think you know. We really can't say anything."

"Consider the issue closed," Marcus said and everyone nodded agreement.

"Where is Weltsmirtz now?" Debbie asked.

Brian tried to answer but he found himself stuttering... "He's uh uh uh out out..."

Iva helped him out. "Weltsmirtz is still at large. Somehow he escaped before the police arrived. But we've arranged for Brian to have a twenty-four hour bodyguard."

The sound of a throat clearing indicated David was about to speak. "This whole thing is incredible, absolutely incredible," he said. "I want to see this tape of Montesano. Is that what the tape player is here for?"

"That's right," Brian said. "Are we all ready?"

Everyone vigorously affirmed they were.

"Then let's watch."

"Oh boy!" Marcus exclaimed, literally jumping up and down and clapping his hands together.

"Isn't there anything else on?" Jeff said as the first images flickered on the TV screen.

"Pipe down," Debbie said.

It was the most memorable recording any of them had ever seen. Savino's nonchalant reference to Alan Sansone's murder roared out like a pile driver and rekindled anger that had been buried for months. When Montesano uttered the words "my bridge" Marcus smacked his fist into his palm and cried out, "I knew it!" Montesano's order to Weltsmirtz to "Kill Werth" was chilling and everyone found themselves stealing a glance at Brian to make sure he was still all right. Brian himself actually derived a certain strength from watching the tape again; he knew he had survived and the ending wasn't written yet. Montesano's tasteless joke about Weltsmirtz having experience in Nazi Germany disturbed only Iva. World War II had ended over thirty-five years ago and its memory was just the stuff of textbooks and movies. To all of them but Iva, Holocaust was only a word.

No one said anything when the tape finished, they all just stood there trying to digest what they had just seen and heard. Brian looked at Iva and she smiled back. He felt he needed to find some way to thank both her and her father in a more substantive way. The Mossad had neatly done what the entire safe stealing fiasco had failed utterly to accomplish.

Nuss spoke first. "Wow," he said.

Marcus threw his fist into the air. "We've got them! The Republicans are nailed to the wall!"

"And Sagamore Bridge comes tumbling down," Jeff added.

"But it's illegally obtained evidence," David pointed out.

"Taken care of," Brian said.

"Incredible," David said.

Nurse Annie walked into the room and stopped short when she noticed the crowd. "Hey, you're allowed a maximum of three visitors at a time," she said.

"They're leaving in a few minutes," Brian said.

"They'd better," Annie said, "otherwise I might have to give you another bath." She winked and left.

"She gave you a bath!" Iva exclaimed.

"Yes, but we're just friends," Brian said.

Marcus ignored the diversion. "Listen, where should we take the tape? Certainly not around here."

"We should take it to the U.S. District Attorney in Brooklyn," Brian said.

"Brooklyn!" David said. "They wouldn't have jurisdiction in this case."

"It's been arranged," Brian said.

"I should have figured that," David said.

There was a moment of silence for a moment then Debbie spoke up. "I guess in this case the ends justify the means," she said.

"Niccolò Machiavelli," Marcus said in a quiet voice.

Brian felt embarrassed. He knew he was asking his friends to participate in something illegal, and whether or not it was also immoral was open to debate. "I feel like... uh... uh... " he began, but he stopped in mid-sentence.

"Like Abraham Lincoln," Nuss suddenly burst out. "Remember, you told us in class that President Lincoln totally blew off the Constitution when he ordered the arrest of members of the Maryland state legislature to keep them from joining the Confederacy."

Brian had not felt at all like Abraham Lincoln but Nuss' analogy struck him as something worth contemplation. *How come my students are smarter than I am?* he thought.

"That's one way to look at it," Brian said. "Certainly it's the best way for us right now. But don't forget, Lincoln got away with it because he won."

Iva removed the cassette from the tape player, closed it inside its plastic cover and placed it inside her shoulder bag. "I'm ready to drive to the U.S. Attorney's Office right now," she said. "Anyone want to come along?"

They all wanted to go. Iva kissed Brian and promised to return as soon as possible. Marcus promised to call with a progress report. The room cleared quickly and Brian found himself alone except for Nuss in his wheelchair.

"Want to play some cards?" Nuss asked. "It'll make waiting a lot easier. How about a couple rounds of Go Fish?"

"Sure, I'll play," Brian said.

Chapter XVIII

"Yes—and again, no."

Warren William and Bette Davis teach gubernatorial candidate Guy Kibbee to be vague when he is questioned by the press in ***The Dark Horse*** *(1932)*

OCTOBER 24, 3:30 P.M.

"The Tape" caused quite an uproar from the moment Iva turned it over to the district attorney. Donald Preston, a prosecutor who for nearly ten years had been attempting to indict Montesano for something... anything... kept running the video over and over and calling associates into his office to enjoy the show with him.

"This is pretty cut and dried," Preston told the group. "We've nailed a couple of lower officials over the years but never gotten close to Montesano. Two years ago I thought we were going to get him for mail fraud but he slithered away. But this tape will do it." He tapped the cassette's box. "Yup, this will definitely do it." He rubbed his eyes and sniffled, and it became evident he was on the verge of tears. "I do believe we've got him," he added, still not seeming to believe it.

"And Mayor Savino?" Iva asked.

"And Mayor Savino," Preston affirmed.

"Weltsmirtz?" Marcus asked.

"As good as convicted. Of course, someone's got to catch him first." Preston paused and took a moment to look all of them in the eye. "Of course, you've all got to forget you ever knew anything about this tape. As far as anyone knows it was our operation from the start. A judge will post-date a warrant."

"If it ever comes up I promise we'll all plead the third," Iva said. She was better with Israeli law.

"If somehow it does get out how we really got this tape, no one will ever believe it and it will be impossible to prove," Preston said. "I think we're safe."

"How soon can you..." Marcus began. "What I mean is... the election is... when will..."

"I understand what you're trying to say," Preston said. "We'll move fast, we have everything we need right here." He stroked the tape cassette as if it was a Cheshire cat. "There's no need to sit on it."

"Will you move to indict before Election Day?" David asked.

"We'll want to talk to Werth and piece things together," Preston replied. "But the answer to your question is yes, we most assuredly will take action well before Election Day."

Two days later, the U.S. District Court in Brooklyn issued warrants for the arrest of Montesano, Savino and Weltsmirtz. Preston, simply because Montesano had been his white whale for so long, at the last minute tipped off a photographer friend employed by the Associated Press. The wire service supplied the world with a picture of Frank and Al being led out of a restaurant by federal marshals, a priceless montage of dumbfounded looks, handcuffs and lobster bibs. *Newsday* carried it on its front page the next day.

The two men were in custody for less than two hours. They were arraigned and released in their own recognizance after each posted a fifty thousand dollar bond.

"We deny everything," Montesano growled to the battery of reporters outside the courthouse.

"And I am definitely still running for reelection," Savino added.

"So many questions flew at them no single one was audible. "No comment," Montesano hissed. "Out of my way!" They elbowed their way to a waiting limousine where a chauffeur, newly hired, opened the door for them.

Although authorities had no clue where to find Weltsmirtz, the case against Montesano and Savino progressed rapidly. Three days after their arraignment they were brought before a federal judge for a probable cause hearing. The two men were formally indicted; both were charged with a litany of offenses including one count of second-degree murder and three counts of solicitation to commit murder. Then after they surrendered their passports, they were allowed to post bail set at two hundred thousand dollars apiece.

The story continued to receive major media coverage. Television newscasts led with it and newspapers gave it banner headlines on the front page. Frank, Al and Brian became national celebrities. At the request of Preston, Brian refused to comment specifically on the case. He said only that he believed the charges to be true and he stuck to that even when confronted personally by the likes of Connie Chung and Ted Koppel. For their part, Montesano and Savino railed over and over that they were being framed by a left-winger desperate to win an election and undermine the United States.

"He's almost certainly a Communist," Savino told the *Washington Post* which declined to print the quote. Henrietta Wilcox left no doubt about her sympathies as once again she used the *Sagamore Record* as her own personal mouthpiece: **SAVINO DENIES VICIOUS SLANDER BY WERTH** blared her latest banner headline.

The general public never saw the "Montesano Tape," the theory being that leaking it would make it impossible to find unbiased jurors for the trial, expected to begin in February at the earliest. Montesano and Savino denied the existence of the tape and claimed the U.S. Attorney's office was involved in a vendetta against them. Even in private Montesano doubted the tape.

"Do you really think they have a tape of us?" Savino had asked him.

"No, impossible," Montesano replied.

"But what if they do?"

"They don't. This is all a game, one big fucking game. And we're going to win it, Al. We always do."

Montesano and Savino had only been indicted, not convicted, and as such they were free to continue in their present positions for the time being. So courted was Montesano's G.O.P. organization that not a single Republican official anywhere ventured a criticism. "No prejudgments, let the legal system run its course," was the Republican spin from the White House on down. The pundits were at a loss to predict the effect the arrests would have on the election. They did not hurt Brian, they obviously helped him, but no one really knew to what extent. Savino was damaged, but enough to lose? Brian remembered the career of New York City's Mayor Jimmy Walker, an absolute reprobate who successfully combined lawbreaking with victories at the polls. He also knew that American history was fraught with politicians who had passed away... died... actually croaked... during their campaigns and been elected to office anyway.

In the remaining few days before the election, the Sagamore Republicans ratcheted up Savino's campaign as much as they could while trying not to make him seem desperate. At giant outdoor rallies the indictments were decried as threats to personal liberty and justice. Radio commercials, up to one every half hour on four area stations, bluntly accused the Justice Department of collaborating with Brian Werth in an attempt to use false charges to discredit two lifelong public servants.

"They are afraid of Al Savino," claimed the ads, "because he is an honest man." For his part Al smiled and waved and denied, and then smiled and waved and denied some more.

"We're not going to let ourselves get beat by lies and innuendoes," Montesano told three hundred city workers and their families who were summoned to Roosevelt Park the evening before Election Day. "We're going to win!"

"I am not running for mayor to benefit myself or any other individual," Savino told the crowd. "I'm running for mayor to protect the United States of America from her enemies!"

Red, white and blue fireworks exploded overhead and the band broke into "You're a Grand Old Flag."

More than two hundred people showed up at the **WERTH FOR MAYOR** general campaign meeting the afternoon before the election. The Sagamore Moose had offered the use of their auditorium and Brian had gratefully accepted. The whole scene had the aura of a Hollywood movie premier; an overflow crowd lined the walls of the hall while photographers pushed to the front to immortalize the event. Marcus banged a gavel and introduced Brian. Cheering erupted and strobe lights popped as he took the stage. He instinctively started to raise his right hand to wave to the throng, but he winced and lowered it immediately. His shoulder still throbbed so his left hand would have to handle the waving.

"We're looking good!" Brian yelled into the microphone causing the cheering to raise itself a notch. When the tumult showed no signs of abating after a full minute, he felt his face beginning to flush red; the hero worship embarrassed him though he imagined it would not be so bad once one got used to it. He waved his good arm to get them to quiet down. "Thank you! Thank you everyone, but we've still got one more day!"

The applause trickled off. "I want you, Brian!" a young woman yelled out as if she was addressing Burt Reynolds. Everyone laughed and a few of the more astute noted how politics and show business were first cousins.

"Thank you," Brian began. "As we come down to the wire, there are a few things I would like to say and a number of individuals I would like to thank specifically."

He mentioned each member of his Executive Committee by name. They all received loud applause, especially Nuss who was still in the hospital. Then Brian thanked all the volunteers and everyone in the past few months who had offered their support in one form or another. Next he talked off the cuff, projecting his words, crisp and clear, using oratorical skills honed even further by the campaign. *The day before the election is a time to project confidence and make everyone feel good,* Brian had decided. "We've got a real shot to win tomorrow, and I know we will," he continued. This line got huge applause. "But most important of all, we've all got to remember what this campaign stands for." There was more applause though not as loud. Next, Brian went on to hammer yet again at Montesano's bridge; it was no longer a joke, people were beginning to believe him. In the same vein, he decried the corrupt Republican machine that had been allowed to dominate Long Island government for so long. Once more with feeling he cautioned that blind conservatism was too easy a response to the pressures of difficult times, "The Republican right believes in giving up. They say all government is automatically bad. I say if it's broken, we'll fix it. We'll never abandon the people." Then he added that single-issue political action groups—like the Baby Protectors—often do much more harm than good. "Our forefathers knew what they were doing when they put the separation of Church and State into our Constitution. No matter what the issue, we must never forget that."

With the shock of having their current mayor indicted on murder charges, most people in the room listened intently, almost desperately so, to Brian's every word. He noted their intensity and was moved by it; never had he generated such intensity as an educator. All eyes stared at him. He was in command.

"We must not forget the lessons of history," Brian was inspired to say. "And we must never let go of our youth. We learned many important lessons growing up in the sixties. But in remembering we must not ignore the future. If we stick together and work hard, our future will be better." To his surprise the line got applause and he noticed to his left Roger Dunlin had tears in his eyes. "We're going to win tomorrow," Brian continued, raising his voice. "We're going to beat Savino!" There was more applause. "Once again, I want to thank all of you for your support. What we're doing is important. We will succeed. Good-bye and..." *Yes, it's right.* "Peace." He flashed a peace sign then turned his hand around into the Winston Churchill's traditional **V for Victory** salute. "Peace and Victory both!"

Brian's speech worked to perfection. The crowd heard what they wanted to hear and they rose to their feet in a standing ovation. A lot of peace signs flashed back. More than a few of the yuppies cried, some remembering Vietnam or Woodstock or both, some just reflecting on their youth that was forever gone. Some of them felt young again, and it felt good.

Marcus started to escort Brian up the center aisle of the auditorium but the crush of the audience stopped them in their tracks. Well-wishers pushed toward them and there was a danger someone might trip and get trampled.

"Let's go out the back through the kitchen," Marcus said.

"Right," Brian replied.

They turned and started to go out the back but after a couple of steps Brian stopped in his tracks. Marcus stopped also and they faced each other. They were both thinking the same thing.

"Rosey," Brian said to Marcus.

"Robert," Marcus said.

They stared at each other.

"This is ridiculous," Brian said.

"Yeah, but let's squeeze our way out the front anyway," Marcus said.

"I agree," Brian said. "This is too weird."

They turned around and proceeded to elbow their way through the friendly crowd. Inside the kitchen, Wilhelm Weltsmirtz cursed and started to unscrew the silencer on his revolver.

The rest of the Executive Committee divided the volunteers into groups and began to map Election Day strategy. Pamphlets were handed out for distribution at the city's busiest polling places—from at least a hundred feet away as required by law. Phone canvassers received lists of people to call to remind them to vote—Democrats this time, to get out the sure vote—and carpools organized to offer rides to the polls for any elderly or handicapped who requested them. Excitement and expectation permeated the room.

Once they got out front, a reporter asked the candidate what he thought his chances were. "Good, real good," Brian replied.

He meant it. He honestly thought he was going to win though he understood nothing in politics was ever certain. History had taught him that. *I might lose,* he thought, *but if I were a betting man I'd bet on me.* The volunteers bustled around him. Their spirit infected his and he felt like he could run forever.

"Would you please come on to bed?" Brian yelled to Iva who was in the bathroom. "I'm too nervous about tomorrow to sleep. I need some companionship." He was trying to decide whether or not he wanted sex.

"I'll be right there," Iva yelled back.

He was in a playful mood and decided to tease her. "For crying out loud, what are you doing in there? Why do women always take so long in the bathroom? Guys don't, they're in, they're out... it's no big deal. Women sometimes have to read an instructional booklet just to figure out what the heck they're doing."

Iva stuck her head out. "If you're in such a hurry, you can go out into the garage and seduce a lug wrench."

Brian smiled and put his hands behind his head. He almost always enjoyed it when they razzed each other. "Are you having one of those woman things, dear?" he said in his most obnoxiously sweet voice. Brian called Iva's period a "woman thing" whenever he wanted to make her mad. She hated the expression and sometimes retaliated by referring to his penis as "that cute little pencil dick."

This time she walked solemnly out of the bathroom. "For your information," she said, "I haven't had my..."

"Would you just come on to bed," Brian interrupted. "Tomorrow's the big day."

"Okay," Iva replied. She slipped under the covers next to him.

Her hands and feet were freezing and Brian shivered. He grabbed her hands and started rubbing them. "Come on, warm up," he whispered.

"Brian..."

"I know exactly what you're going to say."

"You do?" She doubted that he did.

"Yup."

"What did you think I was going to say?"

"Go ahead and say it."

"No, you go ahead and say what you thought I was going to say," she told him.

"Okay, you were going to say you're still going to love me whether or not I win tomorrow."

Iva sighed and hugged him. "That was it," she said.

"I wonder if I'll win tomorrow?" Brian mused, staring up at the ceiling.

Iva lifted herself up on one elbow. "Remember when Alan Sansone said the American people love to vote the scoundrels out? Tomorrow, I think it will happen."

"Maybe the people will think we're the scoundrels with false charges and phony evidence."

"I don't think so," Iva said. "Oh!" she exclaimed, remembering something and hopping out of bed.

Cold air seeped under the covers and Brian shivered again. He ruled out sex for the night.

"What are you doing?" he asked.

Iva took an envelope off her bureau and handed it to him. "Someone gave me this to show to you. The National Rifle Association says they mailed out five thousand of these."

Brian ripped it open. Inside was a picture of Al Savino posing next to a dead deer strapped to the roof of a car. Wearing a Mexican sombrero and with a rifle slung over his shoulder and two belts of ammunition crisscrossed on his chest, he looked just like Pancho Villa. A caption underneath the picture lauded Savino for his stance on gun control and accused Brian of caring only about the rights of criminals.

"Ha, this is great!" Brian cried. "A guy indicted for murder posing with his gun and something else he's killed. Boy did those NRA assholes backfire on this one!"

"It is not a subtle subtext," Iva said, remembering what her English professor always used to say.

"As good an example of poetic justice as anything I've ever seen," he said.

"The picture has a doppelgänger," she added, continuing to reference her former teacher.

"It sure does," Brian agreed. He put the picture on his bedside table and turned off the light.

"Tired?" Iva asked.

"Exhausted. Let's go to sleep and wake up tomorrow and find out where we stand."

Iva did not answer. She rested her head on his chest and closed her eyes. Brian closed his eyes and within a couple of minutes they were both fast asleep.

Chapter XIX

"I'm going to run. You can't stop me.
I'm going to run even if I don't get a single vote."

Broderick Crawford is defiant after his son is beaten up and a rock thrown through his window in ***All the King's Men*** *(1949)*

ELECTION DAY, 6:00 A.M.

Brian and Iva got up at six in the morning on Election Day. Together they prepared an ode to cholesterol—bacon, eggs, home fries, toast, orange juice and coffee—and bustled about like expectant children on Christmas morning. Marcus called at six-thirty to inform Brian that all polling places had opened half an hour earlier without incident. "And our own Election Day strategy is progressing as planned," he added. Brian thanked him and asked him if he had voted yet.

"Sure did, first one on line," Marcus replied.

"Who did you vote for?" Brian asked.

"Savino. I had second thoughts at the last minute."

They both laughed and Brian told his friend he would be at the headquarters as soon as he voted himself at seven sharp. He knew he had to be prompt; he was a media star now and he had promised to appear at the early time so reporters could get their footage of the candidate voting in time for the morning news broadcasts.

Marcus told him to make it snappy and reminded him that, "The campaign is not officially over until the polls close at nine tonight." On this the final day Brian planned to visit a senior center, bowling alley, and two supermarkets for the road.

"See you at the headquarters sometime this morning," Brian said. "And thanks."

He noticed as he started to pull on his pants that Iva suddenly seemed depressed. He guessed what was wrong.

"Don't worry about it," he said, sitting next to her.

"I can't help it," she said.

"It's not that important."

"But it is," Iva insisted. "To be so much a part of your campaign and not even be allowed to vote..."

Brian kissed her cheek. "Citizens of foreign countries are not allowed to vote in our elections. The United States is funny that way."

"I know but I still feel terrible," Iva said. "I want so badly to vote for you."

Brian snapped his fingers, walked over to her bureau and took out two silk scarves. He quickly fashioned two slings, pulled them around his neck and put his arms through. "Look, I'm handicapped," he said. "I can't work the voting machine myself, they'll have to let you help me."

"Yippee!" Iva cried, leaping to her feet. "Let's get going!"

Abigail Weaser had served as poll captain at the Sagamore Intermediate School—Brian's local polling place—since Kennedy/Johnson had defeated Nixon/Lodge in the wee hours of November 3, 1960. This morning the turnout was heavy and the line to enter the voting machines snaked down the hall. She slid her reading glasses down her nose and looked disdainful when Brian walked up with his makeshift injuries; she had seen more than her share of that type of stunt over the years.

"I fell off my roof," he told her.

"Of course you did, dear," Abigail replied.

She did not contest Brian's request to have Iva assist him in the voting booth—election law allowed for the handicapped to have help. Brian and Iva walked in together and Iva threw the handle sideways to close the curtain behind them. The curtain would reopen and their vote officially counted when they threw the handle back.

"There it is," Brian said. He pointed to his name, one among a row of local office seekers. "It's beautiful, this is a thrill."

Al Savino had been endorsed by both the Republican and Conservative parties so his name appeared twice on the ballot. The second endorsement was only a slight advantage, meaningful only if the race turned out extremely tight. Brian had not been offered the Liberal party endorsement because they had given it mechanically for the last five elections to a retired orthodontist named Bruce Koken. Koken had never been a factor in the race; in fact, in early September he had suffered a stroke and been comatose ever since, but his name remained on the ballot regardless. Brian and Iva both wondered how many votes the invalid would get.

"Well, let's vote," Brian finally said. He took off his slings. "You can help me."

"You want to vote straight Democratic?" Iva asked him.

"Nope. There's a judge, O'Connor, and he's been around since I was a kid. He's Republican but independent-minded and a good guy. Vote all Democratic except for Francis O'Connor." He felt a strange sense of loyalty to the local party organization that had offered him virtually no support. Most of the Democrats were jerks, almost as bad as the Republicans, but the lesser of two evils made much more sense than abstention.

They both flipped down all the appropriate levers. Iva flipped Brian's lever down for a moment then flipped it back up. "I just wanted to see how it would feel," she said. "You do it for real."

Brian voted for himself.

"Brian, I love you," Iva said.

"I love you, too."

They kissed passionately inside the booth. There were snickers from the people on line who could tell what was going on from the tangle of legs visible beneath the curtain. Abigail Weaser put her hands on her hips, stamped her foot and huffed, "Honestly!"

Breaking their clinch, Brian and Iva both put their hands on the big lever and... together... pushed it sideways the way it came. Their vote was official. The curtain opened and the cameras got pictures of Brian and Iva smiling and waving and looking confident.

"That was quick and easy," Brian said once they were outside. "Let's go home. I have time for a quick run before I head down to the headquarters."

Iva was sitting at the kitchen table when Brian's appearance in the doorway made her think she was having a nightmare. His pallid complexion made him resemble a walking corpse, a zombie. She did not immediately move or speak. *This has got to be a dream,* she thought, *so I'll just sit here and wait for what comes next.*

"Help me," Brian whimpered.

Oh God, this is real.

She leapt up and ran to him.

"Brian, what happened?"

He shivered uncontrollably.

"Weltsmirtz. He missed. I had to go in the water."

"Oh God, come on. You've got to get warm right away."

Iva tore Brian's clothes off and made him lie in the downstairs bathtub. Firmly, she sponged him all over with tepid water that she gradually made warmer. The tub filled and his color returned but she kept insisting he flex his hands and feet. Slowly and painfully, Brian regained the feeling in his fingers and toes.

"I'm going to be all right, let me just lie here for a while," Brian finally said.

"What the hell happened?" Iva demanded. This time she wanted a detailed answer.

Brian told her everything. Iva was furious.

"Where was Agent Macy?" she snapped.

"Not his fault. I told him I was going right to the headquarters and he should meet me there. All I wanted was a nice peaceful run around Sagamore Bay on Election Day."

"It was stupid to go alone."

"I know, I'm sorry."

"How's your shoulder?"

"Hurts like a son of a bitch. I just need to rest for a while."

Brian stayed in the tub for over an hour. When he finally toweled off and dressed, he looked almost his old self.

"Physically recovered," he announced to Iva.

"Are you emotionally recovered?" she asked.

"Tomorrow," Brian replied. "Tomorrow it will all be over."

Iva noticed a slight trembling in his hands and she could tell he was trying to hide how frazzled and exhausted he was. *Today is the last day,* she reminded herself, *thank the Lord.*

Brian and Iva literally bumped into David on the steps of headquarters; they were coming, he was going.

"Hi, happy Election Day," David said. He had a box of **Werth for Mayor** flyers under his arm.

"Thanks," Brian replied, "same to you."

"Where you off to?" Iva asked.

"To check on the volunteers. Some of them take a coffee break when I'm not around to crack the whip."

Brian and Iva both smiled and slapped him on the back. They did not doubt the existence of that whip; David's assistance in the campaign had been a godsend.

"I'll be down there this afternoon," Brian told him.

"Great, see you then." David started away.

"David," Brian called after him.

David turned around. "Yes?"

"How do you think it's going?"

David took a deep breath and seemed satisfied. "I think it's going very well, very well indeed."

"How do you know?" Brian and Iva both asked simultaneously.

David took another deep breath. "Because I can breathe," he said.

"What?"

"Huh?"

"Listen, this may sound silly," David confided, "but on every campaign I've worked on, and I've worked on quiet a few, when my sinuses are clear on Election Day... my candidate wins. It's been true every single time, excluding Phoenix where my sinuses never bothered me." He took several rapid-fire breaths. "See? No pain, no blockage... this election's in the bag."

"It's in your nose," Iva said.

"See you this afternoon," Brian said.

"Okidoke," David replied. He waved and took off.

"... just a tad eccentric," Brian said sotto voce.

"A tad?" Iva replied.

Marcus opened the door and stuck his head out. "Hi," he said. "Great day for an election." It actually was a great day, sunny and in the sixties. "It should be a large turnout," Marcus added.

"Which is better for our side, a large or small turnout?" Iva asked.

Brian and Marcus looked at each other. "Well, we've debated that point extensively taking into account all the latest theories in the field of political science..." Marcus began.

"And we've concluded we have absolutely no idea," Brian finished.

"Oh," Iva replied, looking up at the cloudless sunny sky, "then it is a very nice day."

"Hopefully it is," Marcus said.

They went inside the headquarters. It was crowded and busy; phone canvassing proceeded against one wall, flyer collating against another, and the click-swish click-swish of the new photocopy machine persisted unendingly. When they saw their candidate, each volunteer took time to say hello. Brian warmly returned every greeting; he knew he owed these people a lot, a debt that could only be repaid by his winning and becoming a good mayor.

Debbie pulled him aside and pointed to a map on the wall. Little red pins identified every busy pedestrian area in town. "We're passing out literature at each one of these locations," she said.

"That's tremendous."

"Good luck tonight."

Brian kissed her on the cheek. "You've been just wonderful through everything," he said. "I can't ever thank you enough."

Debbie brushed her hair back and looked away, unable to face the gratitude straight on. "This campaign has meant a lot to me," she said. Her voice was close to breaking. "I've had fun, there's been friendship, teamwork, working for a good cause and..." She wanted to add that she now loved his best friend but she could not quite do it, so she stopped and brushed her hair back again. "Oh for gosh sakes, I sound like a movie."

Brian knew what she could not bring herself to say. He kissed her on the cheek, again. "You sound real to me," he said. "Thank you."

Across the room Jeff was on the phone ordering supplies for the evening's ***VICTORY*** or ***BETTER LUCK NEXT TIME*** party. Brian strolled over and overheard his friend's end of the conversation.

"The Budweiser is fine," Jeff said into the phone. "And remember we'll need ten kegs if Mr. Werth wins and only three kegs if he loses." He turned around and realized Brian had been listening. "Make it ten kegs no matter what," he said quickly and hung up the phone.

"Ten kegs is an awful lot of beer," Brian said. He wanted to thank his friend for paying for the party out of his own pocket, on top of everything else he had done.

"We'll need ten kegs," Jeff replied. He wanted to tell his friend the past few months had been one hell of a great time, even if his car did stall occasionally.

"You'll be at the party tonight, won't you?" Brian asked him.

"Of course."

"Ten kegs!" they said together, laughing and slapping five.

Suddenly the drone of an airplane reverberated around them. This would have attracted no attention except the noise did not move on, it got louder and louder and seemed to circle the building. Everyone ran outside, curious about what was going on.

A single engine World War I vintage biplane soared about a hundred feet above the headquarters. An orange and blue banner trailed from its tail: **SAVINO FOR MAYOR FOR AMERICA**. Brian and his friends were being treated to their own personal demonstration of the Republicans' Election Day blitzkrieg.

"An airplane!" Iva yelled above the noise. "That's not fair." It was only one of three they would learn later.

"How much does it cost to rent one of those things for a day?" Brian yelled.

"More money than we can afford, that's for sure," Jeff yelled back.

"Why do they have to rub it in our faces?" Debbie wondered, putting her hands over her ears.

"Those sons of bitches," Marcus muttered, wishing he could get his hands on a surface to air missile. Suddenly the Red Baron wannabe started to wave. He really did resemble a World War I flying ace sitting there in an open cockpit with goggles and a white scarf trailing in the wind. Instinctively, most of those on the ground waved back. Then the pilot bent down out of sight for a moment and came up holding a small rectangular package wrapped in plain brown paper.

"What the hell is that?" Marcus said.

"I wonder..." Brian replied.

They did not have time to ponder for long. The pilot threw the package out of the plane and it plummeted directly towards them. Everyone flattened themselves to the ground expecting a bomb, but there was no explosion. The package crashed into the roof of the headquarters and clattered harmlessly to the ground. The plane kept circling.

The ever-present Agent Macy of the Mossad walked over and picked up the package. "Everyone keep back," he said.

"What are you doing?" Iva yelled. "Put that thing down and get the hell away."

Macy looked at her but did not immediately do anything. *Maybe she's right,* he thought, *what the hell am I doing?*

Brian got up off the ground, brushed himself off and walked over to Macy. He took the package out of Macy's hand before the agent could react.

"Give me that," Brian said. "I've had it. This is bullshit. I'm sick and tired of running from these bastards." He started to rip off the brown paper.

"Go slow," Macy said.

"Careful Brian," Iva pleaded.

"I'm going to open it," Brian announced.

"No, it might be a bomb," Iva said.

"I've had it with these bastards," Brian said. "If this was a bomb, it would have gone off on impact. I'm through running scared."

"I'm not," Jeff said, backing up on his hands and knees.

"It's not even my birthday," Brian said, unsuccessfully trying to ease the tension.

Everyone stood up but remained in place, watching silently. Brian used his car key to cut the twine around the package. The wrapping paper peeled back to reveal... a Jack In The Box.

"A Jack In The Box!" Brian exclaimed. "It's just a child's toy."

They all resumed breathing. A few people started toward Brian but Agent Macy yelled, "Keep back!"

"I'm going to turn the handle," Brian said.

"I hope we're not being over confident here," Macy said. "If you die, I'm dead."

Brian did not pay him any heed. He gripped the Jack in the Box and swore to himself he was through being intimidated. Slowly, he turned the handle. Everyone knew the tune...

> All around the Mulberry bush
> The monkey chased the weasel
> The monkey thought it was all in fun
> POP...

Even though it was predictably on cue, they all flinched when a clown popped out of the box. The puppet had been altered; the circus smile remained but there was a bandage wrapped around its head and a typewritten message taped across its chest. It read: **WERTH—YOU LOSE!**

"Well, we all know who it's from," Brian said.

"Right," Macy replied, running for a phone.

Up in the air, Wilhelm Weltsmirtz threw his head back and roared with laughter. He momentarily lost control of the biplane—it fluttered and dipped wildly—which was not surprising since his private pilot's license had expired eleven years earlier.

"I suppose Montesano and Savino will consider this immature stunt a victory," David said.

"Let's hope it's their only victory today," Iva said.

"Those sons of bitches," Marcus kept muttering.

"What does the message mean?" Jeff asked.

"Nothing," Brian said. He held up the Jack in the Box to the pilot and then pitched it, with some extra mustard, into a nearby trashcan. After an obscene gesture from the pilot, the biplane gained altitude and disappeared beyond some treetops.

"Dewey defeats Truman," Brian said.

"What?" Jeff said.

"Never mind," Brian said. He turned to Marcus. "Where am I appearing this afternoon?" he asked, acutely aware of how much more attention an airplane could attract than he ever could on foot.

"Give 'em hell, Brian," Marcus said with a smile as he handed him one last list of whistle stops.

Brian smiled back then turned to the group of volunteers slated to accompany him. "Okay, let's roll!" he said. He was determined to push it to the end—hard.

Chapter XX

"The joy of giving is indeed a pleasure—especially when you get rid of something you don't want."

Pastor Barry Fitzgerald to curate Bing Crosby in ***Going My Way*** *(1944)*

ELECTION NIGHT, 8:55 P.M.

Brian and Iva had to park three blocks from the headquarters because the whole area was packed with volunteers, press and general curiosity seekers. The crowd spilled off the sidewalk onto the street and the police were in the process of closing down that stretch of road. The candidate received an ovation when he was recognized so he shook a few hands and actually kissed a baby who promptly spit up on his shoe. Suddenly, television lights came on and microphones materialized under his chin. "I feel great, never better," Brian proclaimed, "And I'm definitely predicting victory tonight." Then he waved to acknowledge some more cheers and with Iva on his arm, strolled up the steps and inside.

The inside of his headquarters was basically wall-to-wall bodies, very stuffy and short on oxygen. Marcus and David were politely asking those without essential functions to wait outside. Few heeded them. It was fortuitous that just then Jeff pulled up out front with a tapped keg of beer strapped to the trunk rack of his car. Most people went outside for a free drink and stayed out because it was a warm night, not technically an Indian Summer because the temperature had not yet fallen below freezing, but summerlike nonetheless. Jeff poured himself the first beer and then sat back in his front seat to enjoy it.

Inside the headquarters, Brian tracked down Marcus and asked him if there was any word yet on how the actual vote was going.

"The polls just closed a few minutes ago," Marcus replied. "We've got people on the phones to the polling places but it's still too early, the results aren't in yet."

"I guess we just wait," Brian said.

Iva took his hand and noticed how cold and clammy it was. "Wow, you're really sweating," she said.

"You should see my underpants."

"At least you're wearing some."

Brian's last "Hi, I'm Brian Werth, I'm running for mayor," had been delivered about an hour and a half ago in front of a King Kullen supermarket.

"Give me a break," the man had responded, "I already voted for you."

Brian decided right then and there the campaign was over. He took a few seconds to mull it over and realizing he had genuinely done his best allowed himself a moment of satisfaction and pride. He drove home feeling exhilarated, wolfed down a bowl of Rice Krispies, made love—at Iva's suggestion though he was instantly agreeable—showered and changed into his standard Harris Tweed, light blue shirt and tan corduroys.

"Not those pants on Election Night," Iva had said but she had not prevailed. It was no great loss, she realized, her fiancé still cut a handsome figure. Hopefully, the adrenaline pumping through his body could hold at bay for a few more hours the the trauma and exhaustion of the past few months.

Now, at seventeen after nine on Election Night, they were all just a few minutes away from finding out whether Sagamore would have a new mayor.

"Anyone know any good jokes," Brian said, not knowing what else to say.

Thankfully Jeff had just come in and, as always, had a joke. "How many Republicans does it take to screw in a light bulb?" he asked.

"This is stupid," Debbie warned.

"How many," Brian asked.

"Three. One to screw it in, another to deny it, and one more to bang the gavel and shout, *Not guilty.*" The line was incredibly lame—just a switch on an old Polish joke—but Jeff's audience was desperate for anything to break the tension so he got a good laugh.

David walked over. Always the nervous type, tonight he was outdoing himself. "No matter how many campaigns I work on, I still go to pieces Election Night," he admitted. "Look..." He held out trembling hands.

"How are your sinuses?" Iva asked him.

David took a deep breath. "They're fine, still fine."

"Thank God," Brian said, wishing he had a rabbit's foot or some sort of good luck charm. At this point he was not willing to discount any superstition, no matter how silly. Then a hand tapped him on the shoulder. He turned around and was so surprised he actually stumbled a couple of steps backwards. The face he remembered but it did not go with the body.

"Uh... you're Patrolman... uh... Patrolman Bolster," Brian stammered.

"Citizen Bolster now, my boy," he replied. He started to spit but thought better of it and swallowed. "I got my pension, I'm a free man."

Bolster was clad in a shiny brown suit with wide lapels that Brian guessed had last been out of the closet about twenty years ago. A walking stick and a brown derby—way too small for his head and decades out of fashion—added to his absurd appearance.

"Congratulations," Brian said, wishing the man would leave. His presence brought back disturbing memories. *Professor Alan Sansone has been found dead.*

"I was in the neighborhood," Bolster went on, "so I thought I'd stop by and wish you luck. I think it's great the way you've been fuckin' 'em and fuckin' 'em hard."

"Uh... thanks," Brian said. He shot an embarrassed glance at Iva who shook her head back in disgust.

"Oh, and for your information..." Bolster gestured at the room. "... starting next week I own this place."

"What?" Brian said.

"You don't need this place anymore. Your landlord put it up for sale. Me and my wife bought it. It's going to be Bolster's Fresh Fish Store."

Brian winced. His headquarters being turned into a seafood market... it just did not seem right. "Why a fish store?" he asked.

"I've always had a soft spot for the ladies," Bolster replied, and he laughed.

Brian wanted to spit but thought better of it and swallowed. Iva pretended she had not heard.

"Well, thanks for coming by," Brian said.

"You're welcome," Bolster said. Then, without warning, he slapped Brian on his shoulder—the sore one—and whispered in his ear, "Don't forget to watch your ass."

Brian grimaced and, gagging from the combined odors of cigars and scotch, offered assurances that he would, most definitely, continue to watch his ass.

Bolster sauntered to the door and turned to offer a parting word. "Werth, you know if it weren't for me you wouldn't even be here right now." And with that cryptic comment he winked, tapped his walking stick on his hat brim, burped and left.

"What did he mean by that last remark?" Iva asked.

"Never mind," Brian said. "I'll tell you later."

Someone by the door started clapping. Everyone turned to see why and when they did the gesture became unanimous; the appearance of Bill Nuss got a rousing round of applause. He was leaning somewhat unsteadily on Betsy Brewster and a bandage still covered his right temple, but most importantly he was there. Brian ran to him and shook his hand. "Glad you could make it," he said.

"I wouldn't miss tonight for anything," Nuss replied.

"He made them discharge him a day early so he could be here," Betsy said.

Marcus brought over a folding chair. "Here's a ringside seat. Take a load off."

Nuss gratefully accepted the chance to sit down. Betsy produced the pillow she had embroidered and managed to slip it underneath his rear end a split second before it hit the chair.

"He's still tender," she explained.

"I see," Brian said, addressing her breasts. As usual, he knew he was looking there but he could not stop himself.

Few men had addressed her face in years so Betsy did not take any offense. She had always told herself that sort of a thing is really a compliment... a necessary coping strategy because she would have to put up with it for the rest of her life.

"Results any minute now," Marcus said, talking to Nuss but actually staring at the breasts.

"I can't wait," Nuss said. He had grown accustomed to her breasts so he looked at the men. "I saw a plane today plugging Savino," he added, trying to get their attention.

Jeff tore himself away from "Twin Cities" to make a joke. "That was the one that got away. We shot down two of them." Nuss laughed but no one else did and Jeff realized Betsy's breasts might actually be capable of blocking out sound.

Someone behind Brian cleared his throat to get his attention. He turned around and was confronted by a tall humorless man in a tuxedo who scowled and produced a business card that read simply, Mr. Harvey Whetherstone III. Then the man in the tuxedo, who was apparently a butler, stepped aside to reveal a bag of bones in a wheelchair who–judging from his jaundiced complexion–was in the latter stages of liver failure. A tan blanket covered Whetherstone from the waist down and he was so thin it lay nearly flat. The top half of the old geezer sported a rather natty red smoking jacket and an ancient Brooklyn Dodgers baseball cap.

"Mr. Harvey Whetherstone the Third," the man in the tuxedo announced, indicating that Brian should step forward for an audience.

Brian walked over and bent down in front of the old man in the wheelchair. "Mr. Whetherstone, how nice to see you again," he said. "How are you feeling?"

"Werth, I have lung cancer and I'm dying," Whetherstone replied.

The old guy's first words struck Brian as an unduly harsh way to initiate a conversation with someone he did not know very well. He felt an urge to answer with something like *Well, please don't do it here...* but forced himself to remain courteous. "I'm sorry," Brian said.

Whetherstone coughed violently and the man in the tuxedo moved in swiftly to wipe some spittle off his chin. "Just listen to me, Werth," Whetherstone finally said. "It's a done deal. Do you understand me? My lawyers got all the signatures today. I give you credit boy, it was all your idea."

"You mean... " Brian began.

"That's right, Werth. Here are all the papers, signed and notarized..." He handed Brian a manila folder.

Brian opened the folder and rifled through it. Everything seemed legal all right.

"What's this about?" Marcus said.

"Fill us in," Jeff said.

"I... I... I... I think I did it," Brian said in disbelief.

"Did what?"

Whetherstone chuckled. "He beat the bridge, that's what he did. With my help I might add."

"What do you mean?" Marcus said.

"I have donated all my property to the Department of the Interior in Washington," Whetherstone explained as loudly as he could, though those not directly in front of him still had to strain to hear. "They have accepted it: the woods, meadow, wetlands, beachfront, all of it. It will be a federal wildlife preserve. A few of my neighbors have agreed to cooperate and together we're turning over nearly two thousand acres."

"And all the Montesanos in the world will never be able to build on federal land!" David cried.

"Bingo young man," Whetherstone said. He cackled and his breathing made a cracking sound.

"Sagamore is safe!" Marcus yelled, and everyone cheered.

"Wait," Jeff said, "it's hard to believe..."

Whetherstone slowly held up an unsteady hand. "The land is to remain as it is, untouched. The Department of the Interior simply wants it left alone. My friends can still live there and we have a clause in our agreement that automatically reverts the land to our ownership if for any reason changes are to be made to the property. So you see, there's no risk for us."

Brian knelt down on one knee and moved closer to Whetherstone. "You're doing a wonderful thing," he said, and meant it; he was extremely moved.

"It was all your idea, Werth. In that letter you wrote me. Very bold and creative I must say. I'm just happy to save my land. He reached forward and laid a clawlike hand on Brian's shoulder. "Now about the house..." Whetherstone could only speak in a whisper now and his chin sank lower into his chest.

"The mansion," Brian said.

"It's ugly," Whetherstone said softly.

"I beg your pardon," Brian said.

"Admit it, the house is ugly. It's always been ugly from the day we broke ground."

"It is of dubious design," Brian admitted.

"It's fucking ugly," Whetherstone repeated.

"A bit garish," Brian agreed.

"I've donated it to the Lighthouse charity. They're going to turn the whole place into a school for the blind. Those people won't be able to tell how ugly it is."

"That's nice," was all Brian could think of to say.

The man in the tuxedo stepped forward and said, "Mr. Whetherstone is very tired. Please refer any further inquiries to his lawyers." He turned the wheelchair around and pushed it to the door. Brian followed, he wanted one more word.

"Why, Mr. Whetherstone?" he asked. "Why are you really doing this?"

Harvey Whetherstone managed to raise his head high enough to look Brian in the eye. "I'm going to meet Saint Peter very soon," he said. "At least now I'll have something to tell him."

"You've got a lot to tell him," Brian replied. "You're doing a great thing."

"Thanks," Whetherstone said, managing a smile before his chin hit his chest. Tuxedo man wheeled him away.

Brian turned and faced Marcus, David and Jeff. "Not as exciting as a break-in but... hey it worked!"

They all jumped into a four-way embrace. No one said anything; they were all completely overwhelmed so they just hugged. *No bridge, ever!*

"Results coming in!" Nuss called from across the room. Brian and his friends broke their clinch and started over there.

Chapter XXI

"I'm rather surprised myself, but perhaps it's because for the first time in my life I know what I want."

Joan Fontaine to Cary Grant in ***Suspicion*** *(1941)*

ELECTION NIGHT, 9:45 P.M.

Someone gripped Brian's shoulder—not the sore one this time—and pulled him back. It was Iva. "I have to talk to you," she whispered. She took hold of his hand and held it tight.

"But the results are coming in!" Brian said, glancing over his shoulder to where Marcus stood talking on the phone.

"This is important," Iva said.

"The election results are important," Brian replied. He tried to pull his hand free but Iva held firm.

"Brian, please listen,"

He suddenly realized Iva was seriously concerned about something. "What's wrong?" he asked. "Are you sick? Don't you feel well?"

"I'm fine," Iva said, "I think."

Brian led her to a chair and sat her down. He kneeled down in front of her and brushed back her hair. "What is it, Iva? What do you want to tell me?"

"I know this is a bad time. But I can't put it off any longer. I have to tell you this now, before you get the election results. It has to do with keeping our relationship a priority in spite of everything else going on. This is more important than the election."

"What is it?" Brian asked, exasperated.

"Just read me the figures from the two columns," Marcus said into the phone across the room.

Brian started to turn in that direction but stopped himself and continued to look at Iva. She looked in his eyes but could not bring herself to say anything. Over Brian's shoulder she noticed Debbie standing about fifteen feet away watching them.

"Go ahead and tell him," Debbie said. Then she realized she was eavesdropping on what should be a private moment, so she turned away and pretended to become interested in the vote tabulations.

"Tell me what? Tell me what?" Brian pressed.

"I'm..."

"You're what?" A light went off in his head. "Oh God."

"I'm pregnant," Iva said.

She spoke at the precise instant David arrived on the scene with some early returns. He heard her statement and dropped the pile of results he was carrying.

"Ahem... uh... excuse me," he stammered, kneeling down to pick up the papers, some of which had landed under Iva's chair. "I'll get back to you with these." He straightened his glasses and cleared his throat and frantically continued to retrieve what he had dropped. "I'm sorry to bother you. I'll just be going. Ahem. Ahem. Take care. Sorry. Thanks. Good-bye."

Brian had not even noticed David and his gyrations, and it was the first time Iva had ever seen him respond to anything with an open-mouthed gape.

"Close your mouth, dear," she said.

"Would you please repeat what you just said?" Brian asked her calmly and deliberately.

"I said, I'm pregnant."

"You're kidding me," Brian said.

Iva looked hurt. "What kind of response is that?" she said.

"You're really pregnant?" Brian said.

"Yes."

"Really?"

"Brian, yes!"

"You're kidding me!"

"Brian, listen to me," Iva said. "I haven't had my period in two months. I've taken three home pregnancy tests. I got a blood test at the doctor today. I'm pregnant for sure. I thought you'd want to know even before the election results."

"You're kidding me."

"Brian, please."

"But we were always so care... oh." He remembered their interlude on the set of the *H.M.S. Pinafore.*

"That was probably when," Iva confirmed.

"Wow!" he exclaimed. The news was just beginning to register. "How do you feel?"

"I don't know. How do you feel?"

Brian understood then what she needed to hear, and he also knew that he needed to hear himself say the same things. "I feel great," he said. "I love you and you're having our baby. So what if we didn't plan it, it'll be great. We'll get married right away... I'll be a father, you'll be a mother and we'll have the greatest baby in the world."

"I feel wonderful," Iva said.

"I love you," Brian said.

"Same here."

They leaned into each other and kissed. Iva broke away first.

"The election," she said. "Let's go find out..."

"Just stay here and take it easy," Brian said.

"But I want to find out, too."

"No, I don't want you walking around. I'll bring the results over."

"But..."

"No buts, I want you to take it easy."

Iva gave in, it was not time for an argument. Grinning from ear to ear, she folded her arms and sat back. Later, she would make it clear in no uncertain terms that a pregnant woman need not spend nine months as an invalid.

Brian smiled back and stood up. "If it's a boy should we name him Gilbert or Sullivan?" he quipped.

"Let's name him Alan," Iva said.

"Yes, Alan," he replied, chastened. He turned and walked away to find out whether or not he was going to be Sagamore's next mayor.

Marcus waved his arm and motioned him over. "Check this out," he said, handing him a tally sheet:

<u>PRECINCT 7</u>
<u>Savino 391</u>
<u>Werth 379</u>
<u>Koken 33</u>

Brian was dejected. "I lost Precinct Seven," he said. "I lost in my own neighborhood."

Marcus clapped his hands together excitedly. "Come on man, you know what this means. Precinct Seven is by far the heaviest Republican enclave in the city. If you're this close here, you're probably doing well enough elsewhere to win overall."

"Probably," Brian said. "What do you mean, probably?

Jeff slammed down the phone and let loose with an Indian war whoop. "Brian Werth is kicking ass in Precinct Three!" he yelled to the crowd, which cheered the news loudly.

"Precincts One and Two report Werth all the way!" Roger Dunlin chimed in. He looked at the ceiling and said, "Thank you Lord and I might add, it's about time!"

"Precincts Four and Six," David said into another phone. "What? Are you sure? Okay, thanks." He hung up and took a couple of seconds to enjoy everyone's breathless anticipation. "Ahem... three to one in favor of Werth."

Brian ran to David and threw his arms around him. "David ol' buddy, I could kiss your sinuses," he said.

"That is both physically impossible and disgusting," he replied, laughing.

From the vote tabulations that poured into the Werth headquarters from around the city, it became apparent by a few minutes after ten that Brian would win big—probably by over two to one. The word *landslide* did not apply, a more apt description was *annihilation*. Almost every polling place reporting in heralded good news and everyone became hoarse from cheering. When throats grew sore, hugging replaced the yelling and they all embraced each other over and over. Betsy seemed to receive the most hugging, which she understood and took in stride. A lot of people were openly weeping; Brian was not though he knew he probably would before the night was over. Tears were streaming down Roger Dunlin's face and he kept repeating over and over, "I can't believe it!"

"Believe it," Brian told him. "Believe it."

"It's just that we've gotten our asses kicked so badly in the past," Roger said.

"Not this time," Brian replied. "Though I must warn you now that I'm elected I plan to renege on a lot of my promises."

Dunlin stared at him and Brian roared with laughter over his reaction. Roger then joined in the laughter though he admitted for a brief flash he had feared the worst.

"Nothing changes," Brian assured him.

Marcus walked over and they shook hands.

"Hey Marcus," Brian said. "When can I declare I've officially won?"

"Don't expect a congratulatory phone call from that asshole. And it could take days to get an official vote count."

"Days!" Brian echoed, disappointed.

"Everyone look at the television!" someone yelled.

"In that controversial mayoralty race out in Sagamore, Long Island," the anchorwoman said, "with seventy-nine percent of the vote counted it appears Democratic challenger Brian Werth will win a decisive victory over indicted Republican incumbent Al Savino."

The Werth supporters applauded wildly; the news report seemed more real to them than the actual vote counts coming in from the polling places.

"Well, it's official now," Marcus said. "It was on TV."

"I've won," Brian said serenely to himself, savoring the first moment he really believed it.

"Congratulations," Iva, whispered in his ear.

"Same to you," he whispered back.

Close to midnight the victory celebration moved from the headquarters-soon-to-be-fish-store to Geragthy's diner down the street. Brian and Iva knew Billy the owner from their frequent pancake binges, and they had persuaded him to let them take over the place in the event of a victory. Volunteers cleared the tables out of the center of the dining room, kegs of beer were set up and live music commenced. The Off Hour Rockers—Jackie the lead guitarist was an old high school chum of Brian's and Jeff's—had agreed to play for free as a favor and for the complimentary beer. Pancakes flowed freely on a cash only basis and, to the delight of Billy, the over two hundred people who showed up devoured them generously. When the band struck up its first number the multitudes began dancing. The fact that the Off Hour Rockers were not tightly rehearsed—lyrics were a challenge to make out and only a forgiving ear could discern a tune—did not deter the revelers. The drum beat, hard and strong, pumped them along. And if that was not enough, every few minutes Jackie would put down his guitar, take a swig of beer and yell into his microphone at the top of his lungs, "Come on! Come on! Come on!"

Brian moved around the room accepting congratulations and thanking people for their support. Reporters kept asking him to comment on how he felt and he stuck to a simple, "Good, real good." Truthfully, he did not know how he felt, everything was all new and not internalized yet. *And a new baby...*

When one reporter asked him if he harbored any bitterness or resentment towards Al Savino and Frank Montesano, Brian replied, "I sure as hell do."

At half past midnight, Frank Montesano finally lost his temper. "Stop it," Frank yelled, "Stop it right now!" He elbowed an elderly orchestra leader off a platform and kicked over his music stand. "Hot Time In The Old Town Tonight" halted in mid-stanza. "Get the hell out of here now," Montesano hissed. The twenty-piece orchestra silently started to pack up. Next, the Republican leader turned on the crowd: nearly three hundred formally dressed couples on hand to enjoy their bread and circuses.

"All of you!" Frank railed, waving a finger at them. He stumbled backwards and it became obvious he had been drinking. "All of you!" He had their undivided attention. "We lost! We lost! Get out of here! Get the hell out!" He tried to sit in a folding chair but nearly missed it and in anger kicked it away.

"Frank..." One of his associates moved to take his arm.

"Get away from me!" Montesano yelled. "All of you, get away from me."

The Republican faithful solemnly walked to their cars.

The Off Hour Rockers were hot, not good but hot, and their classic Chuck Berry medley had everyone out on the floor sweating. Brian danced continuously, switching partners frequently. To show her a nicer side of American politics, Marcus brought Aida to the party with assurances that, unlike the debate, at a victory celebration there almost certainly would not be an outbreak of violence. And from the way his gaze locked in on her pelvic gyrations, it was obvious he had effectively put the election behind him for the time being. Jeff and Debbie danced with each other in between beer breaks for him. David, after politely checking with the largely immobile Nuss, asked Betsy Brewster to dance. He was able to enjoy about thirty seconds with her before a stream of admirers started cutting in. Roger Dunlin stripped down to his undershirt and convulsed wildly in the center of the dance floor without a partner. Seemingly in a state of euphoria, he kept shouting, "We won! We won! We fuckin' won!"

"Would you buy insurance from that man?" made the rounds.

Iva sat next to Nuss on the sidelines. Brian in his misguided but well-meaning concern for her condition had forbidden her to exert herself on the dance floor. She did not want to put a damper on his victory party by arguing over his excessive protectiveness, so she acquiesced and spent the time chatting with Nuss.

"A great night, isn't it?" Iva said to him at one point.

"It sure is," Nuss replied. Grinning from ear to ear he added, "And I'm on the Executive Committee!"

"Johnny B. Goode" ended and the band broke into a rendition of "You Keep Me Hangin' On" played the way the Vanilla Fudge had covered the song.

"A slow one!" Brian shouted in a reprise of what he had yelled at many a high school dance. He ran over to Iva.

"Let's dance," he said. "It's a slow song, we'll take it easy."

"I guess I'm up to it," Iva said.

Brian and Iva walked out to the center of the dance floor, embraced and starting turning slowly in a circle. They hugged more than danced and had a wonderful time.

Luck was with David, he screwed up his courage and cut back in with Betsy a few seconds before the band switched to "You Keep Me Hangin' On." As he stood there unsure of himself, she gripped him and began to dance "slow." His chin rested right in her cleavage, fortuitous for most but much more than he could handle. He started visibly trembling.

"David, you're shaking," Betsy said.

"I'm cold," he said. "I've got to get a sweater." He pulled back and ran off, and he was instantly replaced.

After about two minutes, Brian and Iva stopped moving to the music, content to kiss and grope at each other in the center of the crowd. She was the first to notice the bulge in his pants.

"Uh, Brian, I think you're getting aroused," Iva whispered.

He stepped back and looked down, deliberately being ridiculous since he did not need to physically see his erection to determine that he had one. "By George, I do believe you're right," he said.

"Brian's got a boner," Iva teased.

"You're being childish," he replied.

"And very immature," she agreed.

He gripped her shoulders. "From now on you will say the Mayor's got a boner," he told her. They laughed at that and resumed grinding away.

Montesano stumbled out of the Colby Hotel's ballroom into an adjacent conference room. He was alone. Tote boards lined the walls but their tenders had long since made themselves scarce, afraid to remain lest they be blamed for the debacle. It was a bad night all around for the Republicans. Not only had Al Savino been soundly defeated, so had most of the other GOP candidates on Long Island. The overall impact of the murder indictments on the voters had been a mass anger that vented itself at the polls. The people had voted the scoundrels out.

"You're all stupid," Montesano said, talking to the names on the wall. "Too stupid for me to deal with. You all lost because you're all stupid." He walked over to a tote board and ripped it down. "I don't need any of you," he mumbled.

Al Savino walked in. He was stone cold sober and he smirked at the reversal of their usual roles. "You're drunk," he said, mimicking the tone of voice he had heard numerous times from his boss.

"You're stupid," Montesano replied.

"That's no way to talk to me," Savino said. "I'm the mayor."

"You're the ex-mayor."

"I'm still the mayor," Savino insisted. "Until January. I'm still the mayor until January."

"You're nothing," Montesano told him.

Al knew Frank was drunk but the insults still hurt. Losing was new to him. "We lost tonight, Frank," Savino said. "We lost tonight. But we'll win again, won't we? Won't we?"

"Oh Christ," Montesano said, thinking about their upcoming trial and how that and the evening's defeats would make it impossible for him to retain his county chairmanship. "I'm going to be out of a job soon, Al," he said, "and so are you. And we're both probably going to jail for a long time."

Savino felt as if he was going to pass out. He had hoped Montesano could somehow make everything all right. "But Frank, I'll be able to run again, won't I?"

Montesano knew that would be impossible. Savino began to sniffle. Staring at perhaps his only true friend, Frank sighed and actually started to feel sorry for him. "Sure Al, you can run again," he said. "Next time you'll win for sure." Then he burped.

Savino burst into tears. "I've got a mortgage and a time share in Florida. Plus there's my wife, three daughters and a new kitten named Buckwheat. I've got to win again, I've just got to."

"You will," Frank said, rapidly sobered by the pathetic display.

Savino sat down, put his face in his hands and continued crying. Montesano walked over and put an arm around him.

"Come on Al, buck up."

"I don't want to be a loser," Savino sobbed. He had never lost an election in his professional life. Few Sagamore Republicans had lost elections.

Frank gripped Al's head and gently pressed it against his stomach. Then he stroked his friend's hair as if he was a puppy. "You're not a loser, Al." Savino sniffled and wiped his nose on his sleeve. "Come on Al, relax," Montesano said softly.

"I don't want to be mayor anymore," Savino finally said. He looked longingly up into Montesano's eyes. "I want to be a judge. Can I be a judge?"

Oh Christ, Frank thought. "Sure, you can be a judge," he assured his weeping comrade, continuing to brush his hair.

A camera flashed. A photographer they only saw for a moment said "Thanks!" and ran from the room. Montesano knew they had been caught in a humiliating pose but he was too drained to chase it down. He could only hope the picture would not be widely distributed.

His worst fears were realized when the photograph made the front page of *Newsday* the following day.

The Off Hour Rockers closed their final set of the evening with a spirited rendition of "Peggy Sue" and, as Buddy Holly turned over in his grave, everyone hopped out to the dance floor for one more dance. Even Nuss waded into the throng to triumphantly wave his crutch. Brian finally allowed Iva to dance to a fast song after she promised not to "jiggle the baby" too much.

It was past four when the Werth victory celebration finally broke up. The ten kegs of beer were empty and everyone was so exhausted that good-byes were mostly a simple "See ya later." Marcus looked at Aida and prayed he would get a second wind. Brian, already operating on his third wind, fell asleep in the car when no fourth wind arrived to rescue him. No matter, it was over, he had won. From behind the wheel Iva reached over and stroked her sleeping mate.

"Sleep, Mr. Mayor," she said.

Chapter XXII

"Ladies and gentlemen, when something like this happens to you and you try to tell how you feel about it, you find that, out of all the words in the world, there are only two that really mean anything—thank you."

Janet Gaynor in the original ***A Star is Born*** *(1937)*

TWO DAYS AFTER THE ELECTION, 3:00 P.M.

The election was history but the headquarters, although on the messy side, still looked the same. But that would soon change. The phone company had been called and told to come and disconnect the phones. Then Brian and his friends would empty the place out: remove the tables and chairs, tear down the posters, sweep up, lock up, and leave with their memories.

"I'm going to miss this place," Brian said, as he glanced fondly around the room that had been his command post for victory.

"So am I," Iva said, remembering plays she had been in during college and how the sets were dismantled so quickly after the run ended.

Brian called the meeting to order. All the members were present including the newest member, Roger Dunlin.

"The first thing I'd like to say," Brian began, "is that..." A pounding on the roof interrupted them. "What the hell is that?"

"They're taking down your sign and replacing it with one that says Bolster's Fresh Fish Store," Marcus explained.

The hammering persisted.

"Don't rush me," Brian yelled at the ceiling. Everyone laughed. "All right, I guess I'll just have to speak up."

"What?" Jeff said.

"Don't start," Brian said.

The first thing he did was thank all of them for their help and support. Then he announced that Marcus had accepted a position as Deputy Mayor and Chief of Staff. Everyone applauded.

"I think its called patronage," Marcus said.

"You're darn right it's patronage," Brian said, adding, "I can't promise your new job will be as exciting as the campaign."

"Don't be so sure," Marcus said.

"Now David..." Brian turned to him. "David has turned down a position on my staff."

David England, naturally, cleared his throat and straightened his glasses. They all watched the ritual fondly, realizing it might be a long time before they would see him again.

"Let me... ahem... explain," he said. "I'm a campaign strategist. I never know what to do after my candidate wins so I always seek out another campaign to become involved in as soon as I can."

"He's found one," Brian said.

"Starting in January I move out to Michigan to direct the campaign of Congressman Chips Cooney who's declared for mayor of Detroit."

"But..." Brian prompted.

"But I'll be back in four years..." David said.

"When I run for reelection," Brian finished. "A lot can happen in four years but as of now I'm looking forward to running again... on my record."

"I'm looking forward to it," David said.

"I think we all are," Jeff said.

Brian looked over at Debbie. She smiled and automatically brushed back her hair. "Debbie here," he said, "is thinking over my offer for her to be Sagamore's Commissioner of General Services. It's a big job and it means she'll be our official watchdog over all the city's municipal employees."

"I am seriously considering it," she confirmed.

Brian desperately wanted her to accept; her exemplary performance during the campaign had more than proven her skills. Debbie was the perfect person for the job but it was not an easy choice to leave a teaching career two years from tenure. Jeff had told him in confidence the odds were pretty good she would go for it, saying, "She'll probably accept. She's found she loves politics and hates teaching long division to little brats."

Marcus, David and Debbie were the only friends to whom Brian offered the spoils of victory. No job he could offer Jeff could compete with the fact that in remaining with his father's masking tape factory, eventually he would inherit it and become a multi-millionaire. Roger's insurance career was successful and too stable for him to want to change. Nuss was still an undergraduate looking forward to law school. And as far as Iva was concerned, giving a job to one's future wife would be just too... well... Republican.

Next, Marcus stood up to address the group. "I have a preliminary vote count," he said. "It's not official yet but the official results probably won't be much different. Are you ready for this?"

"Go ahead," Brian said, beaming because he already knew.

"Werth — 26,318, Savino — 12,776."

Everyone whooped and applauded.

"A two point zero six to one ratio," David added.

"Are Montesano and Savino really through?" Roger asked.

"Well," Marcus said, "Montesano will definitely lose his party chairmanship when the Republican committeemen meet next month. And they'll both be facing some serious jail time after their trial next May."

"Politically their names are mud," David said.

"They may be down for the count, now," Brian cautioned, "but in a few years, who knows? Anything can happen. If it does we'll be ready."

Nuss started to raise his hand but remembered in time he was not in class. He spoke up. "What about the bridge? Was that old guy on Election Night for real?"

"I've been in touch with the Interior Department in Washington and Whetherstone's lawyers several times," Brian replied. "What can I say, it's all on the level. But," he added in a refrain of his assessment of Montesano and Savino, "in a few years, who knows? The most we can say is that right now, at least, there is no bridge and immediate prospects for one are bleak. But gains in politics are usually only temporary, you've always got to be on your guard. It's a good lesson to learn." He was sounding like the teacher he used to be.

"That's something to keep in mind when we're dealing with the Long Island Railroad," Roger commented.

"We will work on that, I promise you," Brian told him.

At that moment, Mr. Antonio Augustinelli, chairman of the Sagamore Democratic Committee, shoved open the front door and made a rather precipitous entry into the room by stumbling into the back of Brian's chair. He tried to right himself but being dead drunk was unsuccessful. He tottered backwards against the wall.

"Good to see you again, Mr. Augustinelli," Brian said.

This was the first they had seen of him since his similar display at their first Executive Committee meeting back in April.

"Aaauuugh." Augustinelli moaned.

"English please," Brian said.

Augustinelli tried to offer congratulations but could not get it out. He passed clear out on his fourth attempt. "Conaaugh... Congrataauugh... Congratulaaauugh... Con..." Jeff and Brian caught him just before his head would have hit the floor. Marcus pushed some chairs together and they laid him out across the seats.

"I told you we wouldn't see him again until we won," Marcus said.

"He'll be able to sleep it off," Iva said. A snore from Augustinelli confirmed it.

"Let's get back to the meeting," Brian said. "I move we keep ourselves completely separate from Augustinelli's organization. All in favor?"

Everyone raised their hand.

"Done," Brian said.

"Maybe we can start a new Democratic organization," Debbie said.

"Absolutely," Brian agreed, casting a quick glance at Jeff. Jeff winked back and they both knew they were looking at a woman who would soon be a former schoolteacher.

Suddenly there was silence. Brian could not think of anything more to say and neither could anyone else. The Executive Committee members looked at each other and realized the election really was all over. Another snort from Augustinelli punctuated the moment.

Then Brian realized there was one more thing he wanted to say. Tears welled up in his eyes. "Before we close down, let's all share a moment of silence in the memory of Professor Alan Sansone," he said. "May he never be forgotten."

For about a minute, thoughts drifted back through the tumult of the past few months to the nice old man with the white hair and wonderful stories. A knock on the door sounded just in time to keep Brian and Iva and some of their friends from needing to wipe their eyes.

A burly fisherman in a yellow rain slicker and black rubber boots entered carrying a large wooden crate. "Here are the lobsters you ordered," he said.

"We didn't order any lobsters," Brian said.

"I know I got the address right," the fisherman said.

"I'm sure you do but we still have this place until tomorrow," Brian said.

"Someone has got to sign for these."

"I'll sign for them," Iva cut in. Then to the group she said, "You're all invited to our house for a lobster feast!"

Everyone was instantly agreeable.

"Yippee... time for my daily dose of mercury," Jeff said *sotto voce*, but not *sotto voce* enough.

"Fuck you," the fisherman said, slamming the door on his way out.

"Okay, let's go. This meeting is adjourned," Brian declared, covering for his friend for the umpteenth time in their lives.

Jeff pried open the crate to reconnoiter what they would be eating. The lobsters were fresh out of the Sound, big and still crawling all over each other. He grabbed one and held it up, and it thrashed its claws and legs about seeming to sense its fate.

"Hey!" Jeff called out. "I've got a great idea how we can sober up Augustinelli real fast." They all roared, picturing the drunken Augustinelli waking up with a live lobster on his chest. Jeff did not go through with it, David talked him out of it citing possible legal ramifications, but it was a great idea nonetheless.

Chapter XXIII

"I had no say in my father's marriage,
so why should he in mine?"

Tyrone Power rejects the advice of his parents in ***The Mark of Zorro*** *(1940)*

NOVEMBER 16, 12:30 P.M.

Brian and Iva were married in the early afternoon in a ceremony officiated by the local Justice of the Peace. They decided against bringing a priest and rabbi together to sanction their nuptials though for a few hundred dollars compromising clerics were available. Neither Brian nor Iva were particularly religious; Iva's pride in being Jewish was almost entirely cultural and Brian really only prayed—as he realized during the campaign—when he was afraid or in trouble. Early in their relationship when they had enjoyed the luxury of time for thoughtful discussions, both agreed they could technically be called Deists. The Big Bang Theory notwithstanding, Brian and Iva both "felt" the existence of an omniscient God, but a God who created the Universe and then stepped back and let Nature, which He had created, take its natural course. Brian had arrived at his belief as an historian when he had encountered the eighteenth century's rational world of the Enlightenment, and he was literally in awe of Thomas Jefferson's seminal writings on the separation of church and state. Iva on the other hand simply could not believe that any so-called benevolent God could allow an errant Israeli airstrike on a Palestinian orphanage to kill all twenty-one children inside.

After considerable reflection, they chose the Wildwood meadow as the site for their wedding... with no apologies for the sixtyishness of it. Brian and Iva both hoped his going back up there for the happy occasion would help him exorcise demons and banish nightmares. It was a small gathering; only Iva's father, Brian's parents and a select group of friends clustered around the couple in the wavy ankle-length grass. Iva wore her arrowhead necklace and Brian, being sentimental, insisted they stand precisely on the spot of his find which, he noted, was only a few feet from where sniper fire had pinned him down on a night that—during his waking hours at least—seemed such a long time ago.

Jeff stood up as Brian's best man and Debbie was Iva's maid of honor. The mid-November weather cooperated; it was sunny and nearly sixty degrees and there were still a fair number of crimson and gold leaves. Dress was nice but nothing fancy. Iva, not showing her pregnancy yet, wore a long ivory taffeta dress while Brian sported a double-breasted navy blue suit. As usual, they made a striking couple. Even the Wildwood mansion appeared almost attractive as it overlooked the joyous celebration on that beautiful afternoon. Almost but not quite. Wildwood would have needed a miracle to really look lovely, something like a total eclipse.

They wrote their marriage vows themselves, simple words that promised love and honor but not obedience. Brian had suggested *grovel at the feet of* as a substitute for the word *obey*, but Iva balked at that so they left it out entirely. Gold wedding bands with tiny arrowheads engraved inside... *I do... You may kiss the bride...* a few tears... it was all very nice, a happy moment for everyone... even Brian's parents and Iva's father.

The elder Werths hosted a reception at their waterfront home after the ceremony. Harvey had forced himself to accept Iva despite the fact she was Jewish, and he had reluctantly concluded that parents who interfered in the love life of offspring were invariably misguided... at least that was how it usually played out in classic movies. Arlene was less reconciled to her new daughter-in-law, but she had weighed all her options and determined that welcoming Iva with open arms was preferable to losing a son—a son she was enormously proud of. The women of the Sagamore Garden Club had been getting more than their fill lately about "My son the mayor." Her dread over the prospect of grandchildren that could conceivably be considered Jewish was, as her husband had admonished, something she would have to get over. Arlene hoped she could, as difficult as it would be.

Conrad Fidele took Brian aside at the reception and shook his hand. "Congratulations, Brian, I mean it, he said. "She's all I've got, take care of her."

"Thanks, I will," Brian replied.

"It was a lovely civil ceremony," Conrad added, accenting the word *civil.*

Brian smiled and noted his father-in-law's eye patch was brushed black velvet, not its usual cardboard-like material. Apparently there was such a thing as a dress eye patch.

"You know, you're already getting to be quite a politician," Conrad continued, smiling as well.

"Sometimes you've got to be if you want to get what you want," Brian said.

They shook hands again and they both felt it... mutual respect and genuine affection.

Marcus strolled by sipping a glass of champagne. Compared to the South Bronx, the regal conditions under which Brian had grown up seemed like something out of a movie. "How old were you when you first got on the subway?" he asked him.

"About eighteen I guess," Brian replied.

"No comment," Marcus said.

David walked over. "Sure is a great view of the water," he said, "and there's never going to be a bridge out there thanks to you."

"Thanks to a lot of people," Brian said.

David nodded and took a deep breath.

"Hey, I'll bet the salt air is great for the sinuses," Brian said.

"Very true," David replied, "very true."

"Where's Iva?" Debbie called from across the room. "She's got to toss her bouquet."

Iva walked in from the hall.

"Time to toss your bouquet," Debbie announced. She went over to where Betsy sat chatting with Nuss and pulled her about twenty feet from Iva. "Okay, turn around and go ahead."

Iva picked up her flowers and tossed them in the air, but her aim was off causing them to sail into the arms of an astonished David England. He reacted as if he had just been pelted with poison sumac and threw them away. The bouquet careened off the wall and this time Debbie made the grab.

"Got 'em," she cried.

"That means Jeff's the next to get married," Iva said.

"God help me," Jeff said.

Everyone laughed but Brian knew Jeff would probably propose marriage to Debbie in the near future. In a heart to heart talk a few days ago, Jeff had confessed his true feelings. And after stalling for months, in that very same conversation Brian had finally blurted out, with no preamble, the words, "Jeff, you're an alcoholic. There, I said it."

Surprisingly, Jeff's response was a simple, "I know."

The stark admission stunned Brian and he did not know what to say next. Fortunately, Jeff did all the talking. "I know," he repeated. "How about we leave it at that for now. That's step one. I know there's eleven more to go. I promise I'll try my best and... uh... thanks."

"You're welcome," Brian had said, thinking about his father who still lied to himself. "And thank you for everything."

Iva knew Debbie would accept Jeff's proposal of marriage, and she also knew that Debbie had been struggling with Jeff over his drinking problem for months. Getting him to admit his alcoholism was Debbie's doing and she confided to Iva that, knowing Jeff as she did, step one was enough for her to make a commitment. "What can I say, I love the guy," Debbie had said. "No more going to bars to meet men. Being with Jeff makes me feel I don't need that anymore."

That's one definition of love, Iva had to admit.

Bridget McDonough, an undocumented immigrant from Scotland and the Werths' live-in maid for nearly forty years, answered the door when the bell rang. The late arriving guest was dressed impeccably in black tie and tails, and he carried in his hands a package wrapped in silver paper about the size of a shoebox. A white gauze bandage circled the top of his head and he wore a neck brace... size double XL.

"Good evening," the late arriving guest said. "I have a gift for the newlyweds."

"How nice," Bridget replied, completely disarmed by the visitor's proper bearing. "Won't you come in?" She opened the door and stepped aside.

"Thank you," the man said, entering the house. "Here's my card."

Bridget took his card and said, "Mr. Weltsmirtz, please follow me." He followed her down the hall to where, in the doorway to the living room, Bridget delivered a formal introduction to all those present at the reception.

"Ladies and gentlemen, Mr. Wilhelm Weltsmirtz," she announced, reading from his card.

Weltsmirtz' appearance stunned them all. No one moved or spoke.

"Good afternoon, everyone," he said, noticing Brian and Iva sitting next to each other on a couch. He walked over and, still in shock, they allowed him to sit down in between them. Groaning and in obvious pain, Weltsmirtz took a sip from his brandy flask.

Still, everyone just looked at him.

Weltsmirtz turned first to Iva. She met his gaze and said nothing. Next, he faced Brian. Their eyes met and Brian felt the extent of his capacity for hatred, but his body seemed frozen.

"My congratulations to you, Brian," Weltsmirtz said. "My congratulations and at the same time my condolences." He patted the silver box on his lap. "Of course you realize that now this is personal for me. I'm going to end it," he added, closing his eyes and sitting up straight.

Events happened fast. Conrad walked in from the hall and immediately yelled, "Weltsmirtz!" He began to strip off his jacket with the intention of strangling the man to death with his bare hands.

Brian guessed the package was a bomb. He grabbed at it and engaged in a tug of war that he won when Iva threw her elbow into Weltsmirtz' eye. Brian then leapt to his feet and found himself in the middle of the room with a bomb in his hands. He knew he had to get rid of it immediately, but he had no idea where.

"Throw it out the picture window," David yelled.

"It's not open," Brian said.

"It is now," Marcus said, picking up a chair and throwing it through the glass. The window shattered leaving a jagged hole in its center. Brian ran to it and, shot-put style, heaved the package outside.

"Get down!" Brian and Marcus yelled.

Everyone ducked. Brian had to pull his mother to the floor because she was dumbfounded and unable to move. Iva literally tackled her father because he was pummeling Weltsmirtz with his fists and oblivious to everything else.

Two seconds later, the bomb went off. Debris flew through the room but they were all on the floor beneath it. No one was hurt.

Conrad leapt to his feet first. He grabbed the bloodied Weltsmirtz by the collar and pulled him off the floor. "I'm going to kill you," he told him. He placed his hands around Weltsmirtz' throat and started to squeeze.

"Papa don't," Iva cried. She jumped up and tried to pull him away, but she was unsuccessful and his grip tightened. Weltsmirtz' eyes rolled back and he made gurgling sounds.

"You killed my wife," Conrad said.

"Papa, you're confused. Stop it!" Iva pleaded.

Brian, Marcus and Jeff ran over and between the three of them they were able to pry him away. Weltsmirtz fell limp to the floor but Conrad continued to try and get at him. Brian gripped his father-in-law under the arms in a bear hug, but still he struggled. Iva, in tears, begged her father to stop. Conrad did not heed her words but finally relaxed because he was exhausted. Brian let him go.

"Listen," Brian told him. "We're not going to murder anyone. We're going to do this legally."

"I'll call the police," David said, running out.

"And an ambulance," Marcus called after him. "He knelt down next to Weltsmirtz to feel for a pulse. There was one, but weak.

"He killed my wife," Conrad gasped.

"Oh Papa, you're upset," Iva said. She ran over and hugged him, and for the first time in her life she felt she was stronger than he was. "You're tired, Papa, you need to rest."

Conrad looked in her eyes and reality seemed to come back to him. "I know, I'm sorry," he said.

"Please try to forget," Iva whispered in his ear. Then she pressed her head against his chest and wondered what she could do to help a man who held inside so much hatred and loneliness. *God, he seems so old,* she thought.

Harvey called the Werth family physician who, because he was a golf partner, rushed over. There were no physical injuries to any of the wedding guests but when the doctor proffered Valium there were more than a few takers; Brian's mother and David took double doses. Harvey Werth stuck with scotch. The police arrived and, showing a newfound respect for the mayor-elect, promised Weltsmirtz would be promptly turned over to the proper authorities and tried for murder along with Montesano and Savino.

After they were satisfied everyone was going to recover from their harrowing experience, the newlyweds announced they were heading home to prepare for their honeymoon. After apologies and good-byes back and forth, Brian and Iva and their wedding guests all walked to their cars.

Jeff had the final words with his friend. "It was a lovely reception," he told him. "The crazed maniac with the bomb was a nice touch."

Brian had to laugh. "Jeff, we're growing up," he said.

"You mean we're grown-ups now?" Jeff said.

That's right, we're finally grown-ups."

"Well, I can handle it if you can."

"I can handle it," Brian replied. "Take it easy."

"Tape it... I mean, see you around," Jeff said.

Chapter XXIV

Andy Hardy: "The next ten years of my life are the best."

Judge Hardy: "The next ten years of anybody's life are the best."

Mickey Rooney and Lewis Stone in ***Life Begins for Andy Hardy*** *(1941)*

BRIAN'S AND IVA'S WEDDING NIGHT, 8:45 P.M.

They had it all mapped out. Brian would run for reelection once then the Werth family would move to Israel for a year or two so Iva could teach on a kibbutz. Brian suggested it the night before their wedding; Iva knew he would, otherwise there could have been no marriage.

"It's something you have to do, isn't it?" Brian had said.

Iva nodded. "Yes."

"Then we'll go."

"But what will you do while we're there?" she asked.

"Write my memoirs," he said.

"You're going to write your memoirs?"

"Local boy fights against all odds to break the machine and save Long Island. How does it sound?"

"Unbelievable."

"That's for sure," Brian replied, shaking his head in wonderment.

She walked over and kissed his cheek. "We'll do whatever we must to stay together, right?"

"Right." He returned her kiss on the cheek. "You know, after Israel I might want to get my doctorate in molecular biology or work in advertising on Madison avenue or... "

"I get the point," Iva said. "Areté."

"Areté," Brian affirmed.

"I've always wanted to write and illustrate a children's book," Iva admitted.

"You will, that's what it means."

They embraced for a moment and then proceeded to stuff clothes into suitcases bound for Greece; Iva had informed Great Neck Academy of an incontinent aunt in Philadelphia with fluid on the brain—"something pathetic no one will question"—who would require at least two weeks of personal care. They were strapped for cash but they had both closed their savings accounts and scrounged enough to get by.

Bright and early the next morning, Brian shifted his Mustang into first gear and started them rolling down their driveway. "How are we doing on time?" he asked.

"Flight time in two and a half hours," Iva replied. "And then dinner in Athens."

"You're going to love Greece," he told her.

"I'm sure I will," Iva said, adding, "You're going to love Israel."

"I'm sure I will," Brian said.

"And you're going to love me," she said.

"Hopefully a lot and for a long time," he replied.

Their car turned onto Skunks Misery Road. Instantly, a police motorcycle turned on its siren and flashing lights. Brian cursed and pulled over.

"That does it, now I'm mad," he said.

"Just now you're mad?"

"Well, I'm mad again. I'm the mayor-elect. I don't have to take this." He got out of his car and walked back to the policeman.

"Now listen here," Brian began. "I'm going to be the mayor in a few weeks and I have no intention of putting up with any..."

"Congratulations on your victory, sir," the officer said with a grin from ear to ear that made him appear about fourteen years old. "I was just wondering... uh... Mr. Mayor... uh... sir... if you might wish a motorcycle escort to the city line."

"A motorcycle escort?" Brian said.

"Yes sir, I'll speed you right through."

I'm on my honeymoon, what the heck, Brian decided.

"I accept Patrolman... uh..."

"Patrolman Bud Armstrong, sir!" the young man yelled in a tenor voice.

"Thank you Patrolman Armstrong, I'll remember this," Brian said.

"Yes sir!" Armstrong replied. He took a step back and offered a smart salute.

Brian started to return the salute but at the last moment turned it into more of a wave. "Let's roll, I've got a plane to catch," he told the youthful officer.

Back in the car Iva asked, "What was that all about?"

"I think a member of the Byzantine palace guard just told me he's switching sides," Brian said.

"That was nice of him," Iva said.

"Yes it was," Brian agreed. "Now check this out, we've got a police escort."

Brian and Iva followed the motorcycle off Skunks Misery and onto Shore Road. The waves of Sagamore Harbor broke crisply on their left and then they passed the fishing pier and remembered for a moment. Ahead lay the airport and the Acropolis and Israel and areté and the rest of their lives together. Iva turned and looked at Brian who stared straight ahead behind the wheel. Then she closed her eyes and brushed her fingertips over her Indian arrowhead necklace... *for it is our destiny that one day we shall journey far from our upland meadow, you and I, and, together, touch the stars.*

CPSIA information can be obtained at www.ICGtesting.com
Printed in the USA
BVOW012055180213

313593BV00001B/1/P

9 781457 515194